CONTENTS

Linda Ford lives on a ranch in Alberta, Canada, near enough to the Rocky Mountains that she can enjoy them on a daily basis. She and her husband raised fourteen children—four homemade, ten adopted. She currently shares her home and life with her husband, a grown son, a live-in paraplegic client and a continual (and welcome) stream of kids, kids-in-law, grandkids, and assorted friends and relatives.

Books by Linda Ford

Love Inspired Historical

Big Sky Country

Montana Cowboy Daddy
Montana Cowboy Family
Montana Cowboy's Baby
Montana Bride by Christmas
Montana Groom of Convenience
Montana Lawman Rescuer

Montana Cowboys

The Cowboy's Ready-Made Family
The Cowboy's Baby Bond
The Cowboy's City Girl

Christmas in Eden Valley

A Daddy for Christmas
A Baby for Christmas
A Home for Christmas

Visit the Author Profile page at Harlequin.com for more titles.

They skated until they were alone in the silence. Buck held her hands and skated backward so he could watch Kathleen's face.

"Are you planning to return to college soon?"

"I have no definite plans. Mother seems better some days, but then she gets worse if anything upsets her, so I do my best to keep things calm in the house."

"That sounds like a huge responsibility."

"It doesn't feel like a responsibility when it's done out of love."

He understood then she would never choose someone or something over loyalty to her parents. Although he admired the trait, it left him feeling lonely. One skate caught on the ice and he fell and landed with a thud that shook the air from him.

Kathleen saw he couldn't breathe. "Buck, take a breath." She shook him a little. "Come on. You're scaring me."

He sucked in air, then let it out in a gusty exhalation.

"Are you okay?"

It felt good to know she would worry so about him. He sat up and grinned.

"I'm fine, sweet Kathleen. Just fine."

Linda Ford
Winnie Griggs
Karen Kirst

Once Upon a
Thanksgiving
&
Married by Christmas

HARLEQUIN® LOVE INSPIRED®CLASSICS

 LOVE INSPIRED BOOKS

Recycling programs
for this product may
not exist in your area.

ISBN-13: 978-1-335-45465-2

Once Upon a Thanksgiving & Married by Christmas

Copyright © 2019 by Harlequin Books S.A.

Season of Bounty
First published in 2011. This edition published in 2019.
Copyright © 2011 by Linda Ford

Home for Thanksgiving
First published in 2011. This edition published in 2019.
Copyright © 2011 by Winnie Griggs

Married by Christmas
First published in 2014. This edition published in 2019.
Copyright © 2014 by Karen Vyskocil

www.Harlequin.com

Printed in U.S.A.

SEASON OF BOUNTY

Linda Ford

O give thanks unto the Lord; for he is good:
for his mercy endureth for ever.
—*Psalms* 136:1

Among the things I am thankful for is my family. Each and every one of them holds a special place in my thoughts. This book is dedicated to them:

I am privileged to have every one of you in my family and in my heart. May you realize how much you are loved and how much we have to be thankful for.

Chapter One

Hopewell, Montana
November 1890

Kathleen Sanderson cracked open the door. Before her stood a rough-looking man twisting a battered Stetson in his hands. His bent head revealed overgrown, untidy brown hair. Her glance took in the trail-worn, dusty, shearling-lined coat.

"Rosie, I know you told me to stay away, but I need your help." He raised his head to reveal demanding brown eyes that widened before they bored into Kathleen. "You're not Rosie."

"True. She's busy with the baby. If you'll wait—"

"Buck." Rosie's voice rang with shock as she joined Kathleen in the doorway. "I thought I'd made myself clear."

"I'll take the baby." Kathleen lifted nine-month-old Lilly from her mother's arms and retreated to the far end of the room, wishing the house was larger so she could escape and let these two work out their differences without her as audience. Yet this way her curiosity might be satisfied.

"Buck," Rosie continued, keeping her words low but not disguising her concern, "I told you I don't want to be associated with—" Her voice dropped to a whisper. "You know... Go away before you ruin everything."

Buck lifted his head, glanced past Rosie, saw Kathleen and shuttered his feelings, but not before she'd seen stark misery. He didn't shift his gaze away, making it impossible for her to get a satisfying breath. Then he returned his attention to Rosie and her lungs expanded with a whoosh.

"I wouldn't be here if I knew what else to do." A beat, two, in which Kathleen wondered if Rosie found his statement as demanding as she did.

"Rosie, I have a son and he's ill. I can't chase after cows or live in a bunkhouse with a sick kid. You're my sister. My only relative. Surely you'll help me for the sake of my son."

Rosie gasped. "You're married? Without even letting me know?"

"Not married. I adopted the boy. Help us?"

"I don't know." Rosie glanced over her shoulder toward Kathleen as if seeking some signal one way or the other from her.

Kathleen sensed how troubled Rosie was. Understood something about this man made her tremble.

She shifted Lilly to her hip and moved to Rosie's side to indicate her support, but it wasn't clear in her mind if she meant to encourage Rosie or her brother. "Rosie, how would you feel if it was one of your boys?" She had two—Mattie, two and a half, and Junior, four years old—who both nosed around the corner of the bedroom where they'd been playing to eye this stranger at their door.

Buck sent Kathleen a grateful glance before he appealed to Rosie. "I'd help you. You know it." The emotion in his tone caught at Kathleen's heart. A man who cared deeply. Her heart buckled and bowed with feelings she didn't recognize. Had never before in her nineteen years experienced.

Buck stepped aside. "Look at him."

A child of no more than six or seven slumped on the back of a pinto horse, wrapped up against the elements until he could barely move. Kathleen wondered for a moment if he was alive. Then he swayed, righted himself to keep from falling and lifted his face. Black eyes. A pale, thin face framed by black hair and a gray knitted hat.

"He's an Indian." Rosie's tone carried a hefty dose of disbelief and shock.

"Half-breed." The way Buck said it made Kathleen think he must have said so enough times to grow weary of making the explanation.

"You adopted him?"

Buck nodded. "I'll tell you the whole story if you let us in. He needs to be warm and dry."

Rosie rocked her head back and forth and gave careful consideration to the faces of each of her children.

"Rosie," Kathleen urged, knowing this was none of her business, yet not able to turn her back on a man and child needing help. More than that, who needed a welcome.

Not everyone would understand her concern. She

knew that well enough. If her parents saw this pair on the street they would turn their backs and pretend they didn't exist. They'd rush Kathleen by and try to shield her from seeing them. Her parents had objected strenuously when Kathleen mentioned she would like to befriend Rosie.

"She's not our sort," Father said.

"The children are always grubby," Mother added, shuddering and pressing her lace-trimmed, monogrammed hankie to her nose as if the mere mention of them offended her senses.

"She's alone," Kathleen pointed out, not adding that Kathleen felt almost as alone much of the time. "Her husband is working in a logging camp and she has three little ones." At least Rosie had her babies. Kathleen had no one but Mother and Father. Not for the first time, she wondered why her friends never seemed to last. Was there something about her that made her forgettable? Or worse? Maybe she somehow, unknowingly, repelled people. "I think she appreciates me visiting." She helped as much as she could without offending Rosie.

Father studied her for a moment. "How did you meet her?"

She'd told them before but they hadn't listened. "She was leaving the store with an armload of groceries, trying to hold the baby and keep track of little Mattie, who was set on exploring the display of shovels. She dropped a letter in the confusion and I picked it up and offered to help her get home."

"She lives across town, doesn't she?"

"Yes." He knew that, too, of course. He only wanted to make sure Kathleen realized how inappropriate he

considered her association with someone from the poor
side of town. "She's new in Hopewell and doesn't know
anyone. Everyone needs friends." Neither parent relented, but she knew exactly what to say to get their
permission to visit again. "Aren't we, as Christians,
commanded to welcome strangers?"

Her father's silence meant reluctant acquiescence.

She had been back several times and thought Rosie
welcomed her. On her part, Kathleen enjoyed someone
her age to visit with.

As she thought how they were slowly becoming
friends, Rosie stood at the door, patting her fingertips
together in a rapid dance. "I don't want any trouble." She
flung about to stare into the center of the room. "Once
people learn who Buck is and see his kid…" She didn't
say what she expected would happen.

"Who is he?" Who was this man who took in a half-
breed child and begged an unwelcome invitation to care
for him? It made her long to enter his thoughts and explore them.

She hadn't even finished the question when he said,
"I don't intend anyone should find out I'm here. I won't
stay any longer than I need to. Only long enough for
Joey to get his strength."

"Joey? That his name?"

Buck nodded and smiled, changing his worry into
affection, and if Kathleen wasn't mistaken, a whole
lot more.

She jerked her thoughts back to the present. Why did
she think he seemed a loyal, committed sort of man?
She didn't know anything at all about him except he
faced Rosie on behalf of his sick son. But he'd informed

Rosie he didn't intend to stay. Why not? She wanted
to demand an answer. But it was none of her business.
Just because she wanted someone…anyone…to stay in
her life long-term was no reason to pin her longings on
Rosie's transient brother. Poor unsuspecting man. She
touched Rosie's elbow in appeal. "He needs a friend.
What better friend than a sister?"

Rosie took Lilly and stepped back in silent permission.

Buck trotted to the pinto, spoke softly to the boy and
lifted his arms. The child slid into them so smoothly
that Kathleen caught her breath, as if feeling the weight
of the youngster land against her own heart.

Kathleen opened the door wide and ushered Buck
into the house. She shoved a chair closer to the stove
for him to sit on.

"Thank you." Buck sounded weary and wary. No
doubt he wondered who she was and what role she
played. Then he gave his complete attention to Joey,
slipping the heavy winter wear from him.

The boy shivered, though Kathleen knew by the
bright red spots on each cheek he was fevered. His
breathing whistled in and out.

"I don't want my children sick," Rosie murmured,
and backed away from the door until she reached her
sons.

Buck sighed. "I'm sorry." He looked into Kathleen's
eyes. "But what could I do? What would you do in the
same circumstance?"

"I'd go home."

His eyes crinkled in a mixture of humor and regret.
"This is the closest place to home I have."

Kathleen felt herself being drawn into something in his look. Couldn't say for certain what it was—only that it filled her with sadness that a man should not know a welcome any better than what Rosie offered. "If there's anything I can do to help…"

His smile widened and dipped into her heart. Startled at her reaction, she dropped to her knees to look more closely at his son. "Joey, I'm pleased to meet you."

Joey's unblinking gaze revealed nothing.

"My name is Kathleen Sanderson. I'm a friend of your aunt's. That's her over there, Aunt Rosie. Those are your cousins." She named them.

"Hello." Junior stepped forward, but his mother caught his shoulder and pulled him back.

Kathleen spared Rosie a moment's consideration. Shouldn't she be more charitable toward her brother and this child? If Kathleen had a brother or sister, she would do anything she could to help them. But it seemed Rosie was unaware of the blessing of a sibling.

"Never mind. They'll soon be your friends."

Joey turned his face up to ask Buck a silent question. In the moment of wordless interchange between the pair she sensed a connection, an affection needing no words, yet so evident it brought a sting to her eyes.

Buck cupped the boy's head and pressed it to his chest. "We'll be okay, little buddy."

Joey let out a sigh ending on a gasp as he fought for air.

"How long has he been ill?" Kathleen asked.

"Longer than I care to admit." Buck sat the boy up and brushed the long black hair off his face. "I haven't been fair to him, dragging him along with me. I guess I figured it was the sort of life he was born to." He shook his head. "He deserves more."

"Children get sick. It happens." She longed to reassure him. She ached to give him the welcome Rosie refused. "Now that he's here, he'll start to mend." She touched his cheeks. Hot. Dry. Parchment-paper fragile. Her knuckles brushed Buck's and she jerked back. Pushed to her feet. Turned to Rosie. "He's burning up."

"Sponge him. A good washing wouldn't likely go amiss."

"Rosie, you surprise me." Buck spoke in a flat tone.

Kathleen silently echoed his words as she prepared a basin of water.

"Take his shirt off," Rosie instructed.

Kathleen waited as Buck did so, then knelt at his side and lifted a wet cloth. Joey shrank back, his eyes widening.

"I'll do it." Buck reached for the cloth. Again their fingers brushed. She stilled herself not to react. He paused. Slowly she lifted her head to meet his steady consideration, sat back on her heels as his look went on and on, peeling away protective layers she didn't even realize existed—layers established by her upbringing, of being sheltered to the point she often felt she was a lonely spectator of the world. Her parents had long taught her that their station in life demanded certain requirements of her. Namely, to associate only with appropriate people and marry within their circle, meaning to marry well. Yet nowhere in the approved acquaintances had she seen a man so devoted to a child not his own, from an often despised race. Nor had she ever felt a reaction that made her heart beat so erratically.

She drew back to one of the mismatched chairs around the table and watched Buck sponge Joey, murmuring softly as he worked, sometimes in foreign sounding words. All the while, Joey watched him with utmost faith.

Kathleen knew for a fact a man who could earn such trust from a child was a man worthy of the same kind of trust from others. Yet there was something about him that put Rosie on edge. What could it possibly be?

Buck wondered about the young woman watching him. She didn't seem the kind who normally hung out with Rosie, nor visited in a shack barely big enough for a family. He looked about the room. A battered wooden table. Mismatched chairs. A stove and one cupboard in the kitchen area. Beyond, a rocking chair and a small bookshelf containing two books and a basket of mending. One door next to the bookshelf where Rosie hovered, her eyes guarded. His visit would seriously crowd the place, though the floor provided more than enough room for the pair of them. In his twenty-two years he'd slept in far worse places.

Kathleen Sanderson. She'd said her name with pride and confidence of one familiar with respect. No doubt she would be shocked to learn his identity.

Nor did he intend she should. Marriage had provided Rosie with an escape and he didn't plan to ruin things for her.

Being a cowboy, moving from job to job, had given him his only escape.

Kathleen leaned forward. "He's certainly fond of you."

Buck chuckled. "He's smart enough to know where his next meal comes from."

She blinked as if startled by his frank words. Then laughed. "You're teasing, but I'd say it was more than that."

He looked at Joey who watched him with those dark, unblinking eyes of his. "We've formed a sort of mutual admiration society, haven't we, buddy?"

Joey nodded, his expression still solemn.

Buck cupped his son's head and brushed his thumb along the boy's cheeks. When had they shrunk so badly? "I'm sorry, little guy. I should have realized sooner just how sick you are."

"He needs some nourishing broth." Rosie sighed. "Guess I'll have to get some." She handed the baby to Junior. "You kids stay here and play." Then she marched toward the stove and pulled a pot forward. "Good thing for you soup is about all we eat around here."

Buck chuckled. "I knew you couldn't stay mad at me for long." He turned to Kathleen to explain. "She likes me a lot more than she lets on."

"She hides it awfully well." Her smile lit up her face, sent dancing lights into her blue eyes, riveting him motionless.

He studied her. Blond hair carefully pulled back in a wave ending in a roll at her neck. An oval face that belonged on a cameo, pretty pink lips. Everything about her said *rich, refined*.

What was she doing here?

Her cheeks blossomed rose color, and he realized he'd been staring and tore his attention away.

Rosie pulled a bowl from the cupboard and ladled

in broth and bits of carrots. She set the bowl on the table. "Eat."

Joey pressed into Buck's chest. Buck understood his caution, fear even. He had plenty of reason for it. "Say 'thank you, Aunt Rosie.'"

Joey shivered. But he must learn his manners, so Buck nudged him.

"Thank you, Auntie." The boy's normally soft voice crackled from the effects of his illness.

Rosie sat across the table. "You're welcome."

Buck pulled up to the table close to Kathleen. He knew Joey wouldn't be comfortable sitting on a chair by himself, so he held him and encouraged him to eat.

"This is lots better than what I've been feeding you, isn't it, buddy?"

"I like rabbit." Joey's firm tones informed everyone where his loyalty lay, and Buck chuckled.

"You'd say that if all we ate was gopher."

"I like gopher, too."

Buck laughed and scrubbed his knuckles across the boy's head. "You ever tasted one?"

"Not yet."

Kathleen's soft laughter filled Buck's senses. My, he did like a woman with a gentle laugh. "He's determined to be loyal to you no matter what."

Buck allowed himself a glance of acknowledgment and was immediately warmed by the admiration in her eyes. "He doesn't know any better."

"Yes, I do."

Kathleen and Buck both laughed, sharing something more than enjoyment of Joey's conviction. Something he couldn't name, but it felt like a gift from God.

Strange. He hadn't thought of God, or His gifts or anything of the sort for a long time.

Rosie leaned forward on her elbows. "So how did you and Joey find each other?"

"Bless you, Rosie."

"For what?"

"For saying it like that."

She shrugged. "I have never been able to stay annoyed with you." She shifted her attention to Kathleen. "Does that make me weak?"

"No, Rosie," Kathleen said gently. "It makes you a good sister."

"She is that. We learned to stick together a long time ago, didn't we, sister?"

"Then we found out we were better off not being together." Her words contained more than a hint of warning. "Now tell us about Joey. Unless you'd rather wait."

He understood her unspoken acknowledgment that he might prefer not to speak of it in Joey's hearing. Or before her own children who hovered at the doorway, hearing and seeing everything. "He knows every detail already."

"I was there," Joey pointed out as if they might have forgotten.

Buck wished the little guy could have missed certain portions of the experience, but at least God had protected him. Again, he thought of God. Not once until now had he stopped to consider God protected Joey throughout an ordeal that might have ended much differently. Why was he suddenly realizing it?

He shifted so he could consider Kathleen out of the corner of his eyes. Something about her nudged him toward nobler, kinder thoughts than he'd enjoyed in a very long time.

What would she think after she heard Joey's story? Would she be repulsed? Warmed? He could only hope it would give both her and Rosie a kindly disposition toward his son.

Chapter Two

Kathleen leaned close, not wanting to miss a word of Buck's explanation. Something about the fondness between Buck and Joey made her wonder if a heart could weep with emotion.

Buck settled back in his chair, a distant look in his eyes, as if he lived the past again. "It was a year ago this past spring and I was heading west. Heard a rancher out there needed a few more hands. Figured it was as good a place as any to find work. I rode up a little ridge and stopped to look around. Remember thinking the mountains made a mighty purty sight, glistening with their winter snowcaps under the bright sunshine. Then I brought my gaze closer to hand and saw what appeared to be the remains of a wagon accident. Rode on down to investigate." He paused and swallowed hard.

Kathleen guessed what he'd found had been unpleasant.

"A man and his wife had been killed."

"Bad man shoot Mama and Papa," Joey said, his voice betraying a thread of sorrow.

"The woman was Indian, the man appeared to be a white miner. I gave them a decent burial and marked the place with fragments of their wagon. There were no papers, no identification. Everything had been picked through and scattered."

"Man look for Papa's money. Find it. Steal it." As Joey listed the deeds he kept his attention on his bowl of soup, though he no longer lifted the spoon to his mouth.

Buck squeezed the back of Joey's neck and the boy relaxed visibly. "I knew from the things left that a child had been with them. I hated the thought the murderers had taken him. It was late in the day so I made camp, intending to resume my journey in the morning. During the night I heard something or someone, but the intruder was gone as fast as he came."

"I was hungry," Joey explained.

Buck chuckled. "When I got up I knew no critter had been in my camp. Only things missing were biscuits and beans. So I hunkered down over my breakfast and studied the tracks. Knew it was a child. Guessed it was the one who'd been on the wagon."

"I hide from bad man. Hide from Buck, too. I not know he not be a bad man."

"Took me a few days to prove it. Then I headed to the nearest town. No one knew the dead family. No one knew Joey. He didn't know of any family but his ma and pa. The sheriff made inquiries. But nothing. I asked the preacher what I should do and he said, why not adopt him? So I did."

The way he grinned gave Kathleen an emptiness, as if her life lacked something. She tried valiantly to dismiss the feeling. After all, what could her life be lacking? Her parents provided her with everything she needed. She had been at finishing school getting a privileged education until her mother's illness required she return home to help care for her. As soon as her mother felt better, she'd return to the Eastern college. She hadn't been there long enough to make friends, but when she got back she would. God willing, she'd find a friend who would remain loyal throughout their years at college.

Above and beyond that, she had a living relationship with God. Had never doubted His love and care. Still, had she ever done anything half as noble as Buck had? Had she ever loved anyone like Buck loved Joey? Had she ever been loved like that? Yes, her parents loved her, she had no doubt, but it seemed their love carried heavy expectations.

Buck watched her. His eyes revealed understanding. Warmth.

As if he read her thoughts.

She ducked her head, amazed at how foolish she proved to be. Until this moment she considered herself a commonsense person who didn't think or act rashly.

"Buck my papa." Joey sounded so proud, Kathleen's throat tightened.

She dare not look at Buck again, afraid of the way her emotions clogged her heart. Instead, she glanced at Rosie. When she saw the same glisten of tears in her eyes she felt in her own, she sniffed.

"Yes, I am. And you're my son. Forever and always."

Kathleen couldn't breathe. Couldn't think beyond the stuffiness in her nose. Never before had she known such open affection between a man and his son...his adopted son, though she guessed he wouldn't acknowledge any distinction. He seemed such a decent man.

Rosie blew her nose on a hankie. "You're a good man, Buck, but it doesn't change anything."

Kathleen couldn't imagine why Rosie was so fearful.

"I'm well aware of it. I'm only here until Joey is better."

At that moment, Joey's head nodded. Buck caught him before he planted his face in the bowl of soup. He lifted the boy, tossed his coat on the floor in the corner and was about to put Joey there.

Kathleen gave Rosie a hard look. "Are you going to let him sleep on the floor? The boy is sick. Besides—" she lowered her voice "—don't you think he's been through enough?"

Rosie lifted her hands in a sign of defeat. "I give up. Buck, use the room past the stove. It's our bedroom, but I can't bring myself to sleep there with Bill gone."

Buck jerked to full attention. "He's gone? How long ago?" He shifted his gaze to the children who played in the doorway.

"He left a few weeks ago to work in a logging camp. We came here expecting a job but it fell through. We can't live in the camp so Bill left us here." She glanced about. "This is a nice, solid little house."

Buck let out a noisy gust. "I thought you meant he was gone…gone for good, as in…well, you know."

Rosie grinned widely. "If you could see the look on your face…" She tipped her head back and looked pleased with herself. "I have to admit I enjoyed that. Sort of evens us up for you showing up at my door."

Kathleen couldn't read the look the two exchanged.

Sharing a secret. She felt she intruded into their lives without invitation. She envied them their obvious affection. She wondered if they realized how blessed they were to have each other and their children.

"Consider us even, then. I'm happy to let you do so." Buck shouldered his way into the room. A cold draft blasted through the kitchen.

Junior waited until Buck was out of sight. "Mama, do we have to stay here forever?"

Rosie crossed the room and took Lilly. "Come on over. It will soon be time for supper."

Kathleen glanced out the window. Long shadows slanted across the skiff of snow. She jumped to her feet. "I've stayed far too long. Mother will be worrying." Her coat hung near the stove and she shrugged into it, pulled on her fur hat and mittens.

Buck stood in the bedroom doorway, watching.

She felt his measured consideration. Determined to ignore him, she turned to Rosie instead. "I could come back tomorrow." Perhaps Rosie wouldn't welcome her company as eagerly now that her brother was there. "If you want."

Rosie's lips flattened. "Nobody's forcing you to come."

Kathleen refused to be offended by the woman's remarks. In the few weeks she'd been visiting, she'd learned Rosie didn't expect any offers of friendship. But Kathleen didn't intend to be a fair-weather friend. She patted Rosie's shoulder. "I only asked because I thought you might enjoy spending time alone with your brother." For some insane reason her cheeks warmed. She could well imagine such pleasure.

Rosie nodded. "I'm sorry for being prickly. It's

just…" She darted a look toward Buck. The pair sent wordless messages to each other, then Rosie shrugged. "I'd be pleased if you'd come again."

Kathleen understood Rosie's caution. She, too, had learned to wonder if a friend would visit again. "I'll be back. After all, we have that quilt to work on." She'd noticed a shortage of warm bedding and offered to help Rosie sew a quilt. Rosie had scraps of material and Kathleen intended to supply a woolen batt.

Only when she reached the outer door did she allow herself to look directly at Buck. "It was nice meeting you, Mr.—" She realized he'd never given his surname.

He grinned. "Buck is name enough for me."

"Nice meeting you, Buck." She knew she blushed to speak so familiarly. Her parents would be shocked.

"My pleasure, Miss Sanderson."

The way he said it made her cheeks grow even warmer.

She scurried out and rushed toward home. When had she ever had such a reaction to any man? Never. But then she'd never before met such a cowboy, never seen such a kind smile. Her feet slowed. What was she thinking?

Nothing. Nothing at all, except it would be nice for Rosie to have a man around to take care of filling the wood box and fetching water.

It would be equally as nice for Buck to have a place to care for his son.

Her parents both sat in the drawing room and glanced up as Kathleen hurried in, rubbing her hands together to ease the chill.

"You're very late," Mother said. "I was beginning to worry."

Father lowered the papers he'd been reading and studied Kathleen. "I'm still not comfortable with you going to that woman's shack. It's in a rough area of town. You aren't safe."

Kathleen held back annoyance at their continued resistance to her being friends with Rosie. "There is no danger." For some reason, Buck's image flitted through her mind. There was something about him his sister considered threatening, but she couldn't imagine it was the kind of danger her father meant. "Rosie and her children are very nice people. You would like them if you ever got to know them."

Mother fluttered her hand. "That's not likely to ever happen, is it? We simply don't belong in the same circles."

Kathleen had invited Rosie to attend church with her. Assured her she would be welcome. "I would think rich and poor are both welcome in the church."

"Why, of course they are." But Rosie heard her unspoken qualifier—*just don't expect us to sit in the same pew.*

Having no desire to argue with them or upset them, Kathleen let the topic end. She sank to an ottoman at her mother's knees and took her hands. "How have you been this afternoon?"

"I've managed to sit up and read a bit." Mother's voice quavered. "I'm sure I'm getting stronger."

Father set aside his papers. "Kathleen, I should think you could see your mother needs your care. I don't like you neglecting her when she's not well."

Stung by his criticism, Kathleen remained on the stool beside her mother. "Mother sleeps much of the afternoon. I only intend to be gone during that time."

He glanced at the big grandfather clock ticking out the seconds in demanding rhythm.

"Today was different. Rosie's brother and his little boy showed up, and the time simply slipped away on me."

Father leaned forward in his chair. "A brother? Good. He can take care of his sister and you can find a more suitable pastime." He sat back, satisfied life would fit into his sense of right and order.

"Father, I promised her I would help her sew a quilt. I told her I would return tomorrow. I hope you won't say I can't go." She couldn't imagine returning to the boredom of sitting quietly in an armchair reading as her mother slept.

Father tapped his knee and considered her. "You used to be such an obedient child. I should never have sent you East to that college. They've filled your head with all sorts of radical ideas. I'm glad you've had cause to return home. Given time, I expect you will come to your senses." He flipped the paper in front of his face, signaling he'd spoken his last word on the subject.

Kathleen eased a sigh of relief over her teeth. At least he hadn't forbidden her to return, which left her free to do so. In the future, she would simply return before the afternoon was spent.

She schooled herself not to smile with anticipation of a visit the next day. Nor would she admit, even to herself, that it was the thought of seeing Buck again that brought the smile to her lips.

She only wanted to assess if the affection she'd witnessed was as evident as she remembered. And check if Joey was feeling better.

Buck sponged Joey several more times and fed him more broth throughout the evening. For now he seemed to be sleeping peacefully.

Rosie glanced in on them. "Likely all he needs is a warm bed and decent food."

"I hope you're right." If anything happened to the boy— "I've grown to love him more than I imagined possible."

"It's pretty obvious." She remained in the doorway. "Care to join me for tea?"

He draped an arm across her shoulders. "Just like old times?"

She patted his hand. "Buck, I'd just as soon forget about old times, if you don't mind."

"Yeah. Me, too." They sat across from each other, nursing warm cups of steaming tea. "So who is this Kathleen Sanderson and why is she visiting you?"

Rosie bristled. "What? I'm not fit for the likes of her to cross my threshold?"

He chuckled. "Is that what you think?"

"Sometimes."

"Guess we've both got reason to consider others think that very thing. So who is she and why is she here?"

"Kathleen's father is the richest man in town."

A punch of alarm raced up Buck's spine. Rich men with beautiful daughters were the worst sort. They didn't want the likes of Buck to even be in the same town. "If her father learns who I am…"

"And who I am." Her gaze bored into his—angry at his visit to her home. "You should never have come here. You promised you wouldn't."

"It's only for Joey and then I'll be gone." He glanced about the house. There were days he wished he didn't have to keep on the move. But wishing didn't change the facts. "I'll do my best to keep our secret from Kathleen. I can think of no reason she'd suspect who I am. Why should anyone be suspicious of your brother visiting? Your married name gives no clue as to who we are." He didn't want to think about his past. "Tell me how you met her."

"The Sandersons live in a big house. Even have a cook and housekeeper. Can you imagine paying someone to clean your house? 'Course, it's a mighty big house and dust probably isn't allowed to settle for even a minute. Someday I'm going to ask Kathleen how many rooms there are."

Buck sighed. Seemed he was going to get a detailed description of the house before she explained about Kathleen.

She must have guessed at his impatience. "Won't likely ever see inside the place, now will I?" She shrugged. "Not that it matters. I'm happy enough here, and Kathleen doesn't seem to mind how small and mean my house is." She told about Kathleen helping her home one afternoon as she struggled to corral young Mattie. "Since then she visits me, plays with the kids. Even helps with the dishes if they aren't done when she gets here. Now she says she wants to help me make a quilt for the children." She rocked her head back and forth. "I just don't understand why."

"Have you asked her?"

"I did. All she said was she couldn't bear the thought of me living on the edge of town with no friends. Though from what she says, I think she's as lonely as I am. She'd like me to go to church with her but I can't. If I let myself care about people and what they think, it only hurts the more when they discover the truth." Her eyes hardened. "Someone is likely to, now that you're here. Once they realize our father was—" She clamped her lips together as tears swelled in her eyes.

He filled in the blank she'd left. "A murderer." Saying the word forced him back to reality. "Don't worry. I won't be around long enough for anyone to take notice." Though he wished things could be different. Wished he could offer Joey a real home. Wished he could belong somewhere. With someone. A forbidden dream flashed through his thoughts of home and a woman. He'd had the thought before, and always the woman was faceless. Just a presence. But this time she had a face and voice… those of Kathleen Sanderson. "I will leave as soon as Joey is rested. Before people find out and drive us out of town." He knew his voice had grown hard. Rosie would understand why. They shared a secret with the power to destroy their lives. He understood why Rosie would be cautious about making friends. A person needed to be able to leave when the time came with no regrets, no glancing back over one's shoulder.

Yet he rose the next morning wondering if Kathleen would return as she had promised Rosie.

Rosie noticed how many times he glanced out the window and laughed. "She won't be along for a bit. She never comes until after lunch when her mother is napping."

"I wasn't looking for her."

"Sure you were."

"Only because I wondered if she would come as she promised."

Rosie grew serious. "I always wonder the same thing, but every time she's said she'd come, she has."

Joey sat at the table spooning in thin porridge. "Buck, who you waiting for?"

He turned away from the window. "Nobody. Just checking the weather."

Rosie snorted. "She's not your sort."

"No one is." They both knew what he meant, and he sat at the table to consider his two nephews. Sturdy-looking boys. Made Joey look as thin as he was. "Your boys appear well fed."

"Bill left us with adequate supplies. He'll send money from time to time. We won't go hungry."

"Didn't think we were, either."

"I not hungry." Joey put his spoon down as if to prove he only ate because the food was before him.

Buck smiled. He appreciated Joey's devotion, but not to the extent of him choosing to go hungry. "Finish it up."

Joey hesitated only a moment before returning his attention to the food.

Rosie stood beside Buck. "He seems a little better today."

"I hope so."

But an hour later, after playing with Mattie and Junior, Joey curled up on the floor, exhausted. Buck carried him to bed and sat at his side, watching him. Surely he would regain his strength in a day or two and they could move on. But to where? And what did it matter? One place was the same as the next.

Joey slept through a lunch of soup and freshly baked bread. He was still asleep when a gentle knock sounded.

Buck sat at the table pretending a great interest in the pencil Junior had given him to sharpen, but every sense tingled with awareness as Kathleen stepped into the house, laughing about the wind tugging at her fine woolen coat. She shrugged out of it and hung it on a nail. "Hello, everyone." She smiled at Rosie who held Lilly, leaned over and kissed the baby's cheek, squatted to kiss Mattie's forehead, hugged Junior and then finally lifted her attention to Buck. "Hello to you, too."

"You're a breath of sunshine." He hadn't meant to sound so adoring. He only meant she made everyone smile with her greeting.

Her cheeks flushed a very becoming pink, reminding him of summer sunrises. "I'm just passing on my own feelings of happiness."

Rosie waggled her hand toward Buck. "He meant it as a compliment." She gave Buck a scolding look. "We're all glad to have you visit." Silently she warned Buck not to ruin things for her. As if his very presence wasn't enough to do that.

"I'm relieved to hear it." Kathleen glanced about. "Where's Joey?"

"Still sleeping." Worry grabbed his gut. "He's been sleeping a long time." He rushed into the bedroom, pressed his hand to the boy's forehead, but even without feeling his hot skin he knew the boy was again fevered. "I hoped he was getting better."

Rosie brought in a basin of water, and both women

hovered at the bedside while Buck stripped the boy to the waist and sponged him.

"I don't think this is a good sign," Rosie murmured. "Fevers that return every day generally mean something like lung fever."

"No." Buck wouldn't allow it. "He's just run down. He'll be fine."

"Let's pray for God to strengthen his little body." Kathleen reached for Rosie's hand.

Buck understood Rosie's hesitation. Hadn't their ma prayed for God to intervene? It hadn't happened. Instead she'd died, and he and Rosie had been on their own. But for Joey, his son, he'd storm the gates of heaven if he must. He reached for Kathleen's hand, saw her start with surprise and likely shock, and he pulled back. But she reached out and clasped his hand on one side and Rosie's on the other. From her flowed confidence and faith that poured into his heart. God could heal his boy. He knew it. He believed it. He bowed his head.

"Dear Heavenly Father." Kathleen's voice rang with love and joy. "You love us so much. You are the great healer. Touch Joey. Stop the fever. Show us what part we need to play, that Your name might be glorified. Amen."

He pulled his hand to his knee, kept his head tilted down. He'd never heard such a simple prayer, and yet he felt he had stepped into the throne room of God.

He picked up the wet cloth and continued to sponge Joey. But no longer did his spirit fret.

The fever slowly abated as it had done before. He almost dared believe this might be the last time.

Joey opened his eyes and smiled. "Hi, Buck."

"Hi, buddy. How you feeling?"

"Maybe a little hungry."

Buck's laugher was joined by Rosie's and Kathleen's. "Surely he's on the mend." He turned and gripped Kathleen's shoulder. "Thanks to you."

"No." She shook her head. "Thanks to God." Her look of assurance filled him with a sense of wonder. God actually might care about him. Amazing. Or was it only Joey God cared about?

It was a question he didn't care to answer at the moment.

Chapter Three

Kathleen couldn't believe her boldness at taking Buck's hand to pray. Praying came naturally enough to her. But what made her think it required holding a hand as solid and firm as the ground beneath her feet? Her palm still felt warmer than normal.

But she had no doubt God intervened for Joey's improvement and would continue to do so. She silently prayed it would accomplish much more...that Rosie and Buck would find healing for whatever made them so fearful and kept them away from each other.

Joey ate a bowl of soup, played with the toys for a few minutes, then crawled into Buck's lap and closed his eyes.

Kathleen watched the play of emotions on Buck's face—worry, love, hope. He lifted his eyes to hers and allowed her to see the depth of his feelings. They caught at her heart. Then he ducked his head, pressing his cheek to Joey's black hair.

Emotion clogged Kathleen's throat. This kind of love awed her. Filled her heart with yearning.

She drew in a shaking breath, wondering at the lightness of the air she sucked in, which did little to relieve her need for oxygen.

Lilly slept in Rosie's arms. Young Mattie whined.

"I need to put the little ones down for their nap." Rosie pushed to her feet. "Come along, Junior. Time for you to have a sleep."

"Mama, I want to play with Joey."

Buck looked at his son. "I don't think Joey feels much like playing at the moment. When you wake up he'll likely be ready."

Rosie took the children to the bedroom to settle them.

Kathleen expected Buck to do the same with Joey, but he stayed seated. She forced herself to remain still, though she longed to jump to her feet and pace the room. A crack in the wooden table caught her attention and she ran a fingernail along it.

"Is he asleep?" Buck whispered.

She looked. "I would say so."

"Then I'll put him down now." He shifted the boy and carried him to the bed, covered him carefully, smoothed his hair from his forehead…all ordinary things, yet watching him made her heart ache.

He stepped back, watched his son a moment, then tiptoed from the room and pulled the door part way shut. "I didn't want to put him down until he fell asleep. Seems like the least I can give him is lots of assurance of safety." He returned to the chair he occupied previously and rubbed his hand across his face. "I fear I am an inadequate parent, but I'm all the poor little guy has."

Such hope and desperation filled his voice, she

couldn't bear it. "From what I've seen, you are an excellent father. The way he adores you is proof enough."

Brown eyes met hers, brimming with hunger and longing. "Do you think so?"

He loved the boy deeply and wasn't afraid to show it. The knowledge of such love—human love—gave her the feeling she missed something vital in her life. She feared it would show in her eyes but lacked the strength to tear her gaze away. "I know so."

A slow, intense smile filled his face. "I perceive you are a most generous person in every way."

It was her turn to be surprised. "How nice of you to say so." But how could he know? He'd only just met her.

His chuckle tingled along her nerves like music rushing up her veins. "You're thinking I couldn't possibly know, seeing as we've only met. But yet, I think I am correct." He leaned closer drawing her into an intimate invisible circle including only the two of them, excluding everyone and everything else. "I know you've gone out of your way to make friends with Rosie, and I'm certain it's more than what most women in your group of friends consider ordinary."

She tried to pull her thoughts into order, but all she could think was he admired her for doing something that had indeed brought criticism from others, even beyond her parents.

"You know, I haven't given God much consideration or due in a long time. Since…well, never mind that. But from the moment I stepped through that door—" He tipped his head in the general direction. "I've thought of Him several times. I think it is due to you."

"How can that be?"

"You bring God's presence into the house."

"I—" She didn't know how to answer. "If so, then I am happy to hear it."

His soft smile thanked her. "If only more people were like you." He sat back. "Maybe you can help me."

"I will if I can." Perhaps he would ask her to assist him and Rosie in sorting out their differences.

"I'd like to know if Rosie needs anything. Is she managing okay on her own?"

Not the direction she'd hoped he'd go, but to know he cared so about others filled her with sweet admiration. "She has her hands full, especially when she goes shopping." She told about her first meeting with Rosie and how his poor sister couldn't keep a hand on everything. "Mattie saw the bucketful of shiny shovels, and I suppose he thought they would make good toys. What a clatter when the bucket tipped and they all fell to the ground. The storekeeper came rushing out to see what the racket was. I think everyone stopped what they were doing to look." She laughed. "Poor Rosie didn't think it very amusing, I'm afraid." She thought of what Rosie really needed—to become more a part of the community instead of keeping so much to herself. But before she could voice her thought, Rosie tiptoed from the bedroom.

"Were you two talking about me?" she asked.

Buck sighed. "You were the furthest thing from my mind."

Rosie considered them suspiciously. "I heard you talking while I got the children to sleep, yet the minute I step into the room you are quiet as mice."

Buck grinned. "If you insist on knowing, I was telling her all the family secrets."

Rosie drew up hard and stared at her brother. Then

she laughed, a nervous twitter of a sound. "I know you're joshing. Serves me right for being so suspicious." She turned to Kathleen. "Were you serious about helping me stitch a quilt top?"

At last, something to do with her hands so her thoughts wouldn't continually run off in silly directions. "Of course. Are you ready to get started?"

Rosie fetched a basket of fabric pieces. "I thought to make one for Junior's bed, but I don't intend to take advantage of your generosity or anything."

Kathleen rubbed her hands together. "We can do this. Do you have a pattern in mind?"

The women pulled out fabric and discussed different arrangements. Once they'd chosen a pattern, they cut out a number of squares, then Kathleen started stitching them together while Rosie continued cutting.

"Where did you spend Thanksgiving last year?" Kathleen asked him.

Guess it was too much for Buck to think their project would keep them occupied and allow him the privilege of watching the subtle changes in Kathleen's expression as she chose colors and patterns and aligned the pieces. But he realized he didn't mind talking about the past year. In most ways it was one of the best in his life, with Joey to look after and love. "The two of us spent it in a settler's shack. The pioneer family had moved to town for the winter, and they were glad enough to have someone occupy their place." No doubt such simple accommodations were something she would not rejoice over, but he'd been grateful.

Kathleen and Rosie continued to work, but he felt their

keen interest. "I really never gave Thanksgiving a thought until the owner of the place rode out with a bundle. Said his wife insisted he bring it to the two of us. I let Joey open it. You should have seen his eyes. I don't think he could remember receiving gifts before. Inside was enough turkey for the both of us and plenty of mashed potatoes and gravy. There were two oranges and a toy whistle. We had us a real good day. Just the two of us." He wasn't sure why he kept saying it was only he and Joey, except he wanted to believe it was how he wanted things to be. Even to his own ears it sounded lonely. But he really did have something to be thankful for—a little son and a warm house, even though the latter was temporary.

Thanksgiving was three weeks away. He should be gone again by then, but only if he remained would Joey know a true family celebration. The temptation to stay was strong.

"It sounds sweet," Kathleen said, although her voice seemed tight, as if the words didn't want release.

"It sounds lonely." Rosie, as always, was bluntly honest. They studied each other. He wished he could stay awhile. Perhaps she did, too, but they both knew the risks. People were less than welcoming when they discovered whom their father was. He and Rosie had been driven from more than one place by a violent crowd.

He and Joey must move on.

Kathleen's gaze had not left him all the while he and Rosie shared their silent communication, and now he shifted and met her blue, intense look.

She smiled. "The church is having a special Thanksgiving service. There will be a community dinner to share the bounty of the year. It would be nice if you would attend. I think you'd enjoy it."

Her words fell into a silence, sending ripples through his thoughts. He hadn't been to church since Ma died. He wondered if Rosie had. He'd attended her wedding, held in the parsonage. It was the last time he'd seen her before yesterday, though he sent her an occasional letter. She wrote to him regularly so he knew she and Bill had moved to this town. Bill knew enough to keep one step ahead of the cruel truth of his wife's past. "I doubt I'll be here." Regret deepened his voice but he hoped no one would notice. "Rosie, you should go. It would be good for you and the kids."

Rosie allowed him the briefest glance, but enough for him to see her longing ran every bit as deep as his. "I'll think on it."

"I'll keep asking," Kathleen said.

Buck wondered how she managed to sound so serene, so confident. Not for the first time, and likely not for the last, he wished things could be different so he could get to know her better and discover who she really was.

It wasn't possible. He shifted his thoughts to other things. Like the children. Rosie's were happy and full of spirit. Was Joey on par with them? Was he suffering because of the way Buck lived? Not that he could do a thing to change it.

The children woke and the women put away the sewing. Rosie brought Lilly from the bedroom with her two boys following her. At the same time, Joey came from the other room. The boy's color had improved.

Rosie put Lilly in her chair and the other children sat around the table to eat bread and jam.

"Good food and rest are giving Joey back his strength," he said.

Kathleen's gentle gaze brushed him. "God has given us so many reasons to be thankful."

He nodded. She made it easy for him to believe in God's bountiful blessings.

"I must return home. I promised Mother and Father I wouldn't be as late as I was yesterday."

Buck scrambled to his feet. "I'll walk you home."

"It's not necessary."

Did he detect a hint of something in her voice he was loath to admit? Was she embarrassed to have him walk her home? "My mother, God rest her soul, would expect no less of me."

She considered him briefly then nodded. "Very well, though it really isn't necessary."

He bent to face his son. "Joey, you stay with Aunt Rosie. I'll be back in a few minutes. Okay?"

"You be back for sure?"

"For sure."

"Okay, then." He returned his attention to the slice of bread.

He slipped into his coat and buttoned it, then held the door for Kathleen, who had already said goodbye to everyone in the room. They tramped along the hardened path.

"Do you realize that's the first time I've heard mention of your mother?"

"Even the likes of Rosie and me have a mother and father, though they are both dead now." He regretted his words as soon as they were out and hoped she wouldn't ask about his father.

"I'm sorry for your loss, but you know I didn't mean you wouldn't have parents." She scowled at him, making him feel like a small boy.

"I'm sorry. Sometimes I am too defensive."

"Both you and Rosie. It's like you expect someone to kick you in the teeth for no reason."

Oh, they thought they had reason enough, but he wasn't about to tell her so.

Kathleen turned to him, her expression a mixture of amusement and something more—perhaps regret? "Rosie's very fond of you."

"Like you said, she hides it pretty well."

Her sweet laugh filled his senses. "Tell me what it was like to have a sister growing up."

Her questions almost stopped him in his tracks. It took every bit of his well-developed self-control to move forward, to keep his voice steady, as if the memories weren't filled with a bittersweet taste. "Life was very different then. My parents were alive."

She didn't speak, and he wondered how aware she was of the tension gripping his heart.

"There was a time…" He slowed his words to cover his regret. "When my father laughed with joy and said we had much to be grateful for." How quickly his attitude had changed.

"It sounds nice."

"It was." How long since he'd remembered those better days? Far too long. And he vowed right there in the middle of the trail he would give Joey some memories of good times, and he'd find a way to remind Rosie of those happier days when being thankful didn't require an effort.

"Having a sibling is special."

Did he detect a lonesome note in her voice? He couldn't think it was true. She came from a secure, stable, safe family.

They passed the business section of town and climbed a slight hill to a cluster of large houses.

Kathleen stopped walking. "This is where I live." She indicated a house dominating those around it.

The place was huge. Buck could see why they might need someone to dust and clean. "Just you and your parents live here?" He failed to keep awe from his voice.

"Our cook has quarters here, too."

"Oh, then that explains why you need such a large house."

She grinned. "You know it doesn't. We don't need a big house, but my father thinks it's in keeping with his station in life." Her smile seemed slightly lopsided. "My father has very well-formed ideas of right and wrong."

"And always does what is right?"

"Always."

"That's something to be grateful for, isn't it?" He knew his voice revealed far more than he wanted to. If his own father had always done what was right, not let his anger and frustration drive him to taking things into his own hands in such a gruesome manner…well, his life and Rosie's—and now their children's—would be much different.

Aware that she watched him closely, likely wondering why he seemed so vehement about the idea of right and wrong when they'd been talking about her big house, he again studied the mansion before him. Lots of red brick and white trim around the seemingly endless windows on both the ground floor and second story. "It certainly makes a person stand up and take notice."

"It's just a house. Isn't a house the place where family gathers? Seems to me that what's important. Not the size of the dwelling."

He couldn't take his eyes off the house in front of them. "If you say so."

"I do. Now stop staring at it. You're making me uncomfortable."

He jerked his attention away and toward her. "Why would it make you uncomfortable?"

"Because I don't want to be judged by who my father is or how large the house I live in is. I want to be judged for my own actions." Her words rang with fierceness.

"I wish I could think such was possible." But people would always judge him by who his father was. He couldn't imagine it would be any different for Kathleen, though for vastly different reasons.

She studied him, her gaze searching out hidden meanings in his words, secrets buried deep in his heart. "Can it not be so between us, at least?"

Her question begged so many things from him. Acceptance of her friendship, but more. Openness, sharing of secrets. He couldn't offer what she silently asked for, though he ached to do so. "I wish things could be different."

"Can't you make them so?"

"I can't control what others say or think or do."

"But you can choose who and what you are."

He searched her frank open gaze. He wanted to point out it was easy for her to choose her own path with the protection of her father's name. But he didn't want to spoil the moment.

She continued to study him. "Haven't you done that already to some extent?"

He didn't understand. His choice was to leave before people learned the truth or immediately after they did.

She must have seen his confusion. "Adopting Joey."

"That has never been a hardship." Though partly because Joey fit into Buck's way of life...moving on before people got too critical. But was he doing the child a disservice by constantly moving?

"I must go inside." Kathleen shifted her attention to the house.

"Good afternoon. Thanks for everything."

She turned back to him. Made him happy he'd said something to accomplish that. "For what?"

"For visiting Rosie and being her friend. For praying for Joey. Reminding me of God." *For being Kathleen and sharing your joy.*

She lowered her eyes. "You're welcome." Brought her gaze back to his, smiling widely. "I hope you think about God more often now."

"I surely shall." Every time he thought of Kathleen and he knew that would be often.

"Goodbye now. I'll see you tomorrow." She headed up the brick sidewalk, paused at the door to give a little wave.

He lifted a hand in response, waited until the door closed behind her then headed back to Rosie's, Kathleen's promise ringing in his ears. *See you tomorrow.*

How many tomorrows dare he plan?

He clamped his jaw down hard, making his teeth ache. Not nearly enough.

Chapter Four

Kathleen leaned against the door and waited for her heart to calm. He admired her. Approved of her friendship with Rosie. Of course he would, Rosie being his sister. But his approval meant more to her than she could explain.

She hung her coat on the hall tree and slipped out of her boots into a pair of fur-lined slippers. Central heating filled the whole house with welcoming warmth. Yes, she was grateful for the comforts of her life. Yes, she admired her parents for their moral strength. But some days it all felt hollow, and today was one of those times.

"I'm in here," Mother called from the sitting room.

Kathleen took a deep, calming breath and scolded herself for feeling so restless when she was so blessed. She stepped into the room. "Mother, you're up already. How are you?"

"I do believe I am feeling better evèry day." She sighed in such a way that Kathleen wondered at the truth of her words. "I get tired of being tired."

Kathleen sat on the stool at her knees. "You did something different with your hair."

"Jeannie offered to brush and style it." Jeannie was more than housekeeper. She often did little things to brighten Mother's day. Kathleen would be sure to thank her later.

"It's very becoming."

Mother brushed her hand over her hair. "Who was that young man?"

Kathleen stalled. She didn't want her parents to know too much about Buck, aware they would heartily disapprove of Joey. "That's Rosie's brother I told you about. He insisted on seeing me safely home."

"I see." Mother studied her a long moment. "And yet you've gone back and forth safely the past few weeks."

"I assured him I didn't need an escort, but he insisted his mother would expect him to do so."

"Where is his mother?"

"She's passed away."

"Oh, I am sorry."

Kathleen wished she could talk to her mother about the thousand thoughts racing through her head. Why were Rosie and Buck so secretive? Both parents were dead. How long ago? Was Joey truly on the mend? If he was, would Buck be on his way? Why did the idea tangle her thoughts? What did it all mean? But aware her mother would tell her to forget such people, she didn't voice any of her questions. "I'll go see if Cook needs help." She hurried to the kitchen before her mother could say anything.

But Cook had everything competently under control and allowed her only to finish setting the table. Kathleen did so and stood back to study the formal dining room with its perfectly matched chairs and perfectly matched china and silver. It was all very nice but lacked something that seemed to abound around Rosie's table. Funny—she hadn't been so acutely aware of it until a day or two ago.

When Buck and Joey showed up. When she discovered in her heart an emotion she couldn't name.

Kathleen's father came in, greeted her mother and asked, "Is Kathleen home?"

She hurried from the dining room. "I'm here, Father."

"Good. Good." He settled down with the paper. "I don't want you spending all afternoon at that woman's place."

"Her name is Rosie Zacharias and she is a very nice woman, as you would surely know if you ever visited her."

Father looked over the top of his paper at Kathleen's tone. She instantly repented of her peevishness. "I only meant she's a good mother and a decent person."

Neither parent said a thing, but Kathleen knew she had shocked and disappointed them with her attitude. She had no wish to be disrespectful. In the future she must guard her thoughts and her tongue.

The hours dragged the next morning as Kathleen helped her mother sort through letters from family members. For some reason Mother enjoyed reading them over and over and putting them in chronological order. "I'm sure some day these will constitute a valuable family history."

Kathleen restrained herself from saying she wondered

who would be interested in the chitchat, gossipy things most of the aunts and cousins related. "Today I wore a new chiffon dress. You would love it. Palest blue. One of your favorite colors, as I recall." "I think I neglected to tell you Mamie and Fred have been seen together more often than not. Why, I myself saw them rowing on the lake Sunday." Kathleen had no idea who Mamie and Fred were, or why anyone should care if they went out together in a rowboat.

She sighed at her frustration. Perhaps she was only being petty because she didn't have anyone who would take her out in a boat, which wasn't exactly true. Young Merv, who worked with Father, would surely take her out if she offered him any encouragement. Perhaps not in a boat, though, as there wasn't a decent lake nearby and she didn't fancy a long ride with him to get to one. She secretly thought the man a little too impressed with himself to be interesting.

He never showed the kindness to others that Buck did. Nor the approval Buck had expressed to her yesterday afternoon.

Finally Kathleen's father arrived home for lunch, again taken in the dining room. As soon as they finished and he returned to work, Mother went to lie down. At last Kathleen could don her winter outerwear and hurry to visit Rosie.

The house rang with laughter as she stepped inside. Buck was on all fours on the floor, playing horsey to three boisterous boys.

Mattie tumbled off and pulled the others with him. They landed in a giggling heap. Buck corralled the trio and tickled them. They escaped to tackle him.

Rosie held young Lilly as she watched. Kathleen stood beside her and grinned at the roughhousing.

"They've missed Bill. He played with them," Rosie said.

Kathleen tried to remember if she'd ever played with her father. She recalled only sedate walks during which she held his hand and flashed shiny new shoes. If not for the children of a large family—the Rempels—who lived a few blocks away, she wondered if she would even know what play was. Mary Rempel had been her best friend. Kathleen remembered afternoons of giggling and boisterous games and a pretend house in the bushes of the backyard. When the family moved away, Kathleen knew unabated loneliness until she went to a private girls' school. But even then, her friendships proved transitory. Again, she wondered if it was her fault. Was she lacking some necessary social skill?

Buck rolled to his back, saw Kathleen watching him and grew still, his eyes flashing such warmth and welcome she forgot to breathe. "Hi," he said. The word seemed to come from deep inside his chest.

Was it her imagination that made her think he silently invited her into a special world shared with him?

Of course it was. She gave herself a mental shake. "Everyone seems to be having a fine time."

"It won't last," Rosie predicted. "Not this close to nap time."

Mattie rolled into Junior, and right on cue they started to cry.

"Come on, you two." Rosie led the way to the bedroom. "Bedtime."

Buck sat up on the floor and pulled Joey into his arms. "What do you say, little buddy? Time for a rest?"

Joey pressed his head to Buck's shoulder. "I sleep here?"

Buck nodded. "For a little while, though I think I'll sit in a chair if you don't mind."

"I not mind."

Cradling the boy, he plunked himself on a kitchen chair.

Kathleen realized she still wore her coat and slipped it off. She sat across the table from Buck as Joey's eyes slowly closed. Watching the two of them brought a sting of tears to the back of her nose. "I think he's asleep," she whispered.

Buck nodded. "He's still not up to his normal self." He held the boy a moment longer, then laid him on the bed and covered him before he returned to the kitchen.

She sewed together more quilt pieces and tried not to be aware of his presence. Yet she couldn't stop her eyes from glancing at him.

He leaned his elbows on the table, rested his chin in his palms and studied her so intently she ducked her head and concentrated on taking a small, even stitch.

"Tell me how you celebrate Thanksgiving in your house."

She drew in a steadying breath, grateful for the offer of normal conversation. "I love Thanksgiving. I didn't always. We have a formal meal, sometimes with guests." Mostly they were business associates and not exactly fun company for a young girl. "The mealtimes were often a bit dreary, but since the church started holding a special service with guest speakers and a shared meal, I've loved the day. More and more I appreciate how much God has blessed all of us." Her hands grew still as she sought for words to explain what she meant. "I am in awe of how much God loves us that He sent his son to earth as a baby. Can you imagine sending Joey into a place where you knew he would be shunned and tortured?"

Bleakness filled Buck's face, and she wished she hadn't used his son as an example. She tended to forget he was mixed-race and likely faced prejudice.

"Good reason to spend winters in isolated shacks, wouldn't you say?"

She didn't think so, but how could she explain in such a way she wouldn't be misunderstood? "What I see between you and Joey," she began slowly, forming her thoughts as she spoke, "is a wonderful example of fatherly love and care. I'm convinced you would do anything for his well-being. I think by hiding your relationship, by seeking isolation, you deprive others of witnessing such a fine example. Our society is the poorer for the loss." She could think of nothing more to add, though the words were inadequate for the emotion she tried to convey.

Buck stared at her, swallowed hard. "You make me want to walk boldly into the town's businesses with Joey at my side."

"There's no reason you shouldn't." But was it for his sake and Joey's she wanted him to believe so? Or for her own sake? She let a picture form in her mind of Buck openly being her friend.

"Life isn't so simple for everyone." His expression grew hard, guarded. Again, the evidence of a secret.

She wanted to ask him about it, but Rosie returned and took up needle and thread.

For the next few days, the afternoons passed in the same fashion with the exception that Buck didn't give her an opportunity to say anything more about walking openly and proudly down the street. Kathleen prayed he would believe he could do so or that she would get a chance to discuss it again, because every day she discovered something more she liked and admired about this man—his easy laughter when he played with the children, the way he sprang to his feet to help Rosie. And herself. She ducked her head over her sewing to hide the heat in her cheeks as she thought of how he lifted her coat from her shoulders and hung it on the rack. A common courtesy, yet when his fingers brushed her neck her reaction was far from common. The way her heart lurched against her rib cage made it impossible to think.

Each afternoon, he escorted her home.

"Won't you come in and meet Mother?" she asked on this particular day—a request she'd considered several times before, but because of her uncertainty as to how Mother would react, she'd never yet voiced it. Now she wanted nothing more than for Buck and Mother to meet.

"I don't think it would be wise," Buck said, his expression giving away nothing.

"I think you'd enjoy meeting my mother. And she you."

He shook his head. "There are things you don't know about me. No one here does. Best to keep it that way."

"I wish you'd tell me what they are so I could understand." She didn't care that her request made it sound like she had a right to know, which she didn't—except for the fact that she admired him and cared how he seemed to feel, he must remain an outsider.

A gentle smile lifted his lips and softened his gaze. "Maybe I will some time." Hardness returned so fast, she almost gasped. "You do realize I promised Rosie I wouldn't hang about until people noticed me. I think I am perilously close to reaching that place."

She reached for his arm, stopped herself before she touched him. "You won't suddenly disappear without a word, will you? I've had friends that dropped out of my life like that. I—" Why did she think it would matter how it had shattered her life? But she steadied her voice and continued. "I found it hard to accept. I asked myself all sorts of questions. Was it my fault? Was there something wrong with me? Wasn't I worthy of their friendship?"

His smile touched her. "Kathleen, anyone would be honored to be your friend."

Her thoughts skidded to a halt as his words spread like wildfire through her insides. Honored? Could he possibly mean it?

"I'll tell you before I leave. I promise."

She nodded and relaxed. She had a strong feeling that a promise from Buck was as good as money in the bank. "I'll see you tomorrow, then?"

"I'll be there."

She hurried into the house, a smile curving her lips. How sweet to know he would be there tomorrow. If only she could persuade him to consider more. More than that, he made her believe her lack of friends wasn't due to some flaw in her makeup.

Mother greeted her in the hall. "It's not proper for you to visit a man on the street like that."

"Mother, I wasn't doing anything wrong."

"He's below you." Mother made it sound like Buck belonged in the gutter.

"He's a decent man." Stilling defensive words on Buck's behalf, she hung her coat on the rack, glad of the excuse to avoid meeting her mother's gaze. "Just as his sister is a decent woman."

"Your father and I don't approve of how much time you're spending with this family."

"Mother, I am only extending Christian kindness in a way I feel I should." Yet it was as much for her sake as for theirs that she went. Having Rosie and Buck as friends eased her loneliness. But only one argument would convince Mother. "Jesus didn't make a distinction between the rich and the poor."

"He was God. You are just a woman."

"I can't believe you said that." She slowly faced her mother. "I don't think my being a woman has anything to do with extending friendship to others." Was it only friendship she longed for from Buck? Or did something deeper, wider, more intense beckon? Afraid her cheeks would flash guilty color, she ducked her head to dust her skirt. Friendship was a good start, but she allowed herself to acknowledge she wanted more.

Buck, with his easy love for Joey, Rosie and her children, and with his loyalty to what he believed, filled in the hollow spots in her heart simply by being there.

If only he would stop believing he had to leave.

"Your father is right. That Eastern college has given you strange ideas."

"No, Mother. Reading God's word—" learning to think for herself "—has given me these ideas, and I'd hardly call them strange." She slipped her arm through her mother's. "Now let's not argue. Tell me what you've been doing. Did you finish going through your letters?"

Mother sniffed then brightened at the chance to talk about what she'd done. "I finished them and started to answer some I've neglected. I haven't seen some of these dear people since before you were born, but I don't want to lose contact."

Kathleen encouraged her mother to talk and tried to still the little annoyance that she felt more regard for people whom she hadn't seen in twenty years or so than she did for those who lived only a few blocks away.

Later that night, after she'd gone to bed, she heard her parents talking and guessed she was the subject of their long discussion. She fully expected one of them to insist on her ending her visits to Rosie's. But after lunch the next day, her mother wiped her arm across her eyes in a gesture of weariness and waved her away. "Do what you want. I need to have a nap."

Thankful to be free to continue her visits, Kathleen slipped away.

Joey was stronger, ready to travel. Still Buck made no plans to leave. He couldn't bring himself to do so. Not yet. Not while Kathleen continued to come. He anticipated every visit with restless joy. Her very presence in the house filled it with sunshine and—

Perhaps only his heart felt the vibrations of happiness.

Perhaps if she, for some reason, stopped coming he would be able to leave.

But she seemed committed to regular visits. According to Rosie, she hadn't come every day until recently. Actually, what Rosie said was she hadn't come every day until Buck showed up. She'd said it with a mixture of teasing and annoyance.

"You can't stay. Have you forgotten?"

"You make sure I don't forget."

"If things were different, I would welcome you. You know it."

He nodded. "Things will never be different."

"I know, but I hope my kids can be free of our fear."

His staying put her hope at risk. He should be on his way, but still he stayed. Always giving himself one more day. Promising tomorrow he would tell Kathleen he had to leave. Then finding some excuse not to inform her, thus giving him a reason to linger one more day.

"You'll go to the Thanksgiving service with her, won't you?"

Rosie hesitated. "I'm thinking about it."

"It's your chance to leave the past behind."

"I know. To be honest, Kathleen makes me want to be closer to God."

"Me, too."

A knock informed them Kathleen had arrived. Rosie nodded at him to answer the door. "I've got Lilly." They both knew it was not the reason.

Buck's growing affection for Kathleen would only make it harder to leave. His heart wanted to see her and enjoy her company one more day. One more day to fill his insides to brimming with her sweet presence.

But one more day would never be enough.

Gritting his teeth, he pushed away the temptation to ignore the reality of his life and stay. Let people find out about his pa. Let them do what they wanted. It would be worth it to enjoy day after day of seeing Kathleen... Kathleen with the rich and powerful father.

What was he thinking? Her father had the power to destroy not only his life but also Rosie's and the children's. He had the power to make Kathleen's life miserable.

Buck vowed he'd leave before he'd allow that to happen.

He opened the door and smiled a welcome that echoed in Kathleen's eyes. Could it be she was growing fond of him, too? She'd been outspoken in her admiration, which he found endearing.

Growing fondness on her part put her future at risk, too. Her mere association with him and Rosie could destroy her. He had no wish to hurt her. For her sake he must leave soon.

Just one more day. Even better—a special outing. The idea was perfect.

He lifted her coat from her shoulders and hung it beside his own. Perhaps some of her sweet flower scent would cling permanently to his jacket, and he could think of her every time he donned it. Not that he would need such a reminder. He would carry her in his heart.

"This is wonderful weather for November," he said, setting up the discussion for his intended suggestion. Snow had fallen a week or two ago and the temperature had been cold enough to freeze the ground, but otherwise it was pleasant enough for the time of year.

"Don't be fooled into complacency," Rosie warned. "Things could change any day now."

"All the more reason to take advantage of it while we can."

Kathleen and Rosie both stared at him and the little boys clustered around his knees, but Rosie was the one to demand an explanation. "What did you have in mind?"

"A picnic."

Rosie snorted. "It might only be November but it feels a lot like winter to my way of thinking."

"Why not?" He silently appealed to Kathleen, who showed a flicker of interest. "I could rent a wagon and we could go to a pond. The kids could play on the ice and we could have a big fire. Then enjoy cocoa and sandwiches. How does that sound?" He directed his question to the kids, knowing they would show more enthusiasm than the women.

"Fun," Junior said.

"Fun," Mattie echoed.

"Sure." Joey was more guarded. Perhaps because he'd spent his share of time out in the elements.

Buck turned to Rosie first. "What do you think?"

"So long as it's not cold."

He turned to Kathleen. "You in?"

Her eyes gleamed. "I'm invited?"

"Of course." It was the reason for his idea. "Tomorrow?"

Rosie looked at the little ones. "I could feed them an early lunch so they can have their naps. That way we can enjoy the warmest part of the day."

"Then it's a plan." Buck scrubbed his hands together. One more special memory to take with him when he left.

One more excuse for delaying his departure.

The children were excited about the planned picnic, so Rosie took longer than normal to get them settled for their naps. Buck held Joey and wondered if he would have the same difficulty, but Joey soon nodded off. Buck held him even after Kathleen whispered that he had fallen asleep. He found comfort in the small body curled against him. At least he would have this bit of human contact when he left. The idea provided only a little comfort. Having met Kathleen, he now knew it would never be enough to have Joey, though he loved the boy beyond measure.

After a few minutes, he carried Joey into the bedroom. When he returned, he pulled out a bit of wood he had begun carving.

"What are you making?" Kathleen asked.

"A little horse for Joey. Watching him enjoy the toys Rosie's children have made me realize how few things Joey has. I intend to remedy it."

Her hands grew still. "You're a good father. Are there other things Joey needs that you might have overlooked, do you suppose?"

She didn't need to spell it out. He knew what she meant—the boy needed a permanent home. He agreed. But it didn't change the facts of his life—namely that people weren't prepared to let him enjoy such luxury.

He felt her watching him. Tried to ignore it but his resistance proved fragile. He lifted his head and let her search his thoughts. Yes, Joey needed a real home. So did Buck. In his deepest, most secret dreams, he longed for the acceptance she hinted he deserved.

He knew it was a fleeting mirage.

"Joey and I will survive the best way we know how."

Slowly her expression changed, softening. "I think you are close to wanting to belong."

"Wanting to belong has never been in question." He closed his mouth firmly. He yearned to tell her everything but he dare not. It would surely put an end to her friendship. Not only with himself but also with Rosie, and Rosie didn't deserve to be robbed of Kathleen's acceptance. He pulled his gaze away and concentrated on the horse he shaped. "I think Joey will enjoy this toy."

"I'm sure he will." She didn't say anything for a spell. "Can I bring the hot cocoa for tomorrow?"

"If you like."

Rosie joined them. "I'll make sandwiches. You know, Buck, this is a good idea. I'm looking forward to an outing."

So was Buck, but for entirely different reasons that were selfish and likely dangerous. He should be leaving, not making plans to stay yet another day. Such plans were foolish and fraught with danger.

But for a little while, a precious interruption to his normal life, Buck was going to ignore the warnings of his gut.

Chapter Five

Buck loaded the children in the back of the wagon he'd rented from the livery. Rosie chose to sit in the back with the children. She slanted him a teasing smile as she got comfortable. "I'll let Kathleen sit up front with you." Her teasing vanished into warning. They both knew this interlude must end soon. Before their secret was discovered.

But for now, Buck was happy to ignore the dangers. He helped Kathleen up to the seat and took his place beside her. "Couldn't ask for better weather, could we?"

"It's beautiful."

The sun shone with golden intensity. No breeze stirred the air. Temperatures hovered at the freezing mark. Perfect for ice skating. Perfect for bonfires and winter picnics.

"Sam at the livery barn told me about a pond where people go skating. Said it was a great place for a picnic." Buck laughed. "He said he could name half a dozen couples who began their courting at a skating party there."

Kathleen laughed softly. "I know the place and two

such couples. Of course, they went after dark, so maybe that makes a difference."

"'Spect so." Though he didn't intend to waste any opportunity the afternoon might present. Of course, he didn't have courting and marriage on his mind. He concentrated on guiding the wagon through a gate and down a trail toward a grove of trees. To be perfectly honest, he admitted he might have been considering both if his circumstances were different.

They weren't. But he didn't intend to let that fact rob him of one ounce of enjoyment this afternoon.

The trail led directly to a large opening. Evidence of previous fires blackened the ground. Crude wooden benches circled the burnt area. Soldierlike, bare-branched trees guarded the spot. An ice-covered pond had been partially cleared, as if used just the night before.

"This is perfect." He jumped from the wagon and assisted Kathleen to the ground. If his hands lingered at her waist longer than necessary, no one seemed to notice. He allowed himself the luxury of breathing in her scent, enjoying the reflection of the sky in her eyes, feeling the warmth of the sun from her smile before he stepped away to help Rosie and the children.

The boys squealed in delight and headed for the ice. Mattie could hardly keep his feet under him, but the other two were soon running and sliding, laughing in complete abandonment of joy. Rosie stood to the side watching, Lilly in her arms. The little girl chortled at the boys and Rosie smiled.

Kathleen moved to Buck's side. "This idea of yours is wonderful."

He grinned down at her. "I have them once in a while."

"Have what?" She managed to look confused.

"Good ideas."

Her musical laughter rang through the trees. "I'd say you have them quite often."

He let himself enjoy her praise, let himself hold her gaze while her warm look filled his heart. If only the afternoon could last forever. But he'd waste none of it.

With wood he'd brought with him and kindling gathered from the trees, he built a fire then carried the lunch basket and a knapsack to one of the benches. Kathleen followed with a jug of cocoa.

He'd brought a scoop shovel and headed for the pond. "Who wants a ride?"

The three boys scrambled to his side, slipping and sliding. "Youngest to oldest." Mattie sat on the scoop and Buck pushed him about the ice.

An hour later he was ready for a break. They trooped toward the fire, where Kathleen poured cocoa into mugs for each of them. Rosie handed out sandwiches and cookies.

He sat next to Kathleen, Joey on his other side, and Buck thought life couldn't get any better than this. A son he loved, a woman he—

He stuffed half a cookie in his mouth. Better to stick to what was possible.

"I used to come here with some friends when I was much younger." Kathleen's voice carried notes of regret and sadness.

Wishing to erase those notes, Buck shifted to study her. "Why did you stop coming?"

Her eyes filled with surprise. "You know, I can't say. Part of the reason, I suppose, is the neighbors who took me with them moved away, and I felt conspicuously alone when I came on my own. Then I got involved in other things."

The children finished their lunch and went back to play. Rosie followed them, leaving Buck and Kathleen alone. There were so many things he wanted to know about her. What she'd been like as a girl. The dreams she'd had. Which ones remained. "Tell me what types of things you're involved in."

"Up until this past fall, I spent three years attending a girls' boarding school, where we were strictly supervised. My father would expect nothing else. Of course there were those who found ways to disobey the rules." She shrugged. "I never felt the need. I loved my studies. I took on some extra projects." Her eyes glistened with pleasure at the memory. "One of the teachers led us on a study of the life of Christ. She urged us to see Him at work in this world and base our lives on how He would live."

"You really liked that, didn't you?"

"It was exactly what I needed to find purpose in my life."

"So you became a do-gooder?" Was that her only reason for befriending Rosie?

Her expression flattened. He wished he could bite back the words and bring the joy into her face again.

"I hope not. I wanted to live my life with purpose and meaning, not selfishly or with judgment. I want my life to reflect my gratitude for all God has given each of us."

He touched her hands as they lay still and peaceful

in her lap. "Forgive me for speaking so harshly. From our first meeting, you have made me aware of my need to open myself up to God. Both Rosie and I were raised to love Him, but over the years I've neglected my faith."

Her eyes shone with happiness and she turned her hands into his. He twined his fingers through hers.

"Nothing would make me happier than to know you've returned to your faith." Her soft words felt like a benediction.

"Why is that?" If only he could allow himself to think it was because she cared about him in a personal way. But why was he even contemplating such a joy? He blocked from his mind the way he pictured her looking if she found out the truth about him.

Enough. He would not allow anything to mar this afternoon.

Rosie returned, Mattie at her side. "Play here with Lilly." She shifted her attention to Buck. "The bigger boys are too fast for him. They're having a great time out there."

Further conversation between himself and Kathleen was impossible. Except he had a plan. He spoke to Rosie. "Would you mind watching Joey while Kathleen and I go for a skate?"

"But I didn't bring skates." Kathleen looked so disappointed, he could have kissed her.

"I've taken care of it. Sam lent me some. Says he always keeps a few on hand." He retrieved the rucksack from the bench and pulled out two pairs of skates. "I brought some extra socks in case you needed them."

"Those look like mine," Rosie protested.

"I didn't think you'd mind."

"I don't, but it wouldn't hurt to ask."

He grinned at her. "This way I didn't have to endure any advice." Or teasing. Or warnings.

She waved away his remark. "Enjoy yourself while you can."

"I intend to." Her unspoken warning filled him with even more determination to make the most of the day. "Let me." He knelt before Kathleen, unbuckled her boots and slipped one foot at a time into the skates. He forced himself to act as if it were no different from helping Joey put on a pair of boots, but his chest muscles grew taut, making breathing difficult. Her foot was so small. So dainty. It made him want to protect her. But he was probably the worst threat she'd ever had in her life. He tightened the laces, then sat beside her to do his own. "I warn you, I haven't been on skates in a couple years."

"I haven't been since last winter."

"I suppose you skate like a dancer."

She laughed softly. "I've had lessons, if that's what you mean."

"Wonderful. You'll make me look like a clod."

She rose and held out a hand to him. "Who's watching?"

"I will be," Rosie said. "And I won't hesitate to laugh when my brother lands on his bottom."

Buck didn't give her the satisfaction of acknowledging her teasing. Instead he took Kathleen's hand and led her to the ice.

Joey saw him and slid over. "You going skating?"

"With Kathleen. You stay here with Aunt Rosie. Okay?"

Joey studied him unblinkingly for a moment, then

shifted his study to Kathleen. Buck hoped he wouldn't say something to make her uneasy. But he smiled. "Okay."

Buck reached for Kathleen's hands, holding them so their arms crisscrossed in the usual skating pose. She fit perfectly at his side and matched her strides to his. He hadn't skated in a while, but discovered he had no trouble keeping on his feet. They circled the cleared area several times. She laughed as he stumbled on a corner. He held her steady when she caught her skate on a lump in the ice. A path had been cleared around the perimeter of the pond. He indicated it. "Shall we?"

"I'd love to."

They skated away from the noise, the fire and into a world where they were alone in the silence. He shifted to hold her hands and skated backward so he could watch her face. "Are you planning to return to your college in the near future?"

"I have no definite plans. Mother seems better some days, but then she gets worse again."

"What's wrong with her?"

"The doctor calls it general malaise. I know she's worse if anything upsets her, so I do my best to keep things calm in the house."

He liked the way she grew thoughtful, full of genuine concern for her mother. "You are a good daughter."

"Thank you. I try. After all, I'm their only child."

"That sounds like a huge responsibility."

She smiled gently.

Oh, how he'd grown to love her smile. If only he could capture it in his palms, tuck it in his pocket and carry it with him into the future. Then whenever he was discouraged or lonely, he could pull it out and enjoy the memory of this day.

Unfortunately he knew the memories, although all he'd have, would never suffice.

"It doesn't feel like a responsibility when it's done out of love."

He understood she would never choose someone or something over loyalty to her parents. Although he admired the trait in her, it left him feeling lonely. He forgot to move his feet. One skate caught on the ice. He churned his legs trying to keep his balance. The moment he knew it was futile, he pulled Kathleen to his chest to protect her. His feet went up. His back went down and he landed with a thud that shook the air from him. His lungs hurt. He couldn't make them work.

Kathleen lay across his chest. She pushed back to look into his face, her eyes dark blue and full of things he dared not acknowledge.

She saw he couldn't breathe and scrambled to her knees. "Buck, take a breath." She shook him a little. "Come on. You're scaring me."

His lungs decided to work, and he sucked in air until he wondered how much he could hold. He let it out in a gusty exhalation and lay there.

"Are you okay?"

He hadn't intended to frighten her, but oh, it felt good to know she would worry so about him. He sat up and grinned at her. "I'm fine, sweet Kathleen. Just fine." He got to his feet, pulling her up with him.

Sweet Kathleen, he'd called her, the sound of her name on his lips pleasant as honey. He stood facing her, studying her.

"You aren't hurt, are you?"

"I'm fine." She struggled to bring her thoughts into order. "You took the brunt of the fall."

"Let me check you over." He turned her about, brushed snow from between her shoulders, then brought her back to face him. He took his time examining her face. The warmth of his gaze on her lips brought a toe-to-hairline blush to her skin.

"There's snow stuck to your hair." He brushed it away with his fingers. They seared across her cheek.

She caught her breath as something wrenched inside her—a sweet, fierce sensation of pleasure and hope. Her growing fondness and admiration for Buck bordered on something more profound. A feeling so new and powerful she didn't want to examine it too closely for fear it would abandon her.

"Kathleen." His husky whisper reached into her head, making it impossible to think beyond this moment when time ceased to exist.

His gaze grew more intense as he looked so deeply into her eyes, she felt his gaze touch her innermost secrets. "Kathleen," he breathed her name again, his attention on her mouth.

He lowered his head. She knew he meant to kiss her. He paused—whether to give her time to demure or to reconsider his intention, she couldn't say.

She had no desire to refuse him and tilted her head upward. His lips claimed hers, warm, firm, gentle… almost reverent. She clutched at his upper arms, holding on as the world fell away and there was nothing but them.

He ended the kiss but pulled her to his chest and pressed her face to the spot where Joey found such comfort and welcome, and she found the same. This man was a rock. An anchor. She could trust her very being to him.

"Kathleen, you are a special woman."

She smiled into the soft warmth of his coat. "Buck, you are a special man. A noble and good man."

His chuckle rumbled beneath her ear. "I love to hear you say so."

Love? Could this be love? This wonderful, satisfying, exhilarating sensation of wanting time to stop, everyone else to disappear, her life to begin at this moment? If so, she couldn't imagine anything better in the whole world.

Buck eased her back, took her hands and pressed them tight to his chest. "We need to get back."

"Of course." She'd forgotten the others. Forgotten everything but Buck. But he would never forget Joey. "I wish—"

"Shh." He pulled her closer. "Let's take what God offers us without demanding more."

It sounded like a warning not to expect anything beyond the moment. "Buck, won't you consider staying? Give people a chance to see how good and noble you are?"

He stiffened, tried to hide it. Sighed almost imperceptibly. She knew he didn't intend for her to notice. "Kathleen, I wish I could."

"Is it because of Joey?" She wanted desperately for him to say it was the reason, even though it wouldn't explain why he'd promised Rosie he would stay away even when she didn't know he had a son. "Because you need to give people a chance to accept him."

"Do you think they ever would?"

"Perhaps not everyone, but there are those who would learn to love him for his sake. I'm sure of it." Her voice rang with determination and a bunch of things she couldn't hide—longing for him to stay, a promise to stand at his side on Joey's behalf and so much more.

"I wish I could believe you, but—"

She pulled at his arms, forcing him to face her. "You can. Stay. Give people a chance to accept him. And you." No doubt her eyes revealed everything she felt, but she didn't care. She wanted him to stay. For Joey's sake, of course. For his, too. But mostly for her. She wanted a chance for this fledgling feeling of love to grow and mature. *Please, God, let him see we can have something worth staying for.*

His eyes darkened with pleasure. His grasp on her hands tightened, and his smile flooded with what she hoped was love, or at least affection. Then without warning his expression flattened, grew hard. "You make me want to stay, but believe me, there are reasons I cannot." He pulled her to his side and they continued to skate toward the bonfire.

Why? The question clung to the tip of her tongue. She stared straight ahead, seeing nothing but a shiny blur. Why couldn't he stay? Or at least tell her his reason?

"Kathleen, I'm sorry." Neither of them broke stride in their skating rhythm. "Please believe me when I say I would stay if I could. I would stay for you."

She sniffed, finding small comfort in the hopeless words. She was almost relieved they drew near to the others and Joey shouted out a greeting and raced to their side.

"Hi, Buck. You were gone long time."

"It didn't seem long to me." He squeezed Kathleen's hands to signal his reason. Having him acknowledge he wanted to stay only deepened her pain.

She smiled and chatted as they gathered together their belongings, threw snow over the fire to douse it and returned to the wagon. The trip back to town seemed to take longer than the trip out had, and yet was over before she could think of anything to say to convince Buck that surely the reasons for staying outweighed his reasons for leaving.

They unloaded the children and picnic remnants at Rosie's. Buck turned to Kathleen, his eyes full of regret. "I'll give you a ride home, then return the wagon."

"Fine." She bid the others goodbye. She had only a few minutes to make any sort of appeal. She barely waited for him to sit beside her on the wagon. "I had hoped you might have some regard for me. That our kiss meant something more than a man and a woman falling inadvertently into each other's arms." She made no attempt to keep the hurt from her voice.

"Kathleen, I should not have kissed you, but I don't regret doing so. I do have feelings for you. But I have no right to them."

They both faced forward, mindful they rode through a town full of windows.

"You have the same rights as anyone else. The right to make a home where you choose. We are all equal in God's eyes." She left it there. How many ways could she tell him, ask him to stay without shamelessly begging? Truth is, she would beg if she thought it would make a difference.

"Not everyone is equal in man's eyes." His tone was brittle. Suddenly he turned the wagon off the road in a direction that took them away from her home. "I have to tell you something."

He drove away from town and pulled to a halt beside some sheltering trees, sending protesting birds away. He leaned over his knees. His jaw muscles clenched and unclenched. With a deep sigh he turned.

She cried out at the despair lining his face. "What is it?"

"I wish I could stay. I've found something here with you I've wanted all my adult life, though I didn't know what it was I longed for." His expression softened as he let his gaze drift over her face.

"I've found something, too." She didn't want to lose it.

Buck rolled his head back and forth in a gesture so full of sadness and defeat that she clutched his arm. He pressed his hands over hers.

"Once you hear my story you will agree I can't stay. You won't want me to."

"Can anything be that terrible?"

He nodded.

"My father—" His gaze shifted past her.

She waited. A cold trickle snaked across her shoulders. What could possibly make him so tense?

"My father was a good man." His snort of laughter was mocking. "At one time. He worked in a mill. Liked his work until a new owner bought the place. The new man expected his employees to work unreasonable hours. He took shortcuts that were dangerous. My father—" Word by word, Buck's voice grew more and more harsh. "He was injured at the mill. Broke his leg and was laid up for months. His leg never healed right. When he tried to go back to work, the mill owner said they had no room for cripples."

"Oh, Buck. How dreadful."

He grimaced. "It gets worse." Again his gaze sought distant places where she could not follow. "My mother got ill and needed medicine that Pa couldn't afford. He begged for his job or any job. Again and again he got turned away. One night Ma was suffering so. It was awful to watch. Pa walked about, angry and cursing God and the mill owner. Then he dashed from the house." The breath Buck sucked in seemed to go on forever. "He didn't come home that night. We didn't know until morning what happened. Our pa—" Buck's words were whispered agony. "Took an axe and killed the mill owner."

"Buck." It was a mere breath of a word. "Oh, Buck." Kathleen's heart had stopped beating. Her lungs had stopped drawing in air. The horror of Buck's experience filtered through a red and purple haze of shock.

"He hanged for it. Ma died. And Rosie and I—her only thirteen, me a year younger—were run out of town."

She sobbed once. Wave after wave of shock coursed through her body.

"The first town of many we were chased from. Rosie and her children deserve a chance to be accepted here. I could ruin that for them. That's why I have to leave before anyone finds out."

His words brought an abrupt end to her anguished

shock. "Why must you leave? You're a good man. Let people learn that."

He grabbed her shoulders. "Am I? Or am I my father's son? Perhaps people have a reason to be afraid of me."

She caught his face between her palms and searched his gaze until she found an entrance into his thoughts. "Sins are not inherited. You are a fine, decent man whom I am honored to know."

His hungry look showed he wanted to believe her.

"Buck, you are a good man. I know it, and I think you do, too." She smiled at his look of hope. She must convince him and she leaned closer, pressed her lips to his. Startled a reaction from him. He wrapped his arms about her and pulled her close, clinging to her kiss.

Just as quickly he withdrew, but not before she'd done her best to prove her opinion of his worth. "You're a good man, Buck."

He shook his head. "Even if I believe it…even if you do, others will not. And they can make life unbearable. Believe me."

"Maybe you've never met a Sanderson before. If my father decrees you should be accepted, do you really think anyone in town will argue?" Not that she was naive enough to think everyone agreed with her father. Only that they were careful about how they expressed their differences. Nor did she think she could convince her father to change his opinion about Buck without some very convincing arguments that she would do her best to formulate.

Buck chuckled. "I see there are advantages to having a rich, powerful father. However—"

"I'd like for you to stay. Give it some thought." She was certain his feelings for her were growing as quickly as hers for him. God willing, it would be enough to persuade him to confront his past and put it to rest.

Buck edged the wagon forward and turned them about. "I better get you home before your father comes looking for you."

In a few minutes they reached her house. He pulled the wagon to a stop and hurried around to help her descend.

They stood facing each other, a hundred wishes swirling through her mind and likely revealing themselves on her face. She didn't care. She wanted a chance to love this man.

He squeezed her shoulder for but a touch, then climbed to the wagon. She grabbed the side to keep him from driving away. "Promise me you'll think about what I said."

His smile brimmed with hope. "I'll think about it."

She stared after him until he turned a corner out of sight. Then she made her way up the sidewalk to face her parents, who she guessed would have watched the proceedings out the window.

Chapter Six

Buck didn't realize how much Rosie had read into the situation, though his expression likely gave away a lot. She waited until they'd had their evening meal and the children had gone to bed.

"Okay, brother, what happened between you and Kathleen?"

He examined the nail bed of his thumb. How could he begin to explain how he felt? How much he loved Kathleen and wished things could be different? "I kissed her."

Rosie shoved her cup out of the way to lean across the table. "Have you lost your mind? Do you know who she is?"

He gave her only stubborn denial. "Of course I do. She's Kathleen Sanderson. A very sweet woman."

"She's also the daughter of the richest, most powerful man in these parts." Rosie let out a noisy gust. "He would never let his sweet daughter look twice at a nobody like you. Worse than a nobody—the son of a murderer. And—" She pressed forward again. "He would stop at nothing to discredit you in her eyes. And in the eyes of all the people around here. You know how easy that will be. Why have you let it go so far? Just when I thought I might be able to forget the past."

"No one will ever let us forget the past. But perhaps it's time to stop trying to outrun it."

Rosie bolted to her feet. "You really think you can change things? Stop and think. How many times have we tried before? Having a murderer for a father marks us. It always will." She glanced about the house. "This is one of the best places I've had. I don't want to leave." She stopped at Buck's side and grabbed his face to turn it toward her. "You are going to wreck my life for nothing."

"Not for nothing. For a chance for Joey and me to belong."

She turned away from him. "Belong somewhere else."

He didn't say somewhere else would not be the same. Kathleen wouldn't be anywhere but here. Yet she didn't need him to say the words to know what he thought, and she gave a snort of disgust. "Buck, what do I have to do to get you to leave?"

He struggled between wanting to protect Rosie and longing for the love he'd ached for for so many years, he'd grown almost comfortable with the feeling.

Now, for the first time, he'd found the answer to his loneliness. Perhaps, like Kathleen said, he needed to stay and prove he deserved it.

Kathleen smiled as she stepped into the house. Buck had kissed her. She had kissed him. If the way he kissed meant anything, it wouldn't take much to convince him to stay.

She sighed as she hung her coat. She wished she knew exactly what it would take. But it seemed to be something more than she could offer. The thought clogged her heart. Why couldn't she be enough?

She turned and came face-to-face with her father.

"I came home from work early because I was worried about your mother. I found her sitting alone in the dark. Is it too much to expect you to be here when your mother needs you?"

"I'm sorry." She hurried past him to her mother's side. "Are you ill?"

"I'm very, very weary."

Kathleen rubbed her mother's hands. "What can I do?"

"Stop going to visit that woman." Her father spoke harshly.

Kathleen bowed her head. *Oh, God. Please don't let him forbid me to go.*

He went to his chair and plopped down. "I think it's time you returned to that school I paid for you to attend. It's not like you're helping your mother a lot."

"I'm not sure I want to return."

Mother took her hand. "Maybe if you simply decide to stay home instead of going *there*." She said the word with more than a hint of bitterness.

Kathleen couldn't answer. She didn't want to go back to the college. She couldn't promise she wouldn't visit Rosie. She hoped and prayed Buck would stay. Somehow she had to convince her father to give them a chance. If only he would meet them, she was certain he'd approve of them. But she wouldn't speak her thoughts until she'd had a chance to pray about them and form a plan. *God, help me.*

She spent the rest of the afternoon at her mother's side, reading to her, fixing her tea, locating a certain necklace she thought she'd lost. It wasn't until later in the evening when her mother had gone to bed that she finally withdrew to her own room to consider the events of the day.

But rather than focus on what her father said, and how to convince him to change his mind about Buck and Rosie, her thoughts went back to the afternoon. Buck had kissed her. A kiss loaded with a thousand unspoken promises. Or so she let herself think.

She lay on her back in bed and smiled into the darkness. Surely he'd felt something. Vowing she'd try again the next day to convince him to stay, she fell asleep with a smile on her face.

But the next morning, her mother was too ill to get out of bed.

"This is on your head," Kathleen's father said. "Bringing home dirt from there. Goodness knows what your mother is ill with, thanks to you." He scowled as he prepared to leave for work.

"Mother, I'm sorry." But she had been sick off and on before she started visiting Rosie, and Kathleen was certain she had not brought sickness home with her.

Her mother slept fitfully throughout the morning and sat up in bed for a lunch of clear soup and crackers. "I'm so weak," she murmured as she pushed away the tray without finishing.

"Can I do anything?" Kathleen refrained from glancing at the clock.

"Could you read to me? I really like the story you started the other day."

Kathleen could not refuse her mother, even though it meant she would not be able to go to Rosie's today. She got the book and settled in next to her mother to read. But it was only words she recited. Her mind was not on the story. If only she could send a message to Buck and let him know why she couldn't be there.

But she'd have to wait until tomorrow and an improvement in Mother's well-being.

At the knock at the door, Buck looked up from playing with the boys and helping Rosie. Had the morning passed so quickly? Or was Kathleen early? He knew the answer. It was much earlier than she normally arrived.

He headed for the door, eager to see her and judge if she'd changed her mind about him. He broke stride. What if she'd come to say they could no longer be friends?

He brushed his finger across his mouth. Her kiss said they could be friends and so much more.

Throughout the night, he'd considered if she could be right. Would people give him a chance to start over here if they knew the truth? Or could he expect to hide it from them? He'd mentally explored ways of disguising his true identity. A false name would be easy enough but carried no guarantees. Experience had taught him that nothing did.

He opened the door, his smile wide in greeting. A

man stood before him, scowling. Buck's smile flattened in an instant.

"You would be Buck, I presume. Buck Donahue."

His heart plummeted to the soles of his feet. So much for hiding his name. "And you would be?"

"Samuel Sanderson. I'm Kathleen's father."

"I see. Would you like to step inside?" Not that he felt exactly welcoming at the way the scowling man regarded him.

"I think I prefer to remain here. What I have to say won't take long."

Buck stepped outside and pulled the door shut behind him. He was pretty sure the kids didn't need to hear whatever the man was about to say. Rosie would guess correctly what it was.

Mr. Sanderson cleared his throat and drew himself up tall. Buck saw no resemblance to his daughter. Kathleen wore a countenance of love and joy. Just looking at her made others feel special. Her father made him feel dirty, despised.

"My daughter has been spending a lot of time here. I didn't approve when it was just your sister and her children. But when I heard a brother had arrived…well, it was my duty to discover what sort of person you are." He waited, as if expecting Buck to fill in the details.

He didn't intend to supply one single fact.

"I learned who you are, Mr. Donahue. I know about your father, Michael Donahue. How dare you think you can even breathe the same air as my daughter? I suggest you leave town immediately. We have no use for the likes of you in our presence. Kathleen doesn't care to see you again." He adjusted the lapels on his coat and turned to leave. Then paused. "I expect you'll be on your way by morning."

It wasn't a suggestion. Yet Buck didn't flinch before the man's demanding glare. Kathleen didn't care to see him again? He didn't believe it.

"I won't be run out of town on your say-so." He leaned forward, his eyes burning with determination. "I will not believe Kathleen doesn't want to see me again unless I hear the words from her mouth."

He dared not contemplate hearing such words.

Mr. Sanderson grunted. "You won't see her again, I promise you that." He stomped away without a backward look.

Buck did not return immediately to the house. He knew he must first compose himself so as not to give away anything to Rosie or keen-eyed Joey. A few minutes later he shivered in the cold and stepped inside.

Joey glanced up, studied Buck closely. Before the boy asked a question, Buck got very busy cleaning up the dirty dishes. Thankfully, Rosie had taken Lilly to the bedroom.

He kept busy but the words spoken by Mr. Sanderson circled inside his head like angry hornets.

I know about your father. How dare you? You won't see her again.

But Kathleen cared about him. She would find a way to at least say goodbye.

The morning, which had gone so fast until this point, slowed down to endless ticks on the clock. He could not expect her earlier than normal, but he tried not to hold his breath, to force his heart to beat again and again until the time arrived.

Rosie came from the bedroom. "Did I hear someone at the door?"

"I don't know. Did you?"

She rolled her eyes. "You know I did. Who was it?"

He couldn't bear to tell her. But soon enough the word would be out. "Later," he said, indicating the children clustered about the table.

Her eyes widened. "No. It can't be."

He nodded. "It is."

"I knew this would happen. I warned you, but would you listen? No. You let your heart rule your head. For what? You'll never have her. Instead you ruin my chances."

"Rosie, I'm sorry."

She drew her lips back in resignation as she looked about her small house. "It's not much, but this is my home. I don't want to move."

Joey edged closer, acutely aware of the tension in the air. "You move? Why? This nice house."

Rosie pulled him to her side. "You're right. I guess I'll stay as long as I can."

Buck rubbed his neck and wished life could be different. "Maybe once we're gone it won't matter."

Her eyes filled with sorrow. "It always matters."

"I know. I should have left long ago."

"We go?" Joey's eyes widened. "Where we go? This good place. I like it here. I like cousins. I like Aunt Rosie."

"I know you do. But this isn't home." Would he ever be able to offer his son a proper home?

Only if he stayed.

He straightened. Considered Rosie. Would staying hurt her chances of acceptance?

She watched him, her eyes narrowing. "Are you thinking what I think you are?"

"Probably."

"Then reconsider. I beg you."

"If Kathleen accepts us, don't you think the rest of the community will?"

"Buck, don't start expecting miracles."

He laughed. "Why not? Don't you believe God loves us as much as He loves the Sandersons?"

"I don't think it's God who runs the store and refuses service or who crosses the street to avoid a person."

His enthusiasm died. "You're right, of course." But Kathleen had almost convinced him it was possible to stay here and start a real life.

They ate lunch, but he barely heard a word of the children's talk as he waited for Kathleen to show up.

But it wasn't Mr. Sanderson's warning words taking up the space in his mind. It was the assurance of her sweet smile and total acceptance.

He could barely finish his meal as his anticipation grew. As soon as the children appeared to be done, he jumped up and began to gather the dirty dishes.

Soon the dishes were washed and dried and back in the cupboard. The table had been scoured to within an inch of annihilation. He stared out the window. The weather was clear. No impending storm to keep her away.

Sighing, he turned. Rosie had gone to the bedroom with Lilly and her boys. No doubt they were all sleeping.

Joey refused to go to bed. "I want to wait for Miss Kathleen."

"Have your nap so you'll be ready to visit her when she comes."

"I'll go to bed but I won't sleep." He got the stubborn look on his face that Buck knew well.

Kathleen was late. Something must have happened to delay her. He walked to the window to look out and saw nothing but snow-dusted grass and the empty beaten path leading to the center of town.

He turned to stare at the door. Perhaps she had knocked and he hadn't heard her. In a flurry of hope and despair he crossed the room and threw open the door, only to be greeted by a blast of cold air and nothing more. Quickly, he closed the door and leaned against it.

Time crept past on heavy, dragging feet.

The children came from the bedroom, sleepy-eyed and tousle-haired. Joey looked carefully around the room, as if expecting to find Kathleen in a corner. "She not come?"

"No. She didn't." Her father was right when he said she wouldn't come again. His insides tore open to realize she would turn her back on him because of her father's decision. But all along he'd tried to tell himself this would happen.

Rosie joined them. She gave him a look of sympathy but refrained from saying, "I told you so."

She didn't need to.

He had no more reason to stay. Only one thing would have made him change his mind, and Kathleen had not given him that invitation.

There was nothing he could do about it.

* * *

The afternoon passed on leaden feet as Kathleen read to her mother and spent time amusing her. When she finally dozed, the day was too far gone to dash over to Rosie's. Besides, she hesitated to leave her mother alone. She'd been really down all day.

She slipped from the room and hurried to kneel beside her bed. Why did God allow these delays? She wanted so much to be with Buck. Yesterday she'd felt he was very close to changing his mind about leaving. Her soul calmed as she prayed. Hearing her father enter the house, she returned to the sitting room. "Mother is sleeping. She's been restless all day."

"Good. I need to talk to you alone. Sit down."

She perched on the edge of the chair, wondering what called for such a serious look on her father's face. *Please don't let him forbid me to go to Rosie's.*

He folded his hands in his lap and looked so stern, her nerves twitched. "It's time you heard the truth about your friends."

"You mean Rosie?"

"Yes. And her brother."

She refrained from saying she knew all she needed to know.

"I took the liberty of doing a little investigation about your friends."

"Rosie and Buck," she insisted. "They have names."

"I am deeply disturbed by what I've discovered."

She guessed what he was about to say but kept her peace, knowing he must speak the words before she could offer any defense.

"You were too young to know the details and even

if you weren't, we would have shielded you from such grizzly information, but I think you must now know it all. About ten years ago there was a cold-blooded murder in a mill town in Colorado. I'll spare you the worst part, but let me simply say a man considered himself unjustly dealt with and took matters into his own hands. Revenge, plain and simple. He butchered the man who owned the mill." Father hesitated as if he knew more. "It was beastly. Needless to say, the man was hanged for murder."

She nodded. She'd heard it all from Buck, so it wasn't the shock it might have been.

"That man was named Michael Donahue. To this day, if you mention his name people get angry and upset. He killed a man with high connections and people aren't about to forget it."

Kathleen's father studied her closely. "Did you know your friends are Donahues?"

"Yes, I knew. Buck told me about it."

"You can understand why his offspring are not welcome in any community."

"But why? They had nothing to do with what happened."

"The acorn doesn't fall far from the tree." Her father shook his head as if he regretted his belief.

"Father, I respectfully disagree."

His face grew thunderous. Long ago she had learned to obey without arguing in order to avoid his disapproval, but never before had there been anything she felt so keenly she must defend.

"If you would but meet them, you would see they are both good and noble people who are living honorable lives. When has a child ever been held responsible for a parent's actions? Buck and Rosie were only twelve and thirteen at the time."

Her father rose to his feet, his posture so stiff she knew she had both offended and shocked him with her defense of the pair. "For your protection I don't intend to tell others, so long as that man leaves town."

He heart grew leaden at her father's stubbornness. "They're good people."

"You surely can't still believe that." He sat back down and leaned forward. "Kathleen, I must do what I think is best for you, as I always have. Just as I did with those other friends of yours."

"What do you mean?" She shivered, sensing she wouldn't like what he was about to say.

"You must have guessed what happened to the Rempels and why friends from your school don't contact you."

"No, Father. Tell me why." Cold dread iced her veins at what he suggested.

"I persuaded Mr. Rempel to move on to a better job. Took care of them very well. I allowed only letters from friends I considered appropriate."

"Father, how could you? You've confined me to a lonely life. And I blamed myself. I thought there was something wrong with me that made all my friends disappear." Her voice cracked and she clamped her mouth shut lest she say things she'd regret.

Her father looked confused for a moment, then his expression cleared. "I only did what I thought was best, and I always will."

"Kathleen." Her mother's voice came from her bedroom and Kathleen excused herself, grateful to have a reason to discontinue the conversation. But she might have swallowed thorns at the way her insides bled.

Chapter Seven

Kathleen tried to still her restless concern throughout the night, but she wanted nothing more than to rush to Buck's side and assure him she did not agree with her father.

But first she must spend the morning with her mother who insisted she was well enough to be up. She didn't want Kathleen to read to her. She didn't have any project she cared about doing. "I'm bored. If I felt stronger I would visit one of my friends." She sounded petulant.

"Would you like to help with a project I'm working on? It's a quilt."

Mother brightened. "I might like that."

Kathleen got the basket she'd brought from Rosie's and took out the unfinished top. "I'm helping Rosie make this for one of her children. They don't have enough warm bedding, so they'll truly appreciate it."

Her mother examined the needlework. Each square had been carefully stitched to the next with firm, even stitches that would last a good long time. "This is fine work. Did you do this?"

Kathleen looked at the section her mother examined. "Rosie did that." She moved the quilt. "I did this part."

Mother bent over the handwork. "Both of you do fine sewing."

Kathleen studied her mother. "Are you surprised I stitch a fine seam? Or that Rosie does?"

She fingered the material. "Both, I think. You were taught to do things like needlework and cross-stitch. This is so…"

"Practical?"

Mother's smile was full of self-mockery. "That makes me sound shallow."

"I don't mean to insinuate such. But there is something satisfying about knowing I'm working on a project to keep a little boy warm at night."

Mother took up a needle and thread and began to sew a square into the pattern. "Tell me about the little boy."

"It's Rosie's son, Junior. He's four years old and so grown up in some ways. Mattie, his little brother, is two, and Junior watches out for him."

"There are two children?"

"Three." She told about Lilly next. "And Rosie's brother has a child." She wondered how much to tell, but her heart overflowed. "Mother, I want to tell you about Rosie's brother. His name is Buck and he's adopted a little boy he found alone on the prairie." She repeated Joey's story.

"He's a half-breed child?"

"Yes, Mother." She prayed for wisdom to discuss this. After all, if Buck remained in the area and their relationship developed as she hoped, her mother would have to confront this issue. "That's his heritage, but who he is, what matters to people who know him, is that Joey is a very observant little boy who cares about how others feel. He's very loyal." She repeated some of the things Joey had said to defend Buck. "Buck is a loving, kind father."

Mother studied Kathleen. "This Buck—what do you know about him?"

Her fingers grew still as she met Mother's eyes. "I know all I need to know. I admire him greatly for doing what he knows is right, even though he understands some will frown at his choice to adopt Joey. He's a good man, Mother. I wish you would meet him. I think you'd like him."

The way her mother's gaze darted away told Kathleen she wasn't ready to accept Buck into her home. "Mother, I am growing very fond of him."

"Your father told me about him. His father is a murderer."

"But that isn't who he is. Don't you see? He needs people to see past what his father did to who he is."

"Kathleen, do you really think the community would ever accept him, knowing about his father? And seeing the boy he's adopted? People don't forgive and forget easily."

"I think I am growing to love Buck. I haven't told him so but I will. I don't want to be controlled by what people might say and miss God-given possibilities." There. She'd said it and it felt good and right. "I do not want to disappoint you and Father, but your caution about Rosie and Buck is misplaced and I intend to continue visiting them. If Buck returns my affections as I think he does, I will not reject him because of his father—and certainly not because of his son."

They stared at each other a long moment. Kathleen sensed no disapproval or censure in her mother's gaze. Dare she hope her mother understood the depth of Kathleen's feelings and would honor them?

She reached for one of Kathleen's hands. "I believe your motives are pure and honorable. But I fear this whole thing is out of your hands."

Kathleen jerked back. "What do you mean?"

"Your father visited this Buck—" she broke off as if the word stung her tongue "—yesterday and told him he wasn't welcome in our town."

Kathleen bolted to her feet. "Yesterday!" And she'd stayed home to care for her mother. "I must go. I must stop him from leaving."

"My dear, I expect you are too late."

"I must try." She raced for the door. If Mother forbade her—oh, she hoped it wouldn't come to that. She didn't want to be forced to disobey her mother.

But Mother watched her depart without uttering a word.

Buck stuffed the last of his belongings into the saddlebag. "I hope you will go to the Thanksgiving service. You and the kids deserve a chance to be accepted."

Rosie sat at the table watching his every move, her face a study in misery. "I don't have a lot to be thankful for. If only things could be different for both of us."

Three little boys clustered about Buck. Joey wore an expression of resignation. "We not staying ever, are we?"

The words scraped at Buck's head. He would love to give Joey a permanent home. "Don't make this any harder than it has to be, okay, little buddy?"

Joey nodded. "I go quietly."

Buck chuckled. "You make it sound like a walk to the gallows."

"What's that?"

"Never mind." He shouldn't have used that word and couldn't meet Rosie's gaze for fear she would be upset. "Joey, time to say goodbye."

Joey hugged his cousins and kissed Rosie.

Buck's heart sat heavy in his chest, weighed like ten gallons of cold water as Buck also hugged the children and kissed Rosie. "We'll walk to the livery barn and get our horses." He paused at the door. "Tell Kathleen goodbye for me if you get a chance."

Rosie nodded. "I will."

They both knew she might never get an opportunity. Kathleen may never again visit.

Joey strode at Buck's side, every step filled with determination. His loyalty to Buck meant he would always tuck in his chin and move when Buck moved.

"Buck, it's my fault, isn't it?"

"What is?"

"That we got to leave again. It's 'cause I'm Indian. I hear people say bad things about me. Call me dirty."

Buck stumbled. When had he heard such awful things? Of course, there were those who didn't consider Joey worth common courtesy. If only he could prevent such nasty talk. But he couldn't. And every time they moved on, Buck reinforced Joey's belief. "Buddy, it isn't because of you. It's because of me. Or I suppose, because of my father."

"But your father dead."

"Yes, he is." Someday he would have to tell Joey the whole truth, but not yet.

"Why a dead man tell you what to do?"

He stopped stock-still halfway across the street. Why did his father still control his life? Or Kathleen's father, for that matter? Would people ever stop telling him to move on? Seemed like too much to hope for. "Come on, Joey. We've got things to tend to."

Kathleen paused before Rosie's door and struggled to catch her breath. *Please, let me be in time to stop him.* She knocked.

Rosie answered the door, Lilly perched on her hip. She studied Kathleen from head to toe and back, then stepped aside to allow her entrance. "I didn't expect you again."

Kathleen glanced about the room. Mattie and Junior played on the floor. Her heart hammered a protest against her ribs. "Where is he?"

"He's gone." Rosie tried to sound hard but her voice trembled, gave away her sorrow.

"Gone? I'm too late?" She pressed a fist to her mouth to stifle a moan. "But he promised he would tell me before he left."

"I think all promises are off." Rose's voice tightened. "What did you expect? Your father told him to leave town. Told you wouldn't come again. Then you didn't show up. How did you think he'd take it?"

"I wanted to come yesterday, but Mother was ill. She needed me."

"I expect she did."

Kathleen lifted her face to study Rosie. A dreadful thought formed. "You think she pretended to be sick to keep me from coming?"

Rosie shrugged. "What do you think?"

"I don't know. I suppose it's possible. Today I informed her I intended to keep visiting here." Ignoring the heat stealing up her cheeks, she continued. "I told her I care about Buck. That's when she told me Father had been here. I didn't know until then."

Rosie didn't change her expression. She wasn't convinced.

"You must believe me."

"Buck's life is hard enough without some rich girl toying with him."

Kathleen jerked back. "You think—? No. It's not like that at all."

"Really?"

"Rosie, how can you say that? I thought we were friends." She scrubbed at the tickle in her nose. Things were not turning out at all the way she hoped. She pressed the heels of her hands to her eyes. God help her.

"I don't want to see Buck hurt anymore. He has very deep feelings."

Kathleen grabbed Rosie's hands. "I know. He is a good, honorable man. Tell me where he's gone. I love him and must find him and tell him so. If he won't stay, I'll go with him. I don't care where we go. Please tell me where I can find him."

Rosie studied her a long moment, measuring her

words, no doubt, against her father's. After a bit, she sighed. "He and Joey were going to the livery barn to get their horses. You might catch them if you hurry." She sounded doubtful, but Kathleen didn't pay any heed.

"I'll find him. I will. If he's gone I'll hire someone to ride after him." She dashed out the door and raced across town to the livery barn. Upon arrival, she glanced about the yard, didn't know if to be relieved or disappointed when she saw no one in the pen outside the barn. She stepped inside, giving her eyes a moment to adjust to the dim interior.

The livery man watched her. She gasped in air so she could speak. "I'm looking for a man and a boy. Have you seen them?"

"Would it be a particular man and boy or will any do?"

She laughed a little at the unexpected humor. "A tall, good-looking man and a dark-haired little boy."

He removed his hat and scratched his haystack hair. "Half-breed maybe?"

"The boy is." She waited in an agony of uncertainty as the man considered her answer.

"Uh-huh."

"You've seen them?"

He nodded past her. "Could that be them?"

She turned, saw Buck standing in the shadows grinning at her and sprang toward him. "Buck, you haven't left."

"So I'm a tall, good-looking man? I like that."

She ground to a stop, embarrassment racing up her neck and pooling in her cheeks. "Rosie said you were leaving," she whispered.

He bent to Joey. "Son, go play with the cat you found in the back."

Joey looked from one to the other as if seeking reassurance. "You not going to change your mind?"

"She said I was good-looking."

Joey grinned and dashed off.

Buck resumed his casual stance, one booted foot resting on the toe. Sure didn't seem in a hurry to leave. "Why are you here?"

There wasn't time to play silly games. He had to know what she felt. "To stop you from leaving."

"Why?"

"I think you know the answer."

He pushed his Stetson back, and the light from the door made his eyes look intense. "You didn't come yesterday."

"Mother was ill and I couldn't leave her."

He acknowledged her explanation with a slight tilt of his head. "Your father paid me a visit."

"I know. Please don't think he speaks for me."

He waited, studying her.

She wanted…expected…more—a welcome. A hug at the least. Then she realized what he needed. "Buck, you are a good and noble man. I cannot imagine how difficult life has been for you." Her words were coming out in a jumble. She hoped he could arrange them into a meaningful order. "All these years you have been driven away by people's opinion, but if you stay here I promise you I will stand at your side no matter what people say."

"What about your father?"

She hoped her mother had softened toward the Donahues. Maybe Father would, too. If not, she would do her best to bridge the gap between them. "I will not let him decide who I befriend. What better place to start over than right here where there are already people who accept you?"

"Friends, is it?"

She grinned. "I never said that was all." She took a step closer. "Buck, I think I love you."

"Kathleen, I know I love you." He pulled her into his arms and held her close, his cheek pressed to her head. He eased back, caught her chin in his fingers and lifted her face toward him. Slowly, his eyes adoring her as he lowered his head, he claimed her lips in a kiss so full of love and promise that a sob stalled in her chest.

The kiss ended and she sighed. "You're going to stay then?"

"I am indeed. I've got a job here at the livery barn for the winter. After that, well, we'll see."

"You'd already decided to stay before I begged you to."

He chuckled. "I decided Joey deserves a chance to know family and home and to be accepted. I figured it was time I gave myself the same chance."

A rustle to the side drew their attention to a little boy watching with a guarded expression. "You taking Buck?"

Kathleen held out a hand toward the boy. "I'm taking you both."

Grinning so hard his eyes flashed, he threw his arms around both of them. "I take you, too."

Buck scooped him into his arms and kissed Joey on one cheek while Kathleen kissed him on the other.

She reached for Buck's hand. "People can be so un-fair."

"But others can be so kind. Like you."

After Joey returned to playing with the cat, Kathleen leaned over and kissed Buck. They might face those who would judge Buck or Joey unfairly, but they would stand together and enjoy the good people in life.

A few hours later she prepared to return home. "I volunteered to decorate the church for Thanksgiving tomorrow. Will you help me?"

"Are you sure I should?"

"Very sure."

He kissed her. "I'll be there."

She hurried away to face her parents. She did not look forward to informing them Buck was staying in town and she intended to be his friend and more, but she faced them with determination and gave her little speech. "All I can say is this—Buck is a good man and I am honored to know him. I want your approval, but if you refuse it I must follow my heart." Father looked shocked and she hurried from the room before he could speak.

The next afternoon she met Buck at the church and they arranged the bounty people had brought in all morning—sheaves of grain, huge orange pumpkins, baskets of potatoes, branches of red leaves, jars of beans and beet pickles. "There is so much," she murmured as they stood side by side admiring the rich display.

"This bounty is nothing compared to what's in here." Buck pressed his palm to his chest. "My heart is full to overflowing. First, that a woman like you could love a man like me." His eyes filled with wonder. "Secondly, that I have found a place where I belong."

"You belong right here." She pressed her own palm to her chest. "Where my heart overflows with love and gratitude."

"Gratitude?"

"Yes, for a man such as you to love. And that you didn't leave." She'd told him how her father had sent so many of her friends away without her knowledge.

"I discovered it's hard to walk away from a pretty woman." He pulled her into his arms. "Even harder to walk away from love."

She raised her face. "Isn't it amazing that we discover our love at Thanksgiving?"

"It's really a season of bounty," he murmured before he claimed her lips.

As she prepared for the service that night, she prayed Buck and Rosie would be welcomed as she believed they should be.

She walked with her parents toward the church, thankful they did not take her to task about her decision. The evening was pleasantly warm, unstirred by a breeze. Stars glistened overhead. At the church the milling crowd hummed with anticipation. It had been a bountiful year and people were grateful.

As they drew closer, Kathleen noticed a little boy who looked up at the stained-glass window and said, "He's smiling at me."

Kathleen sniffled as she saw that the child looked into the face of Jesus. She signaled to her parents. "It's Joey, Buck's boy." She glanced about, located Buck standing next to Rosie across the yard. She pointed him out to her parents. "I'm going to welcome them." Without giving either of them a chance to suggest otherwise, she made her way through the crowd to Buck's side and reached for his hand. She greeted Rosie.

Buck smiled and squeezed Kathleen's hand. "Joey is fascinated by the stained-glass window."

"He sees the love of Jesus."

Kathleen felt a nudge at her elbow and turned. "Mother?"

"Would you introduce your friends?"

Bursting with joy at this welcome, Kathleen did so. She looked about for Father. When he saw her silent invitation, he stalked across and allowed himself to be introduced before he backed away. It was a start. After that, several others welcomed the newcomers.

"Thank you," she whispered to her mother.

"You made me realize if I thought more of others and their needs, I'd have less time to dwell on my aches and pains."

Kathleen wrapped her arm around Buck's and they joined the movement toward the door. Tomorrow everyone would sit down with family and celebrate their gratitude. Kathleen would enjoy dinner with her family. Then she'd join Rosie and Buck and their children for another bountiful feast.

Tonight they shared their hearts of thanks with their church family. She sat at his side and sang hymns of Thanksgiving with more joy than she'd ever before known.

And the way Buck smiled down at her, she knew he shared her gratitude.

Epilogue

Kathleen checked the table set for eight. The best china and crystal shone. She wanted these guests to be treated with every honor they'd have bestowed on any of her father's business associates. She turned to her mother. "I'm so grateful that you invited Rosie and Buck and their children for Thanksgiving dinner." This morning her mother announced that Cook had been instructed to prepare more than originally planned, and she'd sent a messenger to Rosie's house to ask them to share the meal with them. Kathleen had hugged her mother with joy and anticipation.

"It seems we are about to be closely associated with them. Besides, I do believe it will be fun to have children at the table for a change."

Kathleen refrained from saying it would be a welcome change for her. Not only the children, but also to have people she cared about sharing the day. "You're sure Father is okay with this?"

Her mother's smile seemed a trifle uncertain. "No matter how your father feels, you can count on him to conduct himself in a hospitable way."

"That's true." She glanced at the mantel clock. Dinner would soon be ready. Suddenly overcome with nervous energy, she hurried to look out the window. Would Buck be comfortable in these formal surroundings? Would he win the approval of her father? Then she sucked in a calming breath. Her father might know how to conduct himself in an acceptable fashion, but so did Buck. More than that, Buck had learned to meet slighting glances without flinching. She prayed it wouldn't come to that. "Here they are." She left the window, then returned. "There's another man with them. Who could it be?" He held baby Lilly in one arm. Rosie clung to his other side. "It must be Rosie's husband. Quick, put out another place." As her mother did so, Kathleen rushed to the door. But her father was there ahead of her.

"I'm the host. I'll invite them in."

So Kathleen waited as her father opened the door. Buck stepped forward and offered his hand. Kathleen's father took it without hesitation. Then Buck introduced the man at Rosie's side. "Her husband, Bill."

"I hope you don't mind that he's come along unexpectedly," Rosie said.

"Not at all," Kathleen assured her.

Bill shook hands with her father. "The boss gave us all a few days off and said to go visit our families. Last chance to get out before Christmas. I jumped at the offer." The way he smiled at Rosie and the children said better than words how much he'd missed them.

Rosie stole a furtive look around the hallway and peeked into the front room. "So this is your house."

"Want a tour?"

"Oh, I couldn't." Then she grinned. "But I'd love to."

"Come along, then. All of you." She led them down the hall. "Father, you, too. After all, it's your house."

Her mother joined them, too, and they traipsed from one room to the next.

Rosie's eyes grew more and more round, but Buck's expression seemed tight. Kathleen edged up to him. "What's wrong?" They dropped back so the others wouldn't hear them.

"I can never compete with this. All I can offer you is a simple home, probably a lot like Rosie's."

She pressed a hand to his cheek. "You can offer me more than that."

He shook his head, not understanding.

"You can offer me your warm love. It's better than anything these rooms can give me."

The tension fled from his eyes. "That I can certainly do."

The others had disappeared into yet another room. Buck took her hands between his and held them to his heart. "Kathleen, I love you more than words can tell. I want to spend the rest of my life with you making you happy, sharing both our joys and our sorrows. Will you marry me?"

Her heart thrilled within her. She'd been a tiny bit worried he might want to hold off asking her this question. But she had no doubts. No hesitation. "I will gladly marry you." They kissed quickly as they heard the others returning. But his eyes promised more later.

Joey rushed to them. "Buck, they got all sorts of rooms but nobody to live in them. Just empty rooms for things." Then his voice saddened. "Grown-up things. No toys."

Kathleen glanced at her father, wondering what he

thought of this assessment of his fine house. He drew back as if the words had hit him in an unfamiliar spot. Then he blinked and relaxed visibly.

"I suppose we are sadly lacking in things for children. Perhaps, young man, you'd like to come shopping with me this week and help me choose things to remedy the situation."

"You really mean it?"

Father nodded. "I never say things I don't mean."

"I'd like to do that," Joey said, "if it's okay with Buck." Buck readily agreed.

Kathleen sidled up to her father. "Thank you."

He squeezed her shoulder but said nothing.

"Dinner is served," her mother called, and they filed into the dining room. A golden roasted turkey sat before her father's place, stuffing spilling from its cavity. Other bowls held heaps of mashed potatoes and a variety of vegetables. The white tablecloth provided a perfect backdrop for the china, crystal and silver. Sunlight streamed from the window and hit the china cupboard, sending shards of rainbow light across the table.

"Oh," Rosie gasped. "It's beautiful." And it truly was.

"Thank you." Kathleen's mother sounded pleased. She indicated where each should sit.

Kathleen and Buck sat on one side of the table with Joey at Buck's side. Buck took her hand under the table and squeezed it.

Her father glanced around the table. "I wish to welcome all of you today. We are honored to have you in our home. Traditionally at this time of year, we share what we're thankful for. I'd like to begin." He turned to Kathleen. "I'm proud and pleased to have a daughter who is bold enough to stand up for her own beliefs. Even against her father."

Kathleen blinked back tears and Buck chuckled, his grip growing firmer.

Bill spoke next. "I am grateful for a job and for a wife and kids to love." His voice choked at the end and Rosie's eyes glistened with tears.

"I am blessed to have a friend like Kathleen," Rosie said, and Kathleen sniffled even as she smiled.

The little boys spoke. Junior said he was glad to have a cousin to play with and Mattie, stumbling over the words, said he liked having a mama and papa. Lilly, too young to speak, sat on her mother's knee and grinned.

Kathleen looked to her mother at the end of the table, wondering if her parent would realize how much she had to be thankful for.

Her mother cleared her throat before she began. "A few days ago I considered myself a lonely, useless woman, but thanks to my daughter—" she reached for Kathleen's hand "—I realize that my vision was too narrow." She indicated the room. "I have so much—a fine husband and a generous daughter. Plus the means to help others, and with my husband's blessing I intend to do more of that in the future."

Kathleen's heart clogged with emotion. "Mother, you make me so proud."

Then it was Kathleen's turn. She could barely speak for the emotions overwhelming her. "I don't know where to begin. I'm grateful for my parents. For my upbringing. I'm grateful for my new friends—"

"You mean me, too?" Joey asked, his voice anxious.

"I mean you and Buck. I love you both very much."

Joey nodded his pleasure and only then did Kathleen let herself meet Buck's eyes. His gaze burned with love and gratitude and a whole lot more that she hoped he'd tell her once they were alone.

Her father tapped the table to bring their attention back to the others. "Buck, what are you thankful for?"

Buck chuckled. "I expect everyone here already knows. It's Kathleen. Her love has set my heart free. Sir." He faced her father. "She has agreed to marry me. Do we have your blessing?"

Kathleen drew in a sharp breath and held it. This was a lot for her father to take in at once. He studied Kathleen for a moment. She could see that he struggled with his desire to have her marry well, in a way that would perhaps improve his position in the eyes of others. "Father, I love him."

He nodded. "Then you have my blessing."

"Thank you."

Buck echoed the thanks.

"And you, young man." Her father turned to Joey. "What are you thankful for?"

Kathleen could see that despite any initial reservations he had, her father was charmed by Joey's directness and keen observation.

Joey flashed a grin to everyone. "I glad for everything and everyone." His eyes settled on the waiting food. "Mostly I very glad we don't have to eat rabbit."

The adults laughed at his comment.

"I think we better eat." Kathleen's father prayed and then began to carve the turkey. Food was passed, and everyone relaxed and visited like old friends.

Kathleen glanced about the table. Never before had

she enjoyed such a Thanksgiving feast in this place. "I am so blessed," she murmured, not caring if anyone heard.

But Buck, attuned to her as he was, leaned close. "God's bounty overflows to us."

She held his gaze a moment, forgetting everyone else. Life with this man would be a continual sharing of God's love. "I love you," she whispered.

"And I love you," he whispered back.

What greater bounty could either of them ask for than this precious shared love?

* * * * *

Winnie Griggs is the multipublished, award-winning author of historical (and occasionally contemporary) romances that focus on small towns, big hearts and amazing grace. She is also a list maker and a lover of dragonflies, and holds an advanced degree in the art of procrastination. Winnie loves to hear from readers—you can connect with her on Facebook at Facebook.com/winniegriggs.author or email her at winnie@winniegriggs.com.

Books by Winnie Griggs

Love Inspired Historical

Texas Grooms

Handpicked Husband
The Bride Next Door
A Family for Christmas
Lone Star Heiress
Her Holiday Family
Second Chance Hero
The Holiday Courtship
Texas Cinderella
A Tailor-Made Husband
Once Upon a Texas Christmas

Visit the Author Profile page at Harlequin.com for more titles.

HOME FOR THANKSGIVING

Winnie Griggs

The Lord upholdeth all that fall, and raiseth up
all those that be bowed down.
—*Psalms* 145:14

To my wonderful family—husband, children, mother, siblings—who have been enthusiastic supporters and all-around cheerleaders for me through the ups and downs of my writing career.

Chapter One

November 1894
Cleebit Springs, Texas

It was now or never.

Ruby Tuggle had been sitting in the hotel lobby when Mr. Lassiter returned from whatever business he'd been conducting. She'd watched him climb the stairs to his room, looking as though he'd had a rough day, and then come back down thirty minutes later, cleaner but still tired-looking.

From her seat in the secluded corner of the lobby she'd had a clear view into the hotel dining room. Watching his profile as he ate his meal, she'd tried to get some sense of the man himself.

She'd memorized the way his dark hair tried to curl around his ears, the way it just barely touched his collar in the back and the slight impression of where his hat had rested. She'd watched the way he politely interacted with Mrs. Dowd when she'd brought out his food, and how he'd kept to himself otherwise.

And the more she studied him, the more solid her gut feeling grew. No doubt about it, he was a good man, and God had put him in her path to help her.

Just now he'd set his cutlery down, sat back and reached for his glass, a sure sign that he was nearly finished with his meal. Soon he would get up and return to his room. If she didn't gather her courage to speak to him now, she likely wouldn't get another chance.

Taking a deep breath, Ruby rose and moved into the dining room. *Heavenly Father, please give me the right words. And, if it's not asking too much, please soften this man's heart toward my need.*

Stopping near his table, she cleared her throat to get his attention. "Excuse me, but can I speak to you for a moment?" Good—her voice hadn't squeaked like it sometimes did when she was nervous.

The man looked up from his nearly empty plate. "Ma'am?"

Her cheeks warmed as her courage wavered. What must he be thinking of her? Approaching him this way would have been considered bold if they were already acquainted. The fact that they were near strangers only made it that much more forward and unseemly.

But it was too late to turn back now. "Mr. Lassiter, is it?"

He nodded, his tobacco-brown eyes continuing to assess her. "That's right—Griff Lassiter."

"My name is Ruby Tuggle," she continued. "You might remember me from this morning?"

Not that *that* particular memory would lend her any additional credibility. She'd dropped a tray of dirty dishes practically at his feet in this very dining room.

The man had been gentleman enough to help her collect the broken dishes and scattered cutlery. He'd even offered her a sympathetic smile when Mrs. Dowd had come out and given her a very public scolding for her clumsiness.

Then she realized she needed to get something straight before she continued. "This isn't about that," she said quickly, "though I do want to thank you again for your kindness. In fact, I don't work here anymore, so it's not hotel business at all. It's a personal matter I'm wanting to discuss with you." Realizing she was babbling, Ruby paused and took a steadying breath.

To her relief, Mr. Lassiter stood. She'd forgotten how very tall and imposing he was up close. The man commanded attention even when he wasn't trying to.

He waved her to the chair across from him. "Please have a seat. Can I order you something?"

Her spirits rose as she sat. This was a good beginning. He *was* a gentleman, and genuinely kind to boot. Now if only she could convince him to help her. "No, thank you. I've already eaten."

He took his seat, placed his elbows on the table and crossed his arms. "What can I do for you, Miss Tuggle?"

"I have a business proposition I'd like to discuss with you, if I may?"

That earned her a raised eyebrow. "I'm listening."

"I understand you own a ranch in the Tyler area and will be returning there soon."

He nodded. "I leave for Hawk's Creek first thing in the morning."

Her hands were clasped under the table so tight she felt the nails bite into her palms. This was it. "Well, I'm planning to travel to Tyler myself and I was wondering if I could hire you to provide me with an escort." *Please, please, please say yes.*

There was a flash of surprise in his expression. "Excuse me for saying so, ma'am, but you don't really know me. Wouldn't you be more comfortable traveling with a relative or family friend?"

At least he hadn't outright rejected her request. "I don't have any family here." Or anywhere else for that matter. "And no friends who could spare time for the trip."

He studied her in silence for a long moment and she did her best not to fidget. Finally he leaned back in his chair. "Mind if I ask what kind of business you have in Tyler that would take you there on your own?"

She bristled a bit at that. It was really none of his business, after all. But she needed his goodwill so she swallowed her pride. "I plan to start a new life." *A new life*—just saying that out loud lifted her spirits. No more facing so much resentment and pity. No more pretending she was happy here. "And I understand Tyler is a large enough place that I could find suitable work to support myself."

He didn't seem happy with her answer. "Miss Tuggle, I hate to rain on your campfire, but it's really not wise for a young lady to strike out on her own like that. Especially in a strange place where she had no friends to turn to should the need arise. And finding suitable work, especially without someone to recommend you, might take time."

"I have enough money to tide me over for a bit." That had a satisfying sound to it, too. Discovering just yesterday that a nest egg had been set aside for her had made her almost giddy just imagining the possibilities. "I'm resourceful enough to take care of myself and I'm not afraid of hard or messy work."

He didn't appear convinced. "You mentioned you don't work here anymore. I don't mean to pry, but if this is just a reaction to that dust-up this morning, you'd likely be better off staying put and working things out with Mrs. Dowd."

Her heart sank as she saw her chances of success begin to fade. But she lifted her chin and tried again. "You're wrong if you think this is a spur of the moment decision. I've been planning to leave here for some time now. This morning's *dust-up,* as you call it, just gave me the final push is all. I'll be headed for Tyler tomorrow, with or without your company." That was partly bluster, of course. But she was just determined enough to contemplate doing it. It was past time to spread her wings.

"Ruby Anne, what do you think you're doing? Get up from there this minute."

Ruby jumped. She'd been so intent on making her case to Mr. Lassiter that she hadn't heard Mrs. Dowd approach.

The stout rolling pin of a woman turned to Mr. Lassiter with an apologetic smile. "Sir, I'm so sorry if this girl has been bothering—"

"On the contrary."

Ruby, already halfway out of her chair, paused as her companion's voice cut across the woman's scold like a knife through lard.

"Miss Tuggle has graciously agreed to join me for dessert this evening," he continued, waving Ruby back down. "Speaking of which, I would appreciate it if you would please bring a bowl of your peach cobbler for each of us when you have a moment." While he hadn't raised his voice, and his expression remained pleasant, there was something in his tone that warned against argument.

Mrs. Dowd stiffened and her mouth snapped shut. Then she offered her best be-nice-to-the-customer smile. "Why, um, yes, of course. I'll get it for you at once."

The woman turned a sharper glance Ruby's way, but didn't linger.

Ruby had never seen Mrs. Dowd move so quickly. She turned to Mr. Lassiter with gratitude and a touch of awe. "Thank you."

He smiled. "It's just a bowl of cobbler."

Oh, it had been so much more than that. But he didn't give her time to elaborate.

"I can see you're determined," he said, returning to their original discussion. "But have you given any thought to the timing? Thanksgiving is a little over a week away and Christmas is right behind that. Surely you'll want to spend the holidays in familiar surroundings?"

She almost rolled her eyes at that. If he only knew. "Not at all. In fact, I believe being settled in a new place, surrounded by new people, is the perfect way to celebrate the holidays. It will definitely give me something extra to be thankful for."

That earned her another probing stare, which she endured without comment.

"How do you plan to travel?" he finally asked.

"I've purchased a small buggy and a horse," Ruby

reported proudly. She'd taken care of that this morning as soon as she'd left the hotel. "I know having to match pace with a buggy will likely slow you down, but as I said, I'm prepared to pay you for your trouble."

He waved her offer aside. "That won't be an issue. I've acquired a young Angus bull today that I'm taking back to Hawk's Creek, so I'll be traveling slow and easy anyway."

Did that mean he was going to agree to her request? "Then you'll do it?"

He raised his napkin and smothered a cough.

She noticed again how tired he looked. "Are you okay?"

He shook his head dismissively. "It's just a bit of trail dust caught in my throat." He took a sip from his water glass, then leaned back again. "As for your other question, there's just one problem. I'm not going to Tyler proper. My ranch is a bit north of there, and since I'll have a bull tethered to my horse, I'd prefer to take the shortest route possible."

"I see." Ruby did her best to swallow her disappointment. Why hadn't he said so right away instead of letting her get her hopes up?

Saying she'd make the trip with or without him was one thing. Actually doing it was another. Not only were there the normal hazards of the road to worry about, but there was always the possibility of getting lost along the way. After all, since the ill-fated day when she'd arrived in Cleebit Springs at age seven, she hadn't traveled more than a mile outside of town.

So what did she do now?

Chapter Two

Griff took the opportunity brought about by Mrs. Dowd's reappearance to study the young woman seated across from him. A slip of a girl with dark hair and bright green eyes, with a face as readable as a babe's. It was hard to tell her age—she had an air of childlike trust about her that made her seem schoolgirlish—yet his instincts told him she was probably around eighteen or so.

Miss Tuggle also had an awkward coltishness about her that reminded him a little of his sister, Sadie. She seemed to have more than a touch of Sadie's stubbornness, as well.

The biggest problem in his opinion, though, was that she was much too trusting for her own good. Sure, *he'd* never take advantage of a young lady, but there were some who'd do it without a second thought. Especially after she'd blurted out that bit about having enough money to tide her over.

Yep, that ingenuousness of hers might be charming to a casual observer, but not to him. A girl like this could be a passel of trouble for whoever had the doubtful honor of looking out for her.

He just didn't want to be saddled with the job himself. He was tired, his head hurt and he had this new bull to get back to Hawk's Creek. The last thing he needed was to have to babysit some wide-eyed girl with big city dreams.

And while Ruby Tuggle was in no way his responsibility at the moment, he was irritated to realize that somehow she was well on her way to making herself so.

Because he kept coming back to the thought that if this had been Sadie...

"There now." Mrs. Dowd took a step back. "Is there anything else I can get for you?"

Griff glanced across the table. "Miss Tuggle?"

"No. I'm fine, thank you."

He was glad to see she didn't appear as nervous in the woman's presence as she had earlier.

He gave Mrs. Dowd a dismissive nod. "I think we're both fine for now."

As soon as the woman was gone, Miss Tuggle leaned forward. "Perhaps we could travel together for part of the way?"

Griff took a bite of his cobbler and had to follow it with a swallow of water. His throat was still scratchy. Hang it all, he just wanted to head upstairs and get a good night's rest. But he knew that wasn't going to happen if he didn't make sure this fool girl didn't go off on her own tomorrow and get herself lost—or worse.

"Actually, I have a better idea."

"Oh?"

He mentally winced at the sudden hope that flared

in her expression. This girl was so transparent. "Since you seem so determined to leave here—"

She nodded vigorously. "Oh, I am."

"At the pace I'll be moving tomorrow it'll take all of nine hours to get to Cornerstone, which is where we would part ways for you to go on to Tyler and me to go to the ranch. That means it would be dusk at best before you actually reach your destination." Assuming she could make it on her own at all. "Which wouldn't give you a whole lot of time to find accommodations for yourself and your horse and buggy before full nightfall."

"Surely there would be someone in town who could direct me to a hotel or boardinghouse."

Did she think everyone in the world was as helpful— or as honest—as her neighbors here in Cleebit Springs? She'd learn different soon enough. "Still, much better for you to arrive in the morning when you're well rested. Easier to get your bearings and be a mite more selective about your accommodations."

Her brow drew down in a thoughtful expression. "I hadn't thought of that."

Of course she hadn't. More proof that she had no idea what she was in for. "There's a church in Cornerstone and the reverend and his wife have been known to provide shelter to travelers when it's needed. What I propose is that I escort you that far and you spend the night with them. Then the next morning either I or one of my ranch hands can escort you into Tyler and see you safely settled in."

Her face lit up. "What a wonderful plan. Oh, I knew you were a true gentleman."

Griff resisted the urge to roll his eyes as he smothered another cough in his napkin. Something about this still didn't feel right. "Isn't there someone I should be talking to or asking permission of to take you on this trip? I know you said you don't have any family here, but surely there's someone who looks out for you? I mean, whom do you live with?"

She drew herself up as if he'd offended her. "I'll have you know I'm an adult—I turned twenty last week. I live over at the boardinghouse and I look out for myself."

Griff was too tired to take this any further. He set his napkin on the table. So she was older than he'd thought. That still didn't make her capable of getting along on her own. "I'd like to get an early start in the morning. Do you think you can be ready at seven o'clock?"

Her indignation immediately turned to smiles. "That won't be a problem. But there is one other thing I should mention."

What now? "And that is?" From the way she hesitated, it was a good bet he wasn't going to like it.

"I plan to take my cat with me," she finally blurted out.

"Cat?" He didn't think much of cats other than as varmint catchers for the barn.

"Yes. Patience is well behaved—mostly, anyway. She won't be any trouble, I promise. You don't mind, do you?"

Patience? Sounded like some fluffy, pampered house pet. "As long as you understand I don't aim to go chasing after the critter if it runs off."

"Oh, I wouldn't expect you to."

"Then I don't see a problem." He stood. "Now, if

there's nothing else, we have a long day ahead of us tomorrow, so if you'll excuse me, I think I'll retire for the evening. I suggest you do the same."

She scrambled to her feet. "Of course. And again, let me say how very grateful I am."

A few minutes later Griff sat on a chair in his room, pulling off his boots. What he wouldn't give to be back at Hawk's Creek right now, in his own room, headed to his own bed.

His own very large, very comfortable, but just as lonely bed.

He shook his head in disgust as he put his left boot on the floor beside his chair and started tugging on the right one. This restless self-pity that had been creeping up on him these past few months was both pointless and beneath him.

He supposed being with the Lipscoms today out at the Double Bar L Ranch had triggered this mood. The family consisted of Barney Lipscom, his wife, his son, his daughter-in-law and three grandkids. When his business with Barney had concluded, Barney had insisted Griff take his noon meal with them. It had given Griff an up-close view of their lives together.

The conversation at the table had been lively, the affection between the family members apparent. Both Mary and Amy were strong women with lives deeply rooted in their family and in the family ranch. They seemed equally at home in the kitchen as in the barn.

And he'd found himself more than a little jealous. It was the kind of life he longed for. Instead, he shared his large home with Inez, the housekeeper and cook who'd been at Hawk's Creek since before he was born.

He loved her as he would a favorite aunt, but she was no substitute for a wife.

To have a wife who would be a proper helpmeet to him, one who loved the rancher's life as much as he did, and with whom he could share, if not love, then a mutual respect.

Was that too much to ask?

Apparently so, since his two attempts had resulted in sound rejection. The ladies in question had eventually decided ranch life was not for them.

Or maybe it was just that *he* wasn't right for them.

Griff tossed his boot across the room, irritated at the direction his thoughts had taken. Self-pity was not productive and definitely not very dignified. If it was his lot in life to face it alone, so be it. Wishing it different wouldn't make it so.

As Griff climbed into bed a few minutes later, his thoughts turned back to Miss Tuggle. If her story was to be believed, it seemed she was even more alone in life than he was. At least he had Inez.

Of course, he wasn't completely convinced she wasn't exaggerating or embellishing on her situation. Young girls seemed prone to do that. Still, he'd given her his word.

He punched his pillow into a more comfortable shape.

Escorting a head-in-the-clouds girl and her fluffy cat...

Just what in the world had he let himself in for?

Griff stepped out of the hotel the next morning in a sour mood. He hadn't slept well and his muscles were stiff and sore. The cold, dreary weather that greeted him didn't help much. All in all, not a good time to be undertaking a long trip on horseback.

True to her word, Miss Tuggle was sitting in her buggy parked outside the hotel, waiting for him.

"Good morning," she said, her expression as bright as that of a kid on Christmas morning. Obviously the prospect of the weather conditions and the length of their upcoming journey didn't dampen her mood any. Or maybe she just didn't know enough to be worried.

But he'd been brought up to be civil. "Good morning. I—"

He paused when he spotted the cat perched beside her. Instead of the well-groomed, well-fed feline he'd expected, this scraggly critter with a coat as gray and mottled as the overcast sky could have easily been mistaken for a stray.

"This is Patience," she said proudly. Then she gave him an apologetic smile. "I'm afraid she doesn't like strangers very much so it might be best if you don't try to pet her."

Now why in the world would he want to pet that scruffy-looking thing? "That won't be a problem."

She nodded and sat up straighter. "We're both ready whenever you are."

"Give me just a few minutes." Griff examined her horse and worn-looking carriage closely—the last thing he needed was to have the horse give out or the vehicle break down on them somewhere out on the road. Especially the way he was feeling this morning. The scratch in his throat was still there and the coffee and biscuits he'd had for breakfast sat heavy in his stomach. He'd be glad to get back to Hawk's Creek, and the comfort of familiar surroundings. And truth to tell, a little cosseting from Inez would be welcome, as well.

One thing he did notice while he was checking her equipment was that, though the buggy was a bit roomier than most vehicles of its type, she was traveling light. The only luggage she had with her was one not-very-large trunk. Did it contain the sum total of her possessions? Or was she literally leaving her old life behind?

Finally satisfied that the horse and vehicle were both sound enough to make the trip, Griff nodded and stepped back.

"It'll do. I need to collect my animals from the livery. Meet me there in a few minutes."

Twenty minutes later he had the bull tethered to the back of the buggy and had loaded a bag of feed in the carriage boot. He climbed up on his horse, gathered the reins and glanced at his traveling companion. She seemed, as Inez liked to say, happy as a pup chasing a stick. Even as he felt the urge to roll his eyes, a reluctant smile tugged at his lips. He supposed he should let her enjoy herself while she could. No doubt her cheery mood would evaporate by the time they were an hour or so into what promised to be a tedious, cold and dreary trip. "Ready?"

She nodded. "I've been ready for this day for ages."

He just didn't understand why big cities held such appeal for some folk. Give him wide-open land any day. "All right, then. Match your pace to mine. And remember, that's valuable livestock tied to your buggy—I don't want to wear him out before I get him to Hawk's Creek."

She nodded again. "Just lead the way."

He pulled his hat down more firmly as he set his horse in motion. Not only were the skies overcast this morning, but there was a nip in the air that hadn't been there yesterday. No hint of rain yet, though. Maybe they'd get lucky and this would be the worst of it.

He watched her closely as they set out, prepared to intervene if she wasn't mindful of his bull. But after ten minutes he relaxed.

"Tell me about this ranch of yours," she asked. "Hawk's Creek, is it?"

"That's right. Some of the richest pasture land in all of Texas—rolling hills, several springs that run practically year-round, lush grazing, prime timber. There's no other place like it. It's been in my family for three generations." And now it was down to him.

"So you've lived there all your life."

"Yep. And I plan to die there, as well." No city—big or small—for him. His roots were planted in Hawk's Creek land and he didn't think he could flourish anywhere else. "What about you? You live in Cleebit Springs your entire life?"

"Most of it. I arrived there when I was seven years old and stayed put until today."

"And now you want to move to Tyler."

She shrugged and kept her gaze on the road. "I'm just ready for a change."

Another restless spirit? Like his brother, Ry. And Belle, his first love. And Martha, his second.

"Do you have any family?" she asked, pulling him out of his thoughts.

He noticed she was quick to turn the discussion away

from herself. "An older brother and younger sister—Ry and Sadie."

"I always wanted siblings." Her tone was wistful. "But my mother died when I was three and my father never remarried." She glanced back his way. "I guess the three of you live on that ranch together, like a real family."

He shook his head as he raised a hand to smother a series of chest-tightening coughs. "Both Ry and Sadie moved on," he said when he'd caught his breath again. "Ry left a long time ago, back when we were both still teens. Went to live in Philadelphia with our grandfather." It had been hard when his big brother chose life back East over life on the ranch, and it had driven a wedge between the two of them, a wedge that had only recently been dislodged when Ry married Josie and moved back to Texas.

"And your sister?"

That was another move he hadn't seen coming. "Sadie got married last year, to a fellow who moved to Texas from New York. It was a whirlwind kind of thing. And, as it turns out, both she and Ry ended up in the same town—Knotty Pine. It's about sixty miles southeast of the ranch." He tried not to be jealous of their closeness. And their newfound happiness.

"So you live alone now?"

He shifted in the saddle, suddenly annoyed with all her questions. "Inez is there."

"Inez?"

"Inez Garner—I guess you'd call her our housekeeper. But she's more than that, more like part of the family. Inez has been at Hawk's Creek since before I was born—I can't imagine the place without her. After my ma died she was the glue that helped hold us all together."

"She sounds like a special lady."

"That she is." Enough of answering her questions—time to ask a few of his own. "What about you? You said you don't have any family—who raised you?"

Was it his imagination or did some of her cheeriness ebb? Maybe he shouldn't have brought up her orphaned status.

"I reckon you could say just about everybody in Cleebit Springs had a hand in raising me," she answered. "After they buried my father—I was seven at the time—the whole community banded together to make certain I was provided for. Different families took turns looking out for me."

Close-knit communities were like that, he supposed—doing what they could to help their neighbors when there was a need. So why was she so eager to give all that up? Seemed shortsighted at best, ungrateful at worst. "Sounds to me as if you had a very large foster family."

"I suppose you could look at it that way."

She didn't seem much taken with the idea. "Folks don't have to be blood kin to be family," he offered. "Inez and I are proof of that."

She gave a noncommittal nod, keeping her gaze straight ahead.

"Might be you'll miss the folks in Cleebit Springs more than you think you will," he said, trying again. "You're going to find out soon enough that folks in large towns tend to mind their own business more often than not and aren't always as neighborly as those in smaller towns."

She shrugged. "Folks minding their own business isn't such a bad thing."

He supposed some lessons had to be learned from experience. And it seemed for her this was going to be one of them.

He only hoped she didn't get hurt too badly when she learned it.

Ruby was glad Mr. Lassiter didn't press further. There was no way she'd agree to call those folks back in Cleebit Springs her family, but she didn't want to speak ill of them, either. Her daddy had taught her to always look for the good in any person or situation, and she'd tried to honor his memory by doing just that. It had been so hard in those first few weeks after he was taken from her, when she'd been dealing with the shock of his sudden, horrific death, when she'd been surrounded by people she didn't know, when the nightmares had come night after night.

But in time the shock, if not the memories, had faded, the people had become more familiar, the nightmares had come less frequently. And that was when her upbringing had kicked in. She'd stopped crying and forced herself to look for any silver lining she could find, in fact had made a game of it.

But even on the best of those days, she hadn't thought of anyone in Cleebit Springs as family. There were lots of good folks there, she knew that. It's just that her memories and relationships with them were all colored by her father's death. Whether right or wrong, she was genuinely happy to know that from this day forward she'd never have to face any of them again. The farther away from Cleebit Springs they got, the lighter her spirits. It had been thirteen long, lonely years since she'd felt so buoyant.

After the silence had dragged on for a bit, Ruby decided it was time for something a bit more cheerful. "Tell me about Tyler."

"I guess it's a fine city, as cities go anyway. What do you want to know about it?"

"Everything." She was determined to look on this as a grand adventure—no matter how discouraging his tone. "Start with what I can expect to find when I get there."

"Well, let's see, there are sawmills, an ice factory, a cotton gin and some fruit-packing plants. There are several other factories, but I don't guess you're much interested in that sort of thing."

"I want to know about *all* of it. I'm going to be looking for work when I get there, remember?"

"All right. Besides the mills and factories, there are stores and shops, some of them huge brick buildings with three floors of merchandise, where you can find just about anything from dry goods to flowers, from hardware to fine jewelry."

He rolled his shoulders. "And there are churches of course, big ones and small ones of just about any denomination you can imagine. There's a busy railway station there along with shipping and freight companies. Oh, and most of the businesses and many of the homes have electricity."

"Mercy! Do the boardinghouses have electricity?"

"I've never visited one, but I imagine they do."

She looked down at her cat. "Did you hear that, Patience? Won't that be a fine thing?"

The cat's only response was a lazy blink.

"I wouldn't call it fine—much too noisy and crowded."

She refused to let her mood be dampened—this was her chance to build a brand-new life, to prove to herself that she could stand on her own. Because she had no one else to depend on. "Crowds don't bother me. What else is there?"

"There's a lot more." His tone indicated he wasn't overly impressed with the list he was reciting. "A courthouse, several hotels, lots of eating places from small cafés to fancy restaurants."

Another fit of coughing interrupted his litany. "If you're interested in more refined offerings," he continued, "there are schools and a library, a newspaper office, two opera houses, a theater and some uppity-sounding social clubs."

Uppity, huh? Did he think that's what she was looking for? But the library—now that *did* sound interesting. She loved to read, but her choices had been limited. Many of the families she'd stayed with had either not had any reading material or had not thought it an appropriate pastime for her. She had exactly three books to her name, safely packed in her trunk. All three had belonged to her father—a Bible, a book about plants and a copy of Mark Twain's *The Prince and The Pauper.* All were dog-eared from the many times she'd read them.

"Sounds like a mighty fine place." She looked over at him. "Do you visit there often?"

"Once or twice a month. Mostly for supplies or to

meet the train." He grimaced. "It's much too crowded for my taste. And besides, there's lots to keep me busy at Hawk's Creek."

Interesting how his voice and expression took on a whole different tone when he spoke of his ranch—deeper, more relaxed. She wondered if he was even aware of how telling that was.

"I don't think I'll mind the crowds so much," she replied. "It sounds like a marvelous place to start a new life."

They rode along in silence for a few minutes, then she cleared her throat. "That's a fine-looking horse you've got there. Does he have a name?"

"Chester." He scowled. "Are you always this chatty?"

Oh, my—he sounded irritable. Probably as much to do with that cough of his as with her. She gave him an apologetic smile. "Actually, no. But since I'm starting out on a new adventure, I find myself full of questions. Sorry if I'm bothering you."

"Sometimes a fella just likes to take a break from talking and hear his own thoughts for a while."

"Of course."

He dropped back to check on the bull and she looked down at Patience, who was now sitting on the floor of the buggy. "Well, at least I have you to talk to."

The cat gave her a long-suffering look, then went back to grooming itself.

"You, too? Well, neither one of you gloomy glumps are going to dampen my mood. It's a wonderful day, just chock-full of silver linings, and I aim to enjoy each and every one of them."

Chapter Three

Griff called a halt around noon. He'd regretted his earlier sour comment within a few minutes of uttering it. After all, it was only natural for Miss Tuggle to be curious about what her future might hold.

The fact that she didn't seem at all cowed by his set-down surprised him. She made occasional comments to her cat, hummed now and then as if she couldn't contain her exuberance and just generally maintained a cheerful demeanor. There didn't seem to be much that could dampen her spirits.

But it'd been a long morning and she *had* quieted considerably these past thirty minutes. Though she hadn't complained, he figured Miss Tuggle was probably ready to get out of that buggy and move around a bit.

"I don't know about you," he said with a smile, "but I'm ready to have a look at what's in that basket you packed."

Her face lit up. "That sounds lovely."

He had the fleeting impression that she was referring as much to the fact that he'd spoken first as to the opportunity to get out of the buggy. "The road widens up ahead by that big oak," he continued. "Why don't we pull the buggy up under the tree and stretch our legs for a little while?"

Within a few minutes he was handing her down. She was surprisingly light and agile. Strange that he hadn't really noticed her eyes before—such a vivid shade of green, flecked with sparks of gold.

He took a moment to steady her once her feet were on the ground and, just for a moment, their gazes locked. Then her cat sprang down and landed at their feet, and the moment passed.

She quickly turned back to the buggy. "I'll get the hamper. It's right—"

He stopped her with a touch to her arm. "Let me get that."

She stepped aside. "Of course." Then she turned away. "I'd better keep an eye on Patience."

"It's been my experience that cats aren't much good at coming when called."

She laughed. "True. But I think she'll stay close when she sees what's in the hamper."

As he stepped back with the hamper, he noticed she was hugging herself. It was definitely colder now than it had been earlier. They probably should make this stop a quick one. The sooner they reached their destination, the better.

She stepped forward and reached inside the buggy. "I also packed a blanket we can sit on while we eat."

"Good thinking." He took her arm to help her over the uneven ground. "It's not exactly picnic weather, but we won't be here long anyway."

He set the hamper beside the tree. "If you can get things set up here, I'm going to give the animals some feed."

"Of course."

By the time he'd given the bull and the two horses each a bit of oats, she had the blanket spread out and had pulled some tin cups and plates out of the hamper. The cat sat beside her, tail swishing slowly, eyeing the hamper as if it were a mouse hole.

Miss Tuggle looked up as he joined her. "I'm afraid the food's not anything fancy, but it should be filling enough."

"No need to apologize. It was good of you to bring anything at all." Besides, he wasn't very hungry. "So, what do we have?"

She started itemizing things as she pulled them out of the hamper. "Some boiled ham slices, a wedge of cheese, two boiled eggs, a couple of biscuits and four nice ripe persimmons."

The cat swiped a paw in the direction of the ham, but Miss Tuggle was faster. She scooped up the cat, holding the affronted feline away from the food. "Oh, no you don't. Wait your turn."

She turned back to Griff, her hand stroking the cat's head. "There's a jug of apple cider in the hamper to wash it down with."

It seemed she'd gone to a lot of trouble. He hoped his lack of appetite didn't hurt her feelings.

She handed him a plate and smiled uncertainly. "Before we start, would you like to say grace?"

Griff paused in the act of reaching for a biscuit. He was embarrassed that he'd gotten out of the habit of praying before meals since Sadie had moved away. Perhaps it was time he remedied that.

He bowed his head. "Thank You, Father, for this food set before us, and for the many other blessings You provide to us each day. Watch over us as we travel. And watch over Miss Tuggle as she begins her new life in Tyler. May she find whatever it is she's looking for."

His companion added an "Amen," then smiled up at him.

Griff pointed to the squirming cat in her arms. "Is that varmint going to let you eat?"

She laughed. "As long as she gets her share. Don't worry, I packed enough." She quickly broke off several slivers of ham and some crumbles of cheese and set them on the corner of the blanket. The cat sashayed over and began eating the morsels as if getting served first were her right.

Griff shook his head. Despite the cat's disreputable appearance, it seemed it was a pampered pet after all.

He turned back to his own plate and cautiously looked over the food. His stomach rebelled at the idea of the ham or the cheese, but he knew he ought to eat something before they got back on the road. He carefully selected one of the biscuits and an egg.

Miss Tuggle frowned when she saw his skimpily loaded plate. "Oh, dear, don't you like ham and cheese? I should have asked ahead of time. Or is it Patience? If cats bother you I can—"

He held up a hand. She might be an overly cheery girl, but she was also quick to accept blame unnecessarily, as well. "I do like ham and cheese. And your cat isn't bothering me. I'm just not very hungry, is all."

"Oh." She was quiet for a while but he could see her worry as she studied him. When he coughed again, she frowned. "Are you sure you're okay? Maybe the folks at one of those farmhouses we passed a ways back would—"

"It's just a cough. I'm fine."

She slipped the cat another sliver of ham. "I lived with Doc Mulligan's family a couple of years ago. He always said a deep cough like yours should be treated right away or it could lead to something really serious."

"That might be true for some folk. But sometimes a cough is just a cough. I haven't been sick enough to slow me down since I lost my first tooth." He lifted the jug out of the hamper. "Hand me those cups and I'll pour us some of this cider." Hopefully she'd get the message that the subject of his health was closed.

She did as he asked and waited until he finished pouring to speak again. "So, did you travel all the way to Cleebit Springs just to fetch that bull?"

At least she'd decided to drop the subject of his health. "Actually, I hadn't planned on getting a new bull at all. I had some business to take care of with Barney Lipscom over at the Double Bar L Ranch." He forced himself to eat another bite of biscuit, then washed it down with a swig of cider. "Barney's been experimenting with Angus bloodlines and was excited about the results he's gotten. He insisted I take one of his young bulls to see for myself."

"That was generous of him. You must be good friends."

"He and my pa were." Griff noticed she'd finished up her meal. "If you're done, we should get back on the road. Sorry we can't make this a longer stop, but I don't like the looks of the weather. The sooner we get to where we're going, the better."

"Of course." She scrambled to her knees, then looked around with a frown. "Now where did Patience get off to?"

Griff stood, eyes scanning the tree line. "She can't have gone far—she was just here."

Miss Tuggle stood as well, biting her lower lip. "I should've watched her closer."

Now what did he do? He'd told her he wouldn't go chasing after her cat, but what if the four-legged troublemaker didn't return in the next few minutes? Could he get Miss Tuggle to go on without her pet? "I don't suppose the critter is trained to come when you call."

She shook her head, then pushed a lock of hair behind her ear with fingers that trembled. "Oh, if something's happened to her—"

Good grief, she wasn't going to cry, was she? "No need to get all worked up just yet," he said quickly. "Why don't you pack up things here and I'll take a quick look around."

"Thank you." She offered him a grateful smile, but the worry never left her expression.

Swallowing a few choice words, he stepped away from the blanket and let his eyes scan the tree line once again. He didn't hold out much hope of finding the feline, though, not unless it wanted to be found. A moment later he got his first clue as to the animal's whereabouts when he heard the excited barking of a dog. It sounded close. Maybe the threat of a dog on its trail would send the cat scampering back in this direction.

"Do you hear that?" Miss Tuggle was at his elbow, the folded blanket in her arms.

"Yes. Don't worry. I'm sure your cat can outrun most dogs. Probably streak out of those woods any minute now."

"She *is* fast."

A moment later Griff frowned. The tenor of the barking had changed. The dog no longer seemed to be moving and it sounded more like baying, as if it had treed its quarry.

Great. Just great.

Griff headed off in the direction of the barking.

Ruby's chin came up. He hadn't really invited her to follow him, but there was no way she was going to stay behind—Patience was, after all, *her* cat. She did her best to keep up with him, but it wasn't easy. His long legs ate up the ground with amazing speed.

Fortunately they didn't have far to go. Just inside the tree line they encountered the dog who was making all that racket. The black-and-brown hound had its front legs braced up against a tree trunk, nose pointed heavenward and howling up a storm.

Oh, dear, was poor Patience up there somewhere?

As soon as the dog spotted them it stopped barking and dropped back down on all fours. Griff put a hand up and Ruby obediently stopped.

He moved forward, slowly, speaking to the animal in a tone too soft for her to make out the words. After a moment the dog's tail began to wag and Mr. Lassiter was able to stoop down and ruffle the animal's fur.

While her companion was busy winning over the

dog, Ruby anxiously scanned the almost bare branches of the tree. She finally caught sight of a furry face peering down at her from what must be a good ten feet above her head. "Look, there she is."

Mr. Lassiter glanced at her, then upward. "It figures," he said drily. "Wouldn't do for her to stop on a lower branch, would it?"

He stood and stared down at the dog, pointing away from the tree. "Get along now."

Ruby grinned as the animal cocked its head to one side, as if trying to figure out if this was some sort of game.

"Get!" He said it more firmly and louder this time, stomping his foot for emphasis.

The dog spun and loped away a few paces before turning back to stare at him.

Mr. Lassiter let out an exasperated breath. "Mutt, I really don't have the time or patience for this."

As if the animal finally understood, it turned and ran back into the woods.

Mr. Lassiter turned to her. "I hope that animal of yours will come when called after all."

She hoped so, too. Moving forward until she was directly under the branch Patience clung to, Ruby set the picnic blanket down and made a downward motion with her hand. "Patience, come on down, sweetie. That big bad dog is gone now, so it's safe."

She kept her gaze on the cat, ignoring Mr. Lassiter's snort at her description of the dog as big and bad. But Patience still didn't budge. "I won't let anything hurt you, I promise. Just come on down so we can get on the road again."

What was she going to do if the cat refused to come down right away? She would never abandon her pet, but would Mr. Lassiter go off and leave them? She tried calling Patience again, letting some of her desperation creep into her tone.

Finally Mr. Lassiter stepped forward. "Enough."

Ruby turned to him, trying to gain a little more time. "Please. She can't stay up there forever. I can go back to the hamper and get a bit of ham. Maybe I can tempt her—"

"I doubt that'll work. And we've already wasted too much time."

"But I can't just leave her here. She needs me." *And I need her, because without her I'd be totally alone.*

"Nobody said anything about leaving her." He tossed his hat on top of the picnic blanket, then, despite the chilly temperature, shrugged out of his jacket. "Here, hold this."

She took the jacket and hugged it against her chest, its warmth strangely comforting. "What are you going to do?" A dozen scenarios played out in her head—everything from him throwing rocks at her poor pet to him climbing up after it.

He momentarily paused in the act of rolling up his sleeves and raised a brow. "What do you *think* I'm going to do?"

She decided to believe the best of him and his intentions. "Go up after her?"

Instead of responding he finished rolling up his sleeves, took his jacket back from her and moved to the tree.

"But—" She missed the feel of his jacket in her arms. "You said you weren't going to chase after her."

"And I'm not." He gave her a considering look as he tied the jacket's sleeves in a chunky knot around his waist. "Are you trying to talk me out of this?"

"No. I just…" He really *was* going to climb up after Patience. The man was a real-life hero. "Please be careful."

He nodded. "Just be prepared for what comes next. I don't aim to climb back down with that critter spitting and clawing in my arms."

Now what did he mean by that? Ruby watched as he grabbed a lower limb and tested its weight. "I must be out of my mind," he muttered. "I haven't climbed a tree since I was a scrawny kid."

She had trouble picturing him as a scrawny anything. Especially right now, what with the way his muscles bunched beneath his shirt as he grabbed hold of one of the lower branches.

Within seconds he was hauling himself up into the network of skeletal limbs. A heartbeat later he was standing on a lower branch and looking for footing on the next tier up. For a big man, he was surprisingly agile. She couldn't help but admire the relative ease with which he maneuvered his way up the tree.

When he paused to control another bout of coughs, however, she had to bite her lip to keep from warning him once again to be careful.

Please God, don't let him fall. I'd never forgive myself if he got hurt because of me and Patience.

But the cough quieted and he continued as if nothing had happened. When he finally reached a branch that put him level with Patience, Mr. Lassiter leaned with his back against the trunk and carefully untied his jacket from about his waist.

She wished she could see what was going on better. "Is Patience okay?"

"She seems fine." His tone held very little sympathy for the object of his rescue.

"Try talking softly to her," Ruby urged. "She's probably scared to death, poor thing." If he'd only handle Patience the same soothing way he had the dog earlier—

Before she could finish that thought, he'd thrown his coat over the cat, scooped her up and had her bundled as cleanly as if he'd tossed her in a sack.

Not that Patience was taking it without a fight. The poor thing was screeching loud enough to be heard for miles and she was writhing so wildly that Ruby wondered how Mr. Lassiter was managing to keep his balance.

"Be careful." She hadn't been able to contain the warning this time. "How are you going to climb back down carrying Patience?"

"I'm not."

What did he mean? Had he gone to all this trouble just to leave—

"Move a little to your left and get ready to catch."

"Catch? Surely you're not going to *drop* her."

"That's exactly what I'm going to do. Don't worry, she won't break. Just make sure you hold on to the critter and don't let her run off again."

"But I—"

"Ready or not."

And with that, the bundle of squirming, screeching feline came falling from above. Ruby managed to catch it, but the impact knocked her down on her backside.

She maintained a tight hold on the bundle but quickly unwrapped it enough to free Patience's head.

"There now, that's better, isn't it?" she cooed. "You just go ahead and spit and howl all you want—you've had a rough time of it and deserve to be upset. Yes, yes, go ahead, protest as loud and indignantly as you like." She continued crooning to her pet, not trying to hush her, merely reassure her.

When she finally looked up, Mr. Lassiter stood a few feet away, staring at her curiously.

When their eyes met he stepped forward and held out a hand to help her up. "Are you okay?"

"I'm fine." She gave Patience a quick hug before accepting his hand. "We both are." Once she was on her feet, they stood face-to-face for a moment, still holding hands. "I don't know how to thank you," she said softly. "That's the kindest thing anyone's ever done for me."

Something flashed in his expression—surprise, sympathy, something else? She couldn't be sure, but she felt the lightest of squeezes to her hand before he dropped it.

"You're welcome, Miss Tuggle. Now—"

"Please, call me Ruby." Her face warmed at her brashness, but she pressed on. "I mean, you've been so kind and I feel that we've become friends, and Miss Tuggle just sounds so formal."

"All right, *Ruby*. And you can call me Griff."

Griff. She liked that. It had a strong, honest quality to it. Heroic. Just like the man.

"Now, as I started to say, we've tarried long enough. We better get going."

"Of course." Her hand still felt the comforting warmth of his touch.

Mr. Lassi—*Griff* turned to retrieve his hat and he grabbed up the blanket, as well.

"I'll get the hamper," he said, slapping his hat on his head. "You just make sure that animal of yours gets in the buggy."

She smiled and turned back toward the carriage. He might pretend to be gruff and dour, but he wasn't fooling her. The man had the heart of a hero.

Chapter Four

Griff rubbed his chin as he watched Ruby move toward the buggy, cat in hand. She was still crooning to the critter, as if it were a hurt child in need of comfort.

The woman was overly sentimental about her pet, not to mention starry-eyed and seriously infected with wanderlust. None of those qualities were ones that would endear her to him—he preferred someone with a more realistic, practical outlook. But he couldn't shake the memory of the look in her eyes just now when she'd thanked him and declared his rescue of her pet the kindest thing anyone had ever done for her. Something about her look and tone at that moment had tugged at him, had made his irritation seem suddenly petty.

She stopped by the hamper and he watched her stoop to reach inside. Pulling out some ham, she fed a sliver to her cat. "This ought to make you feel better," she said in that same lilting tone suitable for a nursery. "Once we get in the buggy I'll give you the rest."

He rolled his eyes, putting down his earlier feeling to a side effect of that irritating cough that had him all out of sorts. His first impression had been the right one—the girl was just plain unprepared for the world she was so desperate to enter.

He grabbed the hamper and followed her to the buggy. By the time he caught up with them, the cat was crouched beneath the buggy seat, chewing on another bit of ham as if nothing out of the ordinary had just happened.

Ruby turned to him with a smile. "I think Patience will be fine now. Oh, here's your jacket."

Griff set the hamper in the buggy then took his coat from her. He shook it out and examined it, frowning at the half-dozen rips in the lining.

Ruby followed his gaze and gave a little cry. "Oh, dear, I'm so sorry—Patience was quite naughty. Naturally I'll pay to have it replaced."

"That won't be necessary. I'm sure Inez can patch it up for me." The sooner this journey was done the happier he'd be. He jammed his arms in the sleeves then offered her his hand. "Now, up you go. The sky's looking more overcast by the minute and we need to make tracks."

"Of course."

He made quick work of handing her up, taking care not to let his hands linger.

She gathered up the reins, her expression mirroring his concern. "You're right about the weather looking gloomy. We'll likely run into rain soon and getting soaked isn't going to do that cough of yours any good." She patted the seat. "Why don't you ride up here with me where there's at least a little protection from the elements? There's more than enough room."

"Thanks for the offer, but it's not raining yet. We might get lucky and miss it altogether. Besides I want to keep an eye on that bull. I can't watch him if I'm inside the buggy."

"What if I let you handle the reins? Then you can go just as slow and easy as you like."

As if there was any question but that he'd take the reins if he climbed in. "Thanks, but I'll ride Chester awhile longer." He stepped back, but then noticed her shoulders flutter. Was she cold? With a frown, he reached back into the buggy and plucked out the picnic cloth, placing it on the seat beside her. "Here, use this as an extra lap blanket."

She held it out. "Maybe you should—"

He didn't let her finish. "Don't argue. I'm used to being out in all sorts of weather—cows and fences need to be tended to year-round—so this bit of nastiness doesn't bother me."

Despite his reassurances to her, Griff eyed the horizon worriedly. Besides being markedly colder, there was a dampness in the air now that didn't bode well for his hope of staying dry. And worse yet, he knew he wasn't quite as okay as he'd tried to convince her. He was coughing more often now and that general achiness had settled into his bones.

He just needed to get home to Hawk's Creek. Inez would take it from there. But first, he had to get Ruby Tuggle safely delivered to Reverend Martin at Cornerstone.

Using the buggy's step, he reached up to loosen the side panels. "In fact, I'm going to fasten down the sides. If it *does* start raining, you'll be better protected."

It would also make conversation between them more difficult.

Now why didn't that thought please him as much as it would have when they'd set out this morning?

He mounted his horse and gave her the signal to set the buggy in motion. By his reckoning they had another four hours of travel ahead of them. And that was assuming they didn't make any more stops or encounter delays. There was no way the rain was going to hold off that long.

Sure enough, thirty minutes later he felt the first drop of rain. It was isolated for the moment, but it wouldn't be for much longer. The urge to move faster was strong but he couldn't do it as long as he had that bull to transport.

Clenching his jaw, he reached a decision. Maneuvering his horse closer to the buggy, he claimed Ruby's attention. "There's a farmhouse just up the road a bit. I'm going to ride on ahead to talk to the owner if you think you'll be okay for a few minutes on your own."

"I'll be fine."

He felt as if he were abandoning her. Ridiculous, because it was straight ahead less than half a mile. "Keep at this pace and pull over by the barn when you get there. All right?"

This time she merely nodded and to his surprise didn't ask any questions about what he was up to.

By the time the buggy caught up with him, he'd struck a deal with the farmer, a man by the name of Fred Callums who had been blessed with an army of children. Griff had counted at least eight faces peering out from various windows and doors before he lost count. Mr. Callums seemed quite eager to care for the bull for the next few days in return for the five dollars Griff offered him. No doubt money was scarce in this very full household.

Within minutes of Ruby's arrival, the bull was untied and led to a paddock by one of Mr. Callums's boys, and Griff had handed over the bag of oats and the money to the farmer himself, along with a promise to send someone to fetch the animal in the next day or two.

He turned to his traveling companion. "If you don't mind, I think I'm ready to take you up on that offer to ride in the buggy."

"Of course."

Was that a hint of relief in her smile? He tied Chester to the back of the buggy where the bull had been a few minutes ago, then climbed up next to her. The cat let out an indignant yowl at being disturbed. So much for the varmint's gratitude for Griff's rescue.

Ruby immediately reached down to pet the animal with a "Hush now" command while Griff matched the cat's glare with one of his own, and the animal finally subsided.

Griff released the brake and gave the reins a flick. "Now, let's see if we can make a little better time."

"That was a good idea, finding a place to stable your bull."

Griff shrugged. "That's one less thing to have to worry about if this storm gets worse." He cut a glance her way. "I'd thought that I might ask them to put you up for the night as well, but when I saw how many were in that household I didn't think you'd be very comfortable there."

She gave him a reassuring smile. "I don't mind sleeping in a barn if it comes to that, but you're right, it would have put them out to have yet another person to look after." He noticed her chin tilt up slightly. "And I'm not as fragile as you seem to think. Short of ice and hail, I'll survive a bit of wet winter weather just fine."

He certainly hoped she was right—he wouldn't want her to get sick while she was under his care.

She reached for the blanket that was over her lap. "Speaking of which, I have two of these. Why don't you take one?"

He waved the offer aside. "Keep it. I'm fine for now."

No way was he going to let her mollycoddle him, especially at the expense of her own comfort.

Ruby compressed her lips in a worried line. It had been nearly an hour since they'd left the Callums place and so far the dark clouds had only managed to produce a light drizzle. But her companion was not looking good. He sat hunched in his seat and his cough was painful to listen to. She'd asked twice again if he wanted to use one of the blankets, but he'd been almost brusque in his refusal. Was it a matter of pride with him? Or did he truly not realize how sick he was?

When the next coughing spasm overtook him she'd had enough. She pulled the top blanket off her lap and firmly placed it on his.

Mr. Lassiter shot her an irritated look, but she glared right back. To her relief he finally nodded and issued a curt "Thank you."

She sensed the weariness beneath his irritation and so refused to take offense. "Would you like me to take the reins for a little while?" she asked.

"I'm fine."

If she'd been standing she would have stomped her foot. "Just *saying* you're fine doesn't make it so. There's nothing wrong with admitting you're sick."

"I told you, I don't get sick." The words were almost a growl and his tone would have been intimidating if it hadn't ended on a particularly nasty cough.

Besides, did he have any idea how absolutely ridiculous that assertion sounded? "I don't think that's something you have absolute control over. And anyway, that cough of yours seems to be contradicting your statement."

His only response was a tightening of his jaw and a quick flicking of the reins.

They rode along without speaking for a while. Finally she broke the silence again, trying for a less volatile subject. "How much longer until we get to this Cornerstone of yours?"

"It's not mine." He shot her a quick look, then softened his tone. "It's about another hour and a half." His lips quirked up in a self-mocking grin. "Why? Are you tired of the traveling or of the company?"

"Just curious." She lifted Patience onto her lap, looking for a bit of moral support. "But you know, maybe you should think about spending the night there yourself, especially if it's still raining when we arrive. The sooner you get dried out in front of a fire the better."

His irritation flared again. "Hang it all, will you *please* stop acting as if I'm about to keel over dead? For the last time, it's just a cough. And since Hawk's Creek is only another thirty minutes past Cornerstone, I'd just as soon dry out in front of my own fire in my own house."

But Ruby focused on the pallor of his complexion and the unhealthy glitter of his eyes rather than his tone. If she wasn't mistaken, he was running a fever. By the time they reached Cornerstone, would he even be capable of going on alone? If not, would she be able to stop him? "Is there a doctor in Cornerstone?"

He shot her another of those glowers and she held up a hand. "I'm just making conversation."

"No," he answered. "About the only thing you'll find in Cornerstone is a church, a schoolhouse and a general store."

That wasn't a town, it was a stopover. "So where do folks around there go for treatment when they get sick?"

He shrugged. "Most families take care of their own when they can. There are doctors in Tyler if it's something really serious." He shifted in his seat, grimacing. "Inez is pretty good with treating folks at Hawk's Creek when we're ailing or get injured."

That comment sent her thoughts down a different rabbit trail. "How many folks live at your ranch?"

He seemed happier with this topic. "Me and Inez, of course. Then there's Red, the ranch foreman, Manny who helps out around the place and three other hands who stay on year-round. We hire on more help during the busier times."

It must be a bigger place than she'd thought. "Is cattle all you deal with?"

"We raise horses, too, but mostly for our own use. There's a small peach orchard and we grow most of our own feed—hay, oats, corn, wheat. But yes, cattle is our main focus."

Ruby absently stroked Patience's head. "And you enjoy it? Raising cattle, I mean."

"Yep. Would have looked for other work years ago if I didn't."

"So what is it that you like about it?"

"Just about everything." He gave her a quick look. "Watching the new calves being born and growing into healthy livestock. Seeing the land green up every spring and burst out with new life. The sweet way the hay and the grain smell when it's harvested. Riding across acre after acre of Hawk's Creek and knowing my father and grandfather rode those same paths before me. And that, God willing, my own children will ride them, too, someday."

She watched Griff's face as he talked, enthralled by the passion she saw there. He truly did love that place and the way of life it provided.

Fifteen minutes later the rain had progressed from a light drizzle to a steady shower. Even worse, a gusty wind had kicked up and was periodically spitting the cold rain in their faces. Griff was visibly shivering. She tucked the lap robe more snugly around him without asking, then offered to take the reins "for a while." It was telling that he didn't put up an argument on either front.

Another ten minutes and she was getting seriously concerned that he wouldn't be upright much longer.

"I think a change of plans might be in order," he said after another spasm of coughs.

"What did you have in mind?"

"If you have no objections, I think it would be better to take you on to Hawk's Creek with me rather than drop you off at Cornerstone."

She felt a little spurt of pleasure at the thought that he wanted to show her his homeplace. "I'd certainly enjoy seeing this wonderful ranch you've been telling me about."

"Of course. But more importantly, if we bypass Cornerstone altogether, there's a shortcut we can take. The road's not quite as good, but it'll cut about thirty minutes off of the trip."

Oh. He was being practical, not neighborly. "Then that's definitely the way to go. I won't get a lick of sleep tonight unless I know you made it safely there."

He managed a smile. "Wouldn't want to be responsible for you not getting a good night's rest." Then he sobered. "Keep an eye out for a large oak with one side sheared off by lightning. A little ways past that you'll see a road branch off to your right. That's our shortcut—it'll take you right to Hawk's Creek."

A few minutes later she spied the milestone he'd mentioned. "There's the scorched tree."

He straightened and focused where she pointed. "That's it. The road we want is just up ahead. See it?"

She nodded and in short order had the buggy moving along the shortcut. It wasn't quite as wide or smooth as the road they'd been traveling before, but it was passable, even in this weather.

"Another thirty minutes and we'll be there," he said thickly.

Would he be able to stay upright that long? "Is there any place we can stop along the way? Any neighbors we'll pass before we get to your place?"

"No." Another bout of coughs. "The first part borders the back side of the Davis place—the house and barn are a ways off in the other direction. The rest of the road borders Hawk's Creek pasture land. The closest shelter is, in fact, my house at Hawk's Creek."

Not the answer she'd hoped for. "All right, then tell me what I'm looking for."

He slumped then roused himself. "You won't be able to miss it." He was mumbling now. "There's an ironwork arch over the entryway with the ranch's name on it."

Sounded easy enough.

Now if she could just keep him from falling out of the buggy until she got them there.

When he swayed again she decided drastic measures were in order. "Scoot over here."

"What?" He seemed to be having trouble focusing on her.

"I said scoot over here. I want you to lean against me to help brace yourself."

"I don't think—"

The man was impossible! "Listen, I've put up with your stubbornness and fool pride up until now but I'm cold and wet and tired and I don't have time for that anymore. And neither do you."

His head came up and he blinked at her.

"You've been none too steady these past few minutes," she continued, ignoring his reaction. "It's obvious you won't stay upright on your own power much longer."

"I can manage until we get there," he said stiffly.

"I doubt it." She wasn't going to sugarcoat this for him. "Even if tumbling out doesn't break your neck, there's no way I could get you back up here once you hit the ground." She took her eyes off the road long enough to glare at him. "Now do as I say and get over here."

He held his position a few moments longer, then slowly slid over until their shoulders touched. He was so stiff she feared he would snap in half at the least bit of jarring.

Did he find contact with her so distasteful? Regardless of his reasons, from the looks of him he wouldn't be able to keep that rigid stance up for long.

"Relax." She tried to keep her tone firm but sympathetic. "Lean against me if you need to. The best thing you can do right now is to focus your energy on staying conscious."

He nodded but his stiffness remained.

In a matter of minutes, however, he was starting to slump again. His head came down on her shoulder and she could feel the heat of his forehead through her clothing. He definitely had a fever.

She had to do what she could to keep him awake. "Griff, I need you to talk to me."

"What? I—" His head came up again. "Sorry."

"No, that's okay. Lean on me if it helps, just stay awake. Why don't you tell me about Inez? You say she's been at Hawk's Creek since before you were born. Was *she* born there?"

"No." His shoulders fluttered in a shiver. "But she was very young when my grandfather hired her." He coughed again and she winced at the painfully raspy sound of it.

But she had to keep him talking. "So he hired her as his housekeeper and she's been there ever since. Is that it?"

"Almost. He hired her to help take care of my grand-mother when she got real sick. The way I hear it, she took over the cooking on her own. Grandmother never did get well again and…once she passed… Inez stayed on to…to run the household."

He was mumbling now and she only caught snatches of the rest of his answer. "…wish…woman like that… keeps her word…someone to stay." He slumped against her again and Ruby reflexively put an arm around his shoulder to hold him upright. No time to think about what his words might mean.

Lord, I need You to help me. Keep Griff from slip-ping down for just a bit longer. Guide me so I don't miss the gate to the ranch. And please don't let anything get in my path. I know that's asking a lot, but I also know there isn't anything You can't do.

Ruby repeated that prayer several times over the next fifteen minutes as the rain came down harder and the wind grew gustier. Her arm and shoulder ached almost unbearably from the effort to hold on to Griff, but she didn't dare take her arm from around his shoulder for fear he would slip down. Her teeth chattered from the cold as the rain blew into the buggy and soaked them both. Griff spoke periodically and tried pulling away from her, but his words were indistinct and his efforts were weak.

Twice she almost pulled the buggy over to wait out the storm, but she knew she had to get her companion to a warm, dry place as soon as possible. And if his in-structions had been correct they had to be getting close.

"Hold on, please, we must be almost there. You're going to be able to warm yourself by your own fire and sleep in your own bed tonight after all, just like you wanted. I promise."

Her only answer was another spasm of coughs.

Please God, don't let me break that promise.

Griff felt disoriented. Time seemed to be jumping around. This was the third time he'd opened his eyes with no recollection of having closed them. And the weather kept getting worse each time with no transition from what it had been before. The rain was really coming down now and he felt chilled to the bone. Something was constricting him, keeping him from moving. That wouldn't do. He tried pushing free but it was no good...

He roused what seemed a few minutes later to the feel of a soft shoulder cushioning his head and an arm around his shoulder. Is that what had held him earlier? He couldn't remember.

His companion was talking under her breath—it sounded like a strange combination of prayer and an exhortation to him to not fall out of the buggy. A sudden catch in her voice, as if on a sob, set off alarm bells in his head. What was the matter? Had something happened to her? He should reassure her. After all, it was his job as her escort keep her safe. And he'd do that just as soon...

Voices. So many voices. They were coming at him from everywhere. But the words were garbled, urgent. He even heard that scraggly cat of hers complaining loudly. Where was Ruby? Then there were hands, lots of hands, grabbing at him, tugging on him, carrying him. The jostling made the pounding in his head worse. But he couldn't let that stop him.

Where was Ruby? Were these hands after her, too? Was she safe? He had to make certain. She'd counted on him.

He struggled, but there were too many of them and they were too strong. Or maybe he was too weak. How could he be so hot and so cold at the same time? It was as if his head was disconnected from the rest of his body.

He called out Ruby's name. She answered, but her voice was so distant. Was she still crying? He couldn't tell.

Then the blackness swallowed him completely.

Chapter Five

Griff bobbed in and out of consciousness for a while, like a cork on choppy water. He wanted to sleep, to find relief from the pounding and the burning and the steel band wrapped around his chest, but the nagging feeling that there was something important he needed to do kept tugging him back to the surface again.

Ruby. She'd been crying. He had to make certain she was okay. But, no matter how hard he tried, his eyelids and arms wouldn't cooperate and down he'd go again.

Finally he drifted up and this time the surface was cool and quiet, and the bands on his chest had loosened. This time he could actually open his eyes, though it was dark here, wherever *here* was.

Then the memories slammed into him—nightmare images of voices and hands, fire and chills, a yowling cat and...

And Ruby! He was supposed to provide her with safe escort. Was she okay? Had she—

"Well, hello there."

She stood over him, a shadowy form in the dimness. Her voice was thick, as if she'd been asleep. Or weeping.

Had something happened to her? If only he could see her more clearly. "Are you okay?"

"I'm fine."

"But you were crying."

"I'm all better now."

"Good." Griff settled back down. There was something heavy on his chest. From the pungent odor, he figured it was one of Inez's poultices. The thing itched and smelled—it had to come off. He just needed a minute to gather his thoughts and his strength...

Griff barely blinked yet sunshine was now streaming into the room.

Ruby appeared at his bedside and smiled down at him. "Good, you're awake again. You had us mighty worried. Now, you just rest easy while I let Inez know you're awake."

"Wait."

She paused and came closer. Close enough that he could see the tired circles under her eyes.

"Is something wrong?" she asked. "Do you need me to get you anything?"

"No. I—" He tried to gather his scattered thoughts. "What day is it?"

"Tuesday."

He frowned. "Tuesday? But that means I lost two and a half days."

Her dimples appeared. "You didn't lose them—you spent both of them right here."

Whatever else had happened, she hadn't lost her

sense of humor. "I guess I owe you a big thank-you for getting me home the way you did."

She waved him off. "I'm just glad that things turned out okay. And Inez has been treating me very well since I arrived, so there's no need for any other thanks." She turned to the door. "Speaking of Inez, I promised I'd let her know the second you woke up. She's been beside herself worrying about you."

After she'd left the room, Griff looked around. This wasn't his bedchamber. In fact, it wasn't a bedchamber at all—it was his mother's sitting room, a room that was rarely used anymore. Someone had pushed the furniture to one side and a bed had been set up near the fireplace.

He winced as he shifted, trying for a more comfortable position. His chest muscles were sore as all get out. And why in the world was his left foot tender? It seemed he'd been a lot sicker—and a lot more out of it—than he'd thought. Pretty lowering to realize he'd put Ruby in a position to have to deal with his troubles.

His sister, Sadie, had always said his stubbornness was going to be the death of him—seems he'd nearly proved her right. Why in the world hadn't he sought out a dry place to wait out the bad weather?

Then again, whatever ailment had laid him low might have overtaken him regardless of the weather. So pushing to get back to Hawk's Creek and Inez's ministrations just might have been the best plan after all.

Feeling better about his decisions, Griff took stock of himself and his surroundings.

The poultice was gone—if it had ever been there in the first place. He wasn't sure how much of the past few days was memory and how much delirium.

He stared up at the ceiling. He had only hazy memories of what had transpired once they'd turned onto that shortcut—just the jostle of the ride, the pounding of his head and his losing battle to stay conscious.

Wait a minute, there was something else—a scolding she'd given him and the feel of her arm holding him snug against her side. Had that really happened? The memory felt real enough. But how could a girl like Ruby have managed his practically dead weight while driving the buggy, especially in that weather?

He still had trouble believing she'd gotten him home when he'd been too sick to get himself here. For a wide-eyed dreamer, she'd sure proven herself resourceful in a pinch. Perhaps the good Lord had actually been looking out for *his* well-being more than Ruby's when He'd put her in his path.

And it was curious that she was still here. Why hadn't she gone on to Tyler? Had she been worried about him? Or was she getting cold feet about her plans for a new life?

Inez bustled in, interrupting his thoughts. "Now ain't you a sight for sore eyes." Her voice was gruff and she looked at him as if he'd been at death's doorstep. "I was beginning to wonder if you were gonna sleep straight through to Christmas."

He gave her a teasing smile. "Now you know you can't get shed of me that easy. I'm too tough to stay down long."

"Too ornery is more like it." She placed a hand on his forehead. "Fever seems to be all gone. How are you feeling?"

His throat and chest ached, but the pounding in his

head was gone and his thinking was clear. "I won't be roping any steers or running any races today, but compared to how I felt Saturday, I'm fine."

She harrumphed. "I think *fine* is a bit optimistic, what with you lying there looking wrung out as wet laundry, but I'm glad to hear you're better."

Griff pushed himself up to a semi-sitting position. "Wet laundry? I'll have you know I'm feeling stronger by the minute." He patted his stomach. "All I need is to get some of your hearty meals in me and I'll be right as rain."

She reached behind him and plumped the pillows. "Don't be expecting steak and potatoes just yet. It's broths and soups for you until you're a bit stronger."

"Yes, ma'am." He smiled innocently up at her. "But it seems to me I'd get stronger a lot quicker with heartier nourishment."

Inez placed her hands on her hips, just as he'd known she would. "Since I'm doing the cooking and the doctorin', with Ruby's help, I'll decide what you need."

What all had Ruby's help consisted of? "I appreciate you looking out for Miss Tuggle the past few days. I hope having her around hasn't added to your work."

"Land sakes, no. In fact, she's been a big help. Spelling me in watching over you, making herself useful in the kitchen."

Ruby had watched over him? For some reason that made him decidedly uncomfortable. "I hope I wasn't too much trouble for you ladies the past few days."

"We managed."

That wasn't exactly an answer. But before he could dig deeper, she changed the subject. "How's your foot feeling?"

"A mite sore, but not anything I can't deal with. I don't recall hurting it though."

"We had some trouble getting you out of the buggy when y'all arrived. Truth to tell, you were delirious with the fever and fought us like a rabid wolf. I'm afraid your foot got banged up in the process. But don't go blaming Red and the guys—it was an accident."

"Seems I'd better be doing more apologizing than blaming." He stiffened at a sudden thought. "I didn't hurt anyone, did I?"

She gave him a sympathetic smile. "I'm afraid you left a few bruises here and there, but nothing worse."

What about Ruby? Was that why he remembered her crying? Please, God, don't let him have hurt her. "I didn't hurt Ruby, did—"

She looked up quickly. "Mercy, no. No worries there. In fact, you seemed to think you were protecting her from goodness only knows what."

Griff released a breath he hadn't realized he'd been holding. At least he didn't have that on his conscience.

"She's quite a girl, isn't she?" Inez added.

Griff nodded. He was beginning to see that himself.

"The good Lord was sure looking after you when He arranged for you two to travel together," she said, echoing his earlier thoughts. "I don't like to think what might have happened if you'd taken ill alone on that road. That girl likely saved your life."

Before Griff could question her further, Ruby stepped through the open doorway, carrying a tray of food. Her cat was right at her heels.

"Here we go," she said cheerily. "Inez's marvelous cooking ought to help fix you right up."

"Mmm-mmm. That sure does smell good." He watched her closely, looking for some sign that she might be leery of him. "What is it?"

"Beef and vegetable broth." Inez answered for her, patting his coverlet before she stepped back. "I expect you to eat it all up."

"Don't worry. I feel like I could eat a whole steer, hooves, horns and all."

"Well, for today you'll just have to settle for the broth. If you behave yourself and rest like you're supposed to, I just might leave some meat and vegetables in it tomorrow."

Ruby watched the interaction between Inez and Griff with surprise and a touch of longing. Griff didn't balk at Inez's solicitousness the way he had with her. The two obviously cared for each other, as if the housekeeper were indeed part of his family, just as he'd claimed. How would it be to have someone in her own life who cared as much for her? The closest emotion she'd felt from her surrogate parents was care born of obligation.

Inez turned to Ruby, pulling her out of her thoughts. "If you don't mind, would you stay here and help Griff with his meal? I want to let Red and the others know that he's feeling better this morning."

"Oh, but I can do that if you—"

Inez waved away her offer. "No, no. I need to talk to Red about something else anyway." She glanced at Griff, then back to Ruby. "I can count on you to stay with him until he finishes every bit of that soup, can't I?"

"Of course."

Ruby faced Griff, feeling suddenly uncertain. She'd spent the past few days taking shifts watching over him in this very room, but an unconscious Griff Lassiter was very different from this alert, watchful man. Suddenly, the memory of holding him tight against her side in the pouring rain during the last twenty minutes of that awful drive was all she could think about.

Pasting a bright smile on her face that she hoped would mask her nervousness, she lifted the tray slightly. "Where would you like me to place this?"

He patted the coverlet in front of him. "Just set it here on my lap and I'll take it from there."

She did as he asked, helped him tuck a napkin under his chin, then pulled a chair up closer to his bedside. "Do you need any help with that?"

"I can manage."

She noticed his hand shook slightly as he ladled up a spoonful, but didn't comment on it. She knew him well enough now to understand he wouldn't appreciate her pointing out such a weakness.

Instead, she kept him company the best way she knew how—chatting. "I had a bowl myself earlier. Inez is quite a cook." She reached down to stroke her cat's head. "I can see why you spoke so highly of her. And I don't mean just for her cooking ability. She's nice." Even knowing Inez would likely have offered the same to anyone, it had warmed Ruby to have someone offer genuine neighborliness, not a handout born of a sense of duty.

Griff scooped up another spoonful. "Couldn't run this place without her." He nodded Ruby's way. "She had good things to say about you, too. I understand you've been lending a hand around here the past few days."

Inez had spoken well of her? Ruby's smile stretched wider. "I like to keep busy. And it was the least I could do in return for Patience and my room and board."

He frowned at that. "We don't usually ask our guests to work off their room and board."

"Oh, I didn't mean to imply Inez *asked* me to work. I pestered her to let me help."

He took another sip of his soup, but he kept his gaze on her and she was having trouble interpreting his expression.

"Sorry if my condition caused you to delay your trip to Tyler," he said finally.

Actually, she hadn't even thought about Tyler since she'd arrived here. "Oh, I don't mind. It wasn't as if I had to be there on a specific date."

"True." Another pause to eat, then, "The last part of that trip home is hazy for me. Care to fill in the blanks?"

She tried to keep her expression even as she remembered just how tense, how frightening the final leg of that ride had been. There were moments when she'd thought for sure he'd slide right off the carriage seat.

But she didn't need to burden him with all of that. Instead she gave him a smile. "You stayed coherent long enough to point out the road I needed to take to get us on the shortcut. Then I just followed it until I found the wrought-iron arch with Hawk's Creek Ranch spelled out." Of course the rain had been coming down so hard at that point she'd had trouble making it out. She pushed that thought aside. "You gave good directions. When I pulled up at the house Inez and some of the ranch hands were waiting on me. Apparently someone spotted the buggy coming up the drive. Then they got you in the house and Inez took over." Ruby grinned. "She's very good at taking charge."

"That she is." He grimaced. "I guess I wasn't much good as an escort after all. Sorry if I gave you a scare."

That was putting it mildly. "I'm just happy it all turned out okay." She sat up straighter. "And you'll be pleased to know that yesterday, when I mentioned the bull we'd left behind at the Callums's place, Red immediately sent someone out to fetch it."

Griff nodded. "Red is a good man."

"And everyone's been just as nice as could be to me. Of course, once they had you settled in, I *did* have to do some explaining as to how I came to be riding with you."

He grinned. "I imagine you did."

She'd been amazed that Inez and the others had heard her out and then took her in as if she were an old family friend instead of a stranger. She wasn't used to receiving such an unconditional welcome.

"I hope you won't think me awful for saying this," she said impulsively, "but if you *had* to get sick, I'm glad I was with you when you did."

He raised a brow and she felt her face warm. That hadn't come out quite right. "I mean, it gave me a chance to spend a little time here at Hawk's Creek. And it's every bit as nice as you described it. I can see why you're so proud of it."

He nodded, obviously pleased with her comment. "There's no other place on earth like Hawk's Creek." Then he cocked his head to one side. "Have you seen much of the ranch itself?"

She shook her head. "I've stayed close to the house."

To be more specific, she'd been staying pretty close to the sickroom—sightseeing had been the furthest thing from her mind the past few days. "But I like what I've seen of it."

"If you've stayed close to the house, then you haven't really seen Hawk's Creek. I'll have to take you for a ride across the place when I get my strength back."

"Oh, I'd enjoy that. But it may be a few days before you're up to a ride."

"You said yourself you didn't have to be in Tyler by any particular date. Or are you in hurry to get there after all?"

"Well, I…" Ruby paused. Was she? She'd lingered here because she wanted to satisfy herself that he was going to be okay. It appeared that was no longer an issue so there wasn't anything to keep her here now.

But, truly, her main goal hadn't been to get to Tyler so much as to get out of Cleebit Springs. And she'd accomplished that. The rest of her fresh start could wait a bit longer.

Ruby smiled. "No, I suppose not. Establishing a new home for myself by Thanksgiving is my only goal. So, as long as I reach Tyler by then, I'm happy to stay here for a few days."

"Then consider yourself our guest for the time being." He pointed his spoon her way. "And none of this 'earning your keep' business, either."

She had no intention of sitting idle for the next few days, but there was no point in getting him agitated by saying so. "Thank you kindly for the invitation." Then she stood. "Now, it looks like you've scraped the bottom of that bowl, so I'll take your tray and let you get a little more rest."

"Rest." He snorted. "I've been *resting* since I got here." But even as he spoke she saw him stifle a yawn.

"You've been fighting a fever since then, which is not at all the same thing as resting. You need to get some real rest if you want to get your strength back. And since you now owe me a tour of the place, I insist." She placed the tray on the chair and reached for the pillows behind his back. "Now, slide down and try to sleep." Not that she figured it would take much trying. He'd probably be asleep before she and Patience made it to the kitchen.

Griff watched her disappear into the hallway, then settled deeper under the covers. He wasn't sure exactly why he'd invited her to stay—gratitude, he supposed. After all, she'd gone through a lot to get him here, and Inez had mentioned how much help she'd been since her arrival.

Ruby Tuggle had to be one of the most deliberately agreeable people he'd ever met. Always trying to please the people she was with, always apologizing when she thought she'd failed, always looking for the bright side of bad situations. Nobody could be that pleasant all the time. What was her story?

He shifted, trying to get more comfortable. Inez hadn't been far off when she pronounced him to be as useful as damp laundry—definitely unfamiliar territory for him. He hadn't been lying when he told Ruby he never got sick. It was embarrassing to realize he'd been laid so low while she was supposed to be in his charge. Seems she'd managed okay on her own, though.

She was either very lucky or more resourceful than he'd given her credit for.

Well, he'd make it up to her once he got his strength back. And then he'd personally see her settled safely in Tyler, and by Thanksgiving if that's what she really wanted. He still didn't understand her reasoning, but if life there was her goal, then he aimed to see she got off on the right foot. Perhaps he should even go so far as to look in on her from time to time. Whenever he was already in Tyler on business, of course. After all, with what she'd done for him, he owed her that much.

This was about paying his debts, he told himself. Nothing more.

Chapter Six

Inez looked up from peeling carrots as Ruby entered the kitchen. "So how's our patient doing?"

"He ate all of his soup and now he's resting." Ruby unloaded the tray of dishes into the sink. "He claimed to be all rested up, but from the looks of him he'll fall back asleep in no time."

Inez gave her a surprised look. "You got him to settle back down, just like that?"

Had she done something wrong? "I thought sleep was what he needed right now."

"Oh, it is. But that doesn't mean Griff will be sensible about it." She shook her head. "I guess you haven't been around him long enough to understand just how stubborn that boy can be."

Ruby smiled. It seemed strange for anyone to call such an impressive man "that boy." "Actually, I did get a taste of that side of him during our ride." She cleared her throat. "I hope you won't mind having me and Patience around a little longer. Mr. Lassiter invited me to stick around for a few more days."

Inez gave her another of those surprised looks, then wiped her hands on her apron. "Good for him. It's been nice to have another female around the place and I'm right pleased to know you'll be staying awhile longer." She moved to the stove with her peeled carrots. "And now that we know he's on the mend, you and I can relax a bit and get to know each other better."

"I'd like that." Feeling as if her world was finally coming to rights after so many years, Ruby began washing the dishes. "But I aim to help out while I'm here. You just let me know what needs doing."

The next time Griff opened his eyes, there were lamps lit and the corners of the room were in shadow. Evening, then—but was it the same day? He turned toward the sound of movement and found Inez rather than Ruby near his bedside.

Surely that was curiosity and not disappointment he felt?

"I thought you might be ready for some supper." Inez nodded toward a tray on the bedside table.

"You thought right." Griff pulled himself into a sitting position. "How long did I sleep this time?"

"About six hours."

At least he hadn't lost another day.

Inez started fussing with the pillows at his back. "You'll be pleased to know there's a bit of substance in your bowl this time. You can thank Ruby for that. I was going to give you another bowl of plain broth but she seems to think you're ready for something a little heartier than that."

Another point in the girl's favor. "Speaking of Miss Tuggle," he said casually, "how is she this evening?"

"I made her sit down a few minutes ago and eat her own supper. That girl has more energy than a wild mustang."

He frowned. "I told her she's a guest here, that she doesn't need to earn her keep."

Inez shrugged as she placed the tray on his lap. "I told her the same thing but she claims she likes to keep busy. Besides, I enjoy the company." She took a seat beside him and pulled some mending from her sewing bag.

Had that been in here earlier? He couldn't remember.

"She tells me you invited her to stay on for a spell."

Griff resisted the urge to squirm under his housekeeper's probing gaze. "The fool girl is planning to move to Tyler all on her own," he explained, "and she doesn't know a soul there. I figure I owe it to her to make sure she gets settled in okay." He swirled the spoon through his soup. "To do that, I need to keep her here long enough for me to get back on my feet so I can take her there myself."

"I see. That makes sense." Inez kept her eyes focused on her sewing. "She also tells me you climbed a tree to rescue that cat of hers."

For some reason Griff felt a touch of heat climb into his cheeks. Was his fever returning? "I didn't have much choice." Why did he feel so defensive? "Ruby wasn't going to leave without her pet and I didn't have all day to hang around waiting for that stubborn critter to come down on its own."

"Well, whatever the circumstances, she's convinced you're quite the hero."

Hero! Of all the foolish, schoolgirl notions. "I'm nobody's hero." Especially after the way he'd fallen apart during the last leg of their trip. Still, there was something about the notion that she'd actually said that…

He caught Inez looking at him with a twinkle in her eye and decided to change the subject. "I guess I was a sorry sight by the time she got me here."

"Mercy me, yes. Wet as a drowned cub and half out of your mind from the fever. I don't know how that girl managed to keep hold of you and handle that buggy in the pouring rain."

Griff paused with the spoon halfway to his mouth. Keep hold of him? So he hadn't imagined that arm around his shoulder. "Seems there was more to this little adventure than I remember," he said slowly. "Want to fill me in?"

Inez didn't look up from her stitches. "Well, the rain had turned from a drizzle to a downpour and it was miserable cold. Not a fit day for man nor beast. We all figured you'd taken shelter somewhere like any *sensible* person would have." The look she gave him was that of a schoolmarm confronting a truant.

Griff felt compelled to explain himself. "Can you blame me for wanting to get back here as soon as possible? After all, no one can take care of me like you can."

"Don't go trying to smooth-talk me, Griff Lassiter. I know your tricks." But her expression had softened considerably.

"Anyway," she continued, "we weren't really looking for you to arrive until the next day. Thank goodness, or I should say thank the good Lord, Red just happened to be looking out from the barn when he spied the wagon coming up the drive. Didn't recognize it, of course, but he figured it had to be something important to bring anyone out in that weather, so he ran out to meet it. Good thing he did, too. Poor Ruby was just about at the end of her stamina what with trying to handle the reins and hold on to you at the same time."

Inez's hands stilled. "It's a wonder that poor child was able to see the gate, much less turn the horse onto the drive."

Griff had given up all pretense of eating. "I didn't realize—"

"Of course you didn't. Thing is, you may have been bad sick, but that didn't keep you from fighting off everyone who tried to help you, mumbling incoherent protests. Red and the boys had a terrible time getting you inside."

Griff groaned. Sounds like he'd made quite a spectacle of himself.

"Poor Ruby was soaked to the skin and her lips were practically blue with cold. I was worried for a while that I would have two patients on my hands."

"She seems okay now." No thanks to him.

"Oh, she's fine. That girl is a lot stronger than she looks." Inez patted his arm. "But there's no reason for you to be too hard on yourself. You were sick and that likely clouded your thinking a mite."

Was that supposed to make him feel better?

"Besides," she continued, picking her sewing back up, "Ruby doesn't blame you. And it all turned out well enough in the end."

Ruby might not blame him but that didn't mean he was blameless. He'd have to find a way to make it up to her.

* * *

Ruby looked up guiltily as Inez entered the kitchen. She'd been down on the floor, slipping Patience a sliver of meat from her bowl of stew. But either Inez didn't notice, or didn't care.

"So was he awake?" Ruby asked as she straightened.

"Yep. And he ate every last bit of his supper. At this rate he'll be up and about in no time."

Inez sounded in remarkably good spirits. Griff must be doing well indeed. Would it seem impertinent if she checked in on him herself?

"The only fly in the ointment," Inez continued, "is that he's feeling restless now. I'm worried he'll try to get up before he should."

"Is there something I can do to help? Would you like me to sit with him for a while?"

Inez gave her a bright smile. "That's a wonderful idea. Actually, why don't you see if there's something more active you can do to keep him occupied?"

That sounded interesting. "Such as?"

"Oh, I don't know. Perhaps a game of checkers, or there's a flute in the study if you play, or maybe get a book and read—"

Ruby's pulse quickened. "Do you have many books here?"

"A fair number." She must have noticed Ruby's excitement because she gave a help-yourself-to-them smile. "They're in the study, which is right across the hall from the room where we put Griff. You're welcome to borrow any of them any time while you're here."

"Thank you. That sounds lovely."

"For now, why don't you see if you can find a book you might both enjoy?"

"Do you know what kind of books he likes?" Ruby was already headed toward the hall.

"As far as I can tell, when it comes to books he likes just about everything."

A man after her own heart. Ruby glanced back at her pet. "Coming, Patience?"

But Inez waved her on. "Leave the cat, she'll keep me company. And I'll pour her up a saucer of buttermilk to keep her happy."

A few moments later, Ruby entered the study, then stopped in her tracks. Being in the possession of her father's three books had made her an exception of sorts in Cleebit Springs. Sure, there were newspapers and catalogs, but other than Bibles and schoolbooks, few of the families had access to very many actual bound books.

But here, in this room, were literally hundreds of volumes. Two entire walls were lined with tall bookcases and all of them were laden with volume upon volume of various sizes and colors. She'd never seen so many books in her entire life. Ruby approached them almost reverently, running her fingers across the spines, reading the titles, imagining the hours she could spend here blissfully lost in such a wealth of information and imagination.

She wasn't sure how long she stood lost in the grandness of it all, until she finally remembered the mission Inez had set her on. She was supposed to be selecting something appropriate to read to Griff.

A few minutes later she hesitated at his doorway. What if he had already fallen asleep? Or worse yet, what if he wished to be alone and saw her visit as an intrusion? What was that he'd said that day on the road—*sometimes a fellow just liked to hear his own thoughts for a while.*

Then again, if he was lying there bored, he might be tempted to get up, and that would never do. She squared her shoulders and gave the door a light tap.

She received an immediate "Come in" reply. Pulling her shoulders back, she tried to decide if she was more nervous or excited by the prospect of visiting with him again.

And decided that it was perhaps a bit of both.

Chapter Seven

When Griff saw it was Ruby at the door, his spirits lifted. "Well, hello. Come to check on the invalid?" he asked as he pushed himself up to a sitting position. The spurt of pleasure he felt at seeing her was due to his need to repay her for her help in getting him home, of course.

She returned his smile. "You're looking less like an invalid by the minute."

Pleased that she'd noticed, he nodded. "Thanks. Regardless of what Inez has to say on the matter, it's not really necessary to keep me bed-bound like this."

"She's only looking out for your best interests."

"I know. That's why I'm humoring her today. But tomorrow I'm getting out of this bed and out of this room, no matter how much she tries to mollycoddle me."

"Do you really think that's wise? You're not—"

"I didn't say I was going to ride out to the back forty. I just want to move around and get a change of scenery."

Ruby held up her hands, palms outward. "No need to get all testy. It's not me you'll need to convince."

"And you don't think I can convince Inez?"

She dropped her hands. "I'll let the two of you battle that out without me." The she grinned. "And don't ask me who I'd favor to come out on top."

He pretended indignation. "I'll grant that Inez can be a formidable opponent. But don't rule me out just yet."

"Oh, I would never *completely* rule you out."

He glanced at the object in her hands. "What do you have there?"

"A book." Then she quickly added, "Inez told me I could borrow it."

"Of course. I was just curious as to which book it was."

"*A Connecticut Yankee in King Arthur's Court.* It's by Mr. Mark Twain. Have you read it?"

"I have." He noticed the way her expression fell.

"Oh. I thought I would read it to you for a while, but if you've already—"

"I'd rather just talk, if you don't mind. Maybe you could read it yourself later and we could compare notes on what we each thought of it."

"All right." She set the book on the side table somewhat wistfully and took a seat. "What would you like to talk about?"

He grabbed the first topic that came to mind. "You enjoy reading?"

"Oh, yes. I own three books myself." Her pride changed to chagrin in an instant. "Of course, compared to what you have here, that must sound meager."

"Not at all. You have to understand, that library was collected by several family members over many, many years. I'm afraid I haven't added much to the collection myself."

"You're blessed to have access to so many volumes."

"I take it you didn't?"

"Other than Bibles, not many of the families in Cleebit Springs have books. But I didn't go entirely without. Mr. Barlowe, who owns the general store, used to get the newspaper from Shreveport and when I lived with his family he would let me read it occasionally. And Mrs. Samuels had a set of encyclopedias that I spent as much time with as I could when I lived with her family."

Sounded as if she'd moved around a lot growing up.

"The books I have were my father's," she continued. "One of them is another of Mr. Twain's books—*The Prince and the Pauper*."

"That's one I haven't read yet. Did you enjoy it?"

"Very much." She brightened. "I'd be glad to loan it to you if you like."

"Why don't you tell me about it?"

"All right." She leaned forward and launched into an enthusiastic discussion of the high points of the story, complete with animated expressions and hand gestures. She seemed to be quite a storyteller in her own right.

Griff interposed questions and comments of his own, as much to keep her talking as for clarification. He was surprised at both her recall and the intelligent way she added asides about her own thoughts on the story.

When Inez stepped into the room, Griff glanced at the clock on the mantel and was surprised to find that nearly two hours had passed.

"Sounds like you two are passing the time enjoyably," Inez commented, "but I think maybe Griff should get some rest now. As should we all."

Ruby popped out of her chair, a guilty flush staining her cheeks. "Oh, I'm so sorry. I lost all track of time. I—"

"No need to apologize," Griff interrupted. Truth to tell he was annoyed at Inez's interruption. He wasn't some schoolboy to be given an early bedtime. "In fact, I was enjoying the story."

"That's all well and good," Inez replied, "but you're still my patient and I say it's time for you to rest."

"I'm not tired." He mentally winced at the petulance of his tone. It didn't help when he spied Ruby's unsuccessful attempt to swallow her grin.

"Well, Ruby and I have had a long day." Inez's tone was tart. "And neither of us got much sleep the past two nights."

A not-so-subtle reminder of the worry he'd caused them.

"Now, before we leave you to your rest," she said as she turned down the wick of the lamp, "would you like me to fix you one of my special teas to help you sleep?"

Griff shook his head and leaned back against the pillows. "No, thanks."

"Good." She made shooing motions for Ruby. "We'll leave you, then."

Griff frowned at her high-handedness, then shifted uncomfortably as his housekeeper shot him a look he couldn't quite interpret. Surely that wasn't amusement?

"Just a minute." Ruby moved back toward the bed

and slipped the pillows out from behind his back. "Slide down and I'll straighten your covers."

"Tucking me in like a babe," Griff said gruffly. "You're as bad as Inez."

But even as he complained, Griff felt oddly warmed by the attention.

Ruby turned to Inez once they were in the hallway. "Honestly, I'm so sorry if I kept him up—"

Inez held up a hand. "No need to apologize. I'm sure your visit did him a world of good." Then she smiled and there was a definite twinkle in her eyes. "Most of my little performance was for his benefit. I wanted to make sure he wasn't in any position to argue with me."

Performance? Ruby gave her head a mental shake. The relationship between these two was more complex than she'd imagined. But there was genuine love on both ends, so she supposed that was what counted.

They paused at the foot of the stairs. Inez had her own set of rooms off the kitchen, away from the family area. She had placed Ruby in one of the guest rooms on the second floor.

"Now, I'm going to head off to my own bed," Inez said. "But if you want to stay up a bit longer, feel free."

They exchanged good-nights and Ruby slowly climbed the stairs, clutching the Mark Twain book to her chest. She'd read for a while before she turned down her lamp tonight. Then she could discuss the story with Griff tomorrow.

She'd certainly enjoyed their discussion tonight. It wasn't often someone sought out her opinion and then really listened to what she had to say. It had been a heady feeling.

Griff Lassiter was a man who was hard to put a label on—gruff and irritable one minute, considerate and gentle the next. But there was no doubting his compassion and integrity.

Strange that such a man had never married. Especially one who seemed so deeply rooted in his land and his family.

As she pushed open her bedroom door, Ruby told herself that that was really none of her business.

Still, the question lingered in her mind long after she'd turned down the lamp and pulled up the blanket.

Ruby looked up from turning the crank on the butter churn as Red entered the kitchen.

"Morning, ladies," he said as he removed his hat and stomped his boots on the rag rug at the threshold. "Another nasty day out there."

Inez wiped her hands on her apron as she moved to the cupboard. "Come on in and let me fix you a cup of coffee."

"No, thanks. I just had a cup at the bunkhouse. Manny tells me Griff wants me to fill him in on what's been going on around here since he left. I assume he's in his office."

Inez headed back to the stove. "Of course. You know Griff—he couldn't wait to get back to work."

Griff had prevailed this morning, getting up right after breakfast to bathe and shave. Afterward he'd headed straight for his office, where he'd been for the past twenty minutes. Ruby had only seen him briefly when she'd brought him a cup of coffee at Inez's request.

Red nodded to Ruby as he passed. "I noticed one of the traces on your buggy harness looked worn. I asked Frank to have a look at it. He'll make sure it's good as new before you need to take it out again."

Ruby was struck again by how thoughtful the folks here were. "Why, thank you. But y'all don't have to go to all that trouble."

"It's not any trouble to speak of. On a day like this there's not much else we can do anyway. And we can't have you breaking down when you're out and about on your own."

And before she could say more he had exited the room.

An hour later Ruby was happily ensconced in the study, curled up in an overstuffed chair, one hand holding an open book and the other hand resting on the cat slumbering in her lap. It felt almost decadent to relax this way in the middle of the day, but the guilty pleasure was one she could happily get used to.

Besides, Inez had run her out of the kitchen, ordering her to take some time for herself.

Patience's lifting of her head was Ruby's first sign that they were no longer alone. Looking toward the doorway, she saw Griff leaning there, watching her.

"Sorry," he said straightening. "Didn't mean to interrupt your reading."

How long had he been standing there? "Oh, that's okay." She uncurled her legs and put her feet on the floor.

"No need to get up on my account," he protested.

She settled back down. Making a quick mental note of the page number, she closed the book. "I hope you don't mind my being in here. Inez ran me out of the kitchen, and the weather's too dreary for me to go outside, so I thought I'd take advantage of your library and do a bit of reading while I still had the chance."

"Of course I don't mind. Spend as much time in here as you like." He moved to the chair across from her and she noticed the slight hitch in his gait. Apparently his foot still bothered him, but he was trying to hide it.

Patience sneezed, hopped off her lap and stalked from the room, head and tail equally high.

"I don't think that animal cares for me," Griff said.

She smiled at his dry tone. "Patience *is* a very discerning animal."

He stared at her a moment as if not certain if she'd been serious. Then he smiled. "So why did you name that pampered rat catcher Patience?"

She raised a brow. "What? You don't think it fits her?" Ruby laughed outright at his expression. "Actually, it's because patience is what was required to win her over."

"Ahh—now that I can believe. So, I take it she was a stray?"

"Uh-huh. I spotted her outside the boardinghouse shortly after I moved in there. Poor thing was skin and bones and had a hurt paw." But Ruby had recognized a kindred spirit beneath the tattered exterior.

"So you took her in."

"Not right away. She wasn't trusting enough for that. But after weeks of leaving food scraps for her and talking softly and being as nonthreatening as possible, she finally quit running away when she saw me. It was a lot longer before I could actually hold her." That had been such a sweet moment. Ruby could still remember that feeling of triumph and joy when she felt Patience begin to truly trust her.

"And now she's your pet."

Ruby grinned. "I don't know if I'd go that far—Patience is much too independent for that. I guess you could say we have an understanding of sorts."

He shook his head. "Seems like a whole lot of trouble for a snooty, scruffy feline."

"You know what they say—appearances can be deceiving. Sometimes it's worth looking closer to see what's inside."

He gave her a strange look at that. But rather than comment, he changed the subject. "What's that you're reading?"

"It's the Mark Twain book I brought to your room last night. I'm really enjoying it."

"So are you going to focus only on Mr. Twain's work, or do you plan to try some other writers while you're here?"

She glanced at the shelves wistfully, wishing she had time to read each and every volume. "I'll admit I was overwhelmed by the bumper crop of choices and just went for the familiar."

He smiled. "Bumper crop, is it?" He moved toward the bookshelves. "Why don't I make some recommendations, if you'll allow me?"

"Oh, I'd appreciate that."

She followed him to the bookshelves where he started pulling books and handing them to her.

"The Twain books are all on this shelf—help yourself to any of them you're interested in. Now these over here are some of my personal favorites."

She read the titles as he handed them to her: *Swiss Family Robinson, The Count of Monte Cristo, A Tale of Two Cities, Around the World in Eighty Days, Castle Nowhere: Lake-Country Sketches, Twice-Told Tales.*

He moved to another bookcase. "These are some of my sister's favorites." He handed her copies of *Pride and Prejudice, Little Women, Sonnets from the Portuguese, Alice's Adventures in Wonderland* and *Black Beauty.*

Then he turned and focused back on her, and the towering stack of books in her arms. "Oh, sorry. Here let me take those." He retrieved them from her and set them on a nearby table.

Ruby stared at the literary feast he'd selected for her. "My goodness, that's quite a pile of books. There's no way I can read all of them while I'm here." Unless she stayed longer than a day or two. Not that she wanted to extend her stay. She was ready to get on with her new life.

He shrugged. "What you don't finish you can take with you when you leave for Tyler. I can get them back from you when you're done with them."

So he expected to see her even after she moved? That thought lightened her mood considerably. It would be nice to have at least one friend in her life. "That's mighty generous. Thank you."

"It's the least I can do. After all, you practically saved my life."

Ruby went very still as the little bubble of joy inside her burst. He was being nice because he thought he *owed* her. Not because he actually wanted to befriend her. Truth was, she'd probably never have seen him again if she hadn't had to help him get home. Was that also the same reason Inez and Red and all the rest of them were being so nice?

Of course it was. She'd been silly to read anything else into their friendliness.

Something of what she was feeling must have shown on her face because he was looking at her with a puzzled expression. She pulled herself together and offered a big smile. "Now, I think I've lollygagged in here long enough. I should go and see if Inez needs any help."

"Inez will be just fine. She likes having her kitchen to herself." He moved to a table near the window where an inlaid checkerboard was displayed. "How about a game of checkers?"

She needed to find a quiet place to gather her thoughts, to start laying plans to leave. "I don't think—"

"You do know how to play, don't you?"

The challenge in his tone snagged her attention. "Of course. When I lived with the McCaulys, Mr. McCauly and his son George used to play every night and sometimes I'd watch them."

"So you've never actually played?" he pressed.

"No," she admitted, "but it looks simple enough."

He laughed. "I believe you were the one who said appearances can be deceiving. Have a seat and we'll see how much you learned." He pulled out a chair for her. "And don't worry, I'll go easy on you the first game or two."

That got her back up. Go easy on her, would he? She marched to the table and sat down. "Very well. But please, don't feel you have to do less than your best on my account." She gave him a sweetly challenging smile. "Because I certainly won't."

Chapter Eight

As he set up the game, Griff pondered her shift in mood. It was as if she'd pulled back and that bothered him, but he couldn't quite put his finger on what had caused it. Going back over their conversation in his mind, they'd been discussing her taking the books with her when she moved to Tyler. Could it be that the mention of Tyler had reminded her of her plans for a fresh start, for adventure and new experiences? Was she chafing at this unexpected delay in her plans?

He'd expected her to be less eager now that she'd spent some time here at Hawk's Creek. But perhaps he'd been wrong.

He forcibly pushed his disappointment away and focused on the game. Ruby proved to be an adept player. He won the first two games, but not as easily as he'd expected. And she managed to surprise him by claiming victory in the third round.

Griff was glad to see she had a competitive streak in her. It demonstrated that there were a few thorns beneath the roses and sunshine facade she projected.

And she'd need those thorns if she was going to make it on her own.

They were halfway through the fourth game when Inez interrupted them. "Here you two are. Lunch is ready."

Griff met Ruby's gaze. "Shall we continue this later? Or do you want to concede now?"

That won him an indignant glare. "From where I'm sitting, this game is still anybody's."

"Then continue later it is." He pushed his chair back, put his hands on his thighs and pushed himself up. "Inez, lead the way."

Inez didn't move immediately. "I know you usually take your meals in the dining room when we have guests, but Ruby and I have been taking our meals in the kitchen the past few days."

Griff waved Ruby on ahead of him. "If Ruby doesn't mind, then the kitchen is fine with me."

As he escorted the two women to the kitchen, Griff was surprised by how natural it felt.

A few minutes later they'd taken their seats, grace had been said and they began serving their plates.

Inez passed Ruby the bowl of butter beans. "Hard to believe that Thanksgiving is just a week from tomorrow. Are you planning to do anything special to mark the day?"

"I'm looking forward to being settled in my new living quarters in Tyler by then. I imagine there'll be a church service I can go to, and maybe there'll be some kind of community celebration."

Inez shook her head. "Sounds a mite lonely if you ask me."

"I'll have Patience and I hope to have made some friends in town by then." Ruby tried for a reassuring tone. "Besides, I'm a fairly self-sufficient person."

Griff wondered about that. Did she really think she could make it alone? A girl like her should have someone to look out for her, to ease, or even share, her burdens.

Ruby looked from one to the other of them. "How do you all celebrate Thanksgiving?"

Griff paused, not quite sure how to answer that.

Luckily, Inez chimed in first. "I always fix a nice meal, but other than that, we haven't really done much of anything to mark the day in years, not since Griff's mother died."

Ruby turned to him. "How did you celebrate when your mother was around?

He leaned back in his chair, remembering. "She and Inez used to plan a big celebration. They'd clean and decorate the house from top to bottom and recruit us kids to help."

"Not that they were very much real help," Inez interjected.

Griff flashed her an unrepentant grin before continuing. "The meal was a fabulous feast. Inez would cook for days. There'd be a pit-roasted calf and a turkey stuffed the way only Inez can. Mother would have my grandfather from Philadelphia send fresh oysters and cranberries and oranges and lots of other things we don't see around here. And there'd be more pies and sweets than people."

"You make it sound like the day was all about the food," Inez said.

Griff grinned. "For a young boy, that was the main attraction." He turned back to Ruby. "But of course it was
about much more than that. We'd invite all the hands and
the folks from the neighboring ranches. If the weather
was nice we'd set up tables outdoors and eat under the
sky. If it was too cold or wet, we'd clear all of the wagons and tools out of the barn and set up in there. After
the meal, Red would play his fiddle and there'd be singing and dancing and storytelling late into the evening."

"It sounds wonderful."

The dreaminess in Ruby's voice and expression had
him giving her a long look. What was with her? One
minute she seemed dead set on setting out on her own
and the next she seemed to have a hankering for roots.

Inez interrupted his thoughts. "You know," she said
slowly, "I'm thinking it's high time we started treating
Thanksgiving as a special day again."

Griff felt his brow furrow. Now what in the world
had brought that on? "First time I heard you mention it."

"Oh, I've been thinking on it awhile. We don't have
to do it up as fancy as we used to, at least not this year.
Keep it to just Hawk's Creek folk, and of course we
wouldn't need to worry about the oysters and such.
After all, we don't have a lot of time to plan."

"Aren't you getting a little ahead of yourself?" Griff
asked. "After all, I haven't agreed to—"

"Your mother was a fine lady and it would likely
break her heart to know you and your family let the
old traditions die."

She had a point. But why bring it up now, after all
these years? "I suppose. Maybe we can talk to Sadie
and Ry about doing something next year."

"Nonsense. Why wait an entire year when we've got seven and a half days to prepare? Besides, I wouldn't mind having an excuse to cook a fancy feast again."

Griff shook his head. "Seems like a lot of trouble for just one day."

"Griffith Michael Lassiter, just listen to yourself. Are you saying you don't have enough blessings in your life to set aside a full day to give thanks? Besides, it'll give the men something to look forward to."

Griff glanced at Ruby's face and saw a touch of longing there. And suddenly he realized Inez was right. He wasn't even sure why he'd protested in the first place. "Okay, I concede. If you want to have a big shindig, I won't stand in the way. In fact, tell me what I can do to help." And he'd find a way to get Ruby to spend it with them.

"You can invite Ry and Sadie to bring their families to join us—make it a true Lassiter Thanksgiving. It would do us all good to have this house full of young'uns again for a bit."

Ruby listened to the two of them plan their family gathering and felt another stab of jealousy. She'd prayed nightly for as long as she could remember that someday she'd have a home and a family of her own. That was another reason she'd been so eager to leave Cleebit Springs—she just couldn't see ever finding a husband there.

"What about you, Ruby?" Inez's question brought her back to the present. "You'll join us for Thanksgiving, won't you?"

Another invitation offered out of a sense of obligation? "That's very kind of you, but it sounds like this is going to be a family event and I wouldn't want to intrude."

"Nonsense, you already said you don't have anyone else to spend it with. And we'd love to have you join us, wouldn't we, Griff?"

Griff met Ruby's gaze head-on. "Of course."

"See?" Inez's voice held a that-settles-it tone. "We'd love to have you here. And I'll be insulted if you say you'd rather spend the day alone than with us."

Ruby noticed it was Inez doing all the asking. Griff only added his voice when prompted. But she'd seen something in his gaze, something that confused her. What was he truly feeling? With an effort she moved her gaze from Griff to Inez. "Really it's very kind of you, and I enjoy spending time here, but I'm eager to get started in my new life."

Inez waved a hand dismissively. "Oh, there'll be plenty of time for that after Thanksgiving."

"Might as well listen to her," Griff said with a drawl. "When Inez sets her mind to something she's like a hound who's treed a possum—she won't stop baying until you say yes."

Ruby tried to read his expression again—did he really want her to stay? Or was he just humoring Inez?

"Not a very flattering description," Inez said drily. "But accurate enough. Besides," she added, "I truly could use your help getting things ready. Lots to be done in a short amount of time."

Ruby wavered. She wouldn't want to leave Inez in the lurch if she really needed help. And the idea of meeting the other Lassiter siblings was tempting.

"You've already agreed to stay long enough for me to show you around the place," Griff added casually. "What's another few days?"

He was right. And now that she understood they were just trying to repay an imagined debt of honor, she wouldn't be in danger of mistaking it for something else. Why not take the opportunity to enjoy herself? "All right. But only if you really do let me help."

"It's a deal." Inez stabbed a chunk of carrot with her fork. "I'll send Frank to town with a telegram for Sadie and Ry."

Griff reclaimed Ruby's attention. "Is there a particular Thanksgiving tradition of yours that you'd like to include in our planning?"

She didn't have to stop and think about that one. She hadn't stayed in one place long enough to establish traditions. "Nothing special. Perhaps I can start making my own traditions once I'm truly on my own."

He looked as if he was going to question her further, but Inez spoke up first.

"If you don't mind my asking, why did you pick Tyler as your new home?"

"Like I told Griff, I don't have any family left and I wanted to start over fresh somewhere new. A big city like Tyler just seems likely to offer more opportunities for me."

Inez frowned. "But aren't you nervous about moving someplace where you don't know anyone?"

Why did everyone think this was a bad idea? "Yes, but in an excited, can't-wait-to-start kind of way. I'm not afraid, if that's what you're asking. And even if I don't know a soul there, I figure the good Lord will be watching over me and that's all I need."

Inez reached over and patted her hand. "You're right, of course. Sorry for being such an old busybody."

"Oh, I don't mind. I guess it *is* kind of unusual for a woman to strike out on her own like this."

"Actually, I did much the same when Griff's grand-daddy hired me to work here. And I've never regretted it for even one minute."

Those words provided a lift to Ruby's spirit, an affirmation that she would be all right. She glanced at Griff to find him studying her, a slight frown on his face.

Inez stood. "Looks like we're all done. I'll start clearing away the dishes."

Ruby stood, as well. "I'll wash."

Griff pushed his chair back. "Since the weather's too wet for me to do anything outdoors, I suppose I could dry."

Inez raised a brow. "Well now, those are words I never thought to hear."

Ruby looked quickly from Inez to Griff before turning to the sink. So he normally *didn't* help clean up after meals? Was he just bored today? Or did he have another reason for staying with them?

The three of them worked in companionable silence for a while. It felt nice, actually. As if they'd worked together like this for years.

Griff finally looked over his shoulder at Inez. "Since I'm back on my feet I figured I'd move back into my own room tonight. I'll get a couple of the guys to help me put mother's sitting room back to rights."

Inez tsked. "I think it might be best if you stay right

where you are for now. Best not to put more strain on that foot of yours than necessary."

Griff frowned dismissively. "I can handle the stairs."

Ruby hid a smile. She could have told Inez he wasn't going to react well to that approach.

Inez, however, didn't seem willing to let the subject drop. "I'm not so sure." She cleared her throat. "By the way, did I mention that Ruby is in the guest chamber next to Sadie's old room upstairs?"

Ruby saw Griff's expression change just a few seconds before she herself realized what Inez had been trying to convey. The heat immediately climbed into her cheeks and she fumbled with the bowl she was washing. Though she trusted Griff to act honorably, and she knew Inez did as well, there were some who wouldn't think it proper for them to be the only two with bedchambers on the second floor.

"You're right," Griff said as he took the bowl from Ruby. "I think it might be best after all if I stay put for the time being. My foot is better, but there's no point pushing it too soon."

Ruby shook her head. "No, really, I can't let you give up your room for me." Her cheeks heated even more as she realized how that sounded. "I mean, I can move into the sitting room after you move upstairs. It won't be any problem at all, and I've slept in far more meager accommodations."

"Don't be ridiculous. No point shuffling everyone around." He set the drying cloth down. "Now, if you ladies can finish up in here, I need to look over some ledgers."

The rest of the day passed quietly enough. Griff stayed holed up in his office for most of the afternoon while Ruby helped Inez plan the menu and shopping list for the elaborate Thanksgiving meal. At supper they came back together and, to Ruby's relief, their interaction was relaxed and easy, just as if that earlier conversation had never happened.

Griff was pleased to see the sun shining from a clear sky the next morning. He'd had enough of being cooped up inside and not even Inez's mother-henning would deter him from riding out.

As soon as breakfast was over he turned to Ruby. "What do you say I give you that tour we discussed?"

Ruby smiled and then bit her lip. "I promised Inez I would help—"

To Griff's surprise, Inez seemed to be on his side. "Nonsense. Getting out in the fresh air will do you both a world of good."

"But—"

"No buts, young lady. I need you to keep an eye on Griff for me. If he goes gallivanting off by himself, there's no telling how he might overexert himself."

Griff spread his arms. "She's right you know. I'm not to be trusted out there on my own."

That won him a smile. "In that case," Ruby said in martyred tones, "my duty seems clear. I accept your offer."

"Good. I'll have the buckboard out front in an hour." He gave her a pointed look. "And leave the cat here."

Ruby nodded. "Of course." Then she grinned impishly. "After all, I can see you aren't ready to be climbing any more trees just yet."

He rolled his eyes at that, but refrained from comment.

"That'll give me time to pack you a picnic lunch,"

Inez interjected. "That way you won't have to worry about hurrying back."

Her words put Griff in mind of the previous picnic he'd shared with Ruby. And actually, thinking back on that, he'd enjoyed himself more than he'd thought he would. Even the tree-climbing incident hadn't been totally without merit. After all, it wasn't every day a man got to play the role of knight errant for a pretty girl's benefit.

Chapter Nine

Later that morning, as Griff drove the buckboard along one of the drier paths through Hawk's Creek, he decided it was time he learned a bit more about Ruby. "You mentioned you moved to Cleebit Springs when you were seven. Where did you live before that?"

She grabbed hold of the wagon seat on either side of her. "I've moved around most of my life. My ma died when I was three, and afterward, Pa just couldn't seem to settle down in one place. We lived in towns all across Kentucky, Arkansas and Louisiana before we landed in Texas."

"Then you landed in Cleebit Springs and settled down."

"Not entirely. I moved around a lot within the town. I told you before that most of the town had a hand in raising me. I lived with a number of families as I was growing up."

Did growing up that way account for her restlessness, her burning desire to move to a new place? Was she one of those who always looked over fences, searching for greener pastures, a person who couldn't be content with what she already had? No wonder she wasn't happy with small-town life.

Which meant she'd never be happy with ranch life, either.

Now where had that thought come from?

He flicked the reins a bit more forcefully than necessary.

"Tell me about your brother and sister," she asked. "You mentioned that they're both married. Do they have children?"

"Yep, they each have a kid of their own and are helping raise another." Had leaving Hawk's Creek been worth it to them? They definitely seemed happy.

"What do you mean, raising another?"

"Ry has a foster daughter. Belle, a family friend who lived here at the ranch when we were younger, passed away a little over a year ago and named him as her daughter's guardian." Had Belle even realized that Griff had loved her? He'd never told her, and then he'd lost the chance when she fell in love with another. It had hurt more than he cared to admit when he learned she'd entrusted Ry and not him with her daughter's life. "Viola is nine years old. Then last year, Ry and his wife, Josie, had a little boy of their own. Named him Travis after my father."

"And your sister?"

"Sadie married a man from New York who moved to Texas to get a fresh start for himself and his young half sister, Penny. Penny's ten now. They also had a baby last year, a little girl they named Susannah." He smiled, remembering. "I went down to Knotty Pine to spend some time with them this past summer. Those are two of the sweetest little babies you ever want to see."

Would he ever have children of his own?

"They sound like lovely people," she said. "And what a diverse family you have. I can't wait to meet them." Her expression took on a wistful cast. "You certainly have a lot to be thankful for."

She was right of course. There was no reason for him to be focused on what he didn't have. He needed to take a page from her book and do more looking for the bright side.

Griff spent the rest of the morning showing her his herds of cattle and some of his favorite spots on the place. There was the pond where he and his siblings had learned to fish, the tree where he and Ry had found a honeycomb and gotten unmercifully stung in their efforts to retrieve it, and the small meadow where his mother had liked to picnic.

Ruby seemed to take genuine delight in the tour, exclaiming over the beauty of the landmarks he pointed out or laughing at his stories. It was such a pleasure to see the ranch through fresh, *appreciative* eyes that he found himself trying to find more and more things to show her or tell her about this place he loved so much. And seeing her face light up with that warm glow when she was enjoying herself was just an added bonus.

Near noon, Griff pulled the buckboard to a stop atop a rise the family had nicknamed Hickory Hill because of the three hickory trees that dominated its crest. He often came here when he wanted to be alone, to think over some tough decision or to just enjoy the view. From here it felt as if a person could see forever.

He set the brake and turned to her. "I thought this would be a good place for us to eat that lunch Inez packed. The ground here should be a lot drier than the flatter land we just drove over."

"It's certainly a lot sunnier than our last picnic spot."

He hopped down and turned to assist her. Once her feet were on the ground, he tucked her hand on his arm rather than release it.

To keep her from stumbling, he told himself. "Before we eat, I want to show you something."

She smiled. "Your tour hasn't disappointed me yet."

He led her to the crest of the hill then waited for her reaction. A reaction that proved quite satisfactory.

"Oh, Griff, the view is breathtaking." She squeezed his arm. "I think this is my favorite place of all the ones you've shown me today." She whirled around, beaming. "But it's all been so beautiful, so alive, even in this season. I can see why you love it here so much."

Did that mean she loved it, as well? "There are spots I couldn't show you today because the ground is still so wet—wouldn't want to mire the wagon. Maybe we'll have another chance to ride out before you leave."

Her smile took on an unexpectedly shy quality. "I'd like that very much." She removed her hand and turned back toward the wagon. "I think I'm ready for that picnic now."

When they reached the buckboard, Griff stepped ahead of her and handed her the blanket. He watched her spread the cloth in the sunniest spot she could find as he retrieved the hamper. What was she thinking? Had she reevaluated what she wanted out of life at all or did she consider all of this just a pleasant interlude on her way to something more to her liking?

And why did the answer to that seem to matter so much?

Not liking the direction his thoughts had taken, Griff set the hamper down on the cloth in front of her. When she opened it, her eyes widened. "Goodness, Inez must have thought she was feeding a half-dozen people."

He smiled. "You should know Inez by now—she doesn't do anything halfway."

She laughed outright at that and then they both dug in.

"Did you and Inez get the whole Thanksgiving Day menu planned out yesterday?" he asked as he reached for a drumstick.

"For the most part. It's definitely an ambitious undertaking. It looks as though she's planning to cook enough to feed an army."

"Like I said, Inez doesn't do anything halfway. Did she let you have much say in the planning?"

"Actually, she took quite a few of my suggestions. She's even going to let me cook one of my own favorites, venison and gingered-parsnip pie. Mrs. Tallmadge is the best cook in all of Cleebit Springs. When I lived with her family, she taught me how to cook it."

Griff considered that as he took a bite of his chicken. "You know," he said carefully, "you've mentioned living with the families of the town doctor, the midwife, the checker players, the general store owner, the encyclopedia lady and now the town's best cook. Exactly how many families did you live with growing up?"

She shifted, as if uncomfortable with his question.

"You don't have to answer if you don't want to," he said quickly.

"No, I don't mind. It's just that the truth is going to seem a bit strange to you."

He raised a brow. "All right, now I'm suitably intrigued."

Just as he'd hoped, she relaxed slightly at his teasing tone. "I told you that most of the townsfolk had a hand in raising me," she began. "I meant that literally. I moved from family to family on a regular basis."

"How so?"

"Every six months there'd be a big ceremony in town where most of the family names were put into a hat and then the preacher would draw one out. Whatever name was pulled, that's the family I'd live with for the next six months. Then, at the end of that time, we'd do it all over again."

He'd never heard of such an unusual arrangement. What had that been like? "Was it hard to live that way?"

She shrugged. "There was as much good as bad in it. One of the best things about it was, if I wasn't happy with where I was, I knew I wouldn't be there for very long."

That seemed a strange, and somewhat callous answer. Was this eagerness for new places an innate part of who she was? Or had the way she'd been brought up made her that way?

Either way, he'd do well to remember that she *was* moving on.

A flash of black-and-red caught his attention and he pointed the red-winged blackbird out to her. They watched it for a while, eating in companionable silence, until she turned to him again.

"Do you mind if I ask *you* a personal question?" she asked.

He smiled. His life was pretty much an open book.

"Since I just got through prying into yours, I don't suppose it would be sporting of me to refuse."

"When you were talking about your brother and sister and their families, I could tell family was important to you. Did you never think about starting one of your own?"

He stilled, feeling sucker-punched by her question. It must have shown on his face because her cheeks reddened and she started backtracking, just as he had earlier.

"I'm sorry. I shouldn't have asked—"

"No, don't apologize. I was just surprised, is all. Yes, I've thought about it. I've just never managed to fall for a woman who loved me back."

"Oh." She started to say something else, then clamped her lips shut.

He found himself curious to know just what it was she'd started to say. "Out with it. I'm feeling expansive today so this is your one and only chance to ask your questions."

"It's just, the way you worded that answer, it made me wonder just how many women you've fallen for."

Did it now? Well, he'd opened himself up for this. "Exactly two." He started to leave it at that, but found himself expanding, almost as if compelled to do so. "I mentioned Belle to you before, the woman who left her daughter in my brother's keeping when she passed. Well, when I was younger I fancied myself in love with her. I was only sixteen at the time, and she was a couple of years older, but I made all sorts of elaborate plans about our future together. Unfortunately, I never told

Belle about my feelings or my plans. She up and married a traveling preacher man."

"Oh, I'm so sorry." She clasped her hands together. "That must have been painful for you."

He shrugged, trying to downplay just how deeply it had cut. "I pined for a while like some lovesick schoolboy, but I got over it." He ran a hand through his hair. "Then I noticed Martha Davis. She was the daughter of one of the ranchers in the area and I'd known her most of my life. But the year I turned twenty, something about her caught my eye in a different way and I started courting her. I thought we were well suited— she knew all about living on a ranch and was sweet and agreeable. Then that summer she went to visit a cousin in St. Louis and decided she liked city life better than ranching. She met someone there, got married and never came back."

Griff sat back, wondering why he'd just told her all of this. She certainly hadn't asked for any details. And he'd never in all these years spoken of it to anyone.

Ruby placed a hand on his arm. "All that means is that neither of these girls was the right one for you. I'm sorry if your heart got broken, but better to find that out before you are irrevocably tied together. You just have to trust that the right person is out there, waiting for you to find her."

As if just realizing what she'd done, Ruby made as if to remove her hand, but he captured it and held it firmly in place, locking his gaze on her suddenly wide-eyed one. Had Belle and Martha broken his heart? Or just his pride? Whatever the case, telling her about his past had left him feeling lighter, freer.

He released her hand and smiled. "Enough of this gloomy talk. If you're done eating, there's one more thing I want to show you before we head back to the house."

And he'd figure out just what that was before they climbed in the buckboard. Truth to tell, he just didn't want to let this little outing end yet.

Ruby got to her knees and busied herself repacking the hamper. She hoped Griff didn't notice that her hands were a bit shaky. She could still feel the warmth and strength of his touch, the depth and intensity of his gaze.

Had something just passed between them? Or was it only her imagination? Wishful thinking perhaps?

That thought stopped her cold. What exactly was she wishing for? She'd told herself not to get too close to these people, that they were thinking of her in terms of someone who'd done them a service, and perhaps as a likable person, but nothing more.

Heavenly Father, please help me remember that he is a good man who is trying to be nice. Don't let me act the fool by thinking it's anything more.

Chapter Ten

Fifteen minutes later they were still riding across the fields. They hadn't spoken much, and the quiet seemed awkward, as if neither was sure what to say next. She was on the brink of saying something, even if it was a comment about the weather, just to break the silence, when he pulled back on the reins to stop the wagon.

Was he ready to show her another landmark?

Before she could comment, though, he raised a hand. "Did you hear that?"

There were worry lines on his brow and she wondered just what he'd heard. Straining her ears, she caught the sound of some sort of animal in distress. "What is that?"

He frowned. "It sounds like a cow bawling. Do you mind if we go check it out?"

"No, of course not."

He set the horse back in motion, turning it in the direction the sound had come from. "It's a good thing this ground is rocky here," he said, "or I'd have to walk."

She didn't say anything, just stared straight ahead,

trying to get some glimpse of the animal making that distressing cry.

Of course Griff spotted the cow first. "There she is."

Ruby stared at the animal who was pacing back and forth near a tree line up ahead. "She doesn't look like she's hurt."

"No, but she's agitated and from the looks of her, her calf has missed its feeding."

Concerned, Ruby scanned the area, looking for some signs of a calf. *Please don't let the poor thing be hurt.*

When they drew closer Ruby realized the cow was on the other side of a gully from them. Griff stopped the wagon and set the brake. "The ground may be rocky, but it's still pretty messy out here. You stay put while I find out what's going on." Without waiting for her response, he jumped down and marched toward the gully's edge.

He returned quickly, his jaw set. "Her calf is down there all right. Fortunately it doesn't look hurt, but the sides are too steep and slippery for it to get itself out."

"Oh, poor thing. What do we do?"

He gave her a surprised look as he removed his jacket. "I'm going to have to drag the critter out of there. Luckily there's a rope in the back of the buckboard."

She watched as he moved around to the back and retrieved the rope. He tied one end to the frame of the buckboard, tested it for snugness, then tossed the rest back in the wagon bed. He came around to the front and looked up at her. "I need to back the buckboard up closer to the edge of the gully. If you'll handle the reins I'll stand at the horse's head. When I give the signal, release the brake, then set it again when I tell you to."

Ten minutes later they had the buckboard positioned

to his satisfaction and he'd thrown the free end of the
rope down the side of the gully.

"So what now?" she asked.

"Now I go down and tie this rope around the calf
and we pull him out of there."

"Is that safe? I mean with your foot—"

He dismissed her concerns. "Other than getting good
and muddy, I'll be fine."

"You're sure there's not anything I can do to help?"
She felt useless just sitting here.

He studied her for a moment. "If you really want to
help," he said slowly, "there is one thing you can do."

Ruby sat up straighter. "Just name it."

"After I get the rope on that calf I'll have to climb
back up and direct the horse so he moves forward nice
and easy. It would help if you kept an eye on the calf
while I'm at the horse's head."

That didn't seem like much of an assignment, but at
least he was letting her help. "Sounds easy enough."

He gave her an approving smile. "Good. Now just
stay put until I climb back out."

She smiled but didn't say anything. As soon as his
head disappeared over the edge, she scrambled down
and moved to where she could watch him at work. He
was using the rope to help in his descent and was nearly
at the bottom.

As if he felt her presence, Griff looked up as soon
as his feet touched bottom. Shaking his head at her as
if she were a wayward child, he turned and moved toward the calf.

Ruby grinned, not at all put off by his reaction. Especially since she'd caught that hint of a smile before he'd turned away.

Watching him work, she was impressed with the confidence and quickness with which he accomplished his task. The man was clearly in his element. In almost no time at all he had the rope secured around the calf.

After a final testing of the knots, Griff quickly started back up. When he reached the top, she offered him a hand but he shook his head. "Don't want to get you muddy. I'm fine."

She stepped back and in moments he was standing back on level ground. He was breathing a bit heavier than normal and was definitely wearing some mud, but he didn't seem at all bothered by either condition. "Okay, I'm going to move to the horse's head. If you'll release the brake as soon as I'm set and then keep an eye on the calf I think we'll have this all taken care of in just a few minutes."

"Is there something I should be on the lookout for?" she asked a few moments later as she released the brake.

"The side of the gully is relatively smooth and slick so there really shouldn't be a lot of problems. Just let me know if it appears that the rope is slipping or if the calf seems to be in any sort of trouble."

She nodded and stepped back to the edge. The operation was surprisingly uneventful. Griff kept the horse moving at a steady pace and the calf eased up the gully's side with lots of bawling but little trouble. As soon as it was up and over the lip of the gully she signaled Griff, who halted the horse.

She moved closer. The calf hadn't gotten to his feet yet. Was he okay? She tentatively extended her hand.

At the same time the calf lunged to his feet. Startled, Ruby took a quick step back and slipped, landing on her backside.

Griff was by her side in an instant. "Are you okay?"

She smiled. "Other than wounded dignity, I'm just fine." Seeing the look on his face, as if he'd expected her to fall to pieces over a bit of mud, she laughed outright and extended her hand. "I'm fine, really. Help me up, please?"

He took her hand and pulled her to her feet. Still slightly off balance, she stumbled forward and he caught her in his arms. He didn't step back immediately and, seeing the look in his eyes, her amusement faded, replaced by something warmer, sweeter. Oh, mercy, but having him hold her like this was so wonderful, so right, so safe. She felt as if she could face just about anything the world had to throw at her if she had *this* to fall back on when it did.

Right now she didn't give a fig whether he felt gratitude or duty or something sweeter. If he tried to kiss her, she'd let him. In fact, she'd welcome him.

Griff released her and stepped back. What was he doing? Ruby had made it abundantly clear she was eager to move to Tyler and start her new life. She was a town girl and wanted a taste of what the big city had to offer. Why did he always find himself attracted to women who had no interest in settling down on a ranch?

He turned to busy himself with untying the rope to hide his agitation. "We'd best get this fellow back to its mama so it can get some lunch."

He watched her from the corner of his eye, noting

the way she stared at him with confusion and something curiously like hurt. To his relief she pulled her shoulders back and focused on his comment. "But the mother cow is on the other side of the gully. How do we get her calf to her?"

Glad to be on safe conversational ground, he pointed off to his left. "If you follow the gully for about a quarter mile that way, it narrows considerably. My pa built a bridge to span it there years ago. That's how the cow got to the other side in the first place."

She nodded. "So we just lead the calf to the bridge?"

"Something like that." He moved to the calf, lifted it and deposited it in the bed of the buckboard. "If you don't mind driving the wagon, I'll ride back here and keep this little guy from jumping out." It would also give him time to get himself back under control.

Because at the moment he wasn't sure if his reaction back there had been the right thing to do.

Or the biggest mistake he'd ever made.

Chapter Eleven

For the next two days Ruby helped Inez get the house ready for Thanksgiving, while Griff declared himself well enough to resume his regular routine. The three of them still got together at mealtimes and Ruby enjoyed listening to Griff talk about his day. What she enjoyed even more were his and Inez's efforts to include her. She wasn't used to people asking for her opinion or listening so intently to what she had to say.

During the midday meal on Friday, a telegraph arrived informing them that both Ry's and Sadie's families had accepted the invitation to return to Hawk's Creek for Thanksgiving. From Griff and Inez's response to the news, Ruby realized neither had been as certain as they pretended they were that Griff's siblings would come. She caught Inez actually humming that afternoon as they were polishing the woodwork in the front hall.

The evenings were becoming Ruby's favorite time of the day. After the supper chores were taken care of, she would take Patience and curl up in the study with one of the books Griff had selected for her and get happily lost in the world of the story. After about an hour or so, Griff would join her and challenge her to a game of checkers.

And while the competition between them was fun, what she really enjoyed were their discussions. He would ask her questions about the book she'd been reading, giving his own opinions on the passages he remembered. They didn't always agree on the finer points, but the debates they had were invigorating rather than confrontational.

On Saturday evening she noticed that even Patience had softened toward Griff. The cat drifted over while they were playing checkers, but rather than approach her, she began stropping herself against one of Griff's legs, purring softly. Even more surprising, Griff absently reached down and stroked the animal as he pondered his next move. Ruby hid a smile, wondering if her opponent was even aware of what he was doing. Apparently he wasn't as averse to cats as he'd claimed.

Strange to think that she'd only known Griff Lassiter for a week and a day. So much about her life had changed in that short time. Even her ideas about what life could be, and of her place in it, had shifted slightly.

There were no more encounters like the ones they'd shared during their outing on Thursday. She was beginning to believe any emotion on his part other than solicitousness had come purely from her imagination.

And she told herself she could be content with his friendship. After all, she'd had very few friends in her life.

On Sunday Ruby attended church service with Griff and Inez. It was sweet and somehow affirming to have

Griff introduce her to his friends and neighbors as a family friend.

She met Reverend Martin and his wife, Olivia. The elderly couple seemed very nice and it hit Ruby as she spoke to them that if things had gone differently last week she would have spent that first night away from Cleebit Springs with them instead of at Hawk's Creek. Had that happened, she would have never met Inez, might never have seen Griff again.

Thank You, Father, for setting me on that frightening but oh-so-rewarding path. My life has been made so much richer because of it.

Later, after lunch, Ruby watched as Griff pushed away from the table and carried his dishes to the sink.

"The weather's been cooperating lately and the ground has dried out considerably," he said, meeting her gaze. "What do you say I give you the second half of that tour?"

Ruby felt her spirits lift. "Oh, that would be lovely." Then she turned to Inez. "After I help with the dishes, of course."

But Inez waved her offer aside. "You two go on and leave this to me." She shook a finger at them. "But I expect you to take care of the supper dishes without me tonight."

Before Ruby could say anything, Griff grinned. "It's a deal." Then he turned to her. "How do you feel about riding horseback?"

She smiled. "I enjoy it, but I haven't ridden in a while." Her father had taught her to ride when she was quite young, but opportunities to ride had been hit or miss since—depending on what family she'd lived with.

"I'll have Mabel saddled up for you, then. She's gentle but not a plodder."

An hour and a half later they had ridden through a wooded area to visit a spot where he and his brother had built a fort out of old lumber, they'd skirted the edge of a pond that had a picturesque stair-step waterfall feeding it and had collected a couple dozen ripe persimmons to bring back to Inez.

Ruby was learning to love Hawk's Creek more and more with each new discovery. Seeing it through Griff's eyes made it doubly precious. She could see clearly now what a part of him this place was. Take him away from here for any great length of time and his spirit, the part of him that made him uniquely Griff, would shrivel like an uprooted plant.

Griff watched the appreciation and delight shine in Ruby's face as she discovered the parts that made up the whole of Hawk's Creek. And it wasn't just the places he showed her. She took pleasure in pointing things out to him as well—like the pair of deer she spotted bounding across a corner of an open field before disappearing into a stand of trees, a large rock formation that she decided looked just like a snail and a hawk circling high above them.

It was so easy to see her in this world.

Only this wasn't the world she seemed to want. But why not? If her life to this point had been so filled with sunshine and butterflies, why did she feel the need to move to a big city where she could lose herself in the anonymity of crowds?

It suddenly seemed important to him to find out.

He led them to a nearby spot that he knew would be perfect for having such a discussion. It was near the tree line so was somewhat sheltered, but open enough that it would be filled with warming sunshine this time of day. There were several large rocks strewn about so there would be dry places to sit. And a stream ran through it, so the sound of gurgling water would provide a serene backdrop. She'd love it.

Sure enough, as soon as the clearing came into sight she gave a little coo of delight. "Oh, Griff, this is lovely."

"Why don't we get down and let the horses drink and graze for a while."

"I'd like that."

They strolled around for a bit, drank water from the stream from cupped hands and talked about the upcoming Thanksgiving feast. Almost by mutual consent they sat on a large rock, and faced the stream.

"It's like a sofa, hand-carved by God for our comfort," she mused, "and set in the middle of the most beautiful sitting room in the world."

Griff leaned back, bracing his weight on his palms. "You have the most fanciful way of looking at the world," he said with a smile.

She shrugged. "It's just as easy to look for the good as the bad in things. And much more productive. My dad taught me that."

That gave him an opening and he took it. "You told me your dad passed away when you were seven. What happened to him?"

She stiffened and her expression went blank. "I'd rather not talk about that."

Whatever had happened, it must have been traumatic. "Had he been ill?"

She shook her head and dug around on the ground for some pebbles, which she began pitching one at a time into the stream.

He should drop this and respect her privacy. But something about her closed-off expression, about the set of her jaw and the tremble of her hands whispered to him that perhaps she needed to talk about this, whatever *this* was.

"So I take it your father's demise is the only wrinkle in your otherwise perfect life."

Her head whipped around and she stared at him with something akin to fury in her eyes. "My *perfect* life. Is that what you think? You have no idea—" Her lips snapped shut.

"Because you haven't told me anything but the good. Yes, you were orphaned at seven and that is a terrible thing for a young child. But it happens to many children. And you had a whole town full of people ready to step in and take care of you. You grew up knowing that you would always have someone looking out for you."

"Those people didn't want to take care of me, no matter how useful I tried to make myself. They did it out of guilt and obligation. That name-drawing ceremony every six months that I told you about—the family whose name was selected considered it a misfortune, not a blessing." She took a deep breath. "I even learned recently that those who didn't 'win' the drawing were obliged to pay a small amount into an account for my future. And most preferred to do that."

Her voice had risen and her expression shouted at him

to drop the subject. But he had to see this through now. "For someone who always tries to see the bright side of things, you are sure giving this a dark turn. Perhaps the townsfolk weren't all vying for the privilege of looking after you. But even if they were making the best of what they saw as a bad situation and trying to spread the burden, they still stood by you and saw that you were taken care of. That has to show some measure of concern."

She glared at him, her hands balled up into tight fists. "You want to know about my life? Okay, here's my story."

Griff settled back, satisfied. Perhaps now he'd understand what made her tick just a little better.

"I told you how my pa couldn't seem to be happy staying in any one place for very long after my mother passed," she began. "Well, that summer I turned seven we were traveling through the Texas backwoods and got lost. It wasn't the first time that happened and Pa usually made a game out of it, calling it a grand adventure. We traveled in a buckboard with several days' worth of supplies and we'd slept in it or on the ground lots of times before. But during the second day of that grand adventure the wagon broke down and we were forced to ride double on the wagon horse while we looked for help."

Griff didn't like the way this story was going. Ruby might have thought the world of her father, but to his reckoning it didn't sound as if the man had given much thought to his daughter's welfare.

"Only we weren't looking all that hard," she continued. "We'd found a small lake where we could swim and fish, and were having a wonderful time camping there. Then, the third night we were there, we heard a group of men approaching our camp on horseback. Pa told me to go hide behind a nearby tree and to not come out until he told me it was safe."

At least the man had had that much sense. Then he realized Ruby had started shaking and her expression was a mask of despair. What had happened that night? Whatever it was, reliving it seemed too much for her. Perhaps this hadn't been such a good idea after all. "Ruby, I'm sorry I pressed you. You don't have to—"

"Yes, I do." She swallowed. "To make a long story short, those men were from Cleebit Springs. They were hunting down a thief who'd come through town and robbed and killed a well-loved matriarch. When they stumbled on my father, they decided he was the guilty party."

Chapter Twelve

Griff's pulse kicked up as he realized some of the horror that was to come for her. But he held his peace, realizing that perhaps she really *did* need to get through this recounting of her personal nightmare.

"I heard all the yelling and cursing and I was scared, but I stayed hidden like my pa had told me. When I finally couldn't stand not knowing what was happening any longer, I peeked out from behind the tree." She swallowed hard and he could tell she was no longer with him. She was that frightened little girl deep in the East Texas backwoods again. He squeezed her hand, trying to anchor her to the here and now. To make certain she knew she wasn't alone this time.

"My father was hanging from the very tree we'd slept under the night before. I was just in time to see the last feeble jerk of his body before he went still."

Griff felt the shock of that revelation slam him in the gut and the gorge rise in his throat. She'd only been seven years old.

She shivered. "I don't remember much of that night

after that—just screaming and screaming until my voice wouldn't work anymore."

He stroked her hair, wishing he could take that pain from her, could pluck those ugly memories from her mind. But she wasn't finished talking.

"Two days later they found the man who had actually committed the crime. They say he looked a lot like my pa, though I never saw him myself. That's when Pastor Hannaly exhorted them all for the sin they had committed and told them it was their Christian duty to see that I was looked after the way my father would have wanted. Since no one family wanted to take responsibility, they came up with the taking-turns system."

There were tears running down her cheeks, but he didn't think she was aware of them. "Oh, Ruby, I'm so sorry you had to go through that. Now that I know, it's even more amazing to me what a sweet, strong, generous person you turned out to be."

She didn't appear to have heard him. "The thing is, no one likes living with a reminder of the sins they've committed. No matter how docile I was, how much in the background I tried to stay, all I saw when they looked at me was guilt and resentment."

A sob escaped her and she tried to smile. "Sorry. I know you don't like crying females."

Griff put a finger to her lip. "Don't apologize." He pulled her to him, hugging her against his chest as he stroked her hair. "You have a right to cry. Sob to your heart's content—no one will hear you but me."

And cry she did—heartrending sobs that seemed to come from the very center of her being. Sobs that shook her and wouldn't let her go.

Griff held her close, whispering soothing words, rocking her in his arms, gently rubbing her back. And berating himself roundly. How many times had he thought her shallow or selfish for wanting to leave Cleebit Springs when she had so many "friends" there? He'd even told her at one point that she was lucky to have such a large foster family. What a self-righteous fool he'd been. He could only imagine how his words must have hurt her. If there was any way at all he could make it up to her, he would.

Finally her crying tapered off, her body stilled its shaking and she went limp in his arms.

"I'm so sorry," she said, her voice muffled against his chest.

"I'm not."

She looked up at that. "I've gotten your shirt all damp and mussed."

"It'll dry." He stroked her hair, loving the soft-as-a-kitten feel of it. "I think you needed that. I'm just glad I could be here to hold you while you got it out."

She stared into his eyes with a watery smile. "I think you must be the kindest person in the whole world."

Is that how she saw him? As a *kind* person? That was something you said about a friend. And he suddenly wanted to be so much more to her.

Griff placed a hand against her cheek, then slowly traced the line of her jaw. "And you must be the loveliest—in every sense of that word."

Her eyes darkened and he heard a little catch in her breathing. Slowly he lowered his head, longing to kiss her but giving her the chance to protest if he was alone in that desire.

But there was no sign of protest, no pulling back. Instead she raised her face and her eyes fluttered closed. That was all the invitation Griff needed.

He dipped his head and kissed her.

He'd promised himself to keep it brief, chaste, that he would only be offering her comfort and affirmation. But when her hand snaked around his neck and she pressed closer, those good intentions went out the window. He deepened the kiss, suddenly wanting to let her know that she would never have to face those memories alone again as long as he was with her. He wanted to let her know that she was cherished and admired and...and what?

When he finally raised his head, Griff felt stunned by the force of the emotions stampeding through him. The only explanation was that he was in love with Ruby. How had this happened? *When* had this happened?

The need to protect her from further hurt, to keep her always safe, and always by his side was almost overwhelming.

Staring down at her he was pleased to note she looked equally stunned. The wonder in her eyes as she stared at him, the softness of her smile, brought out all of his protective urges. There wasn't anything she could have asked of him at that moment that he wouldn't have attempted to do for her. And after the way she'd reacted to the ranch, he had reason to hope she could be happy here.

But he had to take it slow, had to woo her properly. She deserved that.

So he stood and reached down his hands to help her up. "It's getting late. Time to head back to the house."

She dusted off the back of her skirt and then let

him help her mount, that shy softness still shimmering around her.

Griff climbed up on Chester, feeling pretty pleased with the world in general. All in all it had been quite a productive day.

As they started off, Griff set their pace to a comfortable walk and pulled his horse alongside hers. "We'll take a more direct route back to the house than the one we took when we headed out," he told her. "We should be there in twenty minutes or so."

She nodded and they rode in companionable silence for a while, though he caught her watching him from time to time.

"It's getting a mite chilly out here. What say when we get back to the house, I fix us both up a big cup of hot chocolate?"

"You're being much too nice to me."

"Nothing's too good for the woman who saved my life." He'd almost said *the woman I love.*

Moving slowly was going to be a whole lot harder than he imagined.

Ruby's smile froze as his words sunk in. Is that how he thought of her—as the woman who'd saved his life? Nothing more personal? After that kiss, she'd thought— fool!

She nudged her horse into a fast trot, wanting an excuse not to talk, not to make eye contact. A moment ago she'd felt herself the luckiest woman on earth. She'd dared to believe that Griff, a man who'd come to mean more to her than she'd ever dreamed possible, might really love her. She'd opened herself up for the first time in thirteen years, shared all her ugly, painful memories, and he'd treated that pain with a gentleness and respect that had touched her deeply.

And then that kiss—she'd never felt so safe and warm and truly *loved* in her life.

And it had all been done out of a need to repay her, and perhaps a touch of pity.

The soaring happiness she'd felt a moment ago shattered around her in a thousand needle-sharp pieces. And there was no one but herself to blame. She'd known from the outset how it was, had warned her heart not to forget it. But she *had* forgotten and it had cost her dearly. Because she'd given him her heart and it was too late to get it back.

Somehow she got through the rest of the day, finding reasons not to be alone with Griff. After supper she claimed a headache—no pretense there—and went to bed early.

Not that she got much sleep. Staring at the darkened ceiling, she came to a painful but necessary decision in the wee hours before dawn.

Chapter Thirteen

The next morning, as soon as Griff rode out, Ruby faced Inez. "I have decided to leave for Tyler today."

Inez stilled, her expression sobering. "May I ask why?"

Ruby waved a hand, as if waving away any arguments to her decision. "It's best this way. Putting off my leaving will not make it any easier and it's probably best if I don't insert myself into a family gathering."

"You know that to me and Griff you are family."

Inez's simple words were almost Ruby's undoing. But she managed to hold herself together. "That's a very kind thing to say, but at best I am a family friend. And please believe that I will always consider myself your friend."

Inez took a step forward and touched Ruby's arm. "Whatever happened between you and Griff, I'm sure—"

Ruby stepped back, afraid she would shatter at the next touch. "Please. I've made up my mind." She pulled an envelope from her pocket and set it on the counter. "Would you give this to Griff when he returns?"

"Of course." Inez's shoulders slumped. "Will you at

least let me send someone to town with you? Griff will want to know that you arrived safely and have found accommodations."

Ruby wavered for a minute. She'd rather not take anything else from them, but Inez was right. If she didn't accept an escort, Griff would no doubt feel obligated to ride after her and make certain she was okay. "Thank you, that's very thoughtful of you."

Thirty minutes later, Ruby was passing underneath the wrought-iron arch that guarded the entrance to Hawk's Creek, Archie riding on a horse ahead of her. The sudden thought that this was likely the very last time she would pass this way was enough to bring a lump to her throat.

She reached down and stroked Patience's head. "It's just you and me again," she said thickly. "But don't you worry, things are going to work out just fine. Spending Thanksgiving at Hawk's Creek would have been a mistake—we'd have been comparing every other Thanksgiving to that one from then on."

But she wondered who she was trying to convince, Patience or herself? Because whether she attended the Thanksgiving festivities or not, she had a feeling deep inside that she'd be comparing every home she ever lived in from here on out to the one she'd experienced briefly there at Hawk's Creek.

"What do you mean, she's gone?" Griff stared at Inez as if she'd gone mad. There had to be some mistake.

"She left first thing this morning. I sent Archie with her. He should be back soon."

"Why'd you let her go?"

"This isn't a prison. She's free to go whenever she wants." Inez snatched an envelope off the counter and handed it to him. "Here. She left this for you."

A note.

Griff sat down at the table and tore it open.

Griff,

Thank you so much for all the kindness and hospitality you've shown me the past few days. Your efforts to repay me for the small service I did for you were most gratefully received and meant more to me than you will ever know. Spending time at Hawk's Creek has left me with some of the happiest memories of my life. It was the perfect way to begin my fresh-start adventure.

I know I agreed to spend Thanksgiving with you and your family, but I have decided that it really would be best for me to start my new life right away. I hope you will forgive me for leaving without saying goodbye, but I feared you would try to talk me out of this and I am not sure I could have withstood your very considerable powers of persuasion, especially when you are determined to be generous.

Please don't feel obligated to follow me to try to change my mind. You won't succeed and it will only be awkward for both of us. I hope that whenever you have occasion to be in Tyler, though, that you will look me up to say hello.

I do truly wish you every happiness.

Yours, always

Ruby Tuggle

P.S. I took you up on your generous offer to lend me some of your books. Rest assured I will take very good care of them until such time as you should come to collect them.

Griff scanned it a second time, trying to read between the lines and understand what she'd been attempting to convey. Unfortunately, the truth seemed clear. Despite everything, she still wanted to start that new life in Tyler.

How could he have been so foolish? Apparently he'd read something into that kiss they'd shared that just hadn't been there. He should have realized. She'd just been through a very draining experience, had relived the most awful day of her life and then cried until his shirt was drenched with her tears. It had been reaction to that emotional turmoil, nothing more.

She didn't love him, at least not enough to give up her dreams for him.

He should be used to this by now—after all, he'd been through it before.

Except he hadn't. What he'd felt for Belle and Martha had been schoolboy fancies—he realized that now. He'd been taken with the *idea* of being in love and so had decided that's what he felt. But those feelings had been mere shadows of emotion compared to what he felt for Ruby.

"Griff." Inez's voice cut across his jumbled thoughts. "I don't know what she says in that note, or what passed between you to make her feel she had to leave, but I do know that she loves you. I see it every time she looks at you. The same way I see your feelings when you look at her."

"You're wrong. She wanted her life in the city more." He stood. "I'll be working on putting Mother's sitting room back to rights. Let me know when Archie gets back."

He marched out of the room without waiting for a response. He needed to be alone to work off some of this raging drive to follow her. Moving furniture was just the ticket.

There was no one to blame in this mess but himself. She'd been oppressively tied to Cleebit Springs, to people who wished her elsewhere, for most of her life. If being on her own with room to breathe and a future that was hers alone to chart was what she needed, then he wouldn't stand in her way, even if it strangled something deep inside him.

The next day Griff worked himself until he was drenched in sweat and too tired and sore to do more than eat and go to bed. Archie had assured him that Ruby had secured a room in a genteel boardinghouse in one of the nicer parts of Tyler. That had alleviated one of his worries, but he still lay awake most of the night wondering how she was faring being truly on her own for the first time in her life.

Sadie and Ry and their families arrived on Wednesday and Griff tried to put aside his roiling thoughts to give them the welcome they expected and deserved. And it *was* good to have everyone at Hawk's Creek again. Inez had been right—it had been much too long since they'd had a proper family gathering.

The only problem was, for him, there was an important someone missing.

He'd thought he was doing a good job of hiding his unfocused and generally gloomy thoughts, though, until that evening when he stepped out on the front porch to be alone for a minute. Within moments Sadie had followed him.

"All right, brother mine, let's hear it."

"Hear what?"

"Whatever it is that has you in this pensive mood. Is there something wrong with the ranch operations?"

"No. Everything here is just fine."

"Then it's something else." She stared at him a moment, then smiled. "Could it be lady troubles? Oh, Griff, have you finally found your true love?"

Griff rolled his eyes. "Now you sound like a fairy tale."

"That's not an answer."

He turned and leaned against the porch rail, trying to keep Sadie from seeing how close to the mark she'd hit. "Don't you have a daughter to see to?"

"Mercy me, it *is* a girl." Sadie joined him at the rail, practically bouncing on her toes. "Who is she and when can I meet her?"

"It's no one you know and you won't be meeting her." He looked out over the front lawn, wondering what Ruby was doing this Thanksgiving eve. "She doesn't feel the same about me," he added reluctantly.

Sadie stilled. "Are you sure?"

"She as much as told me so."

"What's that you have in your pocket? Did she write you a letter?"

Griff realized he must have unconsciously patted his pocket when he answered her. Like a lovesick fool, he'd been carrying Ruby's letter with him, pulling it out to read periodically, trying to figure out how he could have read the woman herself so wrong.

"Can I read it?"

He glared down at her. "It's private."

She kept her hand out. "I thought you might want a woman's perspective on what she wrote."

He started to refuse her again, then found himself pulling the note from his pocket. She'd just keep nagging until he showed it to her, he told himself. Yet a little voice in his head kept whispering that perhaps she *would* see something he'd missed.

Sadie read the letter through and then read it again, finally looking back up at him, a smug smile on her face. "Oh, yes, she definitely loves you."

Griff's pulse kicked up a notch but he knew it was just a false hope. "Thanks for the nice try, Sadie girl, but you can't possibly—"

"Of course I can. The way she talks about your *powers of persuasion* and her pleas for you to not follow her, that's a girl who knows she can't say no to you. The statement that her time at Hawk's Creek left her with happy memories, the regret over leaving without saying goodbye and the hope that you'll visit her, all speak to her deep affection for you. And her closing— *Yours, always*—my goodness Griff, can the girl be any clearer than that?"

"I'd like to believe you, but then why did she leave when we gave her every encouragement to stay?"

"You must have done something to send her running."

That's what he kept telling himself. But for the life of him he couldn't figure out just what it had been.

"Tell me a little about her and how you met," Sadie urged. "She mentions a small service she did for you?"

"I was escorting her to Cornerstone from a town about a days' ride from here when I got sick along the way—coughing, high fever, couldn't stay upright to get home under my own power. She got me here and helped Inez tend to me until I got better."

"Oh, my, that's some small service."

"Exactly. She's rather amazingly generous and spirited."

"And you fell in love with her."

How was it his little sister was making him feel like a schoolboy and she was the teacher? "I did."

"But did you tell her?"

"No. I mean, I only just realized it a few days ago myself. And we'd only known each other a little over a week. I thought it best to go slowly."

Sadie shook her head in disgust. "Men." She raised a brow. "I suppose you did manage to tell her, though, just how grateful you were for all her help."

"Of course."

"I thought so." She held up Ruby's letter. "It's all here, plain as day."

"What's all there?"

"Look at this." She began reading random snippets from the letter. *"Thank you so much for all the kindness and generosity...your efforts to repay me...when you are determined to be generous...please don't feel obligated."*

"So?"

"She thinks you feel gratitude, not love. Though why that should send her scurrying—"

"Not gratitude." Griff felt as though the fog was beginning to part. It was *obligation* she saw in his actions, the kind of oppressive, resentful sense of obligation from others that had haunted her life for years. No wonder she'd left him.

"No?" Sadie sounded deflated.

Griff grabbed her by the shoulder and gave her a resounding kiss on the cheek. "Sadie, my girl, you are the best sister a fellow could ask for."

"Of course I am. But what did I do?"

"You just gave me a reason to hope."

Chapter Fourteen

Ruby looked at the stack of books on her bedside table. Which one would she read today?

Spending a day lost in the pages of a book was something she'd often dreamed about, and now she had that chance. She couldn't help but feel a little tug of longing, though, when she thought of how she had planned to spend Thanksgiving just a few days ago.

Griff's family would all be at the ranch by now. And Inez would have most of the feast prepared with just a few last-minute items still cooking. Would Inez even remember the venison and gingered-parsnip pie Ruby had planned to make? Not that it mattered—there would be more than enough food without it.

Sunshine streamed in through her window, which meant the tables would be set out on the side lawn at Hawk's Creek rather than in the barn.

She glanced at Patience, curled up on the coverlet of her bed. "As soon as it warms up a bit outside we'll go for a walk. I promise."

Before Ruby could open her book, someone knocked

at her door. She looked at her clock—just a few minutes after seven. Mighty early for callers. Especially since she didn't know anyone here.

Ruby opened the door to find Miss Bermont, the boardinghouse proprietor, standing there with a frown on her face.

"Can I help you?" Ruby asked.

"You have a visitor." The woman lifted her chin. "It is quite early in the day for visitors, especially *gentleman* visitors."

Ruby's pulse quickened. She could only think of one person who would come calling. But he'd have had to set out before breakfast… "Did he give a name?"

"Mr. Lassiter."

Why had he come when she'd asked him not to? She should send him away. But, oh, she did so want to see him.

"Well? Should I send him on his way?"

What if it wasn't what she thought? What if Inez needed her for something? She'd never know if she didn't see him. "Please tell him I'll be right down."

Miss Bermont pursed her lips disapprovingly, but nodded. "Very well. But please see that you leave the parlor door open while you are entertaining guests. I run a reputable house here."

"Of course." Ruby moved to the vanity and checked her appearance, fluffing her hair with hands that shook slightly. She moved to the door, then, deciding it might be a good idea to have something to hold on to, turned and picked up her cat. Then she hurried from the room before her courage failed her.

Reaching the parlor door, she took a deep, steadying

breath, then entered with a smile. "Mr. Lassiter, how nice to see you again."

"Hello, Ruby."

He stood there, hat in hand smiling at her, and her knees nearly buckled. The look in his eyes, the warmth of his tone left her breathless and warm and wanting. Oh, but she had it bad. She loved him. Truly, deeply loved him.

And something inside of her was breaking all over again at the thought that he didn't return the feeling.

Trying to get herself back under control, Ruby bypassed the settee and took a seat on one of the high-backed chairs. "Did your family make the trip okay?" she asked, thankful that Patience was tolerating her lap.

"They did. All eight of them arrived yesterday and the house is ringing with their voices. But I didn't come here to talk about them."

She was too much of a coward to ask what he *had* come here to talk about. Instead she nervously tried to fill the pauses. "Shouldn't you be back at Hawk's Creek, celebrating Thanksgiving with all of them?"

"I have something I need to take care of first."

"Oh?" Was he here running errands and had just stopped by to say hello? She wasn't sure how much more of this she could stand. Yet she didn't want to see him leave, either.

He moved to stand directly in front of her. "Yes. I need to tell you that I love you."

Ruby's hand stilled on the cat's back and she stared up at him, afraid she'd misunderstood. "What did you say?"

He knelt down in front of her. "I said I love you. I

don't feel merely obliged, or grateful or honor-bound. I love you, deeply, completely, madly. And I couldn't bear to go another day without making certain you knew it."

"But…but you hardly know me."

"On the contrary, I know you are incredibly generous, and forgiving and strong in ways that humble me. You have spirit and a joyful heart that not even the darkest of circumstances could dim. And I know that you are the one person who makes me feel complete. So you see, I know everything about you that matters. As for the rest, it would be my great pleasure to take the remainder of my life discovering your other qualities."

Was he actually proposing? "Oh, Griff, I do so love you." She let Patience jump down and leaned forward to place a hand on his chest. "I think I began falling for you the first time we met, when you stooped to help me with the dropped dishes." She laughed, a laugh that ended on a sob of happiness. "Your heroic rescue of Patience just sealed the deal."

Griff gathered her up in his arms and gave her a kiss that rivaled that first one they'd shared. When he was done, he tapped her nose. "Now, while I still have a shred of self-control left, go and get your things. We have a Thanksgiving celebration to attend."

She stood, and moved to the door on feet that had wings.

"And Ruby," he called after her, "I mean all of your things. You won't be returning here—you're coming home."

Chapter Fifteen

Griff sat at the head of the long table set out under the clear blue sky. The boards literally sagged under the weight of all the food Inez had prepared. Family and near-family lined both sides.

Ruby sat to his right, glowing with happiness. He still couldn't believe he'd almost let her get away from him. He wouldn't make that mistake again. She'd agreed to marry him and as far as he was concerned, the sooner the better. His family had taken to her just as he'd known they would. Already she and Sadie and Josie were becoming fast friends.

Sadie and her family sat next to Ruby with little Susannah perched on his sister's lap, happily shaking a silver rattle. When she wasn't gumming it, anyway. Eli was whispering something in Sadie's ear, while Penny leaned across the table, talking to Viola.

Ry sat to his left. Ry bounced baby Travis on his knee, trying to distract him from reaching down to grab Patience's tail. Josie, not so hindered as her son, had filched a bit of something from the table and was surreptitiously feeding it to the always-hungry feline. Viola's cat, Daffy, caught sight of them and was making a beeline their way.

On the other end of the table, his Hawk's Creek family, Inez, Red and the others, were just settling into their places.

Griff stood and immediately everyone quieted and gave him their attention. "God has been mighty good to me this year, as I'm sure He's been to all of you, as well. Today being Thanksgiving, I thought it only right we all take turns in sharing some of the things we're thankful for."

He looked around the table. "The things I'm most thankful for are all of you gathered here. For my family, by both birth and marriage, whose love for each other and for me is a true blessing, and who have brought extra joy to all of us by ushering this new generation of cousins into the world. For Inez, who has been like a surrogate mother to us Lassiters, and who encouraged me to renew this tradition of gathering with family and friends to remember how truly blessed we are. May it be the first of many such gatherings to come."

He waited for the general chorus of *Hear, hear!* to die down before he continued. "I'm also thankful for the rest of my Hawk's Creek family, who have stood by me through times of plenty and of want, of drought and flood, ensuring that this place we all love remains strong."

Then he turned to Ruby. "Last, but in no way least, I will get down on my knees every morning and every night and thank God for sending Miss Ruby Anne Tuggle into my life."

He tugged on her hand and drew her up beside him. "Just a few moments ago, Ruby and I had a little talk. We'd like you to all know that you are invited to return here for a Christmas Eve wedding."

Cheers and exclamations erupted from those at the table and most everyone got to their feet to shake Griff's hand and welcome Ruby into the family.

Through it all, Griff kept a firm hold on Ruby's hand, loving the way it fit so perfectly in his. And he said a silent prayer of Thanksgiving, thanking God for sending him this amazing woman who so generously returned his love.

The two of them together, today and always, would see that their home at Hawk's Creek would always be one of love and thanksgiving.

* * * * *

Karen Kirst was born and raised in East Tennessee near the Great Smoky Mountains. She's a lifelong lover of books, but it wasn't until after college that she had the grand idea to write one herself. Now she divides her time between being a wife, homeschooling mom and romance writer. Her favorite pastimes are reading, visiting tearooms and watching romantic comedies.

Books by Karen Kirst

Love Inspired Suspense

Explosive Reunion
Intensive Care Crisis

Love Inspired Historical

Smoky Mountain Matches

The Reluctant Outlaw
The Bridal Swap
The Gift of Family
"Smoky Mountain Christmas"
His Mountain Miss
The Husband Hunt
Married by Christmas
From Boss to Bridegroom
The Bachelor's Homecoming
Reclaiming His Past
The Sheriff's Christmas Twins
Wed by Necessity
The Engagement Charade
A Lawman for Christmas

Visit the Author Profile page
at Harlequin.com for more titles.

MARRIED
BY CHRISTMAS

Karen Kirst

It is of the Lord's mercies that we are not consumed, because his compassions fail not. They are new every morning: great is thy faithfulness.
—*Lamentations* 3:22–23

To my closest friend, Lorie Hedrick.
Thanks for the homeschooling chats at Starbucks
and for providing a godly example of what a wife
and mother should be. I cherish your friendship.

Chapter One

❧

Gatlinburg, Tennessee
December 1881

If the bullet hole in his leg didn't kill him, the snow-storm would.

Caleb swayed in the saddle, stiff fingers clinging to the horn as Rebel stumbled in a drift. "Easy," he breathed, the slight sound swallowed up by fat, white tufts dropping in a thick curtain all around him. Ears flicking, Rebel righted himself. Caleb clamped his jaw tight to smother a moan.

He didn't know which was worse—the incessant pain slowly stealing his consciousness, the bone-numbing cold or the knowledge that he was being hunted.

Hopefully the heavy snowfall would cover his tracks and the trail of blood.

Fighting off a wave of dizziness, he tried to get his bearings. The weakness claiming his body wouldn't be put off much longer. *Concentrate, O'Malley. Find shelter.*

By this point, he'd lost all sense of direction, the towering trees and sloping landscape a white blur as the clouds overhead continued their silent assault. Frustration pounded at his temples. He knew these mountains like the back of his hand. No way could he be lost.

The forest tilted crazily, and he slumped onto Rebel's neck, gulping in frigid air that seared his lungs. "Sorry, boy," he choked out, "doesn't look like we're gonna make it outta this one."

Images of his family flashed against closed lids. His parents. Brothers. Cousins. All the people he loved but wouldn't let close. Josh and Kate were about to make him an uncle for the first time. And from the way Nathan and Sophie acted around each other, they couldn't be far behind. Unlike him, his older brothers were solid. Responsible. They'd be amazing fathers.

And he'd miss all of it.

Would they ever discover what happened to him? Or would they be forced to forever wonder?

Regret flickered in his chest, igniting a tiny flame of resolve. He couldn't give up. He'd brought them enough pain to last a lifetime. If he was going to kick the bucket, the least he could do was give them closure. Caleb eased upright. Urged the big black into motion with a nudge of his boot heel.

The impulse to pray caught him unawares. While he was a believer, he hadn't uttered a single word asking for God's direction for over two years. Not since the sawmill accident. Asking for assistance now just didn't seem right.

The minutes crawled past as they painstakingly descended into the valley, Caleb on alert for sights or sounds that might mean he'd been located. Eventually, though, the burning need to reach home wasn't enough to sustain him, his body unable to withstand the cold or the dangerous lethargy weighing down his limbs.

When the ground dipped and his weight was thrown sharply to the right, he didn't react fast enough. He landed on hard-packed snow. Swirling gloom blocked the gleaming, too-bright world, sucking him into a black void.

Careful not to slosh milk over the pail's rim, Rebecca Thurston shouldered the rickety barn door shut. The thing was more holes and air than solid wood. One more item to add to an already impossibly long list of things that needed attention around here. A foglike sigh puffed around her mouth. While thankful for the home-making skills she'd learned from her mother, she wished she'd shown more interest in her father's responsibilities. Knowing how to shoe horses, mend fences and repair barn doors would come in handy now that the running of the farm fell squarely upon her shoulders.

At her feet, Storm's ears pricked.

"What is it, girl?" Rebecca reached out to pet the salt-and-pepper head, but before her fingers contacted fur, the dog bounded toward the woods behind their cabin, paws flinging snow in all directions. "Storm, come back!"

From beneath her cape's fur-lined hood, she peered up at the leaden sky, blinking away flakes that caught on her eyelashes. Already the snow topped the second fence rung and made walking difficult, the icy powder seeping through her pantaloons and stockings and chilling her calves. White blanketed the rooftops of the barn and outbuildings, as well as the cabin. Icicles glimmered beneath the porch overhang. They didn't normally get snow until after Christmas. Sometimes it wasn't until late January. This storm must've caught a lot of folks off guard.

Bunching her skirt in one hand, she forged ahead, anticipating a steaming cup of coffee and molasses-drizzled flapjacks. Storm's frantic barking shredded the morning's hushed stillness. Rebecca halted. Goose bumps riddled her legs. This was no "I've stumbled upon a skunk and come see how cute it is" bark. What had her so upset? Coyote? Mountain lion? Two-legged intruder?

Swirling snow hindered her vision, wreathing the forest climbing up the mountain in an impenetrable veil. Holding the pail aloft, she hurried to the cabin and lifted the latch. "Amy?"

Her thirteen-year-old sister appeared in the doorway and held her hands out for the milk. Instead, Rebecca set it on the floor. "Bring me Daisy. Hurry."

"What? Why?" Curiosity sparked in her big blue eyes.

"Something's upset Storm. I need to investigate." She extended an impatient hand, palm up. "The rifle, please?"

A frown tugged Amy's sparse brows together. "Hope it's not a wild animal."

Bypassing the table and settee with its faded floral upholstery, Amy went to the stacked-stone fireplace and, going up on her tiptoes, snagged Pa's favorite rifle. One he'd long ago christened Daisy on a silly whim.

Chestnut braids bouncing against slender shoulders, Amy brought it to her. "Be careful."

Her gloved fingers closed over the stock, the heavy weight in her hand reassuring. "It's difficult to see out here. If I'm not back in ten minutes, bang some pots together on the porch. The sound will lead me home."

"What if you don't return?" The smattering of light freckles across her nose and cheekbones stood in stark relief against her pale skin. Ever since the tragic wagon accident that had claimed their parents' lives last year, Amy had become prone to worry.

"I will."

Pulling the lapels of her indigo cape tighter, she left the shelter of the porch. Storm hadn't stopped her alarm, which meant this was serious. She braced the Winchester in both hands. As she neared, a huge black shape took form, startling her. A horse.

"Storm, hush."

The riderless horse shifted his weight and swung his face her direction. The white star between his intelligent black eyes strummed a memory. Her gaze shot to the snow-crusted saddle. Made of dark brown leather, it lacked ornamentation and tooling. Plain and serviceable. She didn't recognize it.

Her dog's barking shifted to a whine. Cautiously she moved around the big black, giving him plenty of space so as not to spook him, and her gaze fell on the object of Storm's distress. Her heart leaped into her throat.

A man. Sprawled on his stomach and half-buried in snow. Dead? Unconscious? Sleeping off too much liquor?

Storm finally quieted and cocked her head, silently imploring Rebecca to do something.

Gun wavering in her suddenly nerveless fingers, she crept forward and extended a boot, lightly nudging the stranger's ankle. No response. She tried again, harder this time. Nothing.

A Stetson lay a few feet from his head. Shaggy hair the color of India ink curled over the collar of his black duster. His boots, though worn-in, were in good condition, as were his fawn canvas trousers. He didn't appear to be a drifter.

"Mister?" Creeping forward, she prodded his shoulder. "Hello?"

Please don't be dead. Setting her rifle within grabbing distance, she crouched down and, yanking off a glove with her teeth, gingerly slipped her fingers beneath his blue-and-white-dotted neckerchief. Relief skittered through her at the faint pulse she detected there. *Not dead.*

But if she didn't get him up and out of the elements, he would be soon.

Taking hold of his shoulder, she tugged, easing him onto his back. One glance at his face, and she landed on her rear.

"No." The strangled denial brought Storm over, her sturdy, furry body leaning into Rebecca's side.

This was no stranger. The jagged, inch-long pink lines fanning from his right eye marked him as the enemy. Caleb O'Malley. The man who'd single-handedly ruined her life.

Bitterness, as familiar as an old friend, wrapped its

tentacles around her heart and squeezed, stifling all reason. She wanted him gone.

"Caleb." Loath to touch him, she poked his shoulder. "Wake up. You need to go home."

Dark stubble skimmed his lean jaw and pouty lips stiff with cold. Stiff and *blue-tinged.*

The first twinge of alarm pierced her hostility. Skimming his well-built body, she gasped at the sight of vivid red blood spatters on the sparkling white powder. He was bleeding. Hurt.

Scrambling to open his duster, her stomach lurched. His tattered pant leg was sodden with blood leaking from a gaping wound in his thigh. The gravity of the situation slammed into her. If she didn't help him, he would die. And despite the heartache his actions had caused her, she wasn't that callous.

Standing, she eyed his long, muscular length. There was no way she was getting him up on that horse. She'd have to drag him.

Hating to leave her weapon behind but seeing no other choice, Rebecca hooked her hands beneath his arms and began to pull. Adrenaline fueled her for the daunting task. By the time the cabin's outline came into focus, her chest heaved from the exertion and her legs trembled with strain.

"Amy!" she hollered over her shoulder.

The door banged open, and her sister appeared on the porch. "It's been exactly nine minutes since you left." Her relief was short-lived. "Who's that?"

"Hurry and put your coat on. I need your help getting him inside."

Amy did as she was told, eggplant-colored coat

scraping the ground and brown lace-up boots crunching. Her jaw dropped. "Is that Caleb O'Malley? What happened to him?"

"I don't know." Rebecca suspected a gunshot wound. "You think you can pick his feet up and help me carry him in?"

With a nod, she went and stood between his legs and took hold of his calves. "He looks different with a beard."

"Let's go."

Though it was awkward, they managed to maneuver him inside and onto Amy's bed, situated against the right wall, opposite the cast-iron stove, dry sink and pie safe.

Rebecca straightened and paused to catch her breath and weigh her options. She didn't like the idea of sending her sister out into the storm, but Caleb's wound needed attention now. His pallor and unresponsiveness bothered her. He hadn't made a single sound during the jarring trek here. "Take Storm and retrieve Daisy. Settle Caleb's horse in the barn. I'll unsaddle him later." Probably best Amy didn't see the gruesome injury up close, anyway.

A hint of misgiving flitting across her round face, Amy glanced at Caleb's inert form dwarfing her mattress and squared her shoulders. "I won't be long."

"Be careful." As Rebecca retrieved a box containing herbs, medicines and supplies from their catch-all cabinet, she checked the mantel clock and made note of the time. "If you're not back in fifteen, I'll come looking for you."

When the door clicked, blocking out the frosty, pristine world and shutting her in with her wounded nemesis, the cozy cabin transformed into a hostile space. Spying blood seeping onto the colorful quilt beneath him, she forced herself to focus on the present. To forget the past. The loss and grief.

He's just a man in need of assistance. He can't do anything more to hurt me.

His boots had to be wrestled off. Chucking them onto the floorboards, she gingerly removed the Colt pistols from his gun belt and used scissors to slit open his pant leg. The coppery scent of blood filled her nostrils, as did those of horse and earth and pine needles, typical for a man who spent most of his days roaming the mountains.

Dashing to the counter, she filled a bowl with cool water—there wasn't time to heat it—and gathered rags. Folding one into a thick square, she returned to the bed and, covering the wound, pressed down hard to stem the flow. Caleb jerked. An anguished moan started way down in his gut and ripped through his lips. Rebecca's gaze flew to his face, which was whiter than the pillow cradling his head, and compassion trickled into her bloodstream. Not enough to forgive him. Never that. But enough to want to lessen his pain.

Winding a long strip of cotton around his thigh to hold the cloth firmly in place, she tied it off and set to work cleaning his leg as best she could. She cut away the ruined material and tossed it onto the floor to dispose of later. Unable to remove his damp clothing without assistance, she settled for piling every available quilt on top of him.

After adding wood to the fireplace and kindling to

the stove's firebox, she set water on to boil. She'd fix him something hot to drink, and later, some thin broth.

"No!" The unexpected plea in his distinctive voice made her jump. "Don't do it. Sheriff…"

Clearly distressed, he tossed his head from side to side. Without thinking, she placed a gentle hand against his forehead and leaned close. "You're safe, Caleb. Rest now."

Long lashes fluttered. Lifted. And she found herself staring down into twin pools of deepest brown, the color of the mysterious broad-winged hawk's wings. His brow knitted with confusion. "Becca?"

Chapter Two

Ice encased every particle of his body...except for his forehead. Her hand heated and soothed. The strokes of her fingers through his hair blazed trails of sparkling heat and sweet comfort he hadn't known in many years. Comfort he had no right accepting.

His lids grew heavy. He forced them open, needing to see her again. Make certain he wasn't hallucinating. "Becca?" he rasped.

"You should try to conserve your energy. You've lost a lot of blood." She spoke matter-of-factly, her lyrical voice detached. Emotionless. The girl he used to know had been so full of light and laughter the air around her shimmered with joyous expectation. But that was before...

Her face swam into focus. Ah, yes. Becca...there could be no mistaking that winsome appeal, the jade-green eyes, the pert nose, apple cheeks and full lips that could quirk into a come-hither smile at a moment's notice. Not that that particular smile had been directed at him. She'd reserved it for his best friend, Adam Tierney. To his shame, he'd sometimes wondered what it might've been like to be the object of her devotion.

He shifted on the soft mattress and liquid fire exploded in his leg, engulfing the right side of his body. Memories slammed into him. The sheriff. Figures huddled around. Being chased. Shot at.

"Caleb?" The hand stilled in his hair.

He couldn't think straight. Darkness clawed at him. *Danger. She was in danger.*

He'd blacked out.

Rebecca snatched her hand away. What had she been thinking, playing attentive nursemaid to this man? It was imperative she maintain an impersonal attitude.

She reluctantly rechecked the wound. Located on the outer thigh, it didn't appear to have nicked any major blood vessels, for the bleeding was already slowing. But what about tissue damage? Were any bones involved? Rebecca's medical knowledge was extremely limited. She could only offer him the basics of care.

Amy swept inside, bringing with her a swirl of wintry air. "I got Daisy—" she pushed her hood back, smiling triumphantly "—and the horse is all settled in."

Rebecca belatedly realized she hadn't removed her own cape. Or eaten. Or had her usual bracing coffee. Quickly covering him, she remarked, "You must be starving. How about a glass of warm milk and toast with cheese? I need to get broth started for our visitor."

"You make it sound like he's a stranger." Her nose crumpled. She replaced the gun on its hooks above the mantel. "Don't you remember how he used to come here with Adam? He'd play any game I asked, even dolls. Not even Adam would do that."

Rebecca deflected the hurtful reminder of happier times, when the three of them—Caleb, Adam and her—were friends. "That was a long time ago."

Removing the loaf of bread she'd made yesterday from the pie safe, she set it on the work surface and grabbed a knife, slicing off two thick pieces and placing them in a pan. Behind her, Amy wandered closer to the bed.

"How bad is he?"

Glancing over her shoulder, Rebecca caught the worry flashing in wide eyes. How to phrase it? Her younger sister was practical-minded and perceptive. The instinct to protect her—stirred to life the day their parents passed away and Rebecca assumed full responsibility—warred with the need to prepare her for the worst.

"I'm not a doctor, so it's difficult to hazard a guess." Pouring the heated milk into a mug, she sighed. "I'll be honest, Amy, it could go either way."

"He's shivering." Her frown deepened. "Can we say a prayer for him?"

She hauled in a startled breath. Pray? For *Caleb?* After he'd destroyed her chance at happiness? If not for his recklessness, she'd be married to her childhood sweetheart by now. Might've even had a child of her own. The sting of shattered dreams left her floundering for an appropriate response. She refused to allow her problems to taint Amy's outlook on life.

"I, uh—" Sliding her wavy, dark hair behind her shoulders, she stepped haltingly toward the bed.

"Would you mind praying? I don't think I can gather my thoughts right now."

While Amy softly uttered words of petition, Rebecca studied Caleb's profile. When they were teens, his boyish good looks and fun-loving manner had drawn girls like ants to a picnic. There was no sign of that boy now. Aloof and cynical, the events of the past two years were etched into his severe features.

She closed her eyes. *Why, God? Why did You bring him here to me, of all people? How can You ask this of me?*

"We won't be able to fetch Doc Owens anytime soon, will we?"

Beyond the window glass, clouds yet dumped snow at a steady rate. Town was a good mile and a half away. "I'm afraid we can't risk it." Returning to the kitchen to finish readying breakfast, she said, "We'll wait and see how things look tomorrow."

But it soon became clear the storm had stalled over their quaint cove, and by lunchtime, the snow had surpassed the third fence rung. No way could Toby, her frail, aging horse, venture out into that. They were stuck.

The notion troubled her. Throughout the morning, Caleb had fretted off and on, mumbling unintelligible things, alternating between sweating and shivering. Once he'd even tried to sit up, only to cry out in agony.

With Amy in Rebecca's bedroom writing in her diary, she tackled the task of feeding him. Placing a bowl of tepid vegetable broth on the bedside table, she scooted one of the heavy walnut dining chairs over and sat down, reluctant to stir him. He needed sustenance, however. And something for pain.

"Caleb?"

His head shifted in her direction, damp hair sliding over one black brow. How she despised the unexpected vulnerability cloaking him and the pull it had on her. She always had harbored soft spots for those in need, be it animal or human, deserving or no.

"I've brought you some broth." She waited, hands clasped tightly in her lap, fingers itching to smooth his furrowed brow.

His eyes fluttered open, the severe discomfort in the brown depths—which had taken on the hue of the burnt-umber watercolor cake in her art chest—a kick in the gut. What had happened out there? An accident? Or was he in some kind of trouble?

"Drink," he pushed past dry, cracked lips.

"First let me prop you up with another pillow." Stretching across him, she snagged an extra and carefully wedged it beneath the first one. "There."

As she fed him several spoons of the fragrant liquid, his dark gaze never wavered from her face, unnerving her. It took all her concentration to hold her hand steady.

"Enough." He turned his face away.

He'd consumed less than half of the bowl's contents. Not much considering his size. Concern slithered through her. Standing, she smoothed the layered quilts over his chest and shoulders. "Are you warm enough?"

He nodded without looking at her, his gaze glued to the log wall adorned with Amy's bunches of dried flowers and a single canvas—a floral composition Rebecca had painted many years ago. Amy loved flowers, and Rebecca enjoyed capturing their likeness with her brush. Not as much as birds, though, as evidenced by the paintings cramming the remaining walls.

"I have laudanum to help with the pain. Let me get it for you."

Cool fingers closed over her wrist. She yelped. Jerked away from his touch.

"How did I get here?" His voice was sandpaper rough.

Rebecca stepped out of reach. "My dog found you."

"And Rebel?"

"Your horse is fine."

After breakfast, she'd gone out to the barn and groomed him, the earlier recognition blossoming into full remembrance. Caleb had purchased the fine animal from a farmer on the outskirts of Gatlinburg. Thrilled at the acquisition, he and Adam had brought him over for her to see. Rebel. A fitting name for an owner who'd continually flouted common sense, flying in the face of danger without a thought to the repercussions.

Images of another man lying injured in a bed, his life forever changed because of Caleb's actions, pushed into her mind. *Oh, Adam, why couldn't you have stayed? Given us a chance?*

"You weigh a ton, by the way," she snapped, frustrated at the memories Caleb's presence resurrected. "Amy and I were barely able to get you inside. What happened to you? And why were you on my property?"

He blanched. "I can't stay here." He shoved the covers off, attempted to sit up.

Surprised, Rebecca placed a restraining hand on his shoulder. "What are you doing? You're gonna aggravate your wound."

He weaved to the side, too weak to put up much of a fight. Perspiration glistened on his forehead. "You don't understand. Need to leave. Now."

"Believe me, there's nothing I'd like better," she muttered, "but you're not fit to walk across this room, let alone venture out into the storm." Urging him to lie back, she checked his wound's wrapping. No sign of fresh blood. Good. Covering him once more, she propped her hands on her hips and assumed her no-nonsense voice. "No more trying to get out of bed, do you hear me, Caleb O'Malley?"

He peered up at her through heavy-lidded, pain-glazed eyes. "Yes, ma'am."

Instinctively, she reached out a hand to comfort him, at the last minute curling her fingers into a fist and dropping it to her side. Hang her caramel-soft, too-sensitive heart! How was she supposed to remain impassive to this man's suffering?

I used to imagine it, though. Caleb O'Malley getting his just deserts. Suffering the way he made me suffer.

She winced, shame flooding her. Not like this. There was no satisfaction in this.

That didn't mean she didn't want him out of here at the first opportunity.

She gestured to the kitchen. "The laudanum—"

"No."

Why was he being stubborn? "It will help you rest."

Striding to the pie safe, she retrieved the tiny bottle from the shelf and returned to his bedside, only to find that his eyes had drifted closed and his breathing evened out.

Sinking onto the chair, she watched him sleep. Warring emotions wrestled in her chest—the chief being resentment. After all she'd endured, after everything she'd lost, being forced to care for Caleb felt like pouring kerosene on a wound that had never healed.

She could only hope the storm moved on quickly, and that the doctor could fetch him on the morrow.

A thump wrenched Rebecca out of a nebulous but unsettling dream. For a moment, she lay still, trying to decipher exactly what had woken her. Shadows wreathed the long, narrow bedroom that had once belonged to their parents, and she was just able to make out the familiar shapes of the carved cherry wardrobe and corner writing desk, as well as the washstand by the window.

Amy's soft breathing barely stirred the silence. The younger girl hadn't been the slightest bit upset about giving up her bed. To her, this was fun. A departure from their routine. Rebecca couldn't help but be proud of her. Like all siblings, they had their moments, but much of the time they got along quite well. They were a team, she and Amy, the loss of their parents having drawn them closer than they ever were before.

Rebecca closed her eyes and huddled deeper into the toasty warmth. Must've been a random sound from outside that woke her. Surely Storm would've alerted her if something were amiss.

There. Another dull thud.

Caleb. Pulse thundering, she hauled her legs from beneath the covers and, hardly noticing the cold seeping through her wool stockings, rushed into the living room. Muted light from the fireplace revealed her dog perched on the hearth rug, head up and ears at attention, staring intently at the bed. The *empty* bed.

Sprawled on the floorboards, her patient was making a valiant effort to regain his footing.

"Caleb," she half moaned, half admonished, "you shouldn't be out of bed!"

Crouching beside him, she braced an arm about his broad back. "We have to get you up off this floor."

"It's not safe," he told her as a shudder racked him. "You and Amy… Danger."

Danger? What was he talking about? She framed his cheek, unmindful of the stubble's prickle. It was as she suspected—burning up with fever.

Grim now, she assisted him up and onto the mattress, taking a moment to wrestle his black duster off before urging him to lie back. The sight of a red circle blooming on the white compress struck a chord of fear deep within her. The very real possibility of him succumbing to his injuries, of him *dying,* loomed like a menacing specter. For the first time since she'd discovered him unconscious in the snow, Rebecca was truly frightened.

She wasn't a doctor. She possessed limited nursing skills. What if she inadvertently did something to hurt him or make his condition worse?

Again, she asked God why. Why couldn't he have ended up in someone else's yard? Someone more knowledgeable. More capable. Someone whose life hadn't been sullied by his careless disdain for others.

The very last thing she wanted was to shoulder this particular burden.

He was still agitated, lips moving as his head thrashed from side to side. A couple of words she understood. *Danger. Sheriff. Leave.* He was delirious, of course, but were his warnings grounded in truth?

She paused in applying a fresh compress. "What kind of secrets are you carrying?" Afraid of the answer, she turned back to her task, thankful the bleeding had lessened. Working quickly, she tucked the quilts tight about his long length. Then she spooned up a small dose of laudanum and put it to his mouth.

"You need to take this." Supporting his head, she held him steady as he sipped. Grimaced. Quaked.

When it was gone, she set the spoon aside and eased onto the mattress edge. Closing her mind to the past, if only temporarily, she administered the comfort he needed, gently threading his fine, glossy hair away from his face. Weak firelight glinted in the blue-black strands. He seemed to settle at her touch.

Lightly, gingerly, she traced the slashing black eyebrows with her fingertips. Then, more daringly, she traced the hard contours of his face—the jutting cheekbones, strong jawline and chin—all the while avoiding the scar. It was too terrible a reminder of the sawmill accident that had altered the course of their lives.

"Why did you have to involve Adam in your mischief?" she quietly demanded, knowing he couldn't hear her. Knowing, too, that even if her ex-fiancé hadn't accompanied Caleb that fateful night, something terrible would've happened eventually.

Feeling cramped suddenly by her proximity to him, she rose to her feet and interlocked her fingers behind her back. Touching Caleb wasn't supposed to feel good. Perish the thought!

He turned his head as if in search of her. "Not safe," he whispered.

Though sleeping, he wasn't at complete rest. Something was clearly bothering him. Something so big it penetrated his mind's cloak of unconscious. A frisson of unease tightened her shoulder blades. Could they truly be in danger?

There was no disputing the fact that, wherever Caleb O'Malley went, trouble followed.

Chapter Three

Caleb thought he just might burst into flames. Heat licked his insides, a strange heat that had him battling the heavy covers one minute and his teeth clacking together the next. The pain was constant, as if a red-hot branding iron had been plunged deep into his flesh.

If only he could clear the fog shrouding his brain.

The sense that it was no longer night tugged his eyes open. Searching the chilly room, his gaze encountered a woman asleep in a rocking chair situated before the now-cold fireplace, wavy brown hair shot with copper streaks skimming her shoulders and features softened in slumber.

Becca.

For a split second, he was startled to see her. Confused. Why? How? Then the fog dispersed, and he remembered every disturbing detail. *Sheriff Tate.* Caleb had witnessed the cold-blooded murder of Cades Cove's sheriff. And he'd been spotted, which meant his presence put Becca and Amy in grave danger.

"Becca." Spurred by their predicament, he managed to prop himself up on his elbows. "Wake up."

A medium-size, shaggy black-and-white dog of uncertain origins lifted its head to study him with curious eyes. Caleb didn't recognize the pet, which meant he or she had joined the family within the past two years. While not much to look at, the dog must certainly be well loved. Becca was famous for her weakness for strays.

He called her name again, and she jerked upright, jade irises nearly eclipsed by wide, black pupils. She blinked. Focused on him. Sympathy and concern flashed across her face, tucked away the moment she became aware of his regard. All business once again.

Rising with the grace of a dancer, her movements lithe and fluid despite having slept in an awkward position, she seemed to float across the floor. He used to tease her that gravity didn't have as tight a hold on her as the rest of earth's population. Maybe it was her artistic spirit, her ability to see beauty in ordinary things.

Going to the kitchen, she dipped out water for him. Helped him drink the cool liquid, which heated as it slid down his parched throat.

"I need for you to bring Rebel to me so I can get outta here."

Her fingers tightened on the glass. Plunking it onto the bedside table, her brows descended. "I will do no such thing."

Stunned by the conviction in her voice, he slumped onto the pillow. He couldn't recall her ever standing up to Adam this way. No sirree, she'd gone along with pretty much whatever his best friend suggested. Not that Adam would've asked her to do anything questionable. Or risky. That had been Caleb's department.

"I have to get home." He could send his brothers to fetch Sheriff Timmons. "Why won't you help me?"

"You have a life-threatening injury, that's why," she retorted, exasperation twisting her mouth. "For once in your life, accept that you have limitations. You're not invincible, Caleb O'Malley. Thought you would've learned that by now."

The words hung in the air, the implication quite plain. She meant he should've learned his lesson two years ago, the night he'd dared Adam to break into the sawmill yard.

Closing his eyes, he recalled the last time he saw her. Back in August, he and his brother Nathan had been delivering milk and cheese to Clawson's Mercantile when they'd crossed paths. Her derision and anger, entirely justified, had practically reached out and strangled the life out of him.

"I know how difficult this must be for you," he scraped out. "No one would've blamed you if you'd left me to freeze out there. I appreciate everything you've done, but my family can take it from here. No need to impose on your hospitality any longer."

Shock crystalized in the jade orbs. "You think I'm that coldhearted? You think I'd leave you t-to…" She flung out an arm. Emotion rippled through her lithe form. "Just because I despise everything you stand for doesn't mean I'd wish death upon you." Pushing hair away from her face, she turned her back on him. Stalked away from the bed.

"I didn't mean to imply…" He sighed, frustrated at the weakness invading his body again. Waves of it, jumbling his thoughts. "I'm sorry, Becca." *For all of it.*

Slowly spinning on her heel, ivory cotton house-coat flaring around slim ankles encased in thick, gray wool stockings, she shot him a probing look. "What happened to you?"

It appeared as if he was going to have to level with her. If she knew the danger he was putting her and her sister in, she'd no doubt pack him off so fast his head would spin.

"I saw something I shouldn't have." He debated how many details to divulge. Decided she was strong enough to handle the truth. "Sheriff Tate was murdered two nights ago."

Trembling fingers lifted to cover parted lips. Eyes huge in her face, she came closer and sank down on the wooden chair facing the bed. "You saw this?"

Every last gory detail. The helplessness resurfaced in his chest. He'd never be able to oust Tate's horrified expression from his memory. Never. "I was out riding later than usual, had delayed setting up camp because I'd decided to swing by my folks' for a quick visit." No use mentioning he'd planned to stop here first and leave parcels of fresh deer meat, something he'd been doing off and on since that encounter in August. Anonymously, of course. "I stumbled upon a nightmare. At first, they didn't see me. Preoccupied with their prey, I suppose." His lip curled with disgust. "They had him surrounded. On his knees, hands tied behind his back. The leader, she—"

"She?" Becca blurted, dumbfounded. "Surely you don't mean…"

"Knocked me back, too." He shifted, sucked in a

harsh breath at the resulting ache. His leg throbbed in time with his heartbeat.

"Do you need more pain relief?" She scooted closer, her too-perceptive eyes grave.

Beneath the covers, he fisted his hands. "No." His brain was fuzzy enough without adding medicine to the mix. He had to focus on convincing her to help him get home.

"What was a female doing with a gang of criminals?"

"I couldn't hear what they were saying, but to me she looked like…" His jaw tensed, picturing the bitter reproach marring the blonde's features. "She looked like a woman who'd been rebuffed."

"You think she and Tate were involved romantically?"

"Could be. Or she was interested and he wasn't." Only, why kill him if it was a simple rejection? This woman had seemed deeply distressed.

"There has to be more to it than that," she echoed his unspoken sentiments. Tapping her chin, she mused, "Under what circumstances would a woman on the wrong side of the law associate with a lawman?"

"I don't know." Though the lack of answers bothered him, the main issue here was justice. "I do know how to identify them, however, and I aim to do whatever it takes to make certain they pay for what they did. That's why I need to see Shane Timmons."

Concern flowed over her features, and this time she didn't attempt to hide it. "Did they get a good look at you?"

"Hard to say. I was positioned on the edge of a clearing, and there was a full moon. The storm was still south of us. I know for certain they saw Rebel."

She nodded. "With his distinctive markings, he won't be hard to identify."

And if they did glimpse Caleb's face, his scar would make it easy for them to locate him.

"Now do you understand why I have to leave?"

Popping up, she began to pace. "I can't let you go."

His heart suffered a series of palpitations. Oh, he knew she meant it literally, not figuratively. Still, the words hurled him backward in time to when they were teenagers, to when he'd envied Adam's good fortune, had wondered what it would be like to have a girl like Becca—beautiful, sweet-natured, affectionate—head over heels in love with him.

He'd cared about his best friend's girl a little more than he should have.

"You have to."

She whirled on him, hot color splashing across her cheekbones. "I don't *have* to do anything. You are not leaving until you've improved or the doctor comes to take you away."

"Why, Rebecca Thurston, I do believe you've developed a backbone," he drawled, fascinated by this unusual display of temper. Her eyes blazed with an internal strength not present when they'd been friends. What had happened in her life to forge such a change?

He'd noticed, had he? In his mind, she was still the naive, eager-to-please, hopelessly-in-love-with-love young girl with big dreams and an even bigger future. Well, things changed. People changed.

That love-struck teenager was long gone. Did he realize he was the one responsible for her disappearance?

"Yes, well, I'm all grown up now." Sarcasm dripped from her words. "And I'm obviously the only one thinking rationally at the moment."

Caleb didn't immediately respond. The flicker of humor in his eyes sputtered out, and he studied her with his hooded, enigmatic gaze. Seemed she wasn't the only one who'd changed. The old Caleb, rarely serious, had been armed with ready, lighthearted quips to combat each and every call to reason.

"My presence here is putting you at risk." *Why are you placing my safety above your own?* his expression prompted.

Why indeed? He was right to be worried. The murder of a sheriff was a heinous crime, one that wouldn't be taken lightly. Knowing this, the criminals responsible wouldn't stop until they'd located the witness. If they'd seen his scar…

Shivering, she rubbed her upper arms. The fire needed to be lighted, Flossy milked and the eggs collected. Breakfast cooked. Bread made.

But first, this matter had to be settled. *Because no matter what he's done, I can't in good conscience send him out there in his current condition.*

"Even if I brought Rebel to the front door and helped you mount him, you wouldn't make it past the property fence. Your fever is indicative of an infection."

"The bullet could still be lodged in my leg. Did you check for an exit wound?"

Her cheeks heated with embarrassment. "I didn't think to."

"Is this your first gunshot wound?"

"Is it *your* first?"

"My first and only, I hope." His lips compressed into a tight line, as if he was perturbed she'd ask such a thing. But how was she supposed to know what kind of life he'd led? He was rarely home anymore, preferring to spend most of his time hunting and trapping in the high country. A blessing, in her opinion.

"I suppose I'll need to check it," she reluctantly acknowledged.

Tending his wound while he was unconscious was one thing. Having him awake and watching her every move would strain her nerves to the limit.

A lump in her throat, she approached the bed and, folding the quilts back, checked the compress. "I—I'll try not to cause you further pain."

Eyes closed and face averted, he muttered, "Just do what you gotta do."

Gingerly slipping her hand beneath his knee, she lifted his leg, wincing at the breath hissing between his teeth.

"No exit wound." She carefully covered him, heart knocking against her rib cage. She knew what his next words would be before he uttered them.

"The bullet needs to come out."

Dread settled like a pile of rocks in her stomach. "I don't know what I'm doing here, Caleb. I have very little knowledge when it comes to these things. Ma always tended Pa's nicks and scrapes."

Adam's injuries had been tended by a doctor. Her responsibilities had been limited to giving him water and mopping his forehead with a wet towel. And holding his hand, offering her support, her unending devotion—which he ultimately rejected.

"I wouldn't ask you to do this if there was any other alternative." Regret was carved into his austere features.

"Give me a minute." Although she didn't really have a choice, she craved a moment to wrap her mind around the ghastly task facing her.

Crossing to the hearth on wobbly legs, she extracted logs from the firebox and placed them in the fireplace. Lit the fire.

"Time to go outside, Storm." Stumpy tail quivering, Storm followed Rebecca to the door, diving into the snow that was in some places taller than her. The blast of arctic air stole Rebecca's breath. While the snow had stopped, it was clearly too deep to attempt a ride into town on Toby. She'd hoped...

With a heavy sigh, she tied back the cheery yellow curtains on the windows on either side of the door. Tugging the lapels of her housecoat together at the throat, she returned to his side. Stiffened her spine.

"All right, I'll do it."

Chapter Four

"I don't think I can do this." The cold metal tweezers sat awkward and heavy in her damp palm.

Grim-faced, Caleb gripped the mattress edge. His eyes were dark and flat.

"We don't have a choice, do we? Besides, the sooner you get this thing outta me, the sooner I can be on my way."

"That's easy for you to say," she griped. "You're not the one assuming the role of surgeon." Rebecca glanced down, the sight of the jagged wound causing nausea to swirl up.

"I can't do this." She swallowed hard, feverishly sending up petitions for God to rescue her.

"Becca, look at me."

Doing as he ordered, she met a gaze that was now as sharp as a rapier's edge.

"Take a good, long look at this scar on my face. Think back to the night I convinced your intended to sneak into the sawmill, to the night I condemned him to a wheelchair for the rest of his life."

"No." The blunt words sent a shock of icy water through her veins. This topic was not up for discussion. Why bring it up now? After all this time of avoiding the obvious?

His eyes narrowed. "If it weren't for me, you'd be happily ensconced in married life. You and Adam would've already had children by now. He told me how eager you were to build a family with him. How many did he say you wanted? Four?" His ragged voice seemed to taunt her. "Or was it five?"

How dare he toss her shattered hopes, her bleak and broken future, in her face as if they meant nothing? Of course, they didn't mean anything to him. Caleb had been self-centered, refusing to consider how his words and actions affected those around him.

Anger surged, the fiery heat of it flushing the surface of her skin. "You're right. The sooner you leave, the sooner I can forget you exist." Wielding the blunt-tip tweezers, she was prepared to do whatever necessary to rid her home of this odious man.

Something akin to remorse passed over his taut face a second before his lids slid closed, shutting her out. Burrowing his head deeper into the pillow, he braced himself.

Glad she'd decided to send Amy to the barn, Rebecca set her jaw and proceeded to retrieve the lead ball. Caleb flinched, fingers digging into the ticking. His anguished groans bounced off the walls and straight into her heart.

I refuse to feel sorry for him, she silently vowed. *He only has himself to blame for this mess.* The swift reminder that he'd been an innocent bystander was snuffed out by the flames of outrage.

Locating the foreign object, which thankfully hadn't gone deep, she carefully extracted and dropped the hateful thing in a bowl.

"It's out." Heart hammering as the reality of what she'd done slammed into her, she dropped the tweezers onto the bedside table and vowed to dispose of them. She never wanted to set eyes on the tool again.

He didn't immediately respond. "Caleb?"

He lay there, hands still twisted in the ticking, oblivious to his surroundings. The agony of the procedure must've been too much for him.

Emotions knotting beneath her sternum, Rebecca brushed angrily at rogue tears. She absolutely would not cry over Caleb O'Malley.

"By the way, I wanted four," she muttered. "Three boys and a girl."

Head reeling, Rebecca emerged from the cabin just as Amy popped up from the rocking chair positioned beneath the window and nearly made her upend the bloodied water atop her boots.

"Amy! What are you doing out here? You were supposed to stay in the barn." Her breath puffing out in a cloud, the crystal-frosted air seeped beneath her collar and stole up her skirts. She shivered. Then, Caleb's distress still reverberating in her ears, she studied her sister's face for signs of anxiety. "How long have you been here? Did you hear—"

"Nothing. I didn't hear a peep." She held up her hands. "I've only been out here a minute."

Moving to the railing, Rebecca did a slow sweep of the level clearing that contained their barn and outbuildings, then the forested mountainsides rising up on three sides of their quiet cove. For the first time, her beloved forests took on a menacing quality. Even though the fullness of summer had retreated, the parade of spindly branches coated with white powder that sparkled like diamonds in sunlight and the trees she admired for their towering beauty and strength could be hiding outlaws intent on locating the one witness who could identify them.

Setting the bowl on the floorboards, she crouched beside the rocking chair. Leveling with Amy might not be Rebecca's preferred choice, but it would keep her sister safe. "Caleb got hurt because he saw something he shouldn't have. Men are searching for him. Lawless men. Until he leaves, I need for you to stay close to the cabin. Don't wander into the woods alone. If you see someone coming that you don't recognize, holler for me. Go inside and lock yourself in, no matter where I am."

Her brow furrowed. "What did he see?"

Something no one should have to witness. The shadows chasing his eyes, the barely concealed horror, were proof enough of that. "That's Caleb's tale to tell, not mine."

The light smattering of freckles across Amy's nose became more pronounced. "What will these men do if they find him?"

Rebecca hesitated a fraction of a second too long.

"They'll finish off the job, won't they? They'll kill him." Shooting to her feet, Amy set her jaw, a gesture that meant she was convinced her way was right. "We have to keep him safe."

Pushing to her feet, Rebecca said, "He won't be

here much longer. We're taking him into town, to Doc Owens, as soon as he's able to withstand the trip."

"Are you seeing what I'm seeing?" Amy gestured to their surroundings. "There must be at least two feet of snow on the ground, three or more in some places. Toby would never make it out of the cove. Even if we tried to reach town with Rebel, can you honestly say Caleb would survive this cold in his condition?"

She stared at her thirteen-year-old sister, who sounded far more reasonable than Rebecca felt. *That's because, unlike me, she's not desperate to be rid of him.*

"Obviously, he can't be moved today. We'll have to wait and see what tomorrow brings."

I'm begging You, God, please take this burden from me. Make it possible for Caleb to reach the doctor. Or his family's homestead.

Sam and Mary O'Malley believed their son was hunting in the high country, off on another of his prolonged absences. They had no idea he lay gravely injured on the opposite side of town, a stone's throw from home. Rebecca frowned. They should be notified, but at the moment that was impossible. And the least of her worries.

"Is he awake?" Hefting the brimming milk pail, Amy paused before the door.

"No."

"I'll try not to disturb him, then."

Rebecca didn't immediately follow her inside. Instead, she forged her way through the snow in order to dispose of the dirty water behind the cabin, all the while straining for any unusual sights or sounds. Disquiet skittered through her mind. Thanks to Caleb's arrival on her doorstep, she no longer felt safe in her own home.

Hurrying back inside, she found Amy in the kitchen putting the kettle on to heat. Rebecca intercepted her skating glances toward the bed dominated by Caleb's unmoving form. Worry tugged her sister's mouth into a frown.

His presence here was troubling her sister. That wasn't acceptable, particularly considering the long months it had taken Amy to recover from their parents' sudden deaths. One more reason he needed to be moved as quickly as possible.

Forcing her feet to his bedside, Rebecca attempted to remain detached as she took in his skin's chalky whiteness, the shadows beneath his eyes, the pained furrow between his brows signaling his silent anguish. Attempted and failed miserably. This was a man with whom her past was irrevocably intertwined—they'd attended the same one-room schoolhouse since they were children, the same church, the same celebrations, weddings, funerals. Caleb O'Malley was as familiar to her as her own family. They'd been linked, Caleb and her, and Adam had been the glue holding them together.

Rebecca could not rejoice in his suffering. Indeed, it weighed heavily upon her soul.

Reaching out, she settled a light hand across his forehead. Troubling heat seared her. Placing a damp, cool cloth where her hand had been, she wondered how long he'd be out this time. Would the wound heal? Or would infection take over, driving his fever too high? The uncertainty—and yes, even fear for his well-being—stayed with her the rest of the day.

The burning sensation in his thigh, akin to a thousand yellow-jacket stings, sucked him up to the surface of the fiery lake of torment imprisoning him. He gasped for air. His insides, like dry sawdust, clamored for relief, his tongue thick and throat gritty.

Water.

He jerked when something hard and unexpected pressed against the seam of his mouth.

"I have water right here, Caleb." Becca's soft words flowed over him as her arm slipped beneath his shoulders to lend him support as he drank greedily. The cool liquid did little to assuage the thirst raging inside him.

"More."

She moved away, taking her comfort with her, and he forced his lids open. Darkness cloaked the room. A fire spit and crackled in the stone fireplace. Beside the bed, a golden circle of light shone from a single kerosene lamp. Night had fallen.

"I tried to wake you several times." She returned with another cupful, her brilliant green gaze watchful as he depleted the contents. "I was beginning to worry—" She bit her lip, apprehension written across her face.

He must be in pretty bad shape for her to admit concern.

"How's the leg look?" he managed to say, focusing with effort on his brave, if reluctant, caretaker.

"Angry."

"Infected?"

Her brows collided. "Maybe. I'm not certain." Self-consciously shoving a cloud of shiny hair behind one shoulder, she said, "I warned you I have little to no nursing experience."

Unable to keep his eyes open, he recalled her exact expression as she'd peered at his injury that morning. When he'd glimpsed the color leaching from her lips,

the dread tightening her shoulders, he'd grasped for
the only means available of distracting her. Reminding
Becca that he was responsible for the current state of
her life—unwed and alone save her sister, her dreams of
home and family nothing but a bittersweet memory—
had reignited her antipathy toward him while taking
her mind off the ugly task awaiting her.

"Doing a fine job." He pushed the words out, fighting
to stay awake so he could voice his gratitude. "The old
Becca couldn't have done what you did today. Brave."

"You're wrong," she whispered. "I'm not brave.
I'm…scared."

He wanted to open his eyes, wanted to reassure her.
A wave of inky darkness crashed over him, but he
wasn't ready to submit just yet.

"If only I could get to the doctor. He'd have medicine to help you."

"Becca."

The mattress dipped near his hip. The odd but not
unpleasant combination of fresh parchment and lilac
wrapped around him, resurrecting memories of golden
days of laughter and fun, a place in time that could
never be revisited. Amazingly, he felt her slender hands
curl about his, holding secure. Grounding him to her
world, perhaps? While she despised him, her compassionate heart would not desire his demise.

"I'm here, Caleb. I—I'll be here for as long as you
need me."

He tried to thank her. Words eluded him, however.
His mute, black void refused to wait a second longer
to reclaim him.

Chapter Five

Driven to comfort him, she'd uttered the hasty words without thinking. Suddenly the weight of his work-roughened hand was too much, the connection too personal. Pulling away, Rebecca sank against the chair and hugged her middle.

The muted light flickered across his face, making his scar appear more grotesque than it truly was. The night of the accident, she'd overheard Doc Owens saying he was fortunate. If the plank had hit him one inch to the left, he'd have lost his eye. At the time, she hadn't cared one whit about Caleb's injury, not when her fiancé's life hung in the balance.

Oh, the fury that had swept through her when she'd learned what had happened! She'd known, hadn't she? Known it deep in her bones that one day Caleb would go too far. If only Adam had heeded her warnings... but he and Caleb had been as close as brothers. Adam had looked up to his larger-than-life friend.

They shouldn't have been anywhere near that sawmill. They'd had run-ins with the owner, Guthrie Fleming, on two previous occasions—Adam had stubbornly refused to reveal the nature of those run-ins, much to her consternation—and he'd warned them to stay away. Always on the search for the next adventure, Caleb had drummed up the idea of sneaking in after closing hours and messing with Fleming's office. Nothing serious, Adam had later informed her, just enough to aggravate the older man.

They never made it to the office. Foolishly climbing on the plank stacks, leaping from one pile to the next, Caleb had reached the ground when the pile Adam was standing on gave way. He'd sustained a blow to his lower spine in the fall. A blow he couldn't recover from, physically or mentally. Watching her best friend, the man she'd loved and admired and planned a life around, retreat inside himself had been excruciating. Nothing she said or did convinced him that a wheelchair couldn't diminish her love for him. When rational speech hadn't worked, she'd argued, pleaded, cajoled, even railed at him to stop feeling sorry for himself. In the end, he hadn't been able to accept their altered future.

Adam had ordered her to stop coming to the doctor's office. When he'd been moved to his parents' home, she attempted to see him more than once. Finally, his mother had tearfully informed her it was time for Rebecca to allow her son to move on with his life. Then she'd asked for the ring back. The humiliation and defeat were as fresh today as they had been all those months ago.

Rebecca automatically reached for the locket hanging about her neck. Lifting it to eye level, she opened it as she'd done hundreds of times in the year since Adam moved away. His easy smile made her heart burn with disappointment.

"Why, Adam?" *Why were you so determined to walk away from everything we had? From me?*

The bedroom door opened. Rebecca shifted to watch Amy's approach, Storm following in her wake. "How's he doing?"

"The fever doesn't seem to be abating."

Amy frowned. "He looks bad, Rebecca. What if he—" Her throat worked.

Ignoring the painful thump of her heart, she gave Amy's hand a gentle squeeze. "Let's try and stay positive, okay? Caleb is strong and healthy."

"But we have no idea how long he was in the snowstorm. Do you think he might have pneumonia?"

"I don't think so." Breaking eye contact as a feeling of helplessness swamped her, she watched his chest rise and fall. His breathing seemed a bit labored to her. "Pray that the snow melts. Getting him to the doctor is our number-one priority."

"Do you want me to sit with him?"

"No, I'll do it. You need your rest."

"So do you," she pointed out. "You've been tending to him nearly every minute since Storm found him."

The past twenty-four hours had passed in a blur. "I'm fine."

At Amy's quirked brow, Rebecca said, "I'll rest on the settee if I need to. That way I'll hear him if he calls out."

"Fine." Patting Storm's head, Amy said, "Keep her company, okay, girl?"

At that, the dog settled herself at Rebecca's feet.

Amy smiled. "'Night, then."

"Sweet dreams."

When Rebecca was left alone once more with her restless patient, the fire crackling and Storm's mournful eyes fastened on her, she sank forward so that her forehead rested on the mattress.

Lord, You are well aware of the state of my sister's poor battered heart, how she still grieves Ma's and Pa's passing. For her sake, and that of Caleb's parents and brothers, I ask You to please spare his life.

"Becca?"

They were in the sawmill, the three of them. It was summer. Full moon. The humid air hugged her body, close and uncomfortable. From her vantage point beneath the overhang of the low building, she could see Adam standing precariously close to the edge of the planks high above her head. With dawning horror, Rebecca tried frantically to get his attention, to warn him. He ignored her. Crept closer to danger.

No. No, don't. Adam, please stop...

"Becca, wake up."

She gradually became aware of the quilt beneath her cheek, the dog's warmth against her ankle and—surely she was imagining it—masculine fingers lightly skimming her hair?

Caleb. Jolting upright, her gaze shot to a pair of glittering brown eyes. She self-consciously smoothed the mussed strands, assuring herself that the featherlight caress had been part of the disturbing dream.

"H-how are you feeling?" She reached for his mug. "Do you want some water?"

He waved her offer aside. His raven hair was damp at the temples, the longish strands clinging to his neck beneath his shirt collar. "Need paper. Pen."

"What for?"

His gaze, which she now noticed was overly bright, slid away. What was he hiding? "I need for you to take down information."

"What sort of information?" Dismay churned in her middle. Deep down, she suspected what he wanted and why.

"Descriptions," he said, broad chest rising and falling as if he'd just completed a race.

"Of the outlaws, you mean?"

He met her gaze head-on. "Yes."

There was resolve in that gaze. Regret, too, so deep she thought she might drown in it. Jaw knotted with unease, she crossed to the opposite wall to the storage cabinet where she kept her watercolors, handmade paintbrushes and other supplies. Withdrawing a pencil and paper, she returned to her chair and took a bracing breath.

"I'm ready when you are."

"There were five of them…."

As Rebecca penned the details, the fact that he had witnessed a man's death finally registered. And not just any man, a respected lawman. As Cades Cove was only a two-day ride from Gatlinburg, Eli Tate had made several visits to their town. She'd even met him once. Had been struck by his somber demeanor. Local folks said the young sheriff was dedicated to protecting his small community and respected by its inhabitants. Now he was dead.

How helpless Caleb must've felt. He had never been one to remain on the fringe of the action. He certainly hadn't ever stood by while injustice was meted out.

Pencil hovering above the parchment, she jerked up her head. "You tried to intervene, didn't you?"

He didn't blink, didn't flinch in the face of her accusation.

She gripped the pencil tighter. "You honestly thought you could take on a gang of outlaws all by yourself?"

"Tate was unarmed. Surrounded." His frown was fierce. "I had to try."

"What did you do exactly?"

"Doesn't matter." Sighing, he pressed his head farther back into the pillow. "It didn't work."

"You very well may pay for that with your life." Jumbled emotions stabbing at her, Rebecca tossed the pencil aside and strode to the fireplace, seizing the poker and jamming it into the half-burned logs. Anger at his foolishness pounded at her temples.

"If I don't make it, will you take the information to Shane? He'll need it if he's gonna get justice for Tate."

She whirled about to gape at him. The resignation in his handsome features filled her mouth with the metallic taste of fear. Fear for the friend he used to be, not the nemesis he'd become.

"You are not dying on my watch," she said through gritted teeth. No way was she going to have his death on her conscience.

Apology deepened the furrow between his brows. "I'd like for Nathan to have my horse. Josh can have my guns."

"Stop." Hands clenched, she stalked over to the bed

and glared down at him. "If I have to pack you in icicles, if I have to bury you in snow or submerge you in the stream to bring that fever down, I will. You *will* recover, Caleb O'Malley, and then you're gonna walk out of my life and never return, got it?"

Something wet splashed onto his hand. Tears. Becca was crying over him? Didn't she know he wasn't worth it?

"I never wanted this," he said. Relaying the details of the murder had drained him. "I stayed away so you wouldn't have to be reminded. Now here I am causing you pain again."

"I don't need you to remind me of what happened." She angrily swiped at the moisture on her cheeks. "I'm reminded every day that I wake up alone. I'm reminded every time I see his parents at the mercantile or in the church pew. This town is riddled with memories. There's no getting away from them."

The magnitude of what he'd done, the price she'd been forced to pay, seized him. "I'd give anything if I could turn back the clock and return to that night—if I could switch places with Adam, I would." Daring to reach out and splay his fingers over her hand, he whispered, "I'm sorry, Becca."

Grief twisted her features, and she bent her head, a thick fall of hair slipping forward and blocking her profile. To his shock, she didn't snatch her hand away. Instead, she traced the veins crisscrossing the top of his with her fingertip. "I don't wish to discuss this anymore tonight," she said, her voice unsteady. "You need rest."

Caleb's eyes slid shut. Despite the weariness weigh-

ing down his body and the throbbing ache in his leg,
that single touch brought him more pleasure than he'd
known in ages.

"Caleb?" The caress ceased, and he had to bite his lip
in order to refrain from begging her to continue. *That's
what happens when you spend most of your time with
nothing but squirrels and birds for company.*

"Yeah?" Afraid she might see how she affected him,
he kept his eyes closed.

"Promise me you're not giving up. That you're gonna
fight this."

The tremor in her voice forced his gaze up to her
lovely face wreathed in worry. Frustration fueled his
heavenward petition. *Why her, God? Why did she have
to be the one to find me? Haven't I caused her enough
suffering? I deserve whatever comes my way, but Becca
and Amy are innocent. My presence here is putting
them at risk.*

He wondered if God would choose to hear his prayer,
much less deem to answer. After all the pain his actions
had brought to those around him, he harbored serious
doubt his Creator looked kindly upon him. But this was
important. Becca's life very well could be on the line. If
those murderers had seen his scar, if they tracked him
here and he was too weak to protect her...

Caleb gritted his teeth, pushed the disturbing images
out of his mind. He couldn't think about that. Had to
focus on fighting the infection. And, if God decided to
spare his life, he'd do as Becca asked and leave Gatlinburg for good. As much as saying goodbye to his family would kill him—spending weeks at a time in the
mountains in self-imposed isolation, not knowing how

they were faring was its own special brand of torture—
he could no longer risk their well-being. Being lonely
was a small price to pay if it meant they were happy and
healthy and untouched by the irresponsibility inherent
to his nature.

"I'll leave here as soon as I'm able," he told her. "Once
my business is concluded with Shane and I'm certain
you and Amy are no longer in danger, I won't bother
you again. You have my word."

Looking as if she had more to say but thinking better
of it, she merely nodded. "I'll heat you up some broth."
Sweeping gracefully to the tiny kitchen, she set a large
enamel pot on the stove top.

Although he wasn't the least bit hungry, Caleb didn't
call her back to his side. The effect of her innocent touch
yet lingered, and he didn't trust himself not to play on
her sympathy and ask if she'd mind holding his hand
until he slept.

Chapter Six

Rebecca was making her way to the barn the next morning, an empty milk pail dangling from her wrist, when the jangle of horse bells reached her. She froze. Had Tate's murderers come to silence Caleb? Hardened criminals knew better than to announce their arrival, didn't they?

Feeling vulnerable without a means of defending herself, she peered along the narrow lane leading out of their cove. A familiar gold-trimmed black sleigh glided through the fresh dusting of snow that had fallen overnight. Her tension eased at the sight of her neighbors, Louis Harper and his daughter, Meredith. Of course they'd come to check on her.

She and Meredith were the same age and had attended school together but hadn't become close until the death of Rebecca's parents. In the midst of Rebecca's grief, the pretty brunette had reached out to her and Amy, stopping by regularly with fresh-baked desserts. Their friendship had been forged over coffee and pie.

Setting the pail in the snow, she greeted the other

woman with a longer-than-usual hug. Meredith pulled back, lively green eyes dancing with questions beneath her furry cap. "We came to see how you were faring in this weather. Didn't figure you'd try to make it to church services on old Toby. Momma's been feeling poorly this week, so we aren't going, either. You look strange, Rebecca. Are you all right?"

Cheeks and nose ruddy from the brisk air, Louis sloughed through the snow to his daughter's side. "You got enough firewood? I can bring some logs inside if you need me to."

Unreasonably, moisture filled her eyes. Louis Harper had been good friends with her father. Ever since the accident, he'd taken it upon himself to try and ease her burden around the farm.

"Something terrible has happened," she said. "Caleb O'Malley has been shot. H-he's inside."

Eyes going wide, Meredith's crimson mitten flew up to cover her mouth. Louis's bushy, ginger-colored brows pulled together. "When did this happen?"

"I found him Friday morning. Actually, Storm led me to him. If she hadn't, he surely would've frozen to death." Or bled to death, whichever came first.

"You've been caring for him all this time?"

"Yes, I...dug the bullet out."

Her friend stared at her in disbelief. "You're the most squeamish person I know. You hate the sight of blood. How?"

An icy wind barreled down the mountainside and through the cove, flattening their skirts against their legs. Chafing her arms through the cape, she said, "I don't know. It wasn't as if I had a choice. I just did what needed to be done, praying all the while."

Louis eyed the cabin. "Did he tell you who shot him?"

It was a reasonable question. However, she didn't want them drawn into the crisis. Bad enough that she and Amy were involved. "I—I'm not at liberty to say, sir."

"I see." He stared at her thoughtfully. "How's he doing?"

"I suspect his wound is infected. His fever is getting worse by the hour." She twisted her hands. "There are times when he is completely lucid and others when he seems confused. I'm afraid of what might happen if he doesn't get medical attention. With all the snow…" She waved a hand at the wintry scene. "Would you mind taking a look at him?"

"Not at all." The burly figure was already crunching his way to the front steps.

She picked up the discarded pail. "Amy's in the barn feeding the horses. We'll wait out there."

He waved a hand in dismissal. "I'll join you in a moment."

Linking arms, they trekked toward the barn. "I'm in shock right now. I can't begin to imagine how you feel." Meredith brushed aside dark strands that had snagged on her lips. "Caleb O'Malley. Here. And you as his caretaker. How are you holding up?"

While everyone in Gatlinburg knew Adam had broken their engagement, only Meredith was aware of her private struggles. Rebecca strove for a brave face in front of the townsfolk. It wasn't in her nature to play the pitied jilted bride. But she'd been honest with her friend about the lingering bitterness she wrestled with, the feeling of helplessness and hurt Adam's decision had wrought.

"There are so many different emotions inside me right now that I can't distinguish one from the other. I can't understand why God did this. He knows how I feel about Caleb. Why couldn't he have ridden a different direction? Why here? Why me? Haven't I had enough trouble for one lifetime?"

She sounded like a petulant child, she knew, but didn't she have a right to complain? In eighteen months' time, she'd not only lost the love of her life but her dear, beloved parents. As scary as it was to admit, she was *angry* at God.

"I wish I had answers for you." Meredith pressed in close to her side. "If we could transport him to our house, you wouldn't have to deal with him."

Rebecca shook her head. "You haven't seen him, Mer." She sighed. "He's bad off."

When they reached the barn, Meredith held back, brown hair swirling about the shoulders of her cape. "I hate to burden you further, but have you considered what might happen when folks learn of his presence here?"

Confused by her friend's grave expression, she frowned. "What do you mean?"

"You're an unmarried woman. Caleb's an unmarried man. The two of you have occupied the same cabin for two whole days and two very long nights without the benefit of a chaperone."

"He's hardly in any position to damage my reputation! He's gravely ill," she stated with a growing sense of alarm. Withdrawing her arm, she pressed her gloves against her cheeks stiff with cold. "Besides, we haven't been alone."

"I'm not certain Amy counts as a suitable chaperone. Logic doesn't always play into these situations. Remember what happened to Cole and Rachel Prescott? They were locked in the storage room overnight and forced to marry, no matter that it was a cruel prank and not even remotely their fault."

Appalled at the mere idea of being linked to Caleb in that way, she set her jaw. "Nothing, and I mean absolutely *nothing,* could induce me to marry that man."

Despite her conviction, a frisson of unease worked its way down her spine. Meredith wasn't exaggerating. Folks were funny about maintaining appearances at all costs. If there was even the suspicion that something improper had occurred—whether it had or no—marriage was the only way to restore the couple's reputation.

Understanding warred with caution in Meredith's heavily fringed green eyes. "I hope it doesn't come to that."

"It won't. I've given the man shelter and done my best to keep him alive, that's all. End of story."

"You don't have to convince me." She held up her hands, the vivid red wool reminding Rebecca of Caleb's blood pooled in the snow. She bit down hard on her lip as worry swirled afresh in her chest.

"Have you heard from Adam?"

Last night's conversation—and the terrible vulnerability in Caleb's eyes—replaying in her mind, it took her a moment to register the question. Meredith was referring, of course, to the numerous letters she'd sent her former fiancé and the fact he hadn't answered even one.

Shaking her head, she allowed her gaze to roam the white-washed forest beyond the barn, where mighty pines wore skirts of shimmering powder and blue jays' wings flashed brilliantly against the white backdrop. Along with cardinals, blue jays were one of her favorite birds. Tough to get that exact shade of blue on canvas, however. For the painting hanging above her parents' bed, she'd had to experiment to get the right shade. Her mother had adored that painting.

A renewed wave of grief gripping her, she sighed. "I haven't written him in four months. It's obvious he doesn't want to hear from me. Don't know why it took me so long to accept that."

"What you two had was special. Makes sense you wouldn't want to give that up."

"Adam clearly didn't have a problem," she muttered, shivering as another gust of wind slammed into them.

"Well, I for one think it's time you turned your attention to someone else. I've noticed Douglas casting moon eyes at you during church. He'd ask to call on you in a heartbeat if you'd encourage him a little."

"We've had this conversation before. I'm not ready." Tired of dwelling on her sorry state of affairs, she turned the tables on her best friend. "How about we discuss your love life, hmm? Are you ready to tell me who it is you're sweet on?"

Color bloomed in the brunette's cheeks, yet she shrugged as if it was no big deal. While Meredith was more than willing to discuss Rebecca's private affairs, she wasn't as forthcoming with her own.

"There's no chance he'll ever notice me, so why put

a name to him?" Her petite nose wrinkled. "Besides, isn't it more interesting to try and guess his identity?"

"No, it isn't. It's frustrating. And hardly fair given everything I've revealed to you."

Meredith was on the verge of relenting when Mr. Harper appeared on the porch and lifted a hand to get their attention.

At the sight of the deep grooves bracketing his mouth, all thoughts of Meredith's crush fled. Did he have bad news? Perhaps he'd seen something she'd missed, some sign of impending death she was unaware of. By the time he reached them, she'd become numb to the cold, oblivious to the thin, cottonlike clouds stretched across the sky.

"Poor lad is suffering from an infection." He scratched beneath his heavy wool cap and sighed. "Wish I could take him off your hands, but I doubt he'd survive the trip. And Teresa's ill. I wouldn't want to expose him to whatever she has. We have medicine that can help bring the fever down, as well as some herbs and such for a poultice to put on the wound." He hesitated, which was unusual. "Would you like for Meredith to come and stay with you? Even at this late date, her presence might ward off some of the gossip that's sure to erupt once your situation becomes known."

"There's no place for her to sleep. And besides, I know she's doing the cooking and cleaning while Teresa is sick." She met Meredith's worried gaze. "I can't ask you to stop caring for your ma simply to babysit us."

"I could do my chores during the day and spend the nights here. We could make a pallet on the floor."

"Absolutely not." She took her friend's hands in hers

and braved a smile. "I appreciate the offer, really, I do. But I can handle whatever the gossips dish out. You know how these things blow over in a week or two."

"Let's hope you're right." Louis sighed. "Meredith, stay and visit with your friends while I get the supplies. I should return within the hour."

"Yes, sir."

The door scraped open then, and Amy's lips parted. "Mr. Harper. Meredith." Her gaze bounced between the cabin and Rebecca. "Is everything okay?"

"Mr. Harper is going to fetch medicine for Caleb."

"Is he gonna make it?" She directed her question at their father's friend.

"That's in the good Lord's hands, Amy. We'll be praying for him." His frown didn't budge. "I'd best be off."

No one spoke as he made his way to the sleigh. Rebecca belatedly noticed the pail in her sister's hands. "You milked Flossy for me?"

"She was getting antsy." She blew out a breath. "I also fed and watered the horses and mucked out the stables."

"I think that deserves a special thank-you."

Wispy brows winged up. "Hot cocoa?"

Rebecca smiled and nodded. There was enough in the tin for one more cup, two if she thinned it. An extra spoonful of sugar would make up for the lack. Hopefully, the hens she'd delivered to Clawson's three days ago had sold and she'd have enough store credit left over from buying necessities to replenish their supply. And perhaps purchase pearl buttons for the new dress she was working on for Amy for Christmas. The special holiday was fast approaching, and Rebecca was determined to provide her sister with some semblance of holiday spirit.

Taking the heavy pail from her, she motioned over her shoulder. "Let's go inside and get warm while we wait. Mer, there's cocoa or coffee for you. Your choice."

"Ma sent along apple butter and two loaves of bread," she said as they ascended the stairs, pointing to the basket her father had left tucked against the door frame. "We can have a slice now, if you'd like."

Once on the threshold, the toasty warmth surrounding her and the anticipation of Teresa's delicious apple butter were promptly forgotten. Caleb was in trouble.

Caleb thrashed about on the bed, a string of incomprehensible words slipping from his lips. Setting the pail on the dining table without care for the contents, she rushed to restrain him. If he aggravated his injury...

"Stop." His voice was hoarse. *"Don't do this."*

Were these the words he'd uttered when he tried to save Tate's life?

She was having trouble restraining him. Even ill, his strength was no match for hers.

"Can you give me a hand, Mer?"

The brunette approached, more solemn than Rebecca had ever seen her. "What do you need me to do?"

"Hold his ankles."

When Meredith had stationed herself at the foot of the bed, Rebecca scooted up on the mattress and, pressing on his shoulders, leaned in close. The scents of pine and earth yet clung to him, intermingled with the familiar one of burning logs in the fireplace and a trace of floral in Amy's quilt. Beneath all that was the smell of the massive amount of blood he'd spilled. *Trying to save the sheriff.*

On the flip side of his recklessness was a courage few could match. He was quick to protect the weak and vulnerable.

"Caleb, can you hear me?"

His fight with an unseen enemy continued, his large hands clutching at the quilt covering him. *"Danger."*

She laid a hand against his fevered, bristle-edged jaw. A memory, long-suppressed, resurfaced of her and Caleb and a nearly drowned calico kitten they'd fished out of the river. Certain he wouldn't survive, Adam had advised her to leave it to its fate. He'd accused her of being too softhearted. Caleb had had other ideas. Tucking the mewling creature against his chest, he'd carried it here, to her barn, and together they'd worked to keep it alive.

His compassion had known no bounds. The sight of him hand-feeding the tiny animal, lean fingers constantly stroking its fur, had affected her in a profound way. Several days later, when it became clear the kitten would survive, she'd thrown herself against him and hugged him tight. He'd hesitated at first. Then his strong arms had wrapped around her, his heart beating fast beneath her cheek, and it had hit her like a locomotive—Caleb posed a danger to what she had with Adam.

Recognizing her heart's susceptibility, she'd created distance between them, both mentally and physically. She wasn't about to risk the security and comfort Adam Tierney offered for anyone, *especially* not live-as-close-to-the-edge-as-possible Caleb. Though it had taken some subtle maneuvering, Rebecca had been careful not to sit beside him in church or dance with him at the many barn dances the three of them had attended together. He hadn't remarked on the change, but she'd caught him staring at her sometimes with a look of hurt and confusion. Recalling those looks now, she wondered why he'd never confronted her.

"You don't wanna do this," he ground out, urgency underscoring the words. In his fevered mind, he was back there in the mountains, challenging outlaws and trying to save a man's life. Trying and failing.

When his whole body stiffened suddenly and air hissed through dry lips, she imagined the precise moment he was reliving. The overwhelming need to assuage his pain lodged in her chest and, the other occupants of the room forgotten, Rebecca leaned down and gently rested her head on his shoulder, kneading the rigid biceps through the soft cotton shirt.

"It's okay," she said in an urgent, hushed voice. "You're gonna be okay."

He continued to resist his unseen enemies. Rebecca repeated the words until he quieted. She wasn't aware of how many moments passed before Meredith came around the bed and touched a hand to her lower back.

"He's resting now."

Sitting up, she avoided her friend's curious gaze, studying the quilt pattern through increasingly watery eyes.

"Are *you* gonna be okay, Rebecca?"

A world of bewilderment accompanied the other woman's obvious concern.

Lifting her head, she said simply, "He was my friend."

And then she burst into tears. Tears for all that they'd lost, her and Adam and Caleb.

Meredith pulled her upright into a hug. Soon Amy joined their circle. When Meredith began to pray aloud, asking God to heal Caleb and to restore Rebecca's peace, Becca silently thanked Him for such a dear friend. And then her prayers centered on her patient, her friend turned adversary—that he would heal and return to the high country as quickly as possible.

Chapter Seven

Caleb woke hours—or was it days?—later, at once noticing the absence of searing heat. His chest no longer felt as if an elk sat on it, and his head was blessedly clear. Gratitude swelled. Now he could remove himself to town. Rebecca and Amy would be safe.

The rustle of skirts alerted him to the presence of his bedside sentry.

Setting her rug-in-progress and hook on the chair, Becca leaned down to check his temperature. Immediately he was surrounded by familiar scents of paint, paper and the ever-present lilac. His gaze caught on the gold locket dangling from her neck. He didn't recognize it. Had it been a gift from her parents? Or Adam?

"How are you feeling?" Apparently satisfied the fever was gone, she straightened and hid her hands behind her back, all emotion smoothed from her countenance. She couldn't mask the strain caring for him these past days had taken, however. Shadows bruised her eyes.

"In need of a bath, a shave and a huge plate of biscuits and gravy. Not necessarily in that order."

A ghost of a smile lifted her lips. "I see you're feeling more yourself. You're gonna have to wait on the biscuits."

Gliding to the cast-iron stove in the corner, she dipped what looked to be broth into a plain white bowl. Becca made even the most mundane actions appear graceful, her movements like a coordinated dance, and he thought that he could watch her for a lifetime and never cease to be fascinated. Maybe it was her artist's spirit shining through. For as long as he'd known her, she'd been driven to create things.

When they were young, her endeavors had been simple. Dandelion necklaces. Animals crafted from leaves, pinecones and acorns. He'd lost count how many times the teacher had reprimanded her for drawing on her chalkboard instead of listening to his lecture. Caleb had winced with every strike of the ruler across her delicate knuckles. One particular time he hadn't been able to contain himself and, bolting to his feet, railed at Mr. Jones for punishing her for something that was as natural to her as breathing. Caleb had received a lashing for that outburst, but it had been worth the look of hero worship in Becca's wide eyes, fleeting though it had been.

As a teenager, she'd experimented with pottery making, basket weaving and rug hooking. And while she was good at those, sketching and painting were her true passions. The evidence of her talent adorned the walls. Light streaming through the windows on either side of the cabin door set the paintings alight with color. There were more than he remembered. Birds and flowers dominated, with a couple of mountain landscapes thrown in.

She pivoted, and he noticed the traces of paint

smudging her faded blue skirt. Her play clothes, she'd jokingly called them.

"What day is it?"

"Tuesday."

"What?" He immediately sat up, the bed coverings pooling about his waist. His leg screamed in protest. "How many days have I been here?"

"I found you Friday morning."

Five days. Becca looked troubled and well she should. That was five days the gang had had to search for him. He had no idea what direction they'd gone, no clue if they'd noticed the trail of blood he'd left or if they'd glimpsed his scar. Certainly they'd be on the lookout for a horse with Rebel's markings.

"I'm leaving. Now."

Shoving off the heavy quilt, he glanced down and saw that his pant leg had been cut away. Not normally a man prone to blushing, embarrassing heat climbed his neck and stung his ears. Quickly covering himself, Caleb couldn't meet her eyes.

"I have an extra pair of trousers in my saddlebags. Would you mind bringing them to me?"

"As a matter of fact, I do mind."

That brought his head up. The set of her jaw brooked no argument. Still, he speared her with a dark gaze. "You're aware of the danger I've put you and your sister in by winding up here. I need to speak with Shane Timmons."

The sooner he left, the sooner the distress would disappear from her beautiful eyes. She could rebury the past. Once again pretend he didn't exist.

The thought of leaving her, of never seeing her again, made him inexplicably sad, something he refused to dwell on. He had no rights where she was concerned, no claim to her company. He hadn't even allowed himself to think of her these past couple of years. Every time he got a flash of Becca laughing or dancing or sitting alone in a field of wildflowers with her paints and easel, he'd redirected his thoughts to the sight of Adam falling, of his twisted body buried beneath the planks. He didn't deserve her attention. Didn't deserve a crumb of her kindness.

Sliding the bowl and spoon onto the bedside table, she jammed her fists on her waist. "You're not ready to travel, Caleb."

"How's it look outside?" He gestured to the windows.

"It hasn't snowed since Sunday, but the days have been overcast and the temperature hasn't risen above freezing. The snow hasn't had a chance to melt."

"Rebel could make it to town."

"Yes, I'm certain he could. You, however, haven't eaten solid food in days, and I have a feeling you're not taking into account what riding astride would cost you."

The logic rankled. "Tell me, Becca, just how long are you planning on holding my pants—and effectively me—hostage?" he drawled.

Her eyes flared. Spinning about on her heel, she stormed to the corner where she'd stowed the bags and, digging through his things without a care for his privacy, retrieved said trousers and dumped them on the bed.

"There—" she jerked a hand toward the door "—you're free to go. Happy now?" Her chest heaved with indignation.

He sighed. "Look—"

Amy chose that moment to barrel inside, stomping on the rug to rid her boots of wet clumps of snow. "Mr.

Harper is here…." She trailed off as her gaze landed on him. "You're awake." She stared wide-eyed at her sister. "He's awake."

"Yes, so he is."

Head bent, seeming to take an inordinate amount of interest in the floorboards, Becca refused to look at him. No doubt his determination to reach town in spite of his injuries struck her as reckless and foolish. Her fear was not unfounded—it wasn't without risk. What she failed to realize was that their well-being took precedence over his own.

"Hello, Amy." He nodded, inwardly wincing as fatigue washed over him. "Thanks for letting me borrow your bed."

She paused in the unbuttoning of her purple coat, a shy smile appearing. "It was nothing."

Becca's little sister had experienced a growth spurt since he'd seen her last. Her hair was longer and darker, her elfin face had thinned out and, while taller than before, she hadn't developed the grace and confidence that came with young adulthood. He supposed she'd put away her dolls for more worthwhile pursuits. Adam had teased him mercilessly for indulging the girl.

Hooking the coat collar on the one-inch prong, she approached with her hands clasped behind her. "I'm glad you're feeling better. We prayed for you."

We? Did that *we* include Becca? He found that difficult to believe.

"Mr. Harper." Becca went to greet their neighbor coming through the doorway. "Good news. Your medicine worked. His fever broke this morning."

"Praise God." Louis Harper's astute gaze raked Caleb from head to toe. "Your folks will be relieved."

His eyes squeezed shut. *His folks.* He hadn't thought of them since the night he was shot, uncertain whether or not he would make it. Here he was again, about to cause them more grief.

"I'll be happy to take them a message for you." Harper's no-nonsense voice held a note of sympathy. "I'm sure they'll be happy to know you're all right."

All right? That was up for debate.

"Let's go outside for a minute."

A serious-bordering-on-stern man, the disquiet stamped in Louis's round, fleshy face made Rebecca uneasy. What was bothering him? What couldn't he say in front of Caleb and Amy?

Emerging from her room, where she and Amy had waited while Louis helped Caleb get cleaned up, her gaze immediately sought out the bed on the far side of the room. Her patient lay with his head turned to the log-and-chinking wall. She could see the damp sheen in his gorgeous black locks, the clean shirt the color of rich buttermilk encasing his lean torso and impossibly broad shoulders. The hands folded atop his chest struck her as strangely vulnerable and, as it had since the moment she'd turned him over in the snow, compassion warred mightily with long-nursed resentment.

On the porch, Rebecca wound the striped wool scarf that had once belonged to her father about her neck. For a moment, Louis's gaze snagged on it, and he heaved a heavy sigh. She imagined his thoughts ran along the same line as hers—what would her father say about the predicament she found herself in?

"Caleb told me what happened," Louis said. "He's

worried about you. I reminded him not to underestimate your strength. You've got a level head on your shoulders, just like your ma."

Rebecca blinked fast. The kind words were a rare gift. Her parents had doled out praise for both their daughters on a regular basis. Guess she'd taken it for granted. Only now that she'd lived without it for so long did she realize how much their support and approval had meant to her.

"He's bound and determined to leave, despite the fact he'd be risking a relapse."

"He calmed a bit when I offered to fetch Timmons myself. Since he's not fit to travel, I'll bring the sheriff to him."

Their words were loud in the hushed stillness cloaking the cove, the thick blanket of snow sponging up sounds.

"Thank you for your help today."

His expression altered into a reluctance to voice unpleasant things. Uh-oh.

"Rebecca…you realize what your tending to Caleb means for your future, don't you? When the town leaders discover how much time you've spent together without a chaperone, they will no doubt expect you to marry."

Restless with indignation, she stalked to the nearest post and wrapped her arm about it, careful to avoid the glistening icicle suspended from the roof.

"There was a time in my life when I would've caved to such expectations. Not anymore. I will not marry him."

"If you were my own daughter, I'd insist on it." Compassion marked his voice. "This situation has gone way beyond propriety."

"We're innocent of any wrongdoing," she forced out. "The man almost died, Louis."

"I know you're innocent. But it's the appearance of wrongdoing that will spur the leaders to action. I just want you to be prepared." Navigating the snow-encrusted steps, he made his way to his waiting team. "I'll return as soon as I can."

"You'll bring Doc, too, right?" She couldn't be confident Caleb was on the mend until the doctor evaluated him. Hopefully Doc would deem him well enough to be moved. Whether he went to his folks' or to Doc's didn't matter to her just as long as he left.

Lifting a hand in acknowledgment of her question, his wool cap bobbed, a spot of charcoal-gray against the blinding white landscape.

The sound of bells jingling in her ears, she reluctantly went inside and removed her scarf and coat. The bowl on the bedside table sat empty. When she neared his bed, the pleasant scent of clean and soapy male tickled her nose. *Don't be awake,* she silently ordered, but his thick, black lashes fluttered upward and dark brown eyes focused on her.

"Harper leave already?" he asked with a grunt, shifting upward on the mound of pillows.

"Just a minute ago." She twisted the folds of her skirt. "I'm hoping he'll return with Doc."

That beautiful mouth flattened. "I asked him to bring Shane."

"And I asked him to bring Doc."

Unsettled by the clarity in his shrewd gaze, Rebecca started to turn away. Dealing with him while he was ill was quite a different reality than when he was in complete possession of his senses. The dangerous edge was front and center once more, calling to her even as it repelled.

His fingers closed over her wrist, stalling her. "What's wrong?"

Turning back, she cocked a you-can't-be-serious brow, ordering herself to shake free of his hold. But she didn't. The strong, masculine touch felt *amazing*. For a millisecond, she reveled in the prickly tingles fanning up her arm, the tug of want and need overruling the voice screaming at her to remember it was her enemy touching her.

"I meant, what's wrong besides the fact that you're stuck with me," he amended.

Stuck with him. As in *forever*. Images of him and her and a preacher and a church full of disapproving townspeople accosted her.

He must've recognized the unease in her expression, because he quickly tacked on, "Temporarily, of course."

"You're imagining things."

"Am I?"

Caleb had always managed to read her moods. The low, coaxing tone, combined with the imprint of his rougher fingertips against the sensitive skin of her inner wrist, reminded her of the time he'd happened upon her following a particularly upsetting fight with Adam. At the first sight of her tears, he'd grimly pulled her into his arms, fingers ever-so-lightly skimming her back as she poured out her frustration.

One thing she'd forgotten about him—he was a fantastic listener. A trait Adam didn't share. Her heart beat out a dull tattoo.

Was it possible that, in her brokenness following the accident, she'd elevated her and Adam's relationship to near-perfect status, blinding herself to his faults while doing the exact opposite with Caleb? One man couldn't be all good, the other all bad.

Jerking from his grasp, she rubbed the spot where he'd held her in an effort to banish the tingling sensation. Loneliness and the scarceness of human touch was no excuse for weakness around this man.

"I'll be fine just as soon as you're gone," she snapped. "I'm going out to the barn. Amy's in the bedroom reading if you need a drink. Anything else, she can come and get me."

Silence choked the cabin as she stalked away, throwing her cape about her shoulders once again when what she really longed to do was lounge before the fire with a mug of rich-bodied coffee and her latest rug-hooking project. Once safely on the porch, the winter air swirled around her, stealing up her skirts and in between her scarf and collar, cold enough to freeze eyelashes. It wasn't enough to drive her back inside, however.

For the hundredth time, she begged God to end this torment. Her greatest hope lay with Doc Owens's visit. *Please let him deem Caleb fit for travel, Lord.* At this point, she wasn't worried about faceless outlaws. She was worried about Caleb's lingering presence in her home and what that might mean to her future.

Chapter Eight

Caleb tried to focus on the meaning behind Amy's words as she read to him from Charles Dickens's *Great Expectations,* but fatigue made his brain sluggish. He would've slept already were it not for his awareness of Becca's every movement in the small kitchen area as she cleaned the lunch dishes and began preparations for supper. She'd hid out in the barn for more than an hour before finally coming inside to heat up a huge pot of bean soup for lunch. The effects of a full stomach and clean clothing were lulling him into a relaxed state that not even his aching thigh could disrupt.

Amy paused, finger pressed to the page to hold her spot. "What's for supper?"

"Venison stew."

Speculation flared in the pixie face. "Did our secret benefactor deliver the meat?"

Twisting at the waist, Becca shot Amy a quelling look. When her gaze speared him, he stopped scratching at the itchy stubble on his chin and lowered his hand to his lap. Surely she didn't suspect him?

"What's all this about?" he questioned Amy. It would look suspicious if he didn't ask.

Slipping a slim, hand-decorated bookmark between the pages, she closed the book and held it against her chest. Her blue eyes twinkled. "For months now, someone has been mysteriously leaving us packages of meat."

"Is that so?"

When he switched his gaze to Becca, she turned back to the work space littered with spoons, spices and pots, presenting him with her stick-straight spine and tense shoulders. He'd reached out and touched her without thinking earlier and, like a fool, hadn't immediately released her. Clearly a rash mistake. She'd been prickly ever since, the accusation *You ruined my life* squarely back in her eyes.

"You have no idea who it is?"

"None." Amy's twin braids swished as she shook her head. "Rebecca questioned Mr. Harper, but he denied having any part of it."

"It's likely someone from church," Becca said, dropping a handful of carrots into the bubbling pot on the stove. The savory smells that were beginning to fill the room chased away his sleepiness. Although he'd eaten just over an hour ago, he found he could eat again. After days of nothing but broth and water, his appetite was kicking in with a vengeance.

"I think it's a man who's sweet on my sister but is too shy to tell her, so he's leaving her secret gifts."

Caleb coughed. Sweet on Becca? More like meeting a need he knew for a fact she wouldn't accept face-to-face. His thoughts turned pensive. *Was* she involved

with someone? Adam had been gone a long time, over
a year. The men of this town couldn't be blind to her
attributes.

"Amy, really." She pursed her lips.

Amy shrugged. "She doesn't believe that theory,"
she informed him, leaning closer. "Rebecca's not a romantic like me."

Rubbing his hand along his scruffy jaw, he swallowed a retort. *That's not the Becca I knew.* The Becca
he'd known had walked around with stars in her eyes,
quoting Elizabeth Barrett Browning, and been convinced Adam was her storybook hero. Until Caleb
brought reality crashing down on all of them.

"Amy, have you finished your history report?" Becca
stood with a hand on her hip, a towel clutched tightly
in the other. "As soon as this snow melts, it'll be back
to school for you."

The younger girl's shoulders sagged. "I don't understand why I have to study something that happened
over a hundred years ago in a country I will never step
foot in."

"Mr. Crockett obviously thinks it's important or else
he wouldn't have given you the assignment. Besides,
there's a whole world out there. Learning about other
people and places expands your thinking. Life doesn't
begin and end in Gatlinburg, Tennessee, you know."

"I can't wait for Christmas break," she moaned,
trudging toward the bedroom. "Come on, Storm," she
beckoned to the dog, who immediately obeyed. "You
can keep me company in my misery."

Caleb hid a smile. He hadn't liked school all that

much, either. Why read about other people having adventures when you could experience one for yourself?

Thinking like that is what led me to this place, isn't it? Disfigured. Alone. And responsible for burdening his closest friends with a world of hurt and disillusionment.

"You're good with her. Your parents would be proud."

Sorrow flickered and was quickly concealed. "I do the best I can," she said tightly before turning to replace the spice jars on the shelf near the stove.

He'd been packing his bags for another hunting trip when his father had relayed the tragic news of their accident. Instantly, the need to go to her and offer what comfort he could had gripped him. Rebecca had enjoyed a close relationship with her parents, especially her pa. She'd adored Jim Thurston. Caleb had managed to master the impulse to see her that day, but he hadn't been able to stay away from the funeral.

"It was a beautiful service," he murmured, lost in memories and not fully aware he'd spoken aloud.

A large spoon slipped from her fingers and clattered onto the floorboards. "You were there?" Her brows crashed together in confused disbelief. "I didn't see you."

He was silent a moment. "Didn't figure you'd want to."

He'd kept to the edge of the crowd, careful not to show himself and cause her more upset. Aching for her profound loss, he'd longed to stride down the aisle to where she stood in between the twin caskets, shoulders quaking with emotion, and shelter her in his embrace.

"I thought…" Old hurts resurfaced.

Caleb blinked. Had she been disappointed by his supposed absence?

"I tried to stay away," he said quietly, "but I couldn't."

Jerking a nod, she bent to retrieve the spoon and placed it in the dry sink, then continued clearing off the work space as the stew simmered on the stove top. Her stiff movements shouted her wish to drop the conversation.

Caleb closed his eyes, transported to those awful, frustrating weeks afterward. He'd postponed his trip, wanting to be nearby on the off chance she might decide she needed him. Of course, she hadn't. What would she do if she found out he'd resorted to spying on her and Amy by way of his brother? Probably strangle him. Nathan had agreed to Caleb's plea to visit them and report back. After the fourth visit, Nathan had informed him that he was finished. People were starting to get the wrong impression.

The air stirred nearby, alerting him to her presence. He opened his eyes to see her clutching a porcelain mug.

"I remember how you preferred to be clean-shaven. Do you feel up to shaving yourself?"

She motioned to the mirror propped up on the table behind her, the brush, straight razor and box of Colgate shaving soap laid out. Struck by her thoughtfulness, Caleb didn't say anything for a long moment.

"I can help you to the table," she added.

"That won't be necessary," he murmured, tired of being weak in front of her. "If you'll just pull the chair out for me, I can make it on my own steam."

"I'll be right here in case you need me."

"I believe I can make it a couple of feet," he muttered drily, but by the time he finally sank into the hard-backed chair, he was winded and dizzy and his entire leg throbbed.

One look at his face and she huffed a sigh. Picking up the shaving brush, she moved in front of him and dipped up a dollop of shaving soap.

"What are you doing?"

The cool cream swiped along his jawline. "I'm saving you from further injury, that's what."

Her knees brushed against his. The accidental contact incited awareness he could ill afford. He clenched his fists. "You are not going to shave me."

Becca straightened, brush held midair. As if reasoning with a child, she stated calmly, "Hold up your hand."

When he just stared at her, she took hold of his right hand and lifted it. "Hold it out flat."

With a scowl, he did as she instructed. There was no disguising the slight trembling. She arched an I-told-you-so brow. He curled his fingers into a tight fist and lowered it to his lap.

"I refuse to tend any more wounds, Caleb O'Malley, so cease being stubborn and let me do this."

He cocked his head. "When did you get to be so bossy?"

"I grew up."

Right. His actions had had something to do with that. As had Adam's leaving town and her parents' deaths. Life's hard knocks had forged a strength of iron within her. The Becca he'd known had changed, and he was far too curious to discover the new facets of her personality for his own good.

The soft crackling of the fire permeated the silence

that fell between them. He kept still as she applied the cream. The sight of the shining blade in her hand gave him pause.

"Have you done this before?"

Not meeting his eyes, she said, "After the accident, whenever Doc was busy and Mrs. Tierney wasn't around, I would shave Adam."

As she bent to scrape off the first layer of bristles, his thoughts turned to his best friend. Caleb had tried to see him on several occasions, but Adam's parents had refused to allow him anywhere near their son. Couldn't blame them. Still, not being able to see him, to apologize to his face, had stung. To this day, Caleb hadn't delivered the apology his friend so rightly deserved.

Becca had stayed by Adam's side day and night. Throughout the long recovery, not once had she abandoned him. Devotion like that was rare. And Adam had turned his back on it as if it meant nothing.

"Why did he leave?" he asked.

The blade lifted from his skin. Jade eyes penetrated his. There need be no explanation as to who *he* was. "He said he'd changed too much to be the husband I needed him to be."

"You tried to convince him otherwise."

Betrayal flared deep in her eyes. "He didn't believe me."

"Becca, I—"

"No more questions." Her lips firmed. And seeing as how she wielded a sharp weapon in her hand and he was her least favorite person in the world, he complied.

She was just finishing up when boots sounded on the porch, followed by a sharp rap.

Caleb tensed.

"Relax." She laid aside the razor. "It's probably Louis and the others."

But it wasn't Louis or the sheriff or even Doc. It was Reverend Monroe. The sight of him troubled Caleb, though why it should he couldn't quite pinpoint.

"Reverend," she exclaimed. "What are you doing here?"

Rebecca clamped her lips together. That sounded incredibly rude. And a touch guilty? "I—I didn't expect to see you today."

While she liked and respected him, he would surely share Louis's opinion about their situation. A lot of folks in Gatlinburg knew her and Caleb well enough not to suspect them of wrongdoing, but there were those who made it their business to judge and condemn. Knowing that appearances were everything in their society, would he try to convince them it was in their best interest to marry?

Shrewd eyes set in a kind face slipped past her to where Caleb sat wiping the remaining bits of shaving cream from his lean cheeks. It didn't take Reverend Monroe long to assess the cozy, domestic scene. Her stomach clenched. What unfortunate timing.

"I was at Doc's office when Louis stopped by and explained what happened. I wanted to check on young Caleb here, as well as you and Amy."

Through the open doorway, Rebecca saw the sheriff dismounting his horse and Doc descending the squat, black buggy, medical bag in hand.

"That was considerate of you," she forced the words

out. "Please, come in." She pulled the door wider, masking her upset with what she hoped was a casual expression. "Can I take your hat?"

Handing it to her with a nod of thanks, he smoothed his short silver hair and proceeded to slip the buttons of his bulky coat free. This was to be a long visit, then.

"How are you holding up, Rebecca?" he asked quietly.

"Fine. Just fine." She pressed clammy hands to her midsection. "Would you like coffee?"

"That would certainly chase the chill away."

She ignored the questioning look Caleb shot her as she swept past. Going through the motions of heating water and setting out mugs, her hands shook. *There's no reason to be nervous. I've done nothing wrong. Even if the subject of marriage comes up, no one can force me into it. Besides, Caleb would never agree.*

Soon her tiny cabin was overrun with virile males. Doc Owens was extracting bottles and instruments from his battered leather bag. The reverend had taken up residence on the settee, petting a blissful-looking Storm while speaking with Amy, who'd come to investigate the commotion. The aloof and ruggedly handsome Sheriff Shane Timmons held himself apart, sharp gaze missing nothing. There was no sign of Louis.

The middle-aged physician took Caleb's wrist in hand to check his pulse. "I'll need to take a look at that wound, son."

Color etched Caleb's chiseled cheekbones. He was clearly unhappy being the center of attention. No doubt his current state of helplessness grated, too. He'd never been patient with his own limitations, pushing himself to the edge and beyond. She used to think he did it for the thrills. Now she wondered if there wasn't some deeper, hidden reason.

Rebecca approached the wingback chair where her sister sat. "Amy, let's wait in the bedroom while Doc examines Caleb."

Once inside the bedroom, the minutes stretched into a long, torturous hour. Rebecca nodded and grunted in all the right places during Amy's conversation, but her mind was out there with Caleb and the others. She hadn't heard the front door open and close, which meant no one had left. She'd hoped against hope the reverend would say a prayer and take his leave. His continued presence bothered her.

I'm not that naive girl anymore, going along with others' suggestions simply to please them. I'm a strong woman with my own opinions. No matter what's happening out there, they can't force me to wed Caleb.

Throughout Doc's exam and Shane's interrogation, Caleb's attention kept drifting to the reverend, who sat quietly listening. The hint of discomfort in Monroe's posture, the telltale weight of apprehension in his astute gaze, set Caleb's nerves on edge. Something was up. He just didn't know what.

The sheriff tucked the small pad of paper into his pocket. "You've given me plenty to go on. I'll round up a search party when I leave and share this information with the men."

"You'll keep me posted?"

With a nod, Shane retreated to the fireplace, propping an elbow on the mantel as Monroe finally pushed

to his feet and approached the bed. Doc's bulky form
was sprawled in one of the dining table chairs. His unreadable gaze tracked Monroe's progress.

The hairs on the back of Caleb's neck stood to attention. Suddenly he could identify with the animals he
hunted, could feel how it was to be prey. The air grew
heavy with foreboding.

Monroe took up residence at the foot of his bed,
fleshy hands folded neatly at his waist. "There's something we need to discuss with you, son."

Son? Caleb's body went rigid, exhaustion chased
away by surging adrenaline.

"Rebecca took you in and cared for you…nursed you
back to health, you might say, which is a blessing from
God. If she hadn't found you in time—" He cleared his
throat, Adam's apple bobbing. His eyes looked a little
sad. "The problem is your isolation here in this cabin.
You and Rebecca have spent many days and nights
alone together without supervision. And while we—"
he gestured to Shane and Doc Owens "—are confident
nothing untoward occurred, the same might not be said
of everyone in town."

Monroe's words rattled around in Caleb's brain,
refusing to connect into anything sensible. His gaze
probed Doc's face first, then Shane's. The young sheriff
looked slightly annoyed, as if he found the entire conversation ridiculous.

"Of course nothing occurred," Caleb snapped. "Even
if I hadn't been wounded, I would never have compro-
mised Becca in any way."

Had they all conveniently forgotten how much she
detested him?

"Of course you wouldn't. You've both been raised to follow God's principles. You are aware, however, that all it takes to ruin a reputation is the suggestion of impropriety. Rebecca will be subjected to ill-treatment if you do not marry her."

"*Marry* her?" He half snorted, half laughed.

Doc shifted in his chair. "This is hardly a matter to take lightly."

"You have lost your minds if you think Becca would ever agree to marry me." The momentary spark of humor fizzled. "She would willingly suffer gossip and public slights and much more, I'm sure, if that meant avoiding getting tangled up with me."

"And what of Amy?" Monroe said. "Would Rebecca place her in a position to be ridiculed and ignored, especially after everything she's endured with her parents passing at such a young age?"

No need to respond to that. Everyone in this room already knew the answer.

The headboard bit into Caleb's back as he sank farther into the mattress. Rebecca would do anything to protect Amy. Even sacrifice herself.

Monroe came around and perched on the bed's edge, his somber manner turning intense. "You're a good man, Caleb. I know this isn't easy. Sometimes God brings difficult things into our lives in order to make us stronger. Sometimes it's to increase our faith and other times He simply wants us to acknowledge we can't do everything in our own strength. I don't know why this happened, but I trust you will do everything in your power to safeguard your friend and her sister."

Caleb squeezed his eyes shut. "I need time to think."

"There isn't much time, I'm afraid. The longer we postpone putting this situation to rights, the worse the repercussions."

"You're gonna have to be patient." He tried not to glare at the reverend. "And understand this—even if I do decide to heed your warning, no one can force Becca into doing something she doesn't wanna do."

Chapter Nine

"Rebecca?"

Jumping up from the bed, she smoothed her skirts and opened the door. Shane Timmons stood on the other side. Brushing longish blond locks off his forehead, he wore an air of impatience. "Doc's getting ready to leave. He'd like a word."

"Right."

"I want to thank you for everything you did to save Caleb's life. Without his testimony, Tate's murderers would've gone free." Twin flames of determination burned in his hard blue eyes.

"I hope you find them soon."

"Until I do, don't let your guard down." He slapped his Stetson on his head and, with a nod to the others, took his leave.

Her gaze sought out Caleb. Propped up once more in the bed, his lower half wrapped in the quilt, his shuttered expression gave nothing away. She joined Doc at the door. He didn't appear particularly worried. Then again, he didn't look upbeat. He was hard to read at times.

"You did a fine job, Rebecca." Already clothed in his outer garments, he grasped the bag's handle with both hands. "We'll need to watch for signs the infection has returned, but he's young and strong. I'm hopeful the worst has passed. He'll need lots of rest." Indicating the handmade crutches in the corner, he said, "Make sure he doesn't put any weight on that leg. I'll come back in a couple of days to check his progress."

The relief that washed over her receded when it registered that preparations weren't being made for Caleb's departure. "I had assumed you'd want to move him to your office."

He shifted uncomfortably. "Well, now, I think that's something you should discuss with Reverend Monroe."

"I d-don't understand," she stuttered, fighting rising panic. "You're the doctor. Caleb is your patient. You should be the one to make decisions regarding his care."

Dear Lord, please, please *don't let this head where I think it's headed.*

Movement behind her had her whirling to face the reverend. "Rebecca, this is a sensitive situation. I'm sure you can appreciate that fact."

"No, actually, I can't. We haven't done anything wrong. I—I discovered a man *dying* in the snow. Am I to be punished for helping him?"

"Becca."

The command in Caleb's voice snapped her attention to him. He'd moved to sit on the edge of the bed, and what she saw in his eyes frightened her. Resignation. That's what had taken so long. Not Doc's examination or Shane's interrogation. They'd been discussing her reputation and how a hasty marriage could smooth away speculation and gossip.

"We'll figure this out," he said. Tension tightened his clean-shaven jaw, but there was no denying he'd fallen for their appeals to his honor. She could hear them now. *You've cast doubts upon her virtue. Folks will talk. It won't be pretty. Marry her and make it right.*

She felt like a cornered animal, and anger welled inside. "There's nothing to figure out."

"I believe the lady and I need some privacy, gentlemen." While his pallor and the pain etched in his features declared he was unwell, his demeanor brooked no argument.

"There's no need for privacy," she shot back, "because I won't marry you, Caleb O'Malley. Not now, not ever."

"You're making my head spin," Caleb complained, shifting the pillows so that the headboard didn't dig into his back. "Sit down so we can figure a way outta this mess."

Mess was putting it mildly. *Disaster* was more like it. Her frantic pacing wasn't really what was causing this sensation of being suspended from the rafters by his boots; it was the unwelcome surprise Monroe and Doc had dropped on him. He'd had absolutely no warning, no preparation. No words to combat their insinuations.

Marry Rebecca or she and Amy would suffer the consequences.

Him? The man she despised most in this world? Marry Becca? She would never agree. On the off chance she did succumb to their coercion, he couldn't in good conscience bind her to him, not when he knew how she felt about him, knew that every day for the rest of their lives his mutilated face would remind her afresh of the grief and turmoil he'd caused her.

Marrying her or any other woman was not something he was prepared to do. The night of the accident, he'd come to the realization that he was a danger to others. His very nature put those he cared about at risk. Look what happened to his mother last fall—a storm had come up and, because of his careless handling of the team, the wagon tipped, and she'd suffered a badly broken leg. His father had been covered with bruises. In spite of his efforts to stay away, he'd brought trouble to Becca's door. His very presence was putting two innocent lives in danger.

"I can't sit." Stormy green eyes shot daggers at the closed door through which the men had disappeared not five minutes ago. "I'm too wound up to sit." She threw her hands up.

"Becca, please." He pinched the bridge of his nose to ward off the ache building behind his eyes.

With a huff, she plopped into the chair and cast him a baleful glare. One knee bounced with impatience. "Do tell me, Caleb, how do you propose we handle this?"

"I don't have any answers. After all, I just learned of our predicament minutes ago. You, on the other hand, didn't seem surprised. Why is that?"

Long lashes lowered to skim cheeks high in color. "Meredith and Louis shared their concerns with me."

So Doc and the reverend weren't the only ones to spot potential problems. Not good. "And you didn't think I deserved to know? A warning might've been nice."

"I was hoping I wouldn't have to tell you." Defensiveness flared. "Anyway, they're welcome to their opinions. We both know we're innocent. That's all that matters."

Caleb wished he could agree. Indeed, despite her brave words, doubts lurked in the luminous depths. They both knew how small towns operated, how people's minds worked. In situations like this—a single man and woman sharing a small cabin for nearly a week— the tendency was to assume the worst.

She smoothed copper-streaked strands with unsteady fingers. "I don't like that look."

"What look is that?" His brows rose.

"The one where you agree with them." Pointing a finger at him, she surged to her feet. "I will not marry you."

"I don't recall asking," he drawled, schooling his features to mask the prick of hurt her repeated denials caused.

Her hands went to her hair again, twisting and tugging the mass into a thick roll. His fingers itched to take over the job, certain the strands would feel as satiny as they appeared. *Yeah, like I'd ever get the chance.*

"I suppose when the reverend comes tomorrow for our answer, we'll inform him of our decision. That we won't be pressured into a marriage neither of us want."

"Sounds reasonable." The headache bloomed into a full-on assault. He *hated* that he'd put her in this position. "What happens after I leave, though? Will you be able to ignore the inevitable gossip? What if folks shun you?"

Her chin jutted. "I can handle gossip. While there may be some who will be hateful, my true friends will stand by me."

His gaze strayed to the bedroom door. Amy hadn't been happy to be relegated to the room once again. Or had it been the fact she had to resume her schoolwork?

"And what of your sister?" He pitched his voice low. "Kids aren't always as forgiving or tactful as adults. I don't want her to be hurt because of something I did."

He absently rubbed the tiny scars fanning out beside his eye, the sensitive, puckered skin smarting as he did so. If he disappeared into the high country, they'd be left behind to bear the brunt of scandal. He'd escape it all. Something deep inside—his conscience, his sense of honor as a man—balked at the idea. It would be the sawmill accident all over again…others suffering because of his actions.

But what other course did he have?

Becca bit her lip. Clearly she hadn't considered how the thirteen-year-old would handle the fallout. "She's been through so much already…." Troubled, she resumed her pacing, though this time her feet seemed weighted, her steps lagging. Finally, she handed him a determined look. "We'll just have to deal with it the best we can. We don't have a choice."

"It seems I owe you yet another apology," he said quietly, hands fisting on the quilt. "I couldn't fix things two years ago, and I can't fix them now. Either way I turn, you'll be hurt."

"It's not like you pointed Rebel in my direction and chose to black out in my backyard," she conceded.

Now probably wouldn't be a good time to point out

that Rebel knew the way to her farm almost as well as he knew the way home, seeing as how they'd come here time and time again to leave fresh meat.

"I'm sure the gossip will subside after a couple of weeks," she said. "With you gone on another one of your excursions, folks will forget soon enough. Out of sight, out of mind."

Ouch. Was that her way of saying he was forgettable?

"You will still be here, however. You and Amy." He wasn't convinced the matter would dissipate so easily.

"We'll deal with it like we've dealt with everything else—together and with God's help."

There was nothing left to say, was there? If she was comfortable with handling things here without him, then he'd have to go along with it. He only hoped the price Becca paid for helping him wouldn't prove too high.

Caleb stirred, confused as to exactly when he'd drifted off to sleep, slowly registering a presence beside the bed. Shifting his head on the pillow, his gaze met a pair of silver eyes that were dark with worry.

He groaned, braced himself for a lecture. "Nathan."

"I would ask you how you're feeling, little brother." He folded his arms across his chest and leveled him a penetrating stare. "But it's fairly obvious. I'm glad Ma agreed to postpone her visit." Threading fingers through dark brown hair grown longer than usual, he leaned forward and rested his elbows on his knees. "Louis told me you'd been shot, but I didn't realize how bad off you were."

"Doc says I'm on the mend." Scooting up, he bit the

inside of his cheek to keep from grimacing as pain radiated outward from the bullet hole.

"If that's the case, I don't wanna even think about what you must've looked like when Rebecca found you."

Caleb scanned the living and kitchen areas. Judging from the waning light filtering through the curtains, dusk was close at hand. Had he slept through supper? "Where is she?"

"In the barn with Amy."

He massaged his temples, the headache reemerging as he recalled their predicament and the thorough lack of satisfying resolutions.

"Did she take a gun with her?"

His eyes narrowed. "Yes, as a matter of fact, she did. What happened out there, Caleb?"

Nathan listened with grim attention as he relayed the events leading up to his losing consciousness not far from her cabin. "You've told Timmons all this, right?"

"He's gathering up men as we speak. They're leaving at first light tomorrow morning." Nathan didn't need to know about his plan to eventually join the search party. He would only argue against it.

"I wonder if any of Cades Cove's residents are involved."

"It's entirely possible."

Nathan's frown deepened. "We need to get a letter to Evan and Juliana."

Did their cousin and her husband even realize there was trouble? "There's a chance no one suspects Tate's missing. He could've had business in another town."

Business that wouldn't be completed. The image of the young lawman on his knees, head held high and righteous anger burning in his eyes as he faced down death, seized Caleb. Regret clamped like a vise about his lungs. If only he'd devised a better plan, moved faster—

Fingers squeezed his shoulder. "Hey, are you okay?"

Caleb's eyes flew open. Nathan was standing over the bed, face hovering too close. "Yeah, why?"

"You just went two shades whiter than the pillowcase." His mouth flattened as he pointed to Caleb's leg. "I wanna see it."

"And have you keel over like a schoolgirl? There may not be fresh blood, but it ain't pretty." His mouth slanted with self-mocking. "One more scar to add to the collection."

Balancing his weight against the footboard, his older brother studied him. "This couldn't have been easy for either of you."

"Understatement of the year."

"When she answered the door, she looked as if her world had come to an end."

"That's because the powers-that-be are pressuring us to marry."

Nathan's jaw dropped. "*What* did you say?"

"Think about it, Nate. I've spent a week in her home. She's dealt with things an unmarried woman oughtn't. Monroe walking in on her shaving me didn't help matters."

Scrubbing a hand down his face, Nathan shook his head. He, of all people, understood how this would impact them both. "What are you gonna do?"

"What do you expect me to do? One, I'm not fit for marriage. Two, she hates my guts. I couldn't force her to wed me even if I wanted to." When Nathan's brow twitched, Caleb rushed to add, "Which I don't."

"You were close once upon a time. Surely she harbors some tender feelings for you, else she wouldn't have taken you in."

"Becca's not heartless, and you know it. She wouldn't have left me out there to die."

"I don't believe she hates you. She's still angry, that's all."

"It's more than that. The woman can't stand the sight of me, Nate." He sighed. "Help me get home."

"Have you lost your mind?"

"I can ride a horse just fine. I'll rest better in my own bed."

Not that he planned on doing much of that. He'd give his leg a day or so to rest and then he was going hunting. For two-legged beasts this time. Shane Timmons had promised to put all his energy into finding the perpetrators, and Caleb trusted the no-nonsense lawman to do just that. Still, he had a personal stake in this. It was his hide if Shane and his men failed. Better to hunt than to be hunted. Injury or no, he couldn't sit around and wait for trouble to come to him.

"I won't do it." Of course his brother would be stubborn.

"The longer I stay here, the more damage Becca's reputation will suffer. Not to mention those thugs could trail me here."

"What if you leave and they trail you here? What then?"

Caleb fisted his hands. It wasn't impossible, but the odds were greater if he stuck around.

"You have to give up this irrational notion that you can protect the ones you care about by staying away. I tried my best to keep Sophie safe and look what happened… Landon accosted her. When I was out there in the woods, left to die, I came face-to-face with the truth—I'm not in control. God is."

"He also gives us free will to make good or bad choices. My life is littered with bad choices. I can't afford to put anyone else in harm's way. Look at what happened to Ma."

"That was not your fault." Nathan crossed his arms and glared at him. "The storm spooked the horses. If anything, your management of the team prevented her from getting hurt worse." His stance softened. "You need to pray about this situation with Rebecca."

He snorted. "God doesn't wanna hear from me."

"You're wrong, brother. He loves you."

Head pounding and every nerve ending in his leg ablaze with pricks of white-hot heat, Caleb turned his face toward the wall. If he couldn't convince Nathan to help him, he was finished with this conversation. "Tell Sophie and Will I said hi."

"Get some rest." He sighed. "I'll be back soon."

"I'm afraid the news of your injury has already traveled through town."

Reverend Monroe had arrived precisely at ten o'clock, an air of gloom hovering around him and his head-to-toe black suit. Towering beside the bed, he looked expectantly at Caleb. Waiting for him to concede the need for a hasty wedding?

Rebecca shivered as a cold draft slammed against

the door. This day—her seventh with Caleb under her roof—had been marked with a low, impenetrable ceiling of gray clouds and blustery winds. She was beginning to wonder if she'd ever see the sun again.

The reverend's apologetic gaze switched to her. "There's already been talk. At the mercantile, post office. Folks are seeking me out, demanding information. I would like nothing more than to shield you and your sister from unpleasant gossip, but I can't."

"It will pass," Rebecca said.

Of course Caleb, with his honed, hawklike perception, would zone in on the slight crack in her confidence. Anger on their behalf simmered in his hot gaze. "I'm not so sure about that."

"It's not just gossip I'm concerned about. There are those who will deliberately cut you and Amy out of their lives. I know you can likely handle such behavior, but what of your sister?" the reverend said gently. "Considering the difficulty she's had dealing with the unexpected deaths of your parents, I would hate to see her hurt again."

Shoving out of the chair, Rebecca stalked to the fireplace and stared down into the orange-yellow flames, her back to both men. Doubts pummeled her. While it wouldn't be pleasant, she was strong enough to withstand being shunned. Amy, on the other hand, was young and impressionable, practical yet in many ways very sensitive. What if the kids at school treated her differently? Already her parents had been ripped from her. School had become a haven, a place of innocence and security and fun. How would Amy cope if that haven became a place of anxiety and unpleasantness?

Lost in what-ifs and distasteful scenarios, she didn't

hear the movement behind her. Suddenly Caleb's lean, hardened body loomed over her. She couldn't stop a gasp of surprise.

He was upright. Relying on crutches to support his weight, granted, but upright, making it necessary for her to actually lift her face to meet his eyes. His dark beauty hit her like a tangible force—the sleek black hair and glittering brown eyes set in a carved, pale face like a marble statue—perfect in every way save for the angry red lines fanning from his right eye to his hairline. Deep inside her disillusioned, lonely heart, hunger awakened, a yearning for solace and rest, connection and companionship. For just a little while, how wonderful it would be to let someone else shoulder the burden of running the farm and seeing to Amy's needs.

Swallowing hard, she stepped back, away from the temptation Caleb unexpectedly presented. He was not the man to offer her any of those things. *He's the enemy, remember?*

The hard line of his jaw broadcasting his determination, he gazed down at her like a man minutes from facing a firing squad.

"We need to talk."

A warning knell reverberated through her system. "No, we don't."

He ignored her retort. "Despite all the reasons a marriage between us defies logic..." He paused, braced himself. "I think we should consider it."

Chapter Ten

Rebecca gaped at him, half tempted to feel his forehead for signs the fever had returned. But the haze of illness no longer clouded his eyes. He was composed, focused. "Have you lost your mind?"

He grimaced, baring even, white teeth. "Apparently so, considering I've been asked that question twice in as many days."

"You can't be serious." She glanced past him to the reverend, who had seated himself at the table and was staring into his coffee mug, attempting to be as inconspicuous as possible.

Hobbling closer, Caleb leaned in and spoke in hushed tones. "I know how you feel about me. I remind you of everything you've lost. And when I look at you…"

Rebecca's breath stalled. Her heart thumped. Hung suspended. Surged again as his dark gaze roamed her face as if memorizing a map.

"I'm reminded of how greatly I failed my closest friends." He frowned. "But this doesn't just involve us. How we handle this will affect Amy for the rest of her life. I'm prepared to do what's best for her. And for you."

Her focus riveted to his mouth hovering an inch from her nose, she forgot all about the reverend sitting at her table. The spicy scent of the shaving soap still clung to his skin, scrambling her senses. He sounded so…mature. So *un*selfish. Nothing like the careless teenager she'd once known.

"I hardly know what to say," she whispered. "What you're suggesting is, well, it's…" *Crazy. Deranged. Guaranteed to make them both miserable.* "Impossible."

A muscle ticked in his jaw. "Is there someone else besides Adam you're set on marrying?"

Out of habit, she fingered the locket nestled between the buttons of her turquoise cotton blouse. Caleb zeroed in on the movement, and she dropped her hand to her side.

"No, of course not." Unable to sustain his demanding gaze, she stared into the fire. She'd accepted that marriage was most likely not going to happen for her, had considered moving east to stay with her aunt and uncle once Amy was grown and settled. The sea and its many creatures would make delightful subjects for her paintings.

He dipped his head, bringing their cheeks side by side. "Then why not marry me?"

The movement of his lips near her ear snagged strands of hair. Rebecca stilled, terrified to move, mortified by what his nearness was doing to her equilibrium. "It would be a marriage in name only," he whispered, his breath fanning across her cheek, "to satisfy the gossips. I spend most of my time in the high country, anyway, which means I wouldn't even be around to bother you. Your life will go on much the same as it did before. When I'm around, I'll help out with whatever needs to be done."

"And what about you?" she murmured, his shirt collar and throat filling her vision. "Don't you want to wait for a real marriage? One based on love and trust?"

Inching back so that he could meet her gaze, his upper lip curled. He hiked his right shoulder to indicate the scar. "With this mug? I don't think so. Besides, I'm not looking for love. Too self-absorbed." The stark loneliness warring with self-derision in the brown depths cut through her defenses.

"Why would you do this?" She stared deep into his eyes.

His throat worked. "I've let you down in the past. Multiple times. It's my fault we're in this mess, and I want to make it right. Fix it for you the only way I know how."

"You'd be miserable."

"So would you," he shot back. "But Amy wouldn't be, would she?"

She closed her eyes. A lifetime with Caleb wasn't a dream come true. More like a nightmare from which she'd never wake. "I can't."

"I warned them that would be your response."

Forcing herself to look at him, she wasn't surprised when she was unable to read his mood. He'd had plenty of practice masking his emotions. "We can't give them that kind of power over our lives, Caleb. Neither of us wants this. Amy is my responsibility. I'll see to it that she isn't hurt."

"That's just it, Becca. I'm not sure you can prevent it."

* * *

Caleb left that afternoon.

As soon as they informed the reverend of their decision, he offered to fetch Nathan to move Caleb to their parents' home. Given the steely determination in the older man's gaze, it wasn't an offer so much as an order. Their resistance clearly irked him.

Caleb had been quiet, his manner bordering on brooding, as they waited for his brother to arrive. Right before he left, he'd turned back and made her promise to come to him if she encountered any trouble.

Rebecca couldn't get the intensity with which he'd said it out of her head, his seeming reluctance to leave. Probably her imagination. He must be as eager as she was to put this behind them.

Wringing excess water from the sheets Caleb had slept on, she strung them on a makeshift clothesline near the fireplace and tried to ignore the change in the cabin's atmosphere. The weight of the silence was choking, as if his departure had sucked the energy and life from her home.

"See? Refusing him was the right thing," she told herself, maneuvering the sudsy water basin across the floor toward the door. "Caleb has the uncanny ability to shred your good judgment."

Amy was on the stairs, stomping the snow from her boots, when Rebecca opened the door. "Can you give me a hand with this?"

"Okay."

Together, they carried the unwieldy load behind the house. The sun peeked through the clouds, glistening on the melting snow and warming Rebecca's skin. Tipping the water out, Amy blew strands of hair out of her eyes.

"We have practice for the Christmas pageant tomorrow night. Should I walk to church or do you think Toby can manage the trip?"

Rebecca held the empty basin in one hand and kneaded her lower back with the other. "I'd like to go to town. How about we walk in together?"

Storm chose that moment to bound out of the forest, short legs splashing through the stream and startling them both. Amy nibbled at her lower lip. "Are you worried about the men looking for Caleb? Is that the reason you want to come with me?"

Her sister wasn't aware of Rebecca and Caleb's situation, and for once, she wasn't sure what to reveal and what to keep hidden. While she wasn't Amy's parent, it sure felt like it sometimes, and she struggled to know what to do.

"I simply need a change of scenery." Linking arms with Amy, she led her around to the porch. "And there are ingredients I need for the baking I have planned."

"Are we going to make gingerbread cookies again this year?"

Rebecca smiled. Last Christmas had been their first without their parents. She'd hit upon the idea of making gingerbread cookies together, thinking it would be nice to start a tradition of their own. "Would you like that?"

Earnestness sparkled in her blue eyes. "Very much."

Inside, they assembled a simple meal of fried potatoes, ham and corn bread. Neither mentioned Caleb, but she caught Amy's gaze on his empty chair several times.

"You must be relieved to have your own bed again."

"I didn't mind sharing with you." Sliding a stare at the bed, her brow furrowed. "I miss having Caleb around."

"How about I play a game of checkers with you?"

"I thought you were going to paint."

"I can paint later."

Staying busy was the only way to keep their minds off their recent guest. Eventually his brief stay would be nothing but a fuzzy memory.

After they had played five games—with Amy besting Rebecca every time—the younger girl settled on the settee with a book and Rebecca took up her paints and paintbrush, deliberately painting a snowy landscape instead of the beguiling face that refused to leave her mind.

She passed a fitful night, worries presenting themselves in upsetting dreams. Had the trip across town caused Caleb undue pain? Was he getting the proper rest? Eating enough?

Where were the outlaws right this minute? Was refusing to marry him the right decision?

By the time pageant practice rolled around Thursday evening, Rebecca's nerves were stretched taut. Depositing her cloak in the church alcove, she cringed as the kids' chatter filling the main room struck her ears. Her skin felt too tight. Her legs were the consistency of molasses.

Amy dashed down the nearest aisle, braids flapping, and Rebecca stifled the urge to call her back.

Stop being ridiculous. I've nothing to be apprehensive about.

Strolling toward the front, she watched as her sister

joined her dearest friends, Clarice and Laney, who were leaning against the piano. The girls pressed close to Amy and began whispering furiously. A couple of feet away, Oliver and Philip Pelletier laughed and pointed her direction, garnering the other children's attention.

Rebecca stopped and seized hold of the nearest pew. It was like watching a field of parched grass catch fire, the flames leaping from stalk to stalk until the entire expanse had been consumed.

The dawning anxiety on Amy's face confirmed every worry she'd wrestled with since turning Caleb down.

"Rebecca?"

Ripping her gaze away, she had trouble focusing on the beautiful young woman before her. A riot of white-blond curls framed fair features that were a study of concern.

"Megan. Hello."

Megan Beaumont was in charge of organizing the pageant. She was also Caleb's cousin.

"Are you okay?" she said. "You're looking quite pale. Would you like to sit down?"

"I—"

Snippets of conversation among some of the parents drifted over. None of it complimentary. Their speculation as to what had happened between her and Caleb drove hot color to her cheeks.

Megan laid a hand on her arm, her sea-colored eyes intense. "Thank you for helping Caleb."

Rebecca merely nodded, plucking at her suddenly too-snug bodice.

"I'm sorry you've been placed in this situation. My family and I will support you in any way we can."

"I appreciate the sentiment."

She wondered what to do. Stay and endure the stares? Embarrass Amy further by taking her home before practice commenced? It wasn't as if Rebecca was a stranger to gossip. Her broken engagement and Adam's subsequent departure had been the preferred topic of discussion for months on end.

But this felt different.

She wasn't the victim any longer. She was the perpetrator of imagined misdeeds.

"Mrs. Beaumont," a young voice called out, "we have a question."

Megan hesitated, clearly torn. "I have to get practice under way. If you need to talk, I'm always available."

Then she was hurrying to address the child's concerns. Keeping her gaze straight ahead, Rebecca sank onto the bench. Leaving would only make her look guilty.

"We shouldn't have come here."

Rebecca sipped the ginger-laced tea, letting the hot liquid soothe her throat, while sneaking glances at the café's other patrons. The speculative gazes she encountered quickly skidded away, followed by hushed whispers.

Her teacup rattled as she placed it on its saucer. "I told you this was a bad idea."

Across from her, Meredith leaned forward, stark white cup cradled in her hands. "You can't hide out in your cabin forever. This will pass."

At least Plum's wasn't crowded this late in the afternoon. The proprietor, Mrs. Greene, emerged from the kitchen to deliver their cinnamon buns. Her compassionate gaze settled on Rebecca.

"I know you're going through a rough time, dear. I wanted to tell you I admire you for sticking to your convictions. Keep your chin up."

Rebecca's response was cut off by the approach of another patron, Ruthanne Moore, whose husband owned Clawson's Mercantile across the street. "Don't listen to her." She waved a heavily ringed hand. "Unless you want to wind up a lonely spinster."

Mrs. Greene sighed. "Now isn't the time, Ruthanne."

The buxom blonde rolled her eyes. "You brought it up. Besides, it's not like Rebecca doesn't know she's the topic of conversation at every table here."

Meredith caught Rebecca's attention and mouthed, *I'm sorry.*

Ruthanne dropped a hand on Rebecca's shoulder. "Listen to me, honey. That Caleb O'Malley is a fine specimen. Snag him while you still have a chance."

By now, all conversation had ceased, and their table was the focus of everyone in the café. "Thanks for the advice," she mumbled, certain she couldn't force a bite of the sweet treat down. "Mrs. Greene, would you mind wrapping this up? I'll take it home with me."

Brows meeting over her nose, the proprietor nodded, removed the plate and steered Ruthanne away.

Gaze lowered, Rebecca fiddled with the delicate cup handle.

"Don't let it get to you," Meredith urged in a soft whisper. "The news is still fresh. Another month and everyone will have forgotten all about it."

"I don't know, Mer. What if they don't? What if I made the wrong decision?"

After practice last night, Amy had been uncharacteristically quiet. Rebecca's every attempt to draw her out had been rebuffed and, like a coward, she'd allowed the matter to drop.

"I have a feeling this will forever taint my reputation. I'll always be the girl who sheltered a man unchaperoned in my home. There will be questions in people's minds about my moral standing, about my virtue."

"Not in everyone's," Meredith said fiercely. "Your friends, those who've known you your whole life, won't question anything. We'll support you."

"What about Amy? There's no question in my mind now that she will suffer because of my actions."

Meredith was aware of Amy's sensitivity, due to both her tender age and the tragedy that had visited her life.

"If you marry Caleb, you will be the one to suffer."

"Better me than her," she said.

Meredith patted her hand. "If I had siblings, I hope I'd be the kind of sister you are to her."

Mrs. Greene brought the wrapped-up treat. "I put an extra in there for your sister."

"That was thoughtful of you." When Rebecca loosened the strings on her reticule, the older lady put out a staying hand.

"It's on me this time."

They thanked her and gathered their things, ignoring the lingering stares. Strolling along Main Street, Rebecca trained her gaze on the quaint church framed by bare-limbed trees and low, grayish white clouds. The stained-glass windows and festive greenery adorning

the entrance added welcome color to the dreary landscape. Pine and smoke from burning woodstoves sharpened the cold air.

They left the businesses behind and walked along
the dirt road leading to their respective homes. "Caleb
spends most of his time in the high country," she said.
"*If* we were to marry, he wouldn't be around that much."

Meredith twirled the tan-colored reticule dangling
from her wrist. "Good point. And when he is around,
he could fix things around your farm."

She studied the winter-dead forest to their right and
longed for spring's vibrant beauty. Marrying Caleb
wouldn't be *entirely* disadvantageous, she supposed.

They stopped at the entrance to her cove. Meredith's
pretty green eyes were troubled. "What if you married
him and then Adam came back?"

Her breath caught. "Adam has made his feelings clear.
He's not going to change his mind."

Battling a frown, Meredith gave Rebecca a quick
hug. "I'll be praying, sweetie."

Throat thick with gratitude, Rebecca watched as
Meredith continued on her way before entering the cove.
She found Amy on the porch rocker, head in her hands.

Jogging across the yard, she knelt at her feet. "What's
wrong? Are you sick?"

Amy slowly lifted her head, and Rebecca gasped at
the angry scratches lining her left cheek. "What happened?"

Fresh tears joined already dried tracks. "They said
horrible things about you." She sniffled. "I couldn't
stand by and do nothing."

She fought to keep her anger hidden. "Laney and Clarice weren't involved, were they?"

"No. They defended me." Amy looked a little defiant. "Are you mad at me?"

"No, I'm not." She was mad at this entire, nightmarish situation. "However, you're aware that violence isn't the answer."

"The teacher wants you to come and see him Monday morning to talk about my punishment."

"And what about the other girls involved? Are they to be reprimanded, as well?"

Amy nodded, eyes darkening. "Why do they think you should marry Caleb?"

How to explain this? "It's complicated."

The sound of an approaching team had her pivoting in her crouched position. Two men occupied the wagon—one guiding the team, the other sitting in the wagon bed.

"Who's that?"

Rebecca reluctantly pushed to her feet, her stomach a jumble of nervous anticipation. "Caleb."

Chapter Eleven

He was probably the last person Rebecca wanted to see, but he hadn't been able to stay away. Not after news of last night's fiasco and today's school altercation reached him.

Nathan held his crutches out to him, waiting by the wagon as Caleb hobbled closer to the cabin. Draped in her lush, fur-lined cape, black-and-blue-striped skirts peeking out from beneath the hem, Rebecca stood like a soldier at attention, ready for anything he might throw at her. Her copper-streaked hair was arranged in a neat chignon, putting those lovely cheekbones on display as well as the slender column of her throat, the pink curve of her ears.

He'd missed her. Thought about her every minute. Not that he'd ever admit it to her or anyone else.

"I heard about what happened."

Her eyes, such a striking shade of green, hit his, and he faltered at the hint of desperation there. "How?"

"Megan stopped by this morning." He gripped the handles tighter, recalling his outrage as she related the story. "As for what happened at school." He paused, wincing at the sight of the marks on Amy's skin. "Will told Sophie, who told Nathan, who told me."

Will, Sophie's ten-year-old brother and Nathan's brother-in-law, had been upset about what happened. He and Amy were friends.

"Are you okay, Amy?" he said softly.

Tears welled in her eyes. Gaze sliding away, she nodded. To Rebecca, she said, "Do you mind if I go inside?"

Rebecca pressed the wrapped cinnamon buns into Amy's hands. "Mrs. Greene sent you a treat."

"Thanks," Amy mumbled.

When the door clicked behind her, Nathan moved closer. "I'm going for a walk."

"You don't have to go." Rebecca gripped the nearest post.

Was she being polite or simply didn't want to be alone with him?

His brother flashed an enigmatic smile. "I don't mind. Could use the exercise."

When Nathan was some distance away, she returned her attention to Caleb. "Why did you come?"

"Because I knew you'd never come to me, in spite of your promise."

Her lips pursed, but she didn't deny it. "How's your leg?"

"Manageable." He swung closer to the steps. "Look, can I come up there? I'm getting a crick in my neck."

"Would you like to come inside?"

"I think Amy could use some space right about now."

Lifting her skirts, she descended the steps, boots

sinking slightly into the ground moist with snow-melt. "You didn't have to check up on us, you know."

"My offer still stands, Becca."

The color leached from her face. While her features were a composed mask, her luminous eyes were a deep, green, swirling tornado of despondency. "If we marry, it will be as if we're admitting to wrongdoing."

"Folks have already made up their minds about that. Marrying will make things right in the eyes of the community. The gossip will fade. The situation at school will settle."

She stalked away from him, glaring into the distance.

Caleb waited, throat as dry as sandpaper and pulse all over the place.

His future hinged on her answer. If she said no, he'd leave this cove, never to return. No more anonymous gifts. He'd have to find another way to help her out that didn't involve coming here. Once the outlaws were captured, he'd go back to sleeping beneath the stars, his worldly possessions stowed in his saddlebags and nothing but his horse to keep him company. Not the life he'd dreamed of, exactly, but it was what he deserved.

If she said no, he wouldn't be asking a third time.

She hung her head. "Okay."

"Okay?"

Becca pivoted to face him. "Okay, I'll do it."

For a second, his world seemed to dip and twirl, and he gripped the crutch handles until the wood bit into his palms.

"You have to promise to stick to the deal," she continued without emotion. "This is a marriage on paper only. We will live separate lives."

Caleb had to call on all his powers of concentration in order to process her words. He was getting married. To Becca. And all he could feel was fear and guilt. She was his best friend's sweetheart.

Her tumultuous gaze stabbed him. "Promise me, Caleb."

"I promise I'll return to the high country just as soon as Tate's killers are behind bars."

"And what if they evade capture? What then?"

"They won't. I'll personally see to that." Even if that meant he had to scour the thirty-eight states.

"Let me be the one to break the news to Amy."

"Fine. I'll let the reverend know he has a wedding to perform."

Becca grimly nodded. In that moment, Caleb felt cheated somehow. While he hadn't once imagined himself proposing to a woman, he was pretty sure his prospective bride shouldn't be looking at him as if he'd ruined her life.

Weddings meant music and food and pretty dresses and gifts, a celebration to mark the beginning of a couple's new life. She should know. She'd been planning one not so long ago.

Here she was engaged again, only to the wrong groom. The very notion of standing up before her friends and Caleb's family, along with those close-minded people who'd likely questioned their innocence, had made her break out in a cold sweat. She simply could not do it.

So she'd asked Caleb if he'd mind a private ceremony, here in her cabin, with only Amy for a witness. To her immense relief, he'd agreed.

Rebecca had had less than twenty-four hours to come to terms with the fact she was about to become Mrs. Caleb O'Malley.

"Rebecca, are you sure you don't want to wear Mama's wedding dress?"

Amy's disappointed gaze swept her dress of aquamarine overlaid with black netting. She had come into the bedroom to tell her that Caleb and the reverend had arrived. Looking at her reflection in the mirror, Rebecca slid in the final hairpin and inhaled deeply, trying to calm her heartbeat.

"We'll save it for your special day, okay?" she murmured, striving to keep her voice free of emotion.

The sting of discarded plans speared her heart. She'd tried her mama's dress on once. The morning after Adam proposed, she'd watched as her mother had carefully lifted the lace-and-pearl dress from the carved pine chest at the foot of her bed and handed it to her, tenderness and pride marking her expression. How could she possibly wear the exquisite white dress—a reminder of her mother's love for her father and the hope and commitment with which she'd approached her vows— as she pledged to honor, love and obey the one man responsible for tearing her heart apart?

"But you looked beautiful in it. And don't you want a cake? What's a wedding without a cake?"

"Amy, please." She shot her a pleading look. This time, she couldn't conceal the strain she was under. *Of course* she wanted a memorable wedding, one she could look back on with fondness. This wasn't about getting what she wanted, though, was it? This was about unfortunate circumstances and appearances and repairing reputations.

There was a knock on her door. Caleb stood on the other side, strikingly handsome in a black suit that emphasized the breadth of his shoulders and lean torso, inky hair shiny against his skin. Concern—and apprehension?—darkened his eyes.

"Are you ready to do this?"

The reverend appeared at his shoulder. "Good morning, Rebecca. Where would you like to exchange your vows?" He smiled encouragingly.

This was all wrong.

This wasn't how his wedding day was supposed to go.

His bride should *want* to marry him. His family should be here. Becca's friends, too.

What was supposed to be a celebration felt more like a mourning of lost dreams.

When he'd asked her yesterday when she wanted to get married, he'd been expecting her to stall. Throw up barricades. That she'd suggested a quick ceremony would be best was yet another reminder that she'd changed. That he no longer truly understood the woman who was about to become his wife unsettled him, as did the forbidden yearning to delve deeper, to explore her mysteries. He'd promised not to stick around. Just because he was suddenly intrigued with the idea of being married to Becca didn't mean he could renege on that promise.

The reverend was looking from her to him for an answer to his question.

"In front of the fireplace will do," he muttered when it became clear Becca wasn't going to answer.

Maneuvering on his crutches to the striped rug beside the hearth, he propped one against the stones, then turned to balance on the other. Storm didn't seem to mind having her nap interrupted. Stretching her stubby legs, she sauntered over to the settee and hopped up on the muted floral cushion, big eyes curious as Monroe moved into place and blocked her view.

Then Becca was in front of him, gaze glued to the fire, cheeks snowy-white and lips colorless. The complete lack of color in her face spurred Caleb to action. Using his free hand, he reached out and snagged hers. Small. Fragile. Skin so cold it hurt to touch, like the chunks of ice that formed in the mountaintop springs.

Her eyes snapped to his, wide and questioning. Lips parted. When she didn't reject his overture, Caleb applied gentle pressure, thumb skimming her knuckles to create friction. He wanted warmth back in her hand and color in those cheeks. Couldn't very well get hitched if she was passed out cold on the floor, could they?

"Amy." The older man gestured to where she hovered by the chair. "Why don't you come and stand near your sister? You're our witness today."

While Becca's fingers remained limp between his, her molten gaze did not leave his for a second. Not when Amy took up her position. Not when the reverend began extolling the virtues of marriage and commitment and faithfulness. Not when they recited the sacred vows that would tie them together for all eternity.

Caleb got lost in the fathomless depths, found himself yearning to erase the loneliness and patch up the brokenness he glimpsed in her soul. It was a fool thing, really, because he was the last person who could help Rebecca. He couldn't help himself. What made him think he could give her even a thimbleful of happiness?

He was everything she despised—a selfish, rash ne'er-do-well.

"You may kiss the bride."

Those words ripped her gaze away. Becca stared at the reverend, who merely smiled. "It's part of the ceremony."

His new bride looked back at him, defiant, no trace of the sweet, naive girl he'd once known. In her place was a strong woman almost fierce in her independence. Beautiful, desirable in every way, yet unattainable.

Don't you dare, she silently reproached.

It hit him then that this was one opportunity he couldn't let pass. He was not noble. Nor was he a gentleman. Why not act as everyone expected him to? It wasn't like she'd ever allow him close again.

Tugging on her hand so that she stumbled forward, he ignored her outraged gasp and lowered his mouth to hers. The tremor that shook Becca's graceful form threw him. Was it disgust? If so, why did her velvet-soft lips cling to his in unspoken wonder? Why did the hand splayed against his stomach not push him away? Her sweet breath mingling with his, Caleb battled the insane urge to haul her against him and kiss her properly.

Her little sister was watching. That gave him pause.

With great reluctance, he broke contact. Eyes still closed, mouth upturned as if begging for more, Becca swayed. Caleb watched with surprising regret as reason returned. Her lids popped open, and hot-pink color surged up the swanlike column of her neck and into her cheeks. Shock, quickly followed by humiliation and outrage, danced through her magnificent eyes. Jerking her hand from his, she scuttled back.

Looking very pleased with himself, Monroe announced, "Congratulations! You are now husband and wife."

"I—" A trembling hand covered her mouth. "P-please excuse me."

Rushing from the room, the soft click of the bedroom door was as effective as if she'd slammed it. While Amy looked confused, Monroe cast him a concerned glance.

In that moment, he thought she must surely hate him.

Calling herself all sorts of a fool, Rebecca rested her forehead against the windowpane, welcoming the cold filtering through the thin glass as it cooled the heat fizzing along her nerve endings. Caleb's heat. He'd *known* she hadn't wanted him to kiss her, and yet he'd done it, anyway. To goad her? Or was he merely curious?

Whatever the reason, she wished it undone. Her lips recalled the insistent press of his well-formed mouth, her body the deep well of dissatisfaction their brief connection had spawned. *She'd wanted more, had longed to feel his strong arms around her, his hands in her hair.*

Recalling how she'd weaved toward him after he'd pulled away, Rebecca's cheeks burned with fresh humiliation. She couldn't for the life of her fathom why she hadn't protested from the start. Shoved him away. He was her nemesis!

Maybe it was the tender way he'd held her hand all through the ceremony. Maybe it was the way he'd looked at her, as if her happiness mattered—something no one else had seemed to care about since her parents' deaths.

It was shameful how she'd allowed herself to become weak and needy like that. She'd rather be numb than feel anything remotely similar to longing for Caleb O'Malley. Her *husband*.

Knees threatening to give out, she sank onto the corner of the bed and buried her head in her hands. There was no going back now. For better or worse, she was an O'Malley. Caleb's wife. The reality of what she'd done—consigned herself to a loveless, in-name-only marriage—weighed on her heart like a stone. She would never experience the love and affection of a man whose heart cherished her as a wife and best friend. The miracle of childbirth would be denied her, as would the rearing of a precious child.

Maybe I could convince Caleb—

She strangled that notion, instinctively aware that she wasn't prepared to go down that road with him. Not now. Maybe not ever, not even for the sake of a baby.

Above the desk hung a family portrait taken shortly before Rebecca's sixteenth birthday. Amy had taken to wearing pigtails the year before. She was wide-eyed and curious, her precociousness already evident at that age. Her parents, dark-haired and serious, stared back at her. They would expect her to take care of her sister the same as if they'd lived.

"I'm doing this for you, Amy," she whispered. "Only for you."

Chapter Twelve

"You've backed me into a corner."

Caleb studied the checkerboard, painted squares on a burlap scrap laid out on the smooth tabletop, and scraped his fingers along his jaw. "So I have."

The hours since the brief ceremony had stretched endlessly.

When Becca had at last emerged from the bedroom, she'd worn a look of somber acceptance. She'd avoided him, as much as that was possible in the small cabin, busying herself with preparations for supper. And unable to think of a single topic of conversation, Caleb hadn't approached her. Instead, he'd let Amy take charge of his time. She'd read another chapter of *Great Expectations,* then suggested checkers. They were on their fifth game.

Fatigue rendered his limbs heavy, but his thoughts hummed with frantic persistence. *I'm a married man. Becca is my wife. And now I have two females depending on me.* The notion made him break out in a cold sweat. He and responsibility were not on friendly terms.

Ensconced in a rocking chair pulled close to the fire and fully absorbed in whatever she was drawing, Becca acted oblivious to their presence. The copper streaks in her upswept mane shimmered in the flickering light, and her skin had the appearance of a luminescent pearl. His gaze fell on her mouth pursed in concentration, and instantly the memory of their kiss slammed into him, emptying his lungs of breath. He really shouldn't have done it. Because now that he was privy to her sweetness, once wouldn't be nearly enough.

"I can't move," Amy cut into his thoughts. "You win."

Jumping her discs, he captured them for his pile. Then he winked at her. "Wanna play again tomorrow?"

A bright smile replaced the frown. "I'd like that."

When she began to put the pieces away, he pushed himself up, steeling himself against his leg's protest. The pain wasn't as piercing as it had been at first, more of a dull throb pulsing through muscle and tissue and bone. Constant and no less troublesome. He wondered how soon he could withstand long hours in the saddle and if this hasty marriage would impact his decision to go after Tate's murderers.

Surely Becca won't have any objections to me leaving. After all, my guaranteed absence is what got her to agree to this marriage in the first place.

Wandering over to the fire, Caleb wasn't surprised when Becca didn't notice his presence. She'd always been like that when working on a project—oblivious to everything around her.

Curious, he leaned forward. "What has you so captivated?"

She jumped. Guilt darkened her eyes. "I don't think—"

Not about to be denied, he deftly lifted the paper from her limp hands. Turned it over and surveyed the sketch. Hot pain seized his chest, as if a knife had been plunged clean through his heart.

"Adam," he whispered, amazed at the near-perfect likeness of his friend. Hale and hearty, standing upright, the ever-present smile on his face. "This is obviously a before picture."

Becca surged upward, hand outstretched. She was pale, distressed. "Caleb, please—"

"What?" he snapped, suddenly angry. "Afraid I'm gonna damage it? Take it. That's what I get for being nosy."

Dropping the paper into her waiting fingers, he turned and swung past the living area to the door. Shoving his arms into his duster, he jammed his Stetson on his head and left them both staring after him.

The frigid air did little to cool his ire. While a portion was directed at Becca—was it too much to ask that his new bride not daydream about her former fiancé on their wedding day?—most of his anger was focused inward. He'd actually felt betrayed. Hurt. It didn't make any sense. While Becca had assumed his name, she hadn't done so willingly. She didn't belong to him, not really, and she never would.

This is a marriage on paper only. We will live separate lives.

A light wind filtered through the forest and across the cove, her remembered words pelting him like tiny, razor-edged stones. His right crutch sank into the damp earth and he nearly lost his balance. He stopped to let the resulting pain dissipate, taking a moment to study the level expanse between the cabin—lit up from within like a Christmas candle—and shadowy outbuildings framed by the rising mountain in the near distance. Due to the past two days of warming temperatures and steady sun, the yard was a patchwork of grassy patches and clumps of unmelted snow.

Behind him, Becca's dog descended the porch steps and, loping across the yard, came to a stop at his feet. In the lack of moon and starlight, Storm's eyes were difficult to make out, but Caleb sensed her silent regard.

"Needed some fresh air, too, huh?" he murmured.

Somewhere behind the cabin, a sharp crack split the silence. Caleb ducked. Spun on his crutches. Eyes narrowed, heart throbbing, he scanned the inky-black forest. Was it her? The gang leader? One of her henchmen?

Instinctively, he reached for his gun and called himself all sorts of a fool when his fingers encountered the soft material of his waistband. In his haste, he'd failed to grab his gun belt. A mistake that could get him killed.

Pushing himself across the yard, he sidled up against the cabin wall, all the while straining for any sound that would clue him in to what was out there. The moonless night cast the dense forest in murky shadows. The perfect hiding place. He, on the other hand, was out in the open. Vulnerable.

Another crack echoed through the trees, followed by a loud rushing sound. He flattened himself further against the cold logs at his back, anticipating the bite of a bullet into his flesh. None came. Seconds stretched into minutes. Caleb had convinced himself there was no one out there, that what had spooked him was likely a branch breaking beneath the weight of snow, when boots clipped against the porch and Becca's lyrical voice carried around the corner.

"Caleb? Where are you?"

He took one last glance at the forest and hurried to intercept her. "Go back inside," he barked.

Her eyes widened at his abrupt appearance. She raised the kerosene lamp, throwing a greater circle of light onto the ground and him. "You were gone a long time. I was worried...." She trailed off when he lobbed his crutches next to her feet. "What are you doing?"

Planting his left leg on the porch, he gripped the edge of a corner log and hauled himself up, the pain of his injury not even registering in his drive to get her inside. He grabbed her by the shoulders and pushed her toward the door. "Not safe. I heard something in the woods."

"What?" She searched his face with dawning horror. "You think they found you?"

Hobbling on his good leg, he maneuvered them both inside. "Can't be sure, but I'm not taking any chances." Lowering the door latch, he lifted his gun from its holster and double-checked the chamber. Fully loaded. Perfect.

"Where's Amy?"

"In bed." Straight, white teeth sank into her lower lip. "Asleep, I think."

Becca had explained to Amy that, because of his injured leg, it would be best for Caleb to continue sleeping alone. He didn't know what they'd do when his leg was fully healed.

Moving to the window, Caleb ordered, "Go into the bedroom and turn out the lamp."

She ignored that directive. Instead, she sidled up to

peek over his shoulder. Her warm breath slid along his neck. A distraction he didn't need.

"Why aren't you doing as I said?" he asked through clenched teeth.

"I'm not leaving you." She sounded insulted that he'd ask. "You really shouldn't have left those crutches out there. You could reopen the wound."

Huffing a sigh, he didn't respond. What was the use? He tried pouring all his concentration into scanning the dark for nightmares. Next to impossible given her stance not even an inch away, derailing his train of thought. They stood there for what seemed like an eternity. Finally, he shrugged, turned all his weight on his good leg and found himself nearly nose to nose with his wife.

Her pearl-like skin glowed in the near darkness. Wisps had escaped her formal chignon, clinging to her cheeks. Caleb fisted his hands to keep from skimming them behind her ear. Touching Becca was a risk he couldn't afford.

"It must've been the snow." His voice was hoarse, memories of their kiss taunting him. "Too heavy for the branches."

Becca cocked her head, shrewd gaze boring into his. "Is that what you really think, or are you just saying that to make me feel better?"

He smiled grimly. "You married into the right family. With that stubborn streak, you'll fit right in with the O'Malleys."

She appeared arrested by the smile curving his mouth, her gaze glued to it in fascination.

"What?" he grunted.

"I haven't seen you smile in a really long time." Her voice dropped to a husky whisper. "I-it's nice."

"Maybe I didn't have a reason to."

"About earlier," she began, slowly lifting her gaze to his. "I wasn't thinking about what I was drawing, not really. My fingers just kind of took over. I'm sorry I hurt you."

Suddenly his skin felt uncomfortably tight. Emotion pinched his chest. Becca was worried about his feelings. Him. The man who hadn't given *her* feelings, *her* life, *her* future, a second thought two years ago when he'd dared Adam to break into the sawmill. This was proof of her generous spirit.

She made him feel dangerous things, made him long for a life he didn't deserve. A life with her. A real marriage. Caleb knew if he didn't put space between them right this second, he was going to grab on to her and never let go.

"That's the thing." He deliberately hardened his features. "You didn't hurt me. I know your heart will always belong to Adam. That's fine with me, because I don't want it." Plunging ahead despite the tears forming in her eyes, he ground out, "You see, I'm no good with hearts. Or love. Or anything meaningful. It's just my nature. Sorry, you got the defective O'Malley. So don't go spinning fairy tales about me, Becca. You'll be the one to get hurt again."

Outlaws or no, he was heading outside. Because he couldn't stay here with her and watch the effects of his little speech take hold. When all was said and done, Caleb O'Malley was a coward.

Chapter Thirteen

Weak sunlight coaxed Rebecca awake the following morning. While she was able to blink the grittiness from her eyes, there was nothing she could do to rid her head of the cotton-stuffed feeling. She'd lain awake long into the night, worried about Caleb out there in the cold, putting undue strain on his injury and possibly in the sights of his pursuers. Only after she'd heard him come inside well after midnight had she been able to relax enough to drift off into a troubled sleep.

His cutting words had hurt more than she could've imagined. That bothered her. In order for him to possess the power to hurt her meant she first had to care, right? Surely tending his wounds hadn't skewered her common sense or rendered her lonely heart susceptible. Caleb had given her ample reason not to care. Even warned her against it. The defective O'Malley, he'd called himself.

Scowling, she inched from beneath the covers and, doing her best not to disturb a still-slumbering Amy, hurriedly pulled on her lace-up leather boots. Defective, huh? The derisive label struck her wrong. Left her with a sour taste in her mouth.

Out of habit, she reached for the gold locket dangling from the bedpost, fingers closing around the thin chain. Rebecca hesitated. Was it wrong of her to wear a photo of her first love around her neck? Theirs may not be a normal union, but she owed Caleb a modicum of respect. That's why she'd offered the apology in the first place. Certain she'd glimpsed pain in his eyes when he recognized Adam's likeness, she'd been racked with guilt. Wasted emotion, she now knew, considering his distinct lack of interest in the state of her heart.

That's fine with me, because I don't want it.

Caleb didn't want her. No surprise there. Still, did he have to punish her with the fact?

Decision made, she clasped the necklace with an air of defiance and began to brush the tangles from her hair. Opting to tie it back with a sky-blue ribbon, she chose a matching blouse and serviceable nut-brown skirt. The icy water in the washstand shocked her fully awake. Pulling aside the checkered curtain, she surveyed the winter scene. Sunshine or no, winter days always impressed her as sad. Lonely. Bare branches, brittle grass, still and silent landscape. The deep green pine trees imparted a touch of color, thank goodness. Occasionally a cardinal's cheerful red feathers streaked against chalk-white sky.

Where would Caleb be come spring? How often did he plan on staying here between hunting trips? And how long would each stay last?

The unknowns bothered her. She could envision how their marriage would go—she'd get used to his latest absence and achieve a measure of contentment only to have him pop in unexpectedly and ruin everything. She'd be constantly wondering when he'd show up. *If* he'd show up. And if he didn't, she'd wonder if he was injured again. Or de—

No. He'd come too close to dying this week for her to want to go there again.

Yanking open the door, she halted at the sight of him sitting at the table nursing a mug of steaming coffee. His hair was damp, raven strands falling forward over his forehead, and his chiseled jaw was freshly shaven. He was wearing his buttermilk-colored shirt and black trousers.

His unreadable gaze lifted to hers, and he jerked a thumb over his shoulder. "There's fresh coffee on the stove. I set a mug out for you."

"I didn't hear you get up."

The bed was neatly made, his crutches propped between the headboard and small bedside table.

When he refocused on his drink, she walked past on stilted legs, uncomfortable in her own home. *It's kind of nice to have another adult around, though, isn't it?* Memories of her parents were embedded in every item in here, making their absence that much more difficult to bear. As reluctant as she was to admit it, Caleb being here meant she wasn't focused on the solitude.

"I noticed the barn door needs replaced," he said quietly. "And the smokehouse is missing some boards. It would be helpful if you could make a list of all the things that need fixing. Some things can wait until spring, of course, but I'd like to focus on the most pressing issues before I leave for a hunting trip."

Placing a heavy skillet on the stove top, she dropped a spoonful of lard into it and pulled down a bowl for the flapjack batter. His masculine presence filled the space with oppressive awareness. That she was attracted to the handsome hunter struck her as unfair. "How are you supposed to do chores with your leg still healing? You're not supposed to put weight on it."

Of course, Caleb didn't ordinarily do what he was supposed to do. Who knew what damage he'd done last night.

Turning around, she spoke to his broad back. "Speaking of that, it wouldn't be a bad idea for me to check the wound. The bandage likely needs changing."

His shoulders went taut. "I can check it myself."

"Fine." He was determined to be stubborn. So be it. "I'll lay out the supplies after breakfast."

His head bent. "Thanks."

Returning her attention to the work space, she cracked two eggs into the bowl. She heard him getting awkwardly to his feet but didn't expect him to approach her.

"Can I help?"

Jumping at the nearness of his gruff voice, she arched a brow at him. "You won't accept my help, yet you want me to accept yours?"

Color etched his cheekbones. "That's different, and you know it."

Unable to maintain his perceptive gaze, she lowered hers. "You should be resting."

"I know what I can handle, Becca. I…need something to do." He sighed, mussing the hair at his nape. "Not used to being idle."

That much was true. He'd always been filled with restless energy. "What did you have in mind?"

He indicated the heating skillet. "How about I cook the flapjacks?"

She handed him the spoon and, stepping back, watched as he mixed the egg, flour and milk. "Did you teach yourself to cook during your time in the mountains?"

"No. My mother taught us." One shoulder kicked up. "Thought it would come in handy someday."

Retrieving a slab of smoked ham, she began cutting it into thin slices for frying. "How old were you?"

"Fourteen."

A teenager, then. Despite their former connection, there were things she didn't know about him. "Do you enjoy it?"

One corner of his lush mouth kicked up, and he cast her a sideways glance that bordered on humorous. "I don't mind it."

It wasn't a smile, exactly, and yet her heart reacted as if he'd laughed outright, slipping and skidding across the slippery surface of fascination. Caleb thought his scar detracted from his appearance. He was wrong. Handsome even with his lip curled in a perpetual smirk, he was downright lethal when he allowed himself to smile, eyes lit from within with humor that transformed miniature gold flecks to sparkles.

Her hand tightened on the knife handle. "Mama started me early. I think I was four or five."

Caleb dropped spoonfuls of batter into the sizzling lard. "I remember her pumpkin bread. She'd offer us a snack whenever we stopped by."

"Yes." She blinked, fighting waves of grief. "Mama

was very generous. Always seeing to others' comfort." How she missed her kind spirit. Her words of wisdom. "I miss her hugs most of all," she murmured.

A worried line appeared between his brows. Fork poised above the skillet, he gazed solemnly at her. "I didn't mean to upset you. I shouldn't have brought it up."

"I brought it up, not you." Swallowing hard, she worked to regain control. Of herself and the conversation. "Tell me, between you and your older brothers, who's the best cook?"

One dark brow lifted, but he went with the change. "Not me."

Caleb didn't used to harbor such negative views of himself. *Could it be he despises himself for what he did even more than I or Adam do?*

"Who, then?" Continuing to slice the ham, she said, "My guess is Josh."

He concentrated on flipping the small, round cakes. "You'd be right. Josh excelled at everything he tried his hand at," he said dispassionately. "He doesn't have to work hard to achieve success."

For the first time, she found herself considering how being the youngest of three brothers had molded him, especially when Josh and Nathan were both high achievers, competent, hard-working and family-oriented. Was it possible he'd given up trying to measure up to such high standards? Was that why he'd embraced the role of ne'er-do-well?

"What about Nathan?"

"Nathan wasn't all that interested in learning. He didn't apply himself." He shot her a sidelong look. "Ma's words, not mine. Still, he managed to best me."

They fell into an easy silence, working side by side to ready breakfast. Acutely aware of his every move, Rebecca was careful to keep at least six inches between them. She could not allow physical attraction—unwelcome and disturbing as it was—to cloud good sense.

When the food was done, she ordered him to sit and let her carry everything to the table. He didn't take kindly to that.

"I'm not helpless."

"True. You are, however, recovering from a near-fatal bullet wound." She pointed at him. "You may not like to admit to weakness, but I can see the lines of strain bracketing your mouth. The grimaces when you think I'm not looking. The pain's getting to you, yet you're determined to prove yourself."

He rolled his eyes. "I told you, I can manage."

"And you accuse me of being stubborn," she huffed. When he reached for the milk glasses, she said, "You do realize Doc left behind a vial of laudanum."

Eyes flaring, he eyed the milk with suspicion. "You wouldn't."

"Wouldn't I?" Grabbing the platter, she turned toward the table. Strong fingers curved around her upper arm, stalling her. Her breath caught in her throat as he brought his face near. Memories of his kiss bombarded her, and she quivered with trepidation. Or was it anticipation?

"Tell me the truth." His silken voice wrapped her in a cocoon of heat and confusion. "Did you spike my milk, Rebecca?"

Rebecca. He rarely used her full name, which meant he must be extremely irked. Against her better judgment, she lifted her face, bringing their noses and mouths close together. His molten eyes fastened onto hers, at once beautiful and deadly.

"I'm not afraid of you, you know," she whispered.

Black brows slashed upward. "You think I'm trying to frighten you?" He shook his head as if bewildered at such a notion. "All I want is an honest answer."

"No, I didn't."

His sharp gaze roamed her face, stopping on her mouth. Like her, he was probably remembering the ceremony and the kiss he stole. The blood raced through her veins, making her light-headed. The platter wobbled.

Immediately he released her. The disappointment crashing through her made her angry. She absolutely must not want this man. It would only lead to heartbreak—hers.

"I didn't this time," she snapped. "However, that doesn't mean I won't if you insist on pushing yourself too hard."

Anger sparked. He opened his mouth to retort but was interrupted by the appearance of her little sister.

"I'm starving," Amy announced from the doorway. "What's for breakfast?"

"Your family is here," Becca announced later that morning.

Hearing the tremor of disquiet in her voice, Caleb looked up from the checkerboard. Nathan had dropped by after breakfast to ask if they'd mind if the family brought lunch over today. No surprise they wanted to officially welcome Becca to the family.

"All of them?"

Touching a slender hand to her hair, she stuck her face closer to the frosted glass. He was still furious with her, so why he found her pert profile distracting was beyond him.

"Everyone except for Josh and Kate."

Twisting in her seat, Amy looked hopeful. "Is Will with them?"

"Yes."

Her smile brightened as she turned back to Caleb. "He likes checkers, too."

Adopting an affronted air, he sank against the chair back. "Is that a hint you'd rather play with Sophie's ten-year-old brother?"

Looking flustered, she toyed with the ends of one chestnut braid. "No, of course not. It's just that I haven't played with him in a while—"

"Relax, little sis. I'm teasing." He winked just as Becca pivoted to observe them. Her eyes darkened with worry.

Amy gasped. "I am your sister-in-law now, aren't I? And Rebecca is an O'Malley, which means I'm part of your family, too, right?"

"Absolutely." He gestured to the half-finished game. "Okay if we stop now?"

"Sure."

Gaining his feet, he used the crutches to carry him to the door. He didn't need them, but apparently his new wife needed to see him using them. This whole considering another person's point of view was new and not entirely convenient. Caleb still found it hard to believe Becca had threatened to secretly medicate him. On the one hand, it irritated him no end—he was not one to be bossed around—on the other, her spunk impressed him.

When she shot him an irritated look, he drawled, "I am allowed to get up, aren't I? If you recall, I let you and Amy clean the breakfast dishes and even took an hour nap afterward like a good little boy."

Pink danced along her collarbone above her pastel blue blouse's scoop neck. Her hair swept across her forehead and flirted with fine brows, tempting him to test its softness. If he were free to do as he pleased, and his family wasn't about to descend on them, he'd trace her features with his fingertips and follow their progress with soft kisses.

Becca must've read something of his thoughts, because she cleared her throat and edged sideways, closer to the door. Averting her face, she remarked, "Your father has what looks to be a cake in his hands."

"I'm certain Ma couldn't resist making a wedding cake."

She touched her hair again. Tugged on her sleeves. Smoothed her skirt. "They can't be thrilled with this situation."

Caleb battled not to pull her close to his side. "Take a look at their faces." He forced his gaze to the front. "Do they look upset to you?"

His mother looked as pleased as punch. Experience told him that as long as she was content, his father was, too. As for Nathan, Caleb was pretty sure he wasn't thinking about their hasty marriage. Silver gaze glued to his best friend and new wife, Sophie, his expression bore evidence of a lovesick man. For her part, the blond-haired beauty looked happier than Caleb had ever seen her.

Good for them, he thought. After watching firsthand their attempts to fight the pull between them—and his staid brother's near unraveling in the process—he was glad they'd come to their senses.

If he felt a pinprick of jealousy when Nathan brushed a tender kiss on Sophie's cheek, he didn't acknowledge it. Wedded bliss was out of the question for him and Becca. Might as well accept that fact and move on.

His father had reached the steps when Caleb remembered something important. "Becca?"

Reluctantly, her gaze swerved to his.

"They're your family now, too. When I'm gone, promise me you'll go to them if you need anything. They'll help you."

Her petal-pink lips parted, surprise swirling. But he didn't get the requested promise because his parents were on the porch already, their jovial chatter trickling through the door.

Chapter Fourteen

Why did Caleb suddenly look so intense? He acted as if it was of paramount importance that she assure him she'd seek help in his absence. Surely he didn't care that much. After all, he'd all but disappeared not long after the sawmill accident. He wasn't around when her parents died—that he'd attended the funeral had come as a shock—and he hadn't cared to check up on her or Amy since.

Rebecca didn't have long to ponder it because the O'Malleys were filing into her home bearing crates of delicious-smelling food, greeting her and Amy with genuine warmth and fussing over Caleb. While Sam showed Amy and Will the cake—a pound cake layered with strawberry preserves—Mary wrapped her son in a fierce hug.

Looking distinctly out of his element, he returned the embrace, awkwardly patting her shoulder. Rebecca studied her new husband, suddenly far too interested to see how he interacted with his family. When Mary at last released him, a grinning Nathan clapped him on the shoulder.

"You look better, brother. Married life must agree with you."

Caleb's hooded gaze skidded to hers, and he shrugged as if in silent apology. "Becca is the best nurse a guy could ask for," he murmured. Then his eyes glinted dangerously. "She's not as sweet and innocent as she appears, however. Can you believe she forced me to take a nap this morning?"

Silence fell. Rebecca stiffened as several pairs of eyes swiveled to her in astonishment. Then Nathan threw his head back and laughed outright. Mary's smile was accompanied by keen interest, and Sam stroked his chin in deep thought.

Rebecca shot Caleb a withering look. He arched an imperious brow. *Oh, he was going to pay for putting her on the spot.*

Sophie, who was the last to enter, offered Rebecca an encouraging smile. "Don't worry, you'll get used to them soon enough." With a little laugh, she placed a hand on her arm and leaned in and whispered, "You'll have your hands full with Caleb, but I have a feeling you can handle him."

Nathan appeared at his wife's side. "What secrets are you spilling, Soph?"

"If I told you, it wouldn't be a secret, would it?" Grinning affectionately, she gently nudged his ribs.

Curving an arm about Sophie's shoulders and tugging her against his side, the quiet O'Malley brother addressed Rebecca. "Welcome to the family."

Beneath his genuine warmth, concern lurked. He was intimately aware of the turmoil that existed between his brother and her. She masked a wince at the memory of their run-in at the mercantile several months ago. The unanticipated sight of Caleb had sparked the old anger, and she'd uttered hateful things while Nathan looked on in pained silence.

"Thank you," she managed, hating that he'd seen her at her worst. And yet, there was no condemnation in his gaze.

After her parents' funeral, Nathan had been the one who'd come to check on her and Amy time and time again. He'd gone out of his way to be kind. She'd never forgotten his attentiveness. Or Caleb's indifference. Not once had he reached out to her.

Mary joined their circle. "You can't know how thrilled I am to have another daughter-in-law. You and Amy are family now. I know it will take some time to adjust to the idea, but I want you to know you can come to us for anything. Our home is your home."

Her words were so similar to Caleb's that Rebecca found herself searching him out to see if he'd overheard. Apparently so. He'd moved to the table to inspect the cake, but his head was turned to study her.

Ripping her gaze away from his intense scrutiny, she mustered a smile. "I appreciate that, Mrs. O'Malley."

The brown-haired woman held up a hand. "Please, call me Mary. I apologize for the suddenness of this visit, but I needed to see for myself how Caleb was doing. Doesn't matter how old your children get, you still worry about them."

"And you couldn't resist marking the occasion of your youngest son's wedding," Nathan added knowingly.

"Can we eat now, sis?" Will piped up from where he stood close to Amy's chair. "I'm starving."

Sophie's resulting smile was a mix of reproof and indulgence. "Will, mind your manners."

"Actually, I'm starving, too." Nathan rubbed his flat belly and adopted a pitiful air.

Rolling her eyes, Sophie merely laughed. "I guess we'd better feed these men before they pass out from hunger," she told Mary, clearly comfortable with her mother-in-law. But then, as the O'Malley's neighbor, she'd grown up with the three boys and had been a part of the family long before it became official.

Rebecca wondered if she'd ever feel that way. She knew Sam and Mary, of course. Growing up in a small town like Gatlinburg, you saw the same faces at church every Sunday, passed those same people on Main Street. That didn't mean the Thurstons and O'Malleys had been particularly close. While she, Adam and Caleb had been friends, they hadn't spent that much time at the O'Malley place. Mostly they'd roamed the countryside or hung out at Adam's parents' home.

Snapping out of her musings, her mother's training took over and she set out to be an amenable hostess. As her table wasn't large enough to accommodate everyone, Amy, Will, Nathan and Sophie carried their plates to the settee and chairs grouped before the fireplace. That left Rebecca with her husband and parents-in-law. It wasn't as uncomfortable as she'd feared, however, as the focus was entirely on Caleb. Between bites of roasted chicken and biscuits, he answered their questions regarding his injury with an air of long-suffering. Seated directly across from him, she watched him surreptitiously. When the conversation turned to their farm and dairy business, she caught flashes of keen interest beneath his carefully bland features. Why was he acting as if he didn't care when it was clear—at least to her—that he did?

When there was a lull in the conversation, Rebecca ventured a question of her own. "How is Kate?"

Nathan snorted. "Huge."

"Nathan O'Malley," Sophie scolded, although laughter filtered through, "that is not nice."

Married to Caleb's oldest brother, Josh, Kate was due to deliver their first baby shortly after the new year. Rebecca didn't know the sophisticated young lady from New York very well, but Kate had always been sweetly kind whenever they'd crossed paths.

Mary sipped her coffee. "She would've liked to come today and welcome you, Rebecca, but she's been having pains on and off the past three days and the doctor advised her to stick close to home."

Caleb wiped a cloth napkin across his mouth, looking uneasy. "She's not in any danger, is she?"

"Childbirth always carries a certain amount of risk," Mary conceded, "but she's healthy and strong."

"She's tiny compared to Josh," he countered. "What if the baby's too big?"

Sam clapped his son on the shoulder. "Your ma didn't have a bit of trouble with you three. You weighed the most." He smiled at Rebecca, eyes twinkling behind his spectacles. "He was over nine pounds."

Rebecca managed a weak smile. The talk of children had her squirming in her seat. *Please, Lord, don't let their attention turn to us, the newlyweds.*

One thing was clear—Caleb cared about his family's well-being. Rebecca wondered how he dealt with the long absences, how he coped with the worry that surely must accompany not knowing what was happening back home.

"My sister wants three boys and one girl," Amy announced into the silence. "I think three girls and a boy would be better, though."

Nearly choking on her tea, Rebecca set the cup down hard enough to send liquid sloshing onto the saucer. Heat surged and waned in her cheeks.

Fork poised above his plate, Caleb looked stricken.

Rebecca wanted children?

Caleb felt sick. He wasn't fit for fatherhood. He wasn't fit for any kind of relationship. Hurting people was what he did, what he excelled at. No child deserved to be saddled with a father like that.

Across from him, Rebecca sat in frozen misery. This final thing he'd stolen from her, this dream he'd destroyed, was the cruelest one of all. She would've made a wonderful mother.

Appetite gone, he lowered his fork and addressed his father. "Any reports from the sheriff yet?"

His answering frown, along with Nathan's suddenly alert form, drove thoughts of babies from Caleb's head. "Something happened. What is it?"

"We got word this morning that Shane and the search party stumbled upon the gang five miles north of here. They engaged our guys in a gunfight. Hugh Galloway was shot in the shoulder. He held on until they could get him back to town, though. Should be fine."

Caleb's temples throbbed. "Do they know for sure it's the same gang that murdered Tate?"

"They saw a woman fitting the description you gave," Nathan said somberly.

The sound that had spooked him last night couldn't have been them, then. "They all got away?"

"Shane was outnumbered. They had to fall back or risk more injuries." His father's perceptive gaze sharpened. "That doesn't mean we won't get them, son. It'll just take a little longer than we'd like."

Frustration simmered in his gut. He should be out there searching, too. Tate deserved justice. "I need some fresh air."

Pushing to a standing position, he hobbled over to where his crutches were propped against the wall.

"We haven't had cake yet." His ma twisted in her chair to look at him. Beside her, Rebecca was silent, gaze lowered to her lap. She looked miserable.... *Just what a new bride ought to be,* he thought sarcastically.

"You all go ahead."

He'd reached the steps when the door opened and closed behind him. Still shoving one arm into his heavy wool outercoat, Nathan held Caleb's duster out to him. "Don't wanna get pneumonia on top of everything else, do you?"

Heaving a sigh, Caleb laid his crutches against the nearest post and slipped into the long black duster. Then, navigating the steps, used the crutches to slowly round the side of the house and cross to the narrow stream at the edge of the forest. His brother followed, of course.

Side by side, they stood staring at the crystalline

water trickling past. Finally, Nathan spoke. "I don't like that particular look in your eyes, little brother. I've come to know it far too well over the past few years, and I've come to despise it."

"You can't be serious. What *look?*"

Silver eyes narrowed in exasperation. "You're planning on going after them yourself."

"You weren't there," he bit out. "You didn't see an innocent man's life cut short before your very eyes."

Scraping a hand down his face, Nathan relented. A little. "I know you want justice for what they did to Tate. And to you. But going off alone when your leg isn't healed isn't only reckless, it's just plain dumb."

Caleb winced at the word *reckless*. It was a label that would follow him for life, he supposed. "This isn't some snap decision, Nate. I've given it a lot of thought. I'll admit the leg pains me, but I'm confident I can ride without reinjuring it. I can always rest along the way."

"You think taking them on by yourself again is the wisest course? Timmons had men with him, and someone still got hurt."

"Give me a little credit. I'm going to join the search party, not charge into enemy camp like a crazy man."

Lips pursing, Nathan pondered that. "And what about Rebecca?"

"She'll be pleased as punch to see me ride outta here. Probably throw a party."

"I'm not so sure." He shook his head. "I was watching her watch you throughout the meal. There's something there, brother."

"Yeah. Loathing."

"No. Something else. I think you have a chance to

make something of this marriage if you give it some effort."

"Look, you may as well know that Rebecca and I have already decided how this union is going to be. I'm going to give her as much space and distance as she wants. And believe me, she wants a lot. She made me promise this would be a marriage in name only. I'm to spend much of my married life alone on the mountaintops."

The sorrowful expression on his brother's face was too much to bear. Balanced on the crutches, he held up a hand. "I don't have time to discuss this right now. I've got to get packing if I aim to go with Shane. I have to find out when they're heading out again. The sooner those criminals are behind bars, the better."

"You're leaving?" Becca demanded behind them. Startled, both men swiveled to stare at the angry young woman in blue wool. Her narrowed eyes spewed jade sparks. A pine-scented breeze tugged strands, which she ignored, across milk-white cheeks.

Nathan jerked a thumb over his shoulder. "I'll, uh, just go on inside."

Looking as if she'd chewed glass, Becca waited until his brother had disappeared to close the remaining few feet separating them. "When were you planning on telling me? Or were you going to leave a note?"

"I honestly don't know. Hadn't figured that out yet. I'm new to this whole marriage thing, ya know."

Her nostrils flared. "At least you're honest. That's something, I guess," she scoffed.

"Why does it matter? I thought you'd be happy," he said, bewildered.

"Happy? You think I'd be *happy* about you going after the ruthless men who shot you?" She threw her hands up. "About you putting your recovery in jeopardy? I spent endless hours worrying you might die from that bullet wound." Pursing her lips together, she shoved wayward strands behind her ears. "You can't simply disregard all of that and place yourself in danger again."

Her hands were suddenly on his chest—not shoving, but applying pressure nonetheless. Enough pressure that his crutches slipped on the damp earth sloping downward to the stream's edge. Time seemed to slow. What she'd done registered on her face, and she clutched ineffectively at his shirtfront. When that didn't stop his backward motion, her arms snaked around his waist, which only served to knock them both off balance. The crutches went flying.

"Caleb!" she gasped.

One second he was upright, the next he was gazing up at clear blue sky, prickly grass an uncomfortable pillow for his head and hard, cold earth beneath him. Becca was sprawled atop him, mouth agape.

At her priceless expression, laughter erupted deep in his chest. The rumbling, rusty sound surprised them both.

"Caleb, your leg—"

"Is fine," he assured her, still smiling. It stung, but she didn't need to know that.

"What's so funny?" she demanded, balancing herself with one hand on his shoulder and the other on the ground near his ear.

"The Rebecca Thurston I used to know would never have done that."

"It's not Thurston anymore, remember." Her voice dropped an octave, lower lip trembling. "And that girl is long gone."

"Hey." Wrapping an arm about her waist, he tried not to let the sweet scent clinging to her skin distract him. "I happen to like the new you. You're a strong, confident woman." Not to mention so beautiful he found it difficult to think.

Tears welled in her eyes. When she attempted to wriggle away, he locked both arms about her. "Not so fast. Tell me what's wrong first."

"Our clothes are getting dirty." She sniffed, indignant.

"I don't care."

"Someone might see. We look ridiculous."

"Again, don't care."

"You enjoy being difficult, don't you?"

"What I don't enjoy is seeing you miserable," he responded, unoffended. Being difficult came naturally. He wouldn't deny it.

"Caleb," she warned, pushing against his shoulders. "Let me up."

He held her fast, quickly becoming mesmerized by her lips hovering above his. Then he noticed the rogue tear tracking down her cheek.

"I will as soon as you tell me why you're crying."

Chapter Fifteen

He was going to be stubborn about this. She could tell from his mulish expression and the determination burning like stars in his eyes.

Where his hand cupped her side, his thumb caressed a spot beneath her ribs in a back-and-forth motion that was both soothing and searing. She was incredibly aware of the unleashed power in him, a strength that made her feel safe and yet also lured her closer. The disturbing thing was he didn't even have to put forth any effort. Caleb just had to simply *be*. This was what had spooked her all those years ago when she and Adam were still together, the reason she'd distanced herself from Caleb.

The fact that he was now her husband complicated things considerably.

"None of this was supposed to happen. You getting shot and winding up here. Us being forced into this farce of a marriage. It's not fair."

"I learned a long time ago not to expect things to go my way," he said softly. "As much as all this stinks, I'm confident you can handle it."

The admiration in his voice stunned her into admitting what was truly bothering her.

"I don't want you to join the search party."

Why the prospect of Caleb facing down that gang filled her with such foreboding, she wasn't ready to examine, but she had to convince him to stay until his leg healed. While her desire for separate lives hadn't changed, when he did leave, she wanted to say goodbye with the knowledge he could take care of himself. That he was completely recovered.

"That's what has you so upset?" His brows lifted.

Clasping her shoulders, he maneuvered them into a sitting position. The cold ground was an unwelcome shock after his comforting heat. His hip grazing hers, he sat facing her, long legs stretching out in the grass.

"It's too dangerous," she insisted. "Look at what happened to you. And now Mr. Galloway. Wait until you're ready."

"I can't. They won't stick around now that they know Shane is on their trail. Besides, I know what I'm up against this time. I'll be more careful. Better prepared."

"That won't stop me from worrying."

He stared at her. "Don't waste your energy. I don't deserve your concern."

Bleak conviction lined his face. This was no ploy to gain her sympathy. He wasn't fishing for reassurances. He meant what he said, and the knowledge that she'd had a role in bringing him to this place of low self-worth pierced her conscience.

Memories of those initial days following the accident bombarded her. She'd lost count how many times Caleb had come to Doc's asking to see Adam, his face still bandaged, bruised and scratched, only to be turned away by Adam's parents and herself. Between the three of them, they'd made certain he felt the weight of their censure and wrath. Looking back, she realized they'd treated him as if he was a criminal instead of a grieving friend.

It had been an accident, after all, hadn't it? Not an intentional act to hurt Adam. An *accident*. Caleb had loved him like a brother. She'd allowed her own disappointment and hurt to cloud her judgment and, in doing so, had wounded not only herself but Caleb, too.

Squeezing her eyes tight, she pressed her hand against her heart. Guilt felt like an ax wedged deep into the sluggishly beating muscle. Sorrow and regret radiated through her chest.

"Rebecca, what's wrong?" His hands were suddenly cupping her face, his breath fanning across her chin. "Are you ill?"

"No, I'm not ill, I—" Opening her eyes, she met his anxious gaze squarely. "Caleb, I'm so sorry."

He blinked, confusion pulling his brows together over his nose. "For what?"

"The way I treated you after Adam's accident. When you came to Doc Owens's those times wanting to see him." She swallowed, recalling his exact expression the last time he'd come—the self-recrimination, the resignation—and the sight of his slumped shoulders as he'd walked out the door one final time. "I know what Adam meant to you. If I'd been thinking clearly, I would've seen how you were hurting as much as the rest of us. I was wrong to behave the way I did. Please forgive me."

Stunned, Caleb dropped his hands as if burned and

jerked back. He shook his head so hard his hair slid onto his forehead. "You don't owe me an apology. I deserved what I got and more."

"No—"

"Adam's in a wheelchair because of me," he said fiercely, "and you lost the man you loved." He scrubbed his face with a shaky hand. "We should rejoin my family. They're probably wondering what's taking so long."

Shoulder muscles rippling, he grabbed the crutches and hauled himself up with a grimace. His forbidding expression froze the words on her tongue, forestalled the desperate urge to press her case. She'd been foolish to assume a single apology would undo years of reproach, hurled insults and anger. Lots and lots of anger.

I'm so sorry, God. It was as if her eyes had finally been opened to the ugliness inside her soul, the stains of bitterness marring her heart. *Please forgive me.*

She only hoped one day Caleb would be able to forgive her, too.

Brim of his hat pulled low over his eyes, Caleb guided Rebel along Main Street, bypassing wagons parked in front of Clawson's Mercantile. People gathered outside the post office, sharing news bits. Through the plate-glass window to his right, the tables in Plum's Café were mostly empty at this hour of day, the lunch crowd having already dissipated.

Weak sunlight painted the buildings in pastel, washed-out hues and the gently rounded mountain peaks encircling the town a monotone blue. Festive greenery twined with crimson ribbon adorned the storefronts. At the end of the lane, the stained-glass windows in the white clapboard church glistened like polished jewels. The crisp air sliding over his exposed skin carried scents of horseflesh, wet earth and, strangely, roasted chestnuts.

He pointedly did not turn his head to look through the window of Josh and Kate's combined furniture store and photography studio. He wasn't in the mood for another lecture. For one thing, his thigh quivered in agony. Worse than that were the lingering effects of Becca's apology, which had left him emotionally numb and in a state of shock.

He hadn't even been able to muster the wherewithal to give her a proper goodbye. Her dismay as he'd stood at the cabin door and strapped on his gun belt and shoulder holster hit him again, and Caleb thought perhaps he should pen a brief note to her and leave it in his pocket for someone to find in case things went south with the outlaws.

He was about to nudge Rebel toward the sheriff's office when he caught sight of a familiar figure emerging from the mercantile. Changing direction, he came alongside the boardwalk and called out a soft greeting.

"Where you headed, Nicki?"

The statuesque figure dressed all in purple stiffened. Head whipping around, inky-black curls bobbing about her shoulders, his cousin's violet eyes went wide at the sight of him. "Caleb." She gathered up her voluminous skirts and hurried to his side. "Uncle Sam told us what happened. Knowing you as I do, I guess I shouldn't be surprised to see you up and around so soon. Are you okay?"

"Managing." He shrugged.

Nicole's uplifted gaze narrowed. "What's so important you disregarded doctor's orders?"

While fashion pretty much dominated his eighteen-year-old cousin's head, she was not slow-witted. Far from it. "Business that doesn't concern you, little Nicki."

Her lips tightened at the nickname she hated. He grinned. Having grown up together on neighboring farms, Nicole and her four sisters were more like sisters than cousins, which meant he got to tease them as any good big brother would.

Black gloves gripping a lacy reticule, her eyes sparkled with mischief. "And what about your new wife? Does she concern me? After all, Rebecca is part of the family now." Nicole glanced up and down the street. "Did she accompany you, by chance? I'd like to congratulate her on her good fortune."

"She's not here." And just like that he was reminded Nicole could give as good as she got, just like any little sister worth her salt. While he was out stalking deer and setting traps for months on end, his cousins were growing up. Maturing into young ladies who would soon leave home and start families of their own. Juliana and Megan had already found their mates. Nicole, Jessica and Jane wouldn't be far behind. "You and the twins should stop by, though. I think Rebecca and her sister would enjoy the company."

One thin raven brow arched in challenge. "I'd be delighted."

A niggle of uncertainty settled at the base of his skull. "Don't be divulging embarrassing tales to Becca about me. Stick to talk of bonnets and slippers."

"Just for that, Caleb O'Malley, I'm going to tell her about the time you lost at horseshoes and as a forfeit had to dress up as a girl."

"One of these days, a man will come along who you want to impress, and I will return the favor."

"You'll be waiting a long time," she quipped. "Men don't interest me in the slightest."

"I forgot. Your aspiration is to be a businesswoman, not a wife." Then he realized what was different about this encounter. She'd come out of the mercantile empty-handed. "Where are your packages? Did you have so many you had to ship them home?"

Instead of the expected retort, Nicole's gaze dropped to her boots. "Actually, Mr. Moore has agreed to hire me as a shop assistant. I start tomorrow."

Caleb worked to sort through his astonishment. "I thought you'd earned all the funds you needed for your boutique. Weren't you planning to go to Knoxville in March to scout out possible sites?"

Her fingers dug into the reticule. "It'll have to be postponed." Averting her face as she looked toward the barbershop, she said, "Listen, Caleb, I have to get home. I promised Ma I'd finish mending her skirt today."

"Wait, Nicole."

She met his gaze for a split second, mixed emotions flitting across the usually cool features. "I really am glad you're okay. See you later."

Nonplussed, he watched her hurry in the opposite direction. As soon as he returned, he was going to have to do a little snooping around. He *would* find out what was going on with her.

Troubled, Caleb rode across the street to the sheriff's

office, relieved it appeared to be deserted. Dismounting took a toll on him. Putting weight on his right leg shot arcs of lightning up to his hip and down to his heel. He gritted his teeth and, mopping his face with a handkerchief, hobbled through the dirt and onto the boardwalk. Inside the sparely furnished office, Shane looked up from his desk and scowled.

"O'Malley."

"Shane." Nodding a greeting, he said without preamble, "I want to ride out with you and the others."

"You shouldn't be here." He tossed his pencil on the scuffed desk, glaring when Caleb sank into the chair opposite.

"My leg will hold up," he said stubbornly, despite the voice of reason insisting Becca had been right.

"This isn't about your leg." Leaning back, the other man folded his arms across his chest. "I was getting ready to send a man out to your place with a warning to steer clear of town. There was a stranger hanging around last night at the livery asking after a man with a scar."

Alarm set his teeth on edge. "Who did he approach? Where is he now?"

"It was one of Lee's helpers, young Tommy Payne. Tommy told Lee about the conversation as soon as the man left. By the time Lee tried to follow him, it was too late."

Tommy was what? Eighteen or nineteen? "What did he tell him about me?" His pulse grew erratic. How many people knew he and Becca had married?

"Nothing." The look in Shane's hard blue eyes didn't reassure Caleb, however. "That doesn't mean this scum didn't approach someone else and get the answers he sought."

"I have to get home." Surging out of the chair, he ignored the pain and hurried to the door.

"Caleb."

"Yeah?"

His eyes glinted a warning. "I observed the ring leader for twenty-four hours before we made our move. She's not a woman I'd fancy tangling with. I suggest you stay out of sight until she and her lackeys are caught."

Lips tightening, he limped out the door, his thoughts racing ahead of him to the quaint cove where his new home and family awaited. Becca had no idea what kind of danger she was in. He had to reach her before someone else did.

Ensconced before the roaring fire with her half-finished rug, hook and wool in hand, Rebecca studied the emerging picture with a critical eye. The pines behind the cabin looked lopsided, but she wasn't all that motivated to fix them. Her gaze strayed for the umpteenth time to the narrow bed against the wall, where the patchwork quilt had been neatly tucked about the straw mattress and the pillow fluffed.

Caleb was gone. And Rebecca wasn't sure when or even if he would return.

She kept picturing his utter shock at her apology, the denial in his stark gaze. What bothered her most was that he'd left still convinced he was the only one who'd done wrong.

Oh, Lord, I've been so blind.

The unexpected knock startled her, and the rug hook

clattered to the floor. Her heart leaped into her throat. Could it be that he had changed his mind? Maybe his leg had pained him too much and he'd decided to come home.

Draping the rug and wool across the basket at her feet, she smoothed her hair. With Amy visiting at the Harpers' homestead, perhaps she and Caleb would have a chance to finish their conversation. *If* he'd stop being stubborn long enough to listen.

But when she swung open the door, it wasn't her husband standing on her porch. It was a stranger. A woman in a shabby, nondescript dress who appeared to be in her early to mid-thirties. While beautiful, with thick blond hair and eyes the color of blue hydrangeas, there was a hardness to her that set Rebecca on edge.

"Good morning," she greeted cautiously. "Can I help you?"

"I hope so," the blonde said with a shiver, chafing her arms against the wind that swept down the mountain and whistled through the cove. "Would you be able to spare a cup of coffee for a poor stranger?"

Rebecca hesitated. While her instincts rebelled, her mother's training demanded she extend hospitality to those in need.

"Certainly." She tugged the door open. "I'm Rebecca Thur—" She inwardly winced. "O'Malley."

"Samantha Wentworth." She paused as a bearded man stalked around the side of the cabin. "Oh, do you mind if my brother Wendell joins us? It's been an age since we've had decent coffee."

Anxiety knotted in her stomach. Inviting an unknown woman into her home was one thing, but the coldly assessing look in the bulky man's gaze made Rebecca want to slam the door in their faces. Courtesy be hanged.

"I, uh, suppose it'd be no problem." The words sounded stilted to her ears. "Come in."

With no other choice but to turn her back on the pair, she crossed quickly to the cookstove and filled the kettle. Her neck prickled beneath the weight of their stares. The click of the cabin door as it closed felt like a jail cell clanging shut.

"Have a seat at the table," she said over her shoulder, gathering mugs. "What brings you to these parts?"

She pivoted in time to see the pair exchange a long look. Samantha's bland expression was at odds with the hard gleam in her eyes. The way she plopped down on the chair struck Rebecca as more mannish than ladylike. Dusty, scuffed boots peeked out from beneath the frayed hem. "Wendell and I are searching for someone. A man in his early twenties with black hair and an ugly scar near his eye. We have reason to believe he passed this way. Have you seen him?"

Caleb's description of the gang leader resurged in her mind. Young. Blond hair worn in a braid. And she was searching for him.

Her throat closed up as stark fear spilled through her limbs. Her lungs clawed for air. She'd invited a murderer in for coffee. *Why didn't I heed my instincts?* Fighting nausea, she struggled to maintain a facade of calm. Her very life—and possibly Caleb's—depended on it.

"What's he done?" Lifting the kettle, she managed to pour the steaming water into the mugs without spilling it.

"He stole from us. And I don't take kindly to thieves. We want what's ours."

Praying for strength, Rebecca tried desperately to compose herself as she delivered their drinks. Wendell, if that truly was his name, ogled every inch of her. The absence of humanity in his gaze frightened her more than Samantha's cold demeanor. The gang leader wanted Caleb, plain and simple. This man, on the other hand, was interested in far more than information.

And she was vulnerable, with no means of defending herself. No one was around to hear her if she screamed. Thank goodness Amy wasn't home. *Keep her safe, God, please. Deliver me from these evil people.*

Walking on legs that threatened to give out, Rebecca picked up her warm mug and cradled it against her chest. "I understand why you'd want to find him. Did he steal something very valuable?"

Samantha set down her mug, gaze sharpening. Had she picked up on the tremor in her voice? "You could say that. The question remains—have you seen him?"

Rebecca shook her head. Please let her be convinced. "Men with facial scars aren't all that common around here. I'd remember if I had."

The blonde studied her for what seemed like forever. When she finally shrugged, Rebecca released a pent-up breath.

"Too bad. I guess we'll have to keep searching." Pushing upward, she addressed the man still sprawled in the next chair. "You finished with your coffee?"

Black eyes riveted on Rebecca, he frowned. "This is good brew. No reason to rush."

Her mouth tightened with displeasure. "We have a lot of ground yet to cover, Wendell."

"I think I'll keep this kind lady company if you wanna go on. I could catch up."

That can't happen. Please, God. A scream clawed her throat, and she clamped her lips to contain it. She gripped the mug until she feared the handle would snap off. "My husband will be along shortly. He went to town on an errand."

Wendell looked pointedly at her bare left hand and grinned knowingly. Her stomach fell to her toes. He thought she was lying.

"The marriage is a recent one," she managed. "No time to get a ring."

Samantha blanched. "Married, huh? Take my advice, Rebecca O'Malley. Don't ever trust a man."

Chapter Sixteen

By the time Rebel thundered into Becca's yard, Caleb was past the point of rational thought. Fear overrode caution. Instead of taking the time to check for possible threats, he swung out of the saddle, his bad leg nearly giving way when his boots slammed to the earth.

He gritted his teeth against the pain. "Becca!"

Ominous silence cloaked the cove. Where was Amy? Storm should be barking by now. Or at the very least investigating.

The door latch wouldn't budge. "Becca, are you in there?" He pounded on the door with his fist. "It's me—"

There was a scrape of wood as the latch lifted. The door eased inward and there stood his wife looking fragile and dazed, her wide eyes darker than he'd ever seen them. A drop of blood clung to her lower lip.

His stomach turned over. A quick survey showed him the cabin was empty. He kicked the door closed behind him and grasped her shoulders. "What happened?" His voice sounded raw, as if he'd screamed for hours.

Something sharp poked his middle. Dipping his head, he swallowed hard at the sight of the polished blade about to plunge into his belly.

"Becca, the knife."

She blinked, and it was as if a curtain lifted. Horror glistened in the jade depths.

"It's all right." Closing his hand about hers where she clutched the handle, he said softly, "I'm going to put this on the table." When he'd discarded it, he turned back, desperate to touch her, to reassure himself she was unharmed.

"I'm sorry—" She broke off.

"Your lip is bleeding." Very lightly, he brushed the spot away.

"Is it? I must've bitten it."

He settled his hands on the cool, creamy skin at the base of her neck. Beneath his thumb, her pulse was erratic. Hectic. Her gaze clung to his as if he were a lighthouse, and she, a ship adrift in a stormy sea.

"She was here, Caleb," she murmured mournfully. "And she wasn't alone."

His heart stopped. "Who was with her?"

"Wendell. She said it was her brother. I think that was a lie. H-he wanted—" She squeezed her eyes tight. "I was so frightened, Caleb."

Rage built in his chest, choking him. "What did he do?"

"Nothing." Reaching up to clasp his wrists, she looked scared. For *him.* Her reaction told him he needed to school his features. "I've no doubt he would have if Samantha had allowed him to stay." Her brow furrowed.

"He didn't believe I was married because I wasn't wearing a ring."

He felt the blood drain from his head. Becca had been in the company of the very woman who'd gunned down Tate. And the man with her... Images of what could've befallen her bombarded him. That had been close. Too close.

Her fingertips dug into his inner wrists. "I'm okay. I'm safe now that you're here." The fragile air was dissipating, and in her eyes, the fierceness he admired was reemerging.

"Tell me everything from start to finish."

She haltingly relayed the details. When she'd finished, gratitude washed over him. Becca could've easily been hurt. Or taken from him forever. A shudder racking his body, he tugged her against his long length and buried his face in her hair. She looped her arms tightly about his waist. When she snuggled against his chest, he let his fingers stroke the silken fall of her hair. Becca in his arms made him feel whole. After months of being lost, aimless, she grounded him.

Thank You, God, for protecting her. It was a prayer he was comfortable offering. After all, he wasn't asking Him for anything, merely expressing his thanks.

Caleb allowed himself five minutes to revel in this feeling of connection and harmony. Pulling away took every ounce of willpower and then some, especially when Becca looked as if he'd snatched away her favorite drawing pencils.

"I have to go after them."

"Why did you come back? What happened to joining the search party?"

"Shane told me there was a man who'd been nosing around town asking questions. I had to check on you and Amy."

"Amy!" She clapped her hand over her mouth. "She's at Meredith's. What if Wendell and Samantha…"

"I'm on my way."

"I'm going with you." She ran after him and reached for her coat and scarf.

He put a hand out to stay her movements. "It's too dangerous."

"I can't stay here alone," she protested. "Not today."

Caleb soaked in her winsome beauty. Nothing had changed. The girl who'd refused to be driven from his mind despite his best efforts, despite the fact she'd belonged to his best friend, still had the power to affect him.

"If anything had happened to you—" He shuddered and, because he was weak, dipped his head and captured her full lips. It was an intense kiss, fueled by high emotions and lingering fear. Becca's fingers tangled in his hair. When she sighed against his mouth and weaved closer, he gentled the pressure and the embrace morphed into something sweet and tender and devastating.

After the terror of the past hour, Caleb was her safe harbor, her resting place. He was no longer her enemy. He was her husband, at least on paper, and was currently taking advantage of that fact. And she was allowing him to.

His lips were soft, warm and sure, his fingers achingly gentle in her hair, the kiss sparking errant thoughts like what would it be like if their marriage was real?

What if they liked and respected each other? What would happen if they were somehow able to overcome the past and opened their hearts?

But thoughts of that nature were dangerous. While she'd come to terms with the role he'd played in the accident, he was not a man who would safeguard her heart. He wasn't safe and predictable like Adam. In her mind, he'd forever be that irresponsible, adventure-seeking boy who didn't think through the consequences of his actions.

This embrace was nothing but an escape from the loneliness that plagued them both and would lead to disaster if they let it.

Rebecca tugged on a lock of hair at his collar, and he immediately lifted his head, glazed brown eyes bearing witness to his distraction. "Ouch."

"We can't do this." She wished she didn't have to be logical. But she had to be if she wanted to survive this marriage with her sanity intact.

"You're right." Slowly nodding, he stroked her hair again from the crown of her head to the ends. "I know you're right, but I can't promise it won't ever happen again."

She should've been irritated. Instead, the frank words thrilled her. "That wasn't part of our agreement."

"I'll do my best to remember that." He reluctantly released her and lifted the door latch. "Ready?"

The ride to Meredith's was intense. Alert in the saddle, Caleb didn't utter a word, his entire focus on tree-lined slopes rising above them on either side. They were at a distinct disadvantage. Now that the snow had completely melted, a person could hide behind massive tree trunks, dark clothing melting into the landscape's varying shades of brown.

When they approached the Harper cabin, Louis, Meredith and Amy were in the yard tying a small tree to the black-and-gold sleigh. Amy fairly radiated excitement.

"Look, Rebecca." She bounced on her toes. "Mr. Harper cut down a Christmas tree for us. Isn't that great? We can string berries and popcorn and make paper ornaments."

Holding on to Caleb's proffered arm, Rebecca slid off Rebel's broad back. Christmas was the last thing on her mind, but for Amy's sake, she tried to muster some enthusiasm. "That sounds like fun."

Green gaze glittering with questions, Meredith linked arms with Rebecca and tugged her onto the porch as Caleb dismounted and went to speak with Louis.

"You decided to marry him?"

"In the end, I didn't have a choice." She matched her voice to hers. "I had to protect Amy."

"I'm sorry, Rebecca. I know this was the very last thing you wanted." She patted her arm. "You were holding out hope for Adam to come to his senses, and now it's too late."

Rebecca clasped the locket, confusion and guilt waging battle. "Everything is all mixed up, Mer. To be honest, I haven't had much time to think about Adam." *That's because ever since I discovered Caleb wounded in the snow, he's the one who's dominated my thoughts.* "Maybe I'd given up hope without even realizing it."

"You did stop writing him." Meredith glanced surreptitiously at Caleb deep in conversation with Louis.

Amy appeared oblivious to the adults, laughing as she tossed sticks to Storm, who'd accompanied her here. "How are you coping with having him around?"

"He agreed to keep his distance. He prefers his solitude to the company of family, anyway."

It was for the best. Obviously he was experiencing the same mysterious pull as she was, only he didn't fight it quite as hard as he should. Allowing Caleb to hold her, to *kiss* her, was as dangerous and foolhardy as building a fire in the midst of dry forest. So why did the prospect of his extended absences weigh down her soul?

Cocking her head, Meredith looked thoughtful. "From what I can remember, he wasn't like that before the accident. Whenever I saw Caleb, he was either with his brothers or cousins or Adam and you."

"Are you suggesting he doesn't truly want to stay away?"

"You'd know the answer to that better than I would."

Their conversation was interrupted when Meredith's mother, Teresa, appeared and ushered them inside for a hot drink. Seeing their Christmas tree draped in red and white and cloth-wrapped gifts beneath the branches reminded Rebecca that she'd allowed the recent upheaval in her life to distract her from the celebration of Christ's birth. Christmas was only seven days away. Her parents would've wanted her to make this time special for her sister. Husband and outlaw problems notwithstanding.

The smells of nutmeg, cinnamon and molasses hung in the air as Rebecca placed another pan of gingerbread men on the table to cool. They wouldn't have raisins to decorate with this year as they were too expensive, but she'd whipped up a simple icing for buttons and trim. Amy hadn't commented on the lack. She'd been all smiles since they'd returned from the Harpers' with the tree in Louis's sleigh.

"What's your favorite thing about Christmas, Caleb?" Seated at the table, Amy tied strips of gingham together to hang on the tree branches.

He turned from the window where he'd been standing for the past half hour, brooding gaze scanning and rescanning the scene. He hadn't removed his gun belt or holster, testament to his concern Samantha or others in her gang might return. They hadn't paid a visit to Louis and Teresa's. And while folks in their mountain community weren't entirely forthcoming to strangers, there was always the chance someone would let vital information slip. Or Samantha would grow impatient and turn to violence to get the information she sought.

Caleb's scrutiny of Rebecca sharpened, and he frowned. He must've guessed the direction of her thoughts, because the look he gave her said, *Try not to worry.* Limping across the room—he'd given up using his crutches, much to her consternation—he snatched up a warm cookie.

"The sweets are my favorite." He smiled for Amy's benefit and popped it in his mouth. "Mmm, these are delicious."

"Not the gifts?" Amy's fingers stilled on the material.

"Most of the time I got practical stuff like socks and scarves. Although one Christmas my uncle sent me a harmonica. My brothers were green with envy. They begged to borrow it, but I refused. As the youngest kid, there wasn't much that belonged solely to me."

"Do you still play?" Rebecca couldn't recall seeing him with a harmonica.

In answer, he went to the corner and, rustling through his saddlebag, withdrew the tiny instrument. He played a slow, melancholy tune. "I play when I'm in the mountains and the quiet gets to be too much."

His words reminded her of Meredith's assertion. "Don't you get lonely? Don't you miss your family?"

He dropped his gaze, but not before she glimpsed the anguish shining there. "Sometimes." When Amy's smooth brow furrowed, he eased into the chair beside her and fingered a piece of gingham. "Show me how to do this, and I'll help."

"You don't have to," she said.

"I want to."

While Rebecca iced the cookies, Amy and Caleb worked on the decorations. Dusk fell, and lamps set about the room cast a cheerful glow. The hemlock tree emitted a fresh, sharp aroma that defined Christmas. This year's celebrations would be different than all those preceding it. Caleb was an official part of their family now.

She licked a dab of icing off her thumb and let her gaze caress his bent head. Firelight glinted off the blue-black strands and outlined the harsh line of his proud cheekbones. The dark stubble that lent him a dangerous air graced his jaw and chin. He was intent on his work, blunt fingernails flashing as he carefully knotted the strips. That he would volunteer for such a task solely for her sister's sake filled Rebecca with heady warmth and admiration.

He looked up from his work then and caught her

staring. Her cheeks heated even as his eyes darkened with awareness. Why did he have to be so incredibly handsome? And why did he have but to look at her for her to be consumed with this toe-curling, heat-licking-her-insides yearning?

Adam didn't have that effect on me. His kiss was comfortable. Nice. Staid?

She blanked her mind. Comparing the two men would gain nothing. Adam was no longer a part of her life. And Caleb was…well, she was still trying to figure out exactly how he fit.

He lowered the decoration and leaned back against the chair, gray-and-white-striped shirt molding to his thick shoulders and biceps. "What about you, Becca? What's your favorite tradition?"

Replacing the spoon into the bowl of icing, she began to place the cookies on a platter. "I like the music. After Christmas Eve supper, we'd gather around the fireplace and sing carols. My pa had the most beautiful voice. I could listen to him and my mother sing for hours."

"I remember." Amy bowed her head. "Do you sing, Caleb?"

He was studying Rebecca with a sad expression. "Not really."

She nudged the gingerbread men closer together. "I've heard you sing. You have a nice voice. Deep and strong."

"Is that a compliment, Becca?" He managed to look simultaneously amused and puzzled.

Wiping her hands on her apron, she strove for candor. "Lately I've been remembering a lot of things I'd suppressed. For instance, you used to give your sandwich to Wally Dailey whenever he showed up at school without a lunch pail. You've always had a generous heart."

His brows lowered. "I'd hoped no one would notice." Because he'd sought to spare the young man humiliation.

"I doubt many did. I happened to observe the two of you one day sitting near the big maple tree behind the school. After that, I made a point to walk by each time I spied you wandering off by yourselves."

"I thought you were going to meet Adam." His thoughtful tone was at odds with the somber light in his eyes.

"Despite what you might think, my life did not revolve around him."

He looked as if he wanted to debate the issue, but Amy interrupted.

"Sounds like Wally was forgetful."

"Actually, his family was very poor," Rebecca told her.

"Oh." Her expression reflected approval as the significance of his actions sank in. "What else did Caleb do?"

"Nothing interesting." He shifted nervously in his seat.

"I have to disagree. What about the time you stood up to the Williams brothers when they ganged up on scrawny Johnny Westfield?"

"They were bullies."

"There were *four* of them. You didn't let that stop you, though."

"That was brave," Amy said, clearly fascinated. "What happened?"

"It was dumb," he countered, tips of his ears going pink. "I got thrashed."

"Johnny escaped unharmed." Rebecca easily recalled how he'd dashed into the school yard, yelling for help. All the students followed him. Even now, her stomach revolted at the memory of Caleb imprisoned between Lloyd and Samuel Williams while the younger brothers took turns slamming their fists into his gut and face.

"Your sister was the brave one." Enigmatic gaze fastened onto hers, shared memories shimmered between them. "Hollering like a madwoman, she ran straight for my attackers and tackled the first one she came to."

"You didn't!" Amy squealed. "How old were you? Why didn't I hear about it?"

"Sixteen, and you were too young."

"Were you hurt?"

"No. Those boys knew better than to hit a girl. Thankfully, the teacher came and broke it up. Caleb suffered a black eye and busted lip, though."

"It was nothing."

"Not to Johnny. You spared him. Sacrificed your own well-being. You're one of the most courageous men I've ever known."

"I don't have to try and remember good things about you." He leaned forward and braced his forearms against the table edge. "In fact, I have trouble recalling much negative, except for the fact you pretty much worshipped the ground Adam walked on."

Her jaw dropped. "I did not!"

"I was there. It all played out in front of me. Whatever he suggested, you went along with like an eager-to-please puppy. Talk about pathetic."

Anger sizzled between her ears. How dare he! Amy stared at them with open interest. "That is a rude thing to say, especially after I…" She bit down on her lip. *Of course.* Caleb couldn't handle her praise, so he'd done what came naturally. Made her angry in order to distract her.

Maybe she *had* been a little too biddable with Adam. A snippet of a conversation she'd had with her mother filtered through her mind. *Are you sure you're being true to yourself, Rebecca? Having opinions of your own doesn't mean you're disrespecting Adam or that he'll like you any less.*

Caleb folded his arms across his broad chest and arched a brow. "What I'd like to know is why you have no trouble whatsoever standing up to me."

"You're simply trying to bait me."

He paused, clearly taken aback by her calm demeanor. Then his lips firmed. "I meant what I said."

"So did I." Picking up a cookie, she held it out to him. "You possess a lot of admirable qualities, Caleb O'Malley, and I intend to remind you of each and every one of them."

Chapter Seventeen

C aleb nestled the string of bright red berries among
the branches of the squat tree. Situated in the corner beside the catch-all cabinet, it was as wide as it was tall.
The girls didn't seem to mind. Amy's smile was constant, her big eyes sparkling with happiness, and even
Becca looked pleased.

He couldn't recall the last time he'd decorated a
tree. When he and his brothers were younger, they'd
enjoyed helping their ma. As they'd grown older, however, they'd considered it a childish activity. Eventually
she'd stopped asking them to help. Guess she got tired
of the grumbling and eye-rolling.

Helping his wife and sister-in-law was altogether different. Not so much of a chore. He was discovering that
giving them pleasure made him feel good.

"It looks lovely, Caleb."

Each time Becca smiled at him—something that up
until recently was as rare as a flying squirrel sighting—
he felt as though he was flailing in deep water. A vise
clamped onto his lungs. His heart grew full to bursting,
and he had no clear means of rescue.

Her apology had changed things. Ever since that day they'd landed in a heap on the frozen ground and he'd compelled her to confess her troubles, she no longer looked at him with accusation and disdain. He suspected she no longer considered him the enemy, which left him floundering. He had no idea how to respond to this side of her. Frankly, it made him nervous.

Standing next to him, she affixed a white crochet cross to a branch tip. Dozens of crosses adorned the tree, a reminder of the sacrifice the newborn baby Jesus would eventually offer. *Can You ever forgive me, Lord? My shortcomings are too many to name, and I can't hide them from You.*

He touched a finger to one dangling nearby. "Did you make these?"

"Amy and I crocheted them last year. I thought a project like this would help distract us from our loss. It was our first holiday without our parents."

"Did it help?"

"A little." Glancing over her shoulder to where Amy sat sipping tea and surreptitiously feeding Storm bits of her gingerbread, Becca lowered her voice. "The cross represents forgiveness. I still don't have yours, Caleb. Have you thought about what we talked about?"

His insides went cold. This was wrong, *her* apologizing to *him.* "Your reaction to my role in the accident was completely justified."

She laid a hand on his arm, and the touch burned through the cotton. "Can you honestly say my words and actions didn't hurt you?"

Snared in her intent gaze, he found he couldn't be less than honest with her. "I can't."

"I punished you for what amounted to an unfortunate accident." He could see the regret tearing her apart.

"It's okay, Becca." He covered her hand and squeezed. "I was never angry with you. I knew you were hurting."

"You were, too. We all were."

"Are you saying you're willing to forgive me?" His voice was rough, strained. Inside his head pounded the refrain *I'm not worthy*.

She stroked one of the crosses. "For so long, I focused only on how the accident affected me. *My* disappointments, *my* suffering. I wish it hadn't taken me so long to come to this place. I don't blame you anymore."

Overcome with emotion, Caleb didn't trust himself to speak. He'd never allowed himself to imagine this moment because he hadn't believed it would ever happen. He wasn't even certain he could accept her absolution.

"I need some fresh air." Pivoting, he limped to the door and seized his hat and duster. His leg felt stronger, not as sore as before.

"Wait. What if—" She broke off, anxious gaze sliding to Amy. They'd agreed that telling her about Samantha and Wendell's visit would only terrorize her. "It's dark and cold out there. Maybe you shouldn't."

"I won't go far." Caleb swung the door open, and his heart nearly came out of his chest at the figure standing there. "What are you doing here?"

With Amy relegated to the bedroom with a book, Rebecca poured Shane Timmons a cup of coffee and set it on the table in front of him. Nodding his thanks, the rugged sheriff took a bracing sip and waited for her to join Caleb, who was sprawled in the chair opposite looking dangerous and irritated. Concerned, too, although he tried valiantly to mask it.

"I still think it'd be best if you three stay at your parents' until we catch these guys," Shane insisted a second time.

"Tomorrow's Christmas Eve," she protested. She'd never spent Christmas away from this cabin. Couldn't imagine it. "We can't barge in on Sam and Mary."

Caleb flicked her a glance. "We won't. I have my own cabin. It's within sight of the main house, however, and Josh and Kate live behind it."

Rebecca gestured around the room. "We've already prepared everything. The food. The tree. Holidays without my parents are difficult enough. Uprooting Amy now would only make things worse."

The gold star pinned to Shane's chest flashed as he shifted. "I don't mean to sound callous, but your safety takes precedence over Christmas sentiment. I've got men combing the town as we speak. There's no telling when or if someone might let vital information slip that would lead them straight back here."

"The news of our marriage has certainly made the rounds." A muscle jumping in his jaw, Caleb leveled his unflinching gaze at her. "I think we should do as Shane suggests. The plan's not foolproof, but my father and Josh would be nearby if trouble came knocking."

"I don't like this." At least here, she felt somewhat in control. This was her home. She was comfortable. Staying in Caleb's domain would not be the least bit comfortable.

"It's too dangerous to stay here, Becca."

There really was no sound argument to combat their reasoning. Shane was right—practicality trumped nostalgia. The thought of coming face-to-face with Wendell again had her nodding her head in agreement.

Deciding it would be wise to leave under cover of night, they broke the news to Amy, who, instead of protesting, viewed the whole thing as a grand adventure. They quickly gathered necessities and the baked goods that Rebecca had already prepared.

Storm and Amy were bundled in the wagon bed and the sheriff was astride his horse when Caleb hesitated in the doorway. He frowned at the tree cloaked in shadows, the stark white crosses tiny beacons in the gloom.

"I'm sorry we can't take it with us," he told her. He didn't seem all that eager to leave, either.

"It's all right." She tried to sound unaffected when in reality her insides felt hollow. "There's always next year."

She couldn't help but wonder if he would be around to spend Christmas with them or off on a hunting expedition. Would their relationship be the same as it was now? Fraught with uncertainty? Tainted by the past?

He caught her hand and squeezed. "Maybe we'll get back in time to enjoy it a little. There's no rule you have to discard it immediately following the holidays. I can water it when I come to see to the animals."

"That would be nice."

Despite his pronounced limp, Caleb held her arm as they descended the steps. Then he assisted her up and climbed onto the seat beside her. His large body blocked much of the wind during their trek across town. Still, Rebecca felt numb.

Although she knew it was unreasonable, it was as though she were abandoning her parents, that by leaving the home they'd built and inhabited their entire married life, she was leaving their memories behind. Perhaps it would be different if she and Caleb had married willingly, if they loved each other and were an actual couple. But she wasn't assured of his support. This marriage was a farce. And that made staying in his home, surrounded by his family—no matter that they were kind, considerate people—a daunting prospect.

When they arrived at the O'Malley farm and he relayed everything to the older couple, Mary insisted Amy stay in one of the empty rooms upstairs.

"Why should she sleep on the couch when we have perfectly good beds not being used?"

Caleb shifted, his face in the shadow of the porch overhang and therefore unreadable. "It's up to the girls."

Rebecca's tummy did a succession of somersaults. She was not about to share a small cabin with only her husband for company. "Really, Mary, she'll be fine on the couch."

Smoothing her long, brown braid threaded with silver, the older woman said, "After being the lone female in the house all these years, having a young girl around would be a treat for me. Wouldn't it, Sam?"

Propped in the doorway, Sam smiled and nodded.

Amy bounced up from her spot in the wagon bed. "Can I, please, Rebecca?"

Rebecca huddled inside her cape as another bracing wind sliced through her. Continuing to protest would only make things awkward. "All right, but mind your manners."

"I will."

Hopping down, she slung her bag over her shoulder and took the steps two at a time. Mary put an arm around her. "Would you like cookies and milk?"

"Yes, ma'am."

Sam lingered. "Need any help unloading, son?"

Walking around the horses, he shook his head. "No, thanks."

"See you in the morning, then."

The seat dipped beneath his weight. He guided the team past the large barn and various outbuildings toward the woods. There, tucked amid the tree line, was a single-story cabin not unlike her own.

"We originally built this for Josh and his first fiancée." He set the brake.

Rebecca recalled the story that had circulated when Kate first arrived in Gatlinburg. "Kate's sister, right?"

"Francesca."

"But he and Kate never lived here?"

After assisting her down, he walked beside her through the short grass. "Kate stayed here for a while. Then, once they decided to marry, we built them their current house, and I decided to move in here." On the porch, he paused with a hand on the door latch. "Wait here for a minute while I light the fire and make sure there aren't any critters who've taken up residence. Ma sweeps it out occasionally, so it shouldn't be too bad."

Four-legged critters didn't concern her half as much as being alone with him.

Huddled inside her coat, nervousness eclipsing her

exhaustion, Rebecca leaned against the rail and studied the wide fields where fruits and vegetables would flourish come spring and the tree-lined lane on the far side of the split-rail fence, all washed in the moon's luminescent glow. Somewhere overhead an owl hooted. The O'Malleys' farm was all open spaces and rolling fields and sturdy outbuildings, far different than her sheltered cove.

Caleb's boots scuffed against the boards. "There's a bit of dust. No critters that I could see, though."

Snagging a crate from the wagon bed, he loomed before her on his return trip. "I should probably carry you over the threshold. That's what a new groom's supposed to do, right?"

"Good thing you don't do what's expected," she said tartly, sidestepping him and rushing to enter the cabin before he could follow through with the idea.

"It was just a suggestion," he muttered under his breath.

Ignoring him, Rebecca went to stand before the fire, tugging off her gloves and holding her hands out toward the growing flames. The heat felt delicious. Her gaze skimmed upward, past the stacked stones similar to the ones in her fireplace, to the rough-hewn mantel. Her mouth fell open and an astonished gasp slipped out. There, beside the coffee grinder and glass-domed lamp, sat a sorry-looking clay vase with a chipped lip and uneven base.

Picking it up as if it were priceless art, she turned and searched out Caleb, who was sliding another crate onto the exquisitely carved walnut dining table. "I can't believe you kept this."

Expression smoothing when he spotted the vase, he kicked up a shoulder. "What can I say? I'm not the type of person who tosses out gifts."

Sweeping past the extralong, deep green sofa that looked as if it had never been sat on, she met him beside the stove. "It was a horrible birthday gift. I don't know what I was thinking. What seventeen-year-old boy would want something like this?"

"This seventeen-year-old was thrilled to get it." Smoothly taking it from her, he brushed past her and returned it to the mantel.

"Why? It's unsightly. And hardly functional."

His back to her, he gingerly fingered the rough surface. "The fact that you made it with me in mind is what makes it special."

"Oh." He'd held on to it simply because it was a gift from her?

Facing her once more, a nostalgic, almost sad smile curved his lips. "Your world revolved entirely around Adam Tierney. To say that I was stunned you'd spared a thought for me is an understatement. Especially after…" Grimacing, he pinched the bridge of his nose. "Never mind."

The crack about Adam annoyed her. Made her sound pathetic. "That's not fair. You can't start something and not finish it." Making herself comfortable on the sofa, she folded her hands in her lap and looked expectantly up at him.

Gaze hooded, hands braced against his lean waist, he didn't move to join her. Obviously he regretted the slip. "Something changed after we plucked that kitten out of the river. You shut me out. Acted like I had the plague or something similarly disgusting."

And now she regretted pushing the issue. What was she supposed to say? *I kept my distance because I was drawn to you? Because you evoked dangerous feelings in me?*

Rebecca plucked at nonexistent strings on her purple calico skirt. "Must've been your imagination," she murmured.

Tension-riddled silence descended. Caleb advanced toward her, halting when his boot toe connected with hers. Head lowered, she studied the slick, shiny black leather. "Don't bother denying it, Becca," he said coolly. "I wasn't the only one who noticed your odd behavior."

She sank against the cushions. "What are you talking about?"

"Did you think Adam wouldn't notice how all of a sudden you refused to sit beside me? Dance with me? How you made sure to never come within touching distance?" Confusion slid behind his eyes. "He confronted me about it. Demanded to know what I'd done to you. I told him the truth, that I had no idea what I'd done. I still don't."

"He didn't mention it to me." Heart thudding uncomfortably against her ribs, she squirmed in her seat, racking her brain for something to say. There was nothing. No plausible explanation.

His stark gaze raked her face. "Are you going to enlighten me or leave me in the dark?"

Rebecca absolutely could not confess the truth, despite the evidence of his bewildered hurt. Popping up, she stifled the urge to flee his compelling presence.

"You didn't do anything wrong. Let's just leave it at that."

Capturing her chin, he gently lifted her face. "What are you afraid of?"

You, she almost blurted. *The way you make me feel.* "If I'm afraid of anything, it's deranged outlaws intent on finding you."

His lips compressed into a thin line. "You're a terrible liar, you know that?" Releasing her, he strode stiffly for the door. "I'll get the rest of our things."

Deflated, nerves on edge, she stood and strayed to the bedroom located off the living area. The ceiling in this room was much lower, the beams about an inch above her head, and there were no windows. A pine bed covered with a navy, red and white quilt dominated the stark room. Skirting it, she opened the armoire doors and spied his clothes hanging from the rod. His distinctive pine-and-earth scent hit her square in the face, and she tamped down the urge to sniff the nearest shirt. Liar indeed.

Quickly closing the doors, she surveyed the space again. Something was missing. Caleb's personality, his stamp, was not in evidence. Besides the clothes, there was nothing at all to indicate that this was his place. The lack of personal items bothered her.

Didn't he long for a real home? Was living under the stars, moving from campsite to campsite, enough for him?

He entered the room balancing her trunk in his arms. Lowering it to the floor, he turned to leave. "That's the last of it."

"There's only one bed."

Twisting back, he gave her an enigmatic look. "Yep."

"If I'd insisted on Amy sleeping here with us, you and I would've had to share it." Her sister would've expected it. She'd already asked why she and Caleb hadn't switched places considering they were married.

"Yep."

"Why didn't you warn me?"

"In front of my parents?" Arching a brow, he hooked a thumb over his shoulder. "I'll be fine on the sofa."

She edged closer to the bed, resting a hand on the footboard. "I can't take your room."

"Either you sleep in the bed alone or we share it," he calmly stated. "Take your pick."

Not going to happen. He knew it, too. "I'm a restless sleeper. You don't want to share with me."

"Whatever you say." With a shrug, he left her to unpack her things. She stared in dismay at the empty doorway. This whole arrangement was going to try her sanity.

Rebecca took her time unpacking. As strange as it was to hang her dresses beside his shirts and trousers, the mundane task restored her equanimity. When she finally emerged, she found him crouched at the fireplace, prodding the logs with a long poker.

"Since the cabin's been shut up, you might wanna leave the bedroom door open tonight. That way the warmth can reach you."

"And subject myself to your snoring?" she teased without thinking. "No, thanks."

He straightened. "I do not snore."

"How would you know? It's not like the birds and

squirrels would tell you. I, on the other hand, have heard you with my own ears."

"Is that so?" He slowly advanced, and the light of mischief in his eyes fired a thrill down her spine. Mischief was so much better than displeasure.

"It's a horrible sound." She adopted an aggrieved expression, thoroughly enjoying this. "Like ten grizzly bears crammed in a cave together."

One dark brow arched as he bypassed the sofa. "Only ten?"

She tapped her chin. "You're right. It's more like twenty."

Suddenly his hands were on her, tickling along her rib cage, evoking peals of laughter. Rebecca squirmed. Pushed at his hands. The lopsided grin brightening his normally somber face buoyed her spirits. Gave her a glimpse of the lighthearted boy he'd once been.

"Grizzly bears, huh?" He continued his assault until she was out of breath. The moment his hold went slack, she danced out of reach. "You're fortunate, Mrs. O'Malley, that my bum leg is giving out. Otherwise, I'd have you begging for mercy."

Rebecca startled at the unfamiliar title. Somehow, it sounded right falling from his lips. *Don't think that. It was supposed to be Mrs. Tierney,* the part of her heart that was loyal to Adam shouted. Beneath the collar of her blouse, the locket weighed heavily against her skin, a silent warning to guard her heart. Look how easily Adam walked away from her. Caleb had made her no promises, had been clear about his plans to leave.

"I warn you, I'll be listening carefully tonight. I have a feeling I'm not the only one who snores around here."

That soul-shocking grin was still in place, his brown eyes earnest. His shiny black hair fell across his forehead. He looked approachable and carefree, and all she wanted was to prolong the rare moment of fun, the sense of connectedness. But she'd learned her lesson well. She wasn't willing to repeat it.

"You know what? I'm actually not that cold. Guess you'll have to wait and wonder." And with that, she went into the bedroom and shut the door. On him. And on foolish hopes.

Chapter Eighteen

As little as a month ago, Caleb would've said he'd be spending Christmas alone on a remote mountaintop somewhere, feasting on trout and dried jerky, fantasizing about his ma's pumpkin pie and wondering if Kate had made him an uncle yet. How quickly plans changed. He could not have foreseen being back in this cabin that didn't feel like home, with a woman who had no desire to be his wife.

He'd known the moment he called her Mrs. O'Malley that it had been a mistake. It was as if Adam himself had materialized in the flesh—a living, breathing reminder that Caleb was a poor substitute. When she'd reached for the locket out of habit, something had clicked in his mind. There could be no doubt whose likeness that locket bore. Fighting jealousy he had no right feeling, he'd watched her retreat with deep regret. Then he'd lain on the stiff sofa cushions and stared at the rafters until exhaustion claimed him.

He'd awoken before dawn and, worried Becca would be cold, risked bodily harm by entering her room and tucking the quilts more closely about her sleeping form. Of course he'd lingered. Her breathing deep and even, her pearl-like skin a stark contrast to the dark waves tumbling across her pillow, her puckered brow spoke to the problems plaguing her even in sleep.

That brow had given him an idea. And now here he was, nearly two hours later, nursing his third coffee, impatient for her reaction.

At ten minutes to eight, the door at last creaked open. Becca wore a fetching striped dress that hugged her curves and made her eyes pop.

"Good morning," he offered from his place at the window, letting the curtain fall back into place. "I hope you slept well."

"I overslept, didn't I?" She touched a hand to her upswept hair. "You should've woken me. You must be starving."

"I can see to my own needs. Besides, we had a late night. You needed your rest."

Nodding, she hung back, hands fisted at her sides. His thoughts returned to last night's unfinished conversation.

What wasn't she telling him about the past? What had triggered the change in her treatment of him? He'd gone over the handful of days they'd spent in her parents' barn nursing the poor cat to health thousands of times and come up empty. They hadn't argued. On the contrary, without Adam around as a distraction, he and Becca had connected in a way they hadn't before. They'd talked for hours. About everything and nothing. He remembered teasing her. A lot. Simply to see the blush bloom on her cheeks and the sparkle light up her magnificent eyes. If he'd offended her, she'd hidden it well.

"Was the sofa comfortable...?" Becca trailed off, attention snared by the evergreens and holly arranged atop the mantel and the spindly tree in the corner. Floating over to the fireplace, she leaned down to inhale the greenery. The pleasure curving her lips filled him with satisfaction. He'd done the right thing. "Did you do this all by yourself?"

"The place was too bare." He tipped his cup toward the tree. "I'm sure Ma has extra ribbons you and Amy can use if you wanna add some color."

"Thank you, Caleb. I'd forgotten how thoughtful you are."

The brilliance of her smile wrapped around him, suffusing him with a contentment he hadn't felt in years. Could happiness be this easy to achieve? Simply by making Becca smile?

He grabbed another mug from the shelf and, dusting it out, poured her some coffee. "How about I scramble you an egg? Then we can peek in on the expectant parents."

It had been weeks since he'd seen his oldest brother, since Thanksgiving, actually. He was curious how Josh was handling impending fatherhood. Smothering poor Kate, probably.

Becca rummaged through one of the baskets on the table and produced a jar of muscadine jelly. "Not necessary. I'll just have some bread."

He handed her the steaming mug, then gathered a plate and knife for her, which gained him another sweet smile. Oh, yeah. A man could get used to this.

* * *

Christmas morning, Caleb greeted Rebecca with ready-made coffee, a cinnamon bun he'd most likely snatched from his mother's kitchen and two presents. Expression schooled to blandness, he scooted both packages—one a square, small box and the other rectangular in shape—across the polished tabletop.

"Merry Christmas, Becca."

She skimmed a finger across the plain brown wrapping paper. "I didn't realize we were exchanging gifts."

"You're my wife," he said simply, as if that was explanation enough.

Sinking into the chair opposite, she splayed her hands on the smooth wood. "I don't have a gift for you."

She hadn't even entertained the thought. Some wife she was turning out to be.

"I don't need anything." His mouth curled with fleeting humor. "I'm sure my parents will supply me with a year's worth of socks and scarves."

Rebecca couldn't be this close and not be affected by him. Mornings were the worst. The shadow of a beard darkening his jaw and chin called to her fingers to explore the chiseled planes. The hair slipping into his eyes would tickle her skin if she threaded it off his forehead as she longed to do. The brown depths weren't as guarded, as if his nightly dreams yet lingered, clouding reality and weakening his defenses.

It didn't help that he was wearing her favorite shirt, the buttermilk-colored one that complemented his skin and dark hair and eyes, the soft cotton conforming to his broad chest and muscular arms. Caleb's controlled strength was housed in a lean, powerful body that hummed with vitality. One that was capable of incredible gentleness.

She shoved memories of their embrace to the far reaches of her mind.

"Aren't you curious what's in that?" He tipped his head to the larger box she'd rested her hand on.

"Very."

"Then I suggest you open it," he teased.

Despite his reassurances, Rebecca felt bad for not getting him anything. And deeply touched that he'd thought of her. Peeling away the paper, she smiled when she saw the drawing pencils and paintbrushes. He'd always been supportive of her passions. "Not only are you thoughtful, but perceptive, as well. Thank you. I will put these to good use."

"I know you will."

Laying the art supplies aside, she picked up the smaller box with a pinprick of trepidation. It resembled a jewelry box. But that couldn't be right. Caleb wasn't the frivolous type. Or was he?

The silence permeating the room grew heavy with expectation. When she lifted the lid and spotted the unadorned gold band, her gaze shot to his. "What's this?"

Scraping his chair back, he came around and took the box from her limp fingers. Extracting the ring, he silently lifted her left hand and slipped it on. "This may not be a conventional marriage—" his voice was coarse "—but the fact remains that we are husband and wife. No one will have cause to question it now."

Rebecca stared at the ring, which fit her finger perfectly. "This is because of Wendell."

He winced. "In part. The incident made me realize I'd overlooked an important part of our union, and I wanted to remedy the oversight." Fishing in his pant pocket, he withdrew a similar gold band. "Figured I'd get one for myself." He quickly slid it on and returned to his seat, his focus on the contents of his mug.

Rebecca stared at her hand. While the ring fit, the weight of it would take some getting used to. The flash of polished gold seemed to scream possession. How much of Caleb's motivation stemmed from the incident with Wendell and how much from the need to claim her as his own?

I'm reading too much into this, she told herself. *He didn't ask for this marriage any more than I did.*

Scooting the breakfast plate closer, she managed a strained thank-you. Why she felt conflicted about the ring she couldn't pinpoint. *Maybe because I'd envisioned wearing his best friend's ring, not his?*

"As soon as you're finished," he said, "we can go on over to the main house. I'm sure Amy is straining at the bit to open presents." Cocking his head, he indicated the small present laid out on the coffee table. "I've one to give her, as well."

Again, his kindness touched Rebecca, making her odd reaction to the ring dissolve like fog in sunlight. "You're too kind. She'll be pleased."

"I couldn't very well forget my sister-in-law on Christmas, could I?"

Swallowing a moist bite of the sweet, she said worriedly, "Since I didn't know we'd be spending the day with your family, I wasn't able to prepare gifts for them."

"They don't expect you to give them anything."

"Still—"

Caleb covered her hand with his own. His ring gleamed in the early-morning light streaming through the kitchen window. *Looks good on him,* she thought with surprise.

"They would be upset if they knew you were fretting about it, so don't. Please."

"All right."

The O'Malleys had been good to her and Amy. She didn't want to cause them anxiety, especially Kate. They had had a wonderful visit with Kate and Josh yesterday morning. It was the first time Rebecca had spoken with the New York native in an intimate setting, and she'd discovered they had many things in common, including a love of books. They'd spent the better part of an hour speaking of Kate's love of photography and Rebecca's drawing. Josh and Caleb had entertained themselves with talk of farming and furniture.

More than once, Rebecca had caught Caleb's furtive glances at Kate's large tummy. Because she was petite, the baby she was carrying seemed to dwarf her small frame. He'd appeared simultaneously fascinated and horrified. And when his gaze had entwined with Rebecca's, regret had flickered in the dark depths only to be quickly banished. She'd considered broaching the matter with him, but what was there to say? *Have you changed your mind about having babies? Should we try for a family?*

Unaware of the direction of her thoughts, he deposited his dishes in the dry sink. "I will warn you. O'Malley family holidays can be overwhelming. My aunt and cousins are coming, except Juliana and her family, of course. There may be embarrassing childhood tales. If Megan and the girls have anything to do with it, those tales are likely to be embellished to the point of ridiculousness."

"You're nervous about what they might tell me, aren't you?"

"I'm just saying don't believe everything you hear today." Hips leaning against the counter, arms crossed over his chest, he flashed a lopsided grin that had a devastating effect on her equilibrium. Her husband was the picture of health and masculine appeal. The scar couldn't detract from that.

Suddenly she very much looked forward to watching him interact with his family members. That she craved insight into his personality didn't have to mean anything beyond mere curiosity, did it?

"Time to open presents." Lovely in an ice-blue, beribboned dress that matched her expressive eyes, Sophie tugged Rebecca out of the chair and through the doorway leading to the living room. Over her shoulder, she addressed their mother-in-law, who was alone in the kitchen slicing into a pecan pie. "Dessert can wait, Mary. Your husband is about to read the Christmas story."

"I'll be right there," Mary called after them.

Sophie leaned in close. "I don't know about you, but I doubt I could eat another bite after that feast."

Rebecca smiled. As usual, the younger girl's bubbly personality put her at ease. Sophie was one of those people who didn't possess a single critical bone in her body and who made everyone around her feel welcome.

Looking around at her newly acquired family, she acknowledged that everyone here had made an effort to include her and Amy. Even standoffish Nicole.

Rebecca hung back as Sophie went to join Nathan on the stairs. The room was filled to overflowing. Will and Amy sat on the striped rug closest to the decorated tree, their attention on the simply wrapped packages beneath the fragrant branches. A very pregnant Kate occupied one of the wingback chairs. Radiant in a frilly peach dress, she couldn't hide her discomfort or the shadows beneath her eyes. Josh stood behind her chair, concern lining his face as he kneaded her shoulders.

Caleb's aunt Alice was ensconced in the other chair, and Nicole, Jessica and Jane had set up dining chairs directly behind the blue serpentine sofa.

"Rebecca." Megan beckoned with a wave of her hand. "There's room here."

Seated beside her distinguished husband, Lucian Beaumont, the fair-haired young woman indicated the single remaining spot on the sofa. Right beside Caleb.

While the O'Malleys had welcomed her into the fold, they had also observed her and Caleb's interactions with curiosity and open scrutiny. Not that she blamed them, considering their past history and the circumstances surrounding their marriage. Still, the attention made her feel as if she were on display.

"Mary can sit there," Rebecca said. "I'll get another chair."

"Oh, no, dear." Mary came in behind her and patted her shoulder, blue eyes twinkling. "You go sit with your husband."

Caleb's penetrating gaze tracked her slow approach.

While he'd been quiet throughout the meal, she'd gotten the impression he was simply soaking everything in.

There wasn't much cushion space left, so when she sat down her generous skirts spilled over onto his pants and her side wedged into his. He angled his head toward her, a bone-melting smile curling his lips. Her breath hitched. They hadn't been this close since the day Samantha and Wendell had paid her a visit and he'd pulled her into a kiss she couldn't stop reliving in her daydreams. One she wouldn't mind repeating.

On the other side of Caleb, Lucian and Megan exchanged a significant look. Across from them, Josh was watching them thoughtfully. Oh, boy.

Cheeks burning, Rebecca centered her attention on her father-in-law, who was standing beside the fireplace with his large black Bible. As he read from the familiar passage in Luke, relating the events leading up to Christ's birth, memories of her parents pressed in. Sam's resonant voice sounded too much like her father's. Each Christmas morning, he'd read those same verses aloud as she, Amy and their mother listened.

Jim Thurston had loved the Lord. Had cherished his family. Rebecca hadn't once questioned his love for her. How she missed his tight hugs, his booming laughter. Missed seeing him take her mother's hand and dance with her across the room. She felt their absence every day. Why did holidays have to be this difficult?

Tears filled her eyes and slipped down her cheeks. Beneath the covering of her skirts, Caleb's hand found hers. His strong fingers laced with hers and held on tight.

She didn't dare look at him, lest she completely lose control. His silent show of support was the latest in a growing list of admirable traits she'd conveniently forgotten.

His unfailing thoughtfulness, his small kindnesses, were slowly but surely altering her view of him. It was growing increasingly difficult to see him as the thoughtless wrecker of dreams she'd painted him to be.

Sam closed the Bible and, hugging it against his chest, swept the room with his wise, bespectacled gaze. "This year we've welcomed several new additions to our family. Some have come from far away." He smiled at Lucian, who hailed from New Orleans. "And some from right next door." Everyone chuckled as Sophie bussed Nathan's cheek. "We're still waiting for the newest addition. Impatiently, I might add." He gestured to Kate, who blushed prettily. "I've watched each of my sons find happiness."

When Sam's gaze landed squarely on Rebecca, she struggled to maintain a composed air. Surely he didn't believe Caleb was happy with her?

"We have much to be thankful for," he continued. "And must remember to thank God for our blessings. Let's pray."

Rebecca didn't have time to bow her head, because suddenly Caleb was pressing a handkerchief into her free hand. Concern warmed his eyes as they caressed her dampened cheeks. She had the distinct feeling that, if they had been alone, he would've mopped up her tears and pulled her close for a hug.

I want him to be happy.

The thought whispered across her heart like the gentle sweep of a paintbrush.

I'm tired of seeing him suffer.

Surely there were ways to make his life better without falling for the man.

Chapter Nineteen

This was his best Christmas.

Not because of the socks or scarves or pecan pie. Not because he was surrounded by loved ones instead of alone on a mountaintop.

It was all due to a gorgeous, green-eyed female who happened to be wearing his wedding ring.

This was also his worst Christmas. Because next year he wouldn't be here. His wife and sister-in-law would spend the holiday with his family, without him. And he'd know exactly what he was missing.

Taking advantage of Rebecca's momentary solitude—his cousins had dominated her time since the opening of presents began—he slipped his arm through hers.

"Come with me."

Her eyes widened in surprise. "Where?"

"Anywhere there aren't people around."

Her brows went up, but a smile played at the corners of her lush mouth. "That might be hard to do."

"Back porch."

Winding their way through the crowd, they passed through the narrow dining area and into the kitchen. Sure enough, no one else had ventured outside. Becca rubbed her arms as her breath came in white puffs.

"Want me to get your cape?"

Drifting to the railing, attention riveted to the rolling fields and mountains spread out before them, she shook her head. "I can manage without it for a bit."

Leaning against the railing so that he faced her, he was relieved to note the redness about her eyes had disappeared and her color had returned. Seeing her anguish had made him ache with helplessness. "You were upset earlier. I'd like to know why. Did my family make you uncomfortable? Did I do something to hurt your feelings?"

A line appeared between her brows. "Your family has been wonderful. So have you." She studied the muted green grass beyond the railing. "I miss my parents, that's all."

"This is your second Christmas without them."

"Yes."

"I'm sorry. I wish there was something I could do or say to make it better." But he couldn't. He knew that. And next year he wouldn't be around to hold her hand. Regret twisted his gut.

"Am I interrupting something?"

Caleb jerked at the sound of Nathan's voice. He'd been so absorbed in Becca that he hadn't heard his approach. What if it had been one of Samantha's hired goons? Good way to get them both killed. *How about I get my head out of the clouds?*

He turned his head to glare at his too-cheerful brother. "Yes, you are. Go away, Nate."

Becca's hand came to rest on his sleeve. Peering past him, she smiled at Nathan. "Don't listen to him. Have you been to see the new calf?"

Nathan climbed the porch steps and propped a shoulder against the notched-log wall, a maddening grin on his face. "Sure have. He's doing fine." His gaze lowered to where Becca clutched Caleb's arm. "I see you finally got your wedding rings."

Becca's hand fell away. "It was a Christmas gift."

"Good thinking, little brother."

"Is there anything specific you wanted, Nate?" Caleb prompted, irritated for wanting time alone with Becca but unable to deny himself.

Chuckling, Nate straightened and reached for the door. "I'll leave you two alone."

"Wait." Hugging her middle, Becca's tone grew serious. "I never got a chance to thank you for what you did for us."

Nathan's gaze turned quizzical. "I don't understand."

"After my parents' passing, you were one of the few people who continued to check on Amy and me. Your kindness made our grief easier to bear. I'm sorry I didn't mention it before."

Stomach going queasy, Caleb stared at his boots.

Nathan shifted his stance. "Um, about that…"

Caleb's head popped up, and he shot him a *don't you dare* stare.

Massaging his neck, Nathan sighed. "I have to be honest. It wasn't my idea to visit you."

"Nathan," Caleb warned, deliberately not looking at Becca.

"Oh. I—I didn't realize." Shifting slightly away from Caleb, she studied his profile. "Whose idea was it?"

"I think I'll let my brother fill you in on the particulars." In a moment, he was gone, the door closed firmly behind him.

"You put him up to it, didn't you?" she asked softly.

Caleb straightened, set his shoulders. "I needed to know that you were all right."

"Why not come yourself?"

He raised his head and stared at her. "The same reason I didn't let you see me at the funeral. I didn't want to cause you more grief."

"So you sent Nathan in your place."

"Yes."

"I had no idea."

"Are you angry?"

"Angry? Because you cared about my well-being? No." Standing very close to him, wide eyes shining with gratitude and something more he couldn't name, she cupped his cheek. "The truth is, I'm not surprised. Not now that…" She trailed off, apparently unwilling to finish her sentence. "Thank you, Caleb. I'll never forget what you did."

Rebecca escaped inside before she did something rash, like hugging her husband and refusing to let go. Ever.

He hadn't been indifferent. He'd cared. Not only had he attended the funeral, he'd sent his brother in his stead to check on them. She should've guessed.

"This is where I've been sleeping." Amy, who'd snagged her in the kitchen and brought her upstairs, ran a finger along the single bed frame that used to be Josh's. "Look at the view." Smiling, she pointed to the window overlooking the apple orchard. Rounded mountain peaks rose in silent majesty. "Isn't it grand?"

Rebecca smiled at her enthusiasm, glad her sister was content staying with Sam and Mary.

"Don't get too comfortable," she felt compelled to warn. "This is only temporary. We'll be returning to our place as soon as the sheriff deems it safe."

Probably for the best. Uninterrupted time alone with her husband was having a peculiar effect on her. At night, her dreams were filled with him. Unable to recall the exact nature of the dreams, she woke with a feeling of deep dissatisfaction, longing for something she couldn't identify.

Amy turned to her with a slight frown. The afternoon light emphasized the freckles smattered across her nose. "I like it here. I like having my own room. I like the animals, the fact you can see for miles. The truth is, spending time with Caleb's parents makes me miss ours less. Does that mean I'm a horrible person?"

"Oh, Amy, no." Rebecca pulled the shorter girl into a hug and smoothed her loose hair. "Not at all. I—I think they'd be happy we're part of a new family. They wouldn't want us to be alone or sad."

Amy returned the hug. "But we can't stay here, can we?"

"No. However, we can visit anytime. Sam and Mary have made that clear."

"Amy?" Will appeared in the doorway. "We're starting a game of charades downstairs. Wanna play?"

"Sure."

Glad her sister had someone close to her own age around, Rebecca followed the pair down the hallway. A buzz of voices drifted up the stairs. Passing by the last bedroom on the left, Rebecca caught sight of Nicole with a sewing project in her lap. No surprise there. The raven-haired beauty was a whiz with a needle and in great demand around these parts. At eighteen, Nicole O'Malley was more goal-oriented, more driven, than most folks twice her age.

She was very different than her sisters—not only in appearance, but in personality. While Juliana, Megan and the twins were friendly and approachable, it was as if a visible barrier surrounded Nicole that warned others to keep their distance. It wasn't that she was unkind. Just difficult to engage and a little aloof.

She's family now, which means I should make an effort to befriend her.

Crossing the polished wooden floors, Rebecca sank onto the edge of the bed across from the rocker. "That's a beautiful shade of green." She pointed at what looked to be a dress.

Nicole's bow-shaped mouth twitched in what might've been a smile. "I'm glad you like it. It's your wedding present."

Rebecca's mouth fell open. *Not* the response she was expecting. "Honestly?"

The younger girl nodded, coal-black ringlets sliding along her butter-colored bodice. Her attention never left her needle. "Megan purchased the material, and Jane and Jessica donated the trim and buttons. She chose the perfect color. It will look amazing with your eyes."

Flattered, she simply thanked her.

Nicole lifted a dainty shoulder. "I would have liked to have it finished by today, but my new position at Clawson's is eating into my sewing time."

"Caleb mentioned you'd started there. How do you like it?"

"It's bearable. I'm gaining valuable experience," she said, as if that surprised her.

"Have you thought of what you will call your boutique?"

Striking violet eyes lifted to Rebecca's face. "You're the first person to ask me that. As if you truly believe I'll actually have one someday."

"You're talented." She gestured to the dress in Nicole's lap. "Not to mention smart and passionate about your dream. Why wouldn't you succeed?"

Grimacing slightly, Nicole pressed a hand to her temple. "I don't have any prospective names yet," she murmured, avoiding the question. "I'll let you know what I come up with. Perhaps you can help me choose."

"I'd be happy to." Something seemed off, her usual confidence conspicuously absent, but Rebecca wasn't sure how to broach the subject. Wasn't as if they were best friends. Did Nicole even have a best friend?

Pushing upward, Rebecca said, "I'll leave you to your work. Thanks again for the wedding gift."

"We didn't get Caleb anything," she slyly remarked, "but I figure seeing you in this dress will be gift enough for him."

"Oh, no, it's not like that with us...." she hotly denied.

"When you're sewing in the company of others, you tend to tune out their conversations. You learn to hear what people are really saying through their movements, their changes in breathing and facial expressions. I know my cousin and, for him, it *is* like that."

Rebecca fought the need to ask exactly what she'd seen in Caleb's behavior that would lead her to such a conclusion.

"And as irritating as Caleb can be sometimes," Nicole said, and maintained eye contact, "I'd like to see him find peace."

Peace. Happiness. "I'd like that, too."

Problem was, she failed to see how a union such as theirs would ever result in those things.

Chapter Twenty

Caleb carried the last pail of milk to the rear barn wall and poured it into the waiting crocks lined up on the shelf. His thigh trembled with strain. His fingers were stiff from milking all the cows himself. He thought about the hunting trips he'd taken these past couple of years, the countless weeks he'd left Nathan to shoulder the weight of their dairy business alone. He'd consoled himself with the knowledge he was contributing to the family's food supply. Couldn't make up for his physical presence, though, could it? Nathan had needed help, yet he'd never attempted to guilt Caleb into staying.

Mopping his brow with a handkerchief, he secured the lids onto the crocks and went to wash his hands in the barrel. In the stalls lined up on either side of the center aisle behind him, the cows munched on hay, the scent of warm milk familiar and soothing. While he appreciated some aspects of his vagabond lifestyle, nothing could beat the satisfaction that came with working his own land, land that had been in their family for generations—a heritage he was increasingly reluctant to relinquish.

Careful, O'Malley. Thoughts like those could unleash a firestorm of dangerous yearnings...for family, home and hearth, constancy. All things I don't deserve.

One of the double doors swung open, admitting a blast of blustery air that whipped his hair across his forehead and pressed his pant legs against his boots. Becca entered the lofty structure, her graceful form cloaked in her thick wool cape, and he tamped down the immediate pleasure her presence evoked. This move to his cabin—and their uninterrupted privacy—had only served to deepen his awareness of her and stir emotions better left locked away.

Threading the hair out of his eyes, he moved forward to greet her. "You're up early."

Considering their late night, he'd assumed she would need extra sleep. They'd stayed at his parents' until nearly midnight, playing games, singing carols and eating insane amounts of food. *And I loved every minute of it, didn't I? Because anything shared with Becca was better than if I were alone.*

"Did you eat breakfast?"

"Yes, I found the plate you left out for me." She smiled, and he thought how fortunate he was to be on the receiving end of that spectacular smile. He'd never tire of it.

She must've noticed how he placed all of his weight on his good leg, because the good humor faded. "Are you in pain?" She observed the animals in stalls on either side of the aisle and the crocks that needed to be delivered to the mercantile. "You really shouldn't be doing this alone. From now on, I want you to wake me so that I can help."

"I'm fine. And while I appreciate your offer, there's no need. Nathan normally comes over to milk, but I told him to take the morning off."

"You can't expect to do the chores here and at my place, too. Not with your leg still on the mend."

"Your place? I thought it was our place?"

"Don't try and distract me, Caleb." Her eyes narrowed. "Tell me, when is Doc Owens coming to check the wound? Because if it's not today, we're paying him a visit in town."

"It's today." Thankfully. Without knowing what evidence, if any, Shane had gathered concerning the gang's whereabouts, he wasn't about to let her anywhere near town.

"Oh, really? What time?"

"You sound as if you don't believe me…." He sauntered closer, his defenses weakening as they always did whenever she was around. His need to be near her was stronger than the voice of caution inside his head.

Becca jutted her chin. "Time?"

"Between the hours of one and four were his exact words. Satisfied?"

"I will be present for this examination."

"I don't think so." When she opened her mouth to protest, he held up a hand. "However, you're welcome to interrogate Doc afterward." His gaze snagged on a piece of paper she held behind her back. "What's that?"

Uncertainty flitted across her face, and his curiosity inched up a notch.

"I wasn't snooping through your things, if that's what

you're thinking," she rushed to say, the paper fluttering with her gestures. "It's just that I…well, your saddle-bag was lying open beside the door and this would've fallen out if I hadn't—"

Snatching it from her, he glanced at the drawing he'd kept with him since the day she'd given it to him. A drawing of himself—before the scar—and Rebel.

"Why do you carry it with you?" she said. "To remind yourself of happier times?"

"No. It's a warning to never be that stupid and reckless again."

"Caleb." Shadows darkened her eyes. "We all make mistakes."

He skimmed a fingertip over the likeness of his younger, unblemished face. "Sorry you got shackled with a freak."

"Don't say that." His head jerked up at the undisguised anger in her voice. "Back then, you were too handsome for your own good. Some would even say a bit cocky." Time seemed to slow as she lifted her fingers to his face, lightly exploring the twisted, puckered skin. Caleb stood frozen, afraid to blink, loath to breathe. His heart bucked, and every nerve ending in his body stood to attention. The tenderness in her expression mesmerized him. "The scar makes you interesting. Gives your face character."

"Character, huh?" His voice resembled a rusty gate.

"I'd like to do another portrait of you."

"What?" Startled, he stumbled back. "No."

She tilted her head. "Why not?"

He pointed to the scar. "Why would I want this captured on paper?"

"Caleb, I—"

She didn't get to finish because Meredith burst through the doors, all smiles and oblivion and hauling a basket overflowing with goodies. "Here you are! When I went to the main house searching for you, Mary told me I might find you here. I know I'm not due for another hour, but I couldn't wait another minute to bring you and Amy your Christmas presents." She folded Becca in her arms. "I feel like it's been a lifetime since we've talked."

Giving them space, Caleb moved to the corner, carefully refolding the drawing.

"I'll be in the cabin if you need me," Becca told him, clearly torn between frustration and eagerness to spend time with her friend.

"Enjoy your visit."

"We'll finish our conversation later."

"As you wish, darling wife." He bowed like a servant before his queen.

Despite Meredith's look of uncertainty, Becca's smile held a silent promise. "Oh, I do wish, *dear* husband. Until later."

"What did I interrupt?" Meredith demanded, shrugging out of her cape and gloves and hanging them on the coatrack.

"Nothing that can't wait." Rebecca pulled down a tin of tea and a teapot dotted with roses. She needed to focus on something other than her still-tingling fingers, hardly able to fathom she'd allowed herself to touch his scar. Even more shocking, Adam hadn't once crossed her mind. Nor had the accident. "How was your Christmas?"

Unwinding the bright red scarf from around her neck, Meredith draped it across the dining chair and folded her arms. "I don't want to discuss my holiday. I'd much rather talk about what's going on with you and Caleb."

"It's complicated," she hedged, tossing kindling in the firebox and filling the kettle with water. While she wasn't averse to confiding in her friend, she hardly knew how to sort through her jumble of emotions.

"Something has changed. I could see it in the way you looked at each other. More specifically, how *you* looked at *him*. Am I right?"

"Spending time with him has opened my eyes to some things I hadn't wanted to face…like how wrong I was to blame him for what happened. He didn't intentionally hurt Adam. Yes, they shouldn't have been there, but it was an unfortunate accident."

Meredith gaped at her. "Did you tell him this? What did he say?"

"He's finding it difficult to accept my forgiveness. Not surprising considering how I've treated him."

Coming around the table, Meredith hugged her. "That couldn't have been easy. I'm proud of you." She stepped back. "There's something I've been meaning to ask you, though. Don't take it the wrong way."

"What is it?"

"In all this time, not once have I heard you express anger at Adam. Yes, it was Caleb's idea to break into the lumberyard, but Adam chose to break off your engagement. He chose to leave town. He chose not to respond to your letters. Why aren't you angry with him?"

Rebecca grasped the counter behind her for support. The blunt words worked their way into the dark caverns of her soul, exposing buried truths she'd been too much of a coward to confront.

Meredith's forehead creased. "Maybe I shouldn't have said anything."

"No." Eyes closed, she shook her head. "Y-you're right. I just didn't want to accept the truth." She forced herself to meet her concerned gaze. "After we found out that he was confined to the wheelchair, I tried to convince him nothing had changed. That I still loved him and wanted more than anything to marry him. It wasn't enough. Adam rejected me."

"He could've made a different choice," she agreed sadly.

"He could've chosen to stay and fight for us. That he didn't tells me he didn't love me like I loved him." She pressed trembling fingers to her temples. "By funneling all of my anger onto Caleb, I managed to avoid dealing with the hurt Adam's rejection inflicted."

She'd been so unfair to Caleb.

"Do you love him?"

"Caleb? Of course not!"

Dark brows winged up. "I meant Adam."

"Oh. Right. Of course you meant Adam." She toyed with the locket. "A part of me will always care for him."

"Rebecca, are you developing feelings for Caleb? Because I don't think that would necessarily be a bad thing."

"You don't?"

"He *is* your husband. Like it or not, you're stuck with him."

"All I want is for us to be friends."

"I'm not sure I believe you."

Was she that transparent? "He's unpredictable. Reckless." Removing the whistling kettle from the stove, she poured water into the teacups, ignoring the inner voice insisting he'd changed. Grown up. Matured.

"Unpredictability keeps things interesting. Besides, I don't see him dashing off in search of those gang members. He's sticking close in order to protect you. That's not reckless. That's noble."

"He's a rolling stone, Mer. He's not interested in sticking around."

"I disagree." She followed her to the table. "He stayed away all this time because of the accident. I think he'd jump at the chance to stay here with you."

"You're wrong."

She had to be. Rebecca couldn't go wishing for something that would only hurt her in the end. The more time she spent in his company, the more her admiration flourished and her heart, her foolhardy, susceptible heart, yearned for a deeper connection. With him. Only him.

Caleb wouldn't hurt her intentionally. But he wasn't steadfast or dependable, he didn't always do the right thing, the expected thing, and she couldn't give her heart to a man who was determined to leave her.

"I want to go to the mercantile."

Caleb's fork hovered midair, the sorghum molasses dripping from the bite of flapjack onto the plate below. Concern darkened his eyes. "How about you jot down a list and I'll give it to Pa or Josh. They'd be happy to go for you."

While Rebecca understood the need to exercise caution, she would not be consigned to this farm indefinitely. "There are items of an intimate nature on my list, so what you suggest is impossible. I want to go."

"It's too dangerous. You remember what Shane said, don't you?"

Not long after Meredith and her parents had left yesterday morning, the sheriff had ridden over to update them on the latest. "Yes. There've been no reports of Samantha or Wendell in the area."

"Just because there've been no reports doesn't mean they aren't lying in wait for the perfect opportunity to strike."

In her lap, she scrunched the cloth napkin into a tight ball. "Caleb, I like this cabin, but I'm desperate for a change of scenery. Please. I'm not suggesting we roam up and down Main Street. I just want to do a little shopping."

A funny look on his face, he lowered the fork. "You like this cabin?"

That's what he'd focused on? With a sigh, she observed the spindly tree he'd found in the woods nearby, the festive greenery he'd placed around the room in an effort to cheer her, the view of his family's farm she'd grown accustomed to. His cabin was smaller than hers. It lacked personality. And yet, she felt perfectly at home here. Dare she say content?

Her gaze swiveled to Caleb's familiar face and it hit her. The reason she felt this way wasn't because of the cabin itself, but because of him. This was their first home together. Temporary, but theirs. Just him and her. As crazy as it sounded, she actually slept better knowing he was in the next room, his continued presence reassuring. She'd grown to anticipate their morning ritual—somehow he managed to wake before her and would greet her with coffee and that lopsided smile that made her heart dance with joy.

She cleared her throat, attempted to make light of her words. "I do. It's…charming. It's nothing like my home, though."

"No. Of course it isn't." He nodded and lowered his gaze.

Feeling horrible but determined to hold her heart aloof, she said, "Back to the issue at hand. Am I going to town alone or are you going with me?"

"You're determined to have your way despite the danger."

"I will not have my father-in-law purchasing unmentionables for me." She shuddered at the thought.

Caleb sighed. "All right, but we do it my way. We park in the rear and use the storage room entrance. You get what you need. No dillydallying."

"Agreed."

He tossed his napkin on the table. "I'll hitch up the wagon."

On impulse, Rebecca reached out and squeezed his fingers. The cool metal of his gold ring bit into her palm. "Thank you."

"Thank me when we return safely," he shot back.

He abruptly withdrew his hand. When he left the table, cold loss swept over her. Watching Caleb's brothers and their wives, as well as Megan and Lucian on

Christmas Day, had filled her with a disturbing ache and the dangerous wish for a loving, trusting relationship with her husband.

Not possible, Rebecca.

"I'll be ready." Shoving her tumultuous feelings into a box and securing the lock, she gathered up the dishes, deliberately not looking his direction.

He left without another word. Within half an hour, they were riding along the forest-edged lane that led to town. Caleb sat rigid and silent on the wagon seat, his gaze constantly on the move, alert for hidden dangers. Rebecca tried to relax and enjoy the outing. It wasn't easy. Not when memories of Wendell slid through her mind, raising doubts and niggling guilt for pushing Caleb into giving her her way.

By the time they stood ringing the bell on Clawson's service entrance, she was as rigid as he was, spying potential danger in every corner and behind every tree. When he placed a light hand on her lower back, she jumped.

His lips compressed. "Becca—"

Emmett Moore appeared then and welcomed them inside, seemingly unconcerned that they didn't have a delivery.

"Sorry for the inconvenience," Caleb began, "but we thought it best to come this way."

"Sheriff warned me about the gang." He led them past storage shelving and the office. "Worrisome business. Haven't had any strangers in here lately, thank the Lord. I've kept my eyes open."

"We won't be long." Caleb shot her a warning glance

as they skirted the long, wooden counters and approached the aisles.

Seeing his cousin tidying bolts of fabric, she told him, "I'll be over there with Nicole."

His gaze following hers to the far wall, he reluctantly nodded and pointed to the plate-glass window overlooking Main Street. Dressed in head-to-toe black, his scar giving him an edge, he looked fierce. Menacing. Twin Colts gleamed on his lean hips. "I'll keep watch."

Hurrying along, she noticed the other patrons' appraisals hadn't ceased with her marriage. Would their interest, their judgment, ever wane?

Nicole looked surprised to see her. "Rebecca."

"Good morning. Thank you again for the dress." Immediately following supper on Christmas Day, Nicole and her sisters had called her upstairs to present the dress.

"Have you modeled it for Caleb yet?"

"I'm saving it for a special occasion." She wasn't prepared to endure his close inspection. Her stomach fluttered just thinking about it. "Could you point me to the undergarments?"

"Certainly." Nicole swept farther down the aisle, boots peeking from beneath her ruffled rose-hued skirts.

When Rebecca had made her choice, she thanked the younger girl and made her way to the counter. Caleb appeared at her side, insistent on paying for her purchase. Causing a scene was out of the question, so she waited until they reached the back stairs to vent her opinion.

"I can afford to pay for my own necessities." Barely, but he didn't have to know that.

His chin jutted, the brewing storm in his eyes indicative of his lingering ill-humor. "I told you I'd take care of you."

"I can take care of myself." She refused to be a burden. Not when he hadn't willingly taken her and Amy on.

"I'm your husband," he stated plainly, as if that fact alone justified everything.

Is this the attitude of an irresponsible man? a small voice prodded.

"Rebecca." His fingers clamped down on her wrist, and he tugged her close.

Caught off guard, she braced herself with a hand against his chest. "What—"

"Shh." Beneath his hat's brim, his gaze was locked on something behind her. The storm in those brown eyes was fully unleashed now. Tension locked his jaw, stiffened his shoulders. Something was very wrong. Approaching voices registered on the road at the bottom of the stairs. Several males. One female.

Her stomach plummeted. "That sounds like Samantha—"

Caleb didn't speak. He acted. Deftly switching positions so that his back was to the road, he brought his mouth down on hers.

Chapter Twenty-One

Hᴉs lips were fire and heat, driving the threat of danger to the edge of conscious thought. Rebecca understood what this was—a desperate ploy to remain unrecognized—and yet, with his big body sheltering her and his hands heavy, even possessive, on her waist, she struggled to remember that. Heady emotion flooded her soul. Caleb's kiss made her feel reckless, coaxed her to abandon caution and give this marriage a chance. Give *them* a chance.

She slung an arm about his neck, angling closer, seeking his strength and reassurance. The embrace altered almost imperceptibly. He was holding her as if it would kill him to let her go.

It was in that moment she comprehended how much he'd come to mean to her. Despite everything that had passed between them, the old anger and misplaced blame, Caleb had become necessary. Essential to her happiness.

An act of pure folly on her part, because he would ultimately leave her.

Rebecca wasn't certain how many minutes had passed when he lifted his head, hooded gaze burning into her. Neither of them moved. The air pulsed with energy and unspoken questions. When the silence at last registered, Rebecca risked a glance around. The lane behind the businesses stood empty.

"We're alone." Caleb reached up and, gently dislodging her arm, put distance between them.

Disappointment squeezing her chest, she shoved out, "Did you get a good look at them?"

A muscle jumped in his jaw. "It was her. I didn't recognize her at first because she's chopped off all her hair." Ignoring Rebecca's gasp, he seized her arm and urged her down the stairs. "She had four men with her. Too many to confront without putting you at risk."

Recognizing the determined jut of his chin, she asked, "What are you going to do?"

Handing her up into the wagon, he hurried to the other side and hauled himself up. "I'm gonna get you home. Then I'll come back and search for them."

Fear lodged in her throat. "Alone?"

He released the brake. "I'll alert Timmons."

Arms hugging her midsection as the wind rushed past her face, she felt colder than she'd ever felt before. When they reached the wooden bridge above Little Pigeon River, she twisted to look at him. "I'm sorry."

"Don't apologize."

"It's my fault we were almost discovered. If I hadn't pressured you…"

"None of this is your fault." He shot her a fierce look. "You were right. I couldn't keep you prisoner.

Besides, we have them in our sights now. We'll get them this time."

"I wish you would leave the search to Timmons and his men."

His gaze fell on the gold band circling her left finger. "They made it personal when they involved you. With my family to keep you safe, I won't have to worry."

"What about your leg?"

"Doc cleared me to ride, remember?"

Since he clearly wouldn't be dissuaded from his course, Rebecca prayed. Begged, in fact, for God to protect her husband and bring him home safe.

They searched for three days. Seemed as if they were traveling in ever-widening circles about Gatlinburg, each passing hour without results intensifying Caleb's frustration.

"Something's not right." Sitting tall in the saddle, craggy profile washed in moonlight, the sheriff huffed an aggravated sigh. "We should've picked up their trail by now."

"We can't stop." Didn't matter that his leg was one throbbing mass of quivering flesh. Didn't matter that he was distracted by thoughts of Becca and their life-altering kiss. Finding Samantha and her gang was paramount.

"I think they have someone helping them. Someone in town who's giving them shelter."

"Why would anyone do that?"

"Could be one of them has relatives in these parts. Or friends."

"Or they could be threatening someone to hide

them." Caleb's lip curled in disgust. *God, please, lead us to them. I know I don't deserve Your help, but my family won't be safe until these murderers are behind bars. No one in this town will be safe. And Tate's family deserves to see justice served.*

"Let's head back. We're low on supplies, and you could use some time out of the saddle." Timmons nudged his mount into motion.

Caleb reluctantly followed suit, Rebel's hulking form blending with the dense shadows. "What if they slip through our fingers? What then?"

"I understand your frustration, O'Malley, but staying out here any longer is pointless. Once we get to town, I'm gonna do a little digging. See if I can learn of anyone who's currently entertaining guests."

"Need any help with that?" His breath puffed white in the frigid temperatures.

"No." Blue eyes flashed in his direction. "You're gonna stay out of sight." He smiled. "Spend some time with your new wife."

Becca's image cemented itself in his mind and refused to budge. Now that his horse was headed toward home, he allowed himself to anticipate their reunion. Would she be angry over his prolonged absence? Worried? She'd been quiet and subdued as he'd packed his gear. Definitely concerned for his safety, which made his chest tighten up. How deep did his wife's feelings go? For the millionth time, he rehashed every second of that spontaneous kiss.

He'd done it to mask their identity. The outlaws hadn't gotten close enough to get a good look at either of them. Their position on the top of the stairs helped.

He'd counted on Samantha and her gang trying to avoid attracting attention to themselves and moving quickly through town.

But the instant their lips met, everything save for the woman in his arms melted away. Danger was passing within feet of them and still he'd been flung into another world, one where he and Becca were meant for each other, where he was the type of man she'd choose if given the chance. *Fantasy. Pure fantasy, O'Malley.*

She hadn't shoved him away, though, had she? Surely Becca wouldn't have responded the way she had if she didn't feel *something* for him. Something good. Something pure.

And what if she did? What would that change? I don't deserve her. I never will.

By the time his cabin in the woods came into view, his heart was as frozen as his toes and fingers. Uncertain if he possessed the fortitude to interact with another human being, he considered bunking down in the barn loft. But it was nearing midnight and the windows were dark. She would be asleep in her room. The promise of a warm fire and thick quilt beckoned.

He hadn't counted on finding her on the couch, tucked inside his quilt, fast asleep with her cheek nestled into his pillow. Weak light from the dwindling fire flickered across her face, shimmered in her thick brown hair. Although it hardly seemed possible, she was even more beautiful now than when they were teens. Part of that was due to her newfound spunk—he liked that there was spice beneath the sweet facade. Made life interesting. Difficult, too. Living here with Becca was showing him what life could be like if he let someone else close, was making his decision to live a solitary life less and less appealing.

Shedding himself of his guns and duster, he sank onto the coffee table and placed his hat beside him. He watched her until exhaustion made him light-headed. Too cold to move, he leaned forward and rested his head on the cushion. *Just for a minute,* he told himself.

Minutes—or was it hours?—had passed when her soft cry stirred him to wakefulness. Her fingers combed lightly through his hair.

"You're home," she exclaimed, joy and relief evident in her tone. Quilts tumbled to the floor, and she was there beside him on the coffee table, hugging him so tight he could hardly catch a breath. "Are you okay?"

The fact that his stiff muscles ached with lingering cold, and he needed a bath and a shave, and his leg hurt, hardly registered after a greeting such as this. "I take it you're happy to see me?" He managed a half-hearted smile.

Becca cupped his unshaven cheek. "You've no idea how worried I've been. H-how worried we've all been," she amended, letting her hand fall to her lap. "Did you find—"

"No."

Frowning, she pulled the lapels of her housecoat tight at the throat. "You're freezing. Sit on the couch." She tugged on his arm, and he had no choice but to do her bidding. She proceeded to wrap him in blankets from his neck to his feet. When she encountered his dirt-flecked boots, she tugged them off despite his protests and encased his stocking feet in the material.

"Stay there."

As if he could move after she'd trussed him up like a Thanksgiving turkey. He sat still and silent as she took logs from the crate and added them to the fire. Arrayed in a cloud of snowy white, her hair streaming past her shoulders, Becca's loveliness made him ache for what he couldn't have. Crossing the wooden floor, she appeared to glide effortlessly, spine straight and head held high.

She lit the stove. "Hot tea will help. Are you hungry? I made sourdough bread this morning. Or I can reheat the beef stew your ma sent home with me. Since you've been gone, I've been eating my meals with them."

He and Timmons had barely stopped to eat, making due with jerky and sandwiches. "I can wait until morning to eat."

Caleb was glad she hadn't taken her meals alone and that his family was around to keep her company. The heat from the fire and Becca's cocoon was loosening his limbs. His lids were growing heavy. He settled deeper into the cushions and rested his head against the curved cushion edge.

Almost asleep when she appeared before him with a cup and saucer, it took him a minute to make sense of what he was seeing. Something was missing.

"Did you lose your locket?"

Eyes widening, she pressed slender fingers to her neck. "No."

"Where is it, then? I haven't seen you without it since I landed on your doorstep."

When she hesitated, her eyelashes sweeping down to hide her eyes, he said, "You didn't sell it to Clawson's, did you? Because I'll provide whatever funds you need. I don't know how many times I have to tell you that," he reiterated, uncertain why he wasn't rejoicing at its absence. All he knew was that the locket mattered to her.

"I've decided not to wear it anymore."

Caleb floundered for a response. What did that mean? "Why not?"

"Is there anything more that you need?" He could tell by her expression that she wasn't about to satisfy his curiosity. "Because if not, I think I'll go ahead and retire."

"No, nothing." He wasn't going to push her on this. Not now. "Sweet dreams, Becca."

She turned back when she reached the bedroom door. "I'm glad you're home safe, Caleb."

"Mmm." Across the table, Caleb chewed with his eyes closed. "Don't tell Ma, but your biscuits and gravy are the best I've ever tasted."

Rebecca smiled and sipped her coffee. When she'd woken before him for a change, she'd eagerly set about fixing him a breakfast fit for a king. His delighted smile as he'd spied the spread had been reward enough, but compliments were nice, too.

His raven hair was mussed, his jaw covered in dark scruff, and he was wearing the same clothes he'd worn yesterday. Not that it mattered. Her husband could be wearing tattered rags and still have a devastating effect on her.

Three days of not knowing whether he lived or died had rendered her a tad desperate to see his face. Certainly her welcome the night before had been unrestrained. She blamed it on the fogginess of sleep. *So why am I considering going over there and throwing my arms around his neck and refusing to let go until the raging fear for his safety recedes?*

Above the rim of his coffee mug, he noticed her staring. He lowered it to the table. "What are you thinking, Rebecca?"

Rebecca. What must he have seen in her eyes to call her that?

Distract him. Reaching into her apron pocket, she withdrew a slender box and slid it across the table.

"What's this?" He pushed his plate to the side.

"A late Christmas present."

His brow furrowed. "You didn't have to get me anything."

"I know. I *wanted* to."

He lifted the lid. Went still. "A harmonica?"

"I noticed your other one was badly dented," she rushed to add. "When I was with your parents at Clawson's, I saw this one and thought you might like it. However, Emmett assured me that you could exchange it for something else if you wish."

Good thing he wouldn't recognize her grandmother's brooch she'd traded in. She'd considered trading in the locket, but while she no longer wished to wear it, she didn't want her first gift for Caleb to be tied to Adam in any way.

He didn't say anything as he examined it, shiny metal flashing as he turned it this way and that.

"Please don't feel obligated to keep it. I won't be upset if you'd rather have a different gift. It's just that you have everything you need, and I wanted to give you something you would enjoy."

"It's perfect, Becca." His intent gaze slid to hers and,

with a crooked smile, he found her hand on the tabletop and threaded his fingers through hers. "I'll treasure it."

A giddy sort of relief expanding through her midsection, she returned the pressure of his fingers, reveling in the slide of his rougher skin against hers. She licked her dry lips, and his gaze caught the unconscious action. Awareness turned his eyes a rich golden hue, like those of a lion. Memories of their recent kiss thickened the air. His hold tightened, and he eased over his plate. She mimicked his movement, uncaring how wrong it was to submit to this magnetic pull between them.

Someone pounded on the door. "Caleb? Rebecca? You in there?"

They both jumped.

"That sounds like Pa." Disappointment flashed as he nudged his chair out of the way and strode to the door.

Wearing an ear-to-ear smile, Sam stepped over the threshold. "Congratulate me. I'm officially a grandpa," he told his youngest son. "And you're an uncle."

Caleb looked dumbfounded. "What?"

Rebecca threw her napkin on the table and came to stand beside him. "Kate had her baby?"

"Yep. Went into labor last night." Behind his spectacles, tears of pride gleamed. "Victoria Marie O'Malley was born at five twenty-four this morning."

"A girl." Rebecca squeezed Caleb's arm, joy for the special couple making her almost giddy.

"How's Kate?" he demanded, looking more upset than pleased. "And the baby?"

"They're both fine. Come over and meet her. Not sure if you'll get to hold her, though. Depends if you can pry her out of her pa's arms." He chuckled, clearly thrilled to pieces at the arrival of his first granddaughter.

Some of Caleb's tension ebbed. He fingered the scruff on his chin. "I need to bathe and shave first."

"Nah—" Sam waved him off "—as long as your hands are scrubbed clean, I say don't worry about it."

Impatient to see the baby, Rebecca grabbed her coat and scarf. "Come on. I'm dying to see who she looks like."

"Doesn't have much hair," Sam said, "much like her pa when he was a babe."

"What about Caleb? Was he bald, too?" she couldn't resist asking. He tossed her a startled look.

Sam grinned. "Unlike his brothers, Caleb was born with a shock of black hair. Good-lookin' kid. Everyone who saw him said so."

"I'm not surprised," she murmured, "considering the handsome man he's grown into."

Caleb's throat worked and the tips of his ears went red. "Okay, enough of that." Turning his back on them, he pulled on his duster and worked quickly to do up the buttons. Sam winked at her.

A hushed silence cloaked the interior of Josh and Kate's cabin. They waited in the living room while Sam went upstairs to alert the new parents of their arrival. Beside her, Caleb shifted nervously.

"You're not frightened of a little baby, are you?" she teased.

He frowned, grooves on either side of his mouth appearing. "Don't have much experience with them."

"You'll be a wonderful uncle, I'm sure of it."

"I doubt she'll see that much of me." He looked at her askance. "Or have you forgotten our agreement?"

The joy leaked out of the moment. Pain replaced it. As Josh descended the stairs with a tiny bundle in his arms, Rebecca watched the emotions skittering across Caleb's face. Brotherly pride edged with caution. Regret entwined with longing. And when the new father gingerly placed the baby in his brother's arms, she thought her heart would rend in two. The way he gazed at his niece...

Caleb wants to be a father as much as I want to be a mother. It was there on his face for anyone to see.

"She's very quiet. And still. Too still." He shot Josh a look that bordered on panic. "Is she supposed to be this still?"

Standing at the end of the couch, Josh peered down at his sleeping daughter and smiled, one that encompassed pride and love and wonder. "I'm told this is normal behavior for a newborn."

"How's Kate?" Rebecca asked, easing down beside her husband.

"She's resting. Ma is up there with her."

"You look strange," Caleb said darkly. "What aren't you saying? Was she in danger?"

Josh grimaced. Rebecca belatedly noticed his finger-tousled hair and wrinkled shirt, the shadows beneath his eyes. "I won't lie. It was...difficult to see her in that much pain. By God's grace, she made it through. I'm beyond amazed at her strength." His blue gaze fastened onto Caleb's. "Perhaps one day you'll understand what I mean."

Rebecca's cheeks burned. As the years passed, peo-ple would wonder why she and Caleb didn't have children. They wouldn't broach the subject, of course, but they'd assume there were physical problems. They'd never know the real reason. Regret coated her mouth.

Caleb cleared his throat. "Would you like to hold her, Becca?"

Unable to speak, she merely nodded and avoided his piercing scrutiny as he passed the baby to her. Victoria was perfect. Small and pink and weightless as a cloud. Lightly skimming the fine blond hair, Rebecca fought back tears. *I will not feel sorry for myself. I will rejoice with all of my being for Josh and Kate's blessing.*

When the infant stirred, little fingers opening and closing, Rebecca handed her to her father. "She's beautiful, Josh. Please tell Kate I'm thrilled for you both."

He smiled, but his gaze was searching. "I will."

"I'd better go and check on Amy." Rushing to escape, she was midway through the orchard when Caleb caught up to her.

"Becca, wait."

"I'm in a hurry." She kept walking, ducking beneath particularly low branches, disturbing birds. "I want to visit with Amy before I start in on the laundry."

His hand clamped down on her elbow, and he hauled her around to face him. He looked like the mountain man she'd rescued that day in the snow, wild and untamed and dangerous. Definitely dangerous. The gray, overcast skies above rendered his collar-length hair a richer black, his eyes a more intense brown. Behind him, the naked branches of the apple trees marched along the field of pale green grass. The orchard would be breathtaking in the spring. She wished she could paint it, but by then he'd be gone and she'd be at her place in the cove.

"We need to talk."

"Can't it wait?"

"No, it can't." He stood so close she had to tilt her head back to meet his gaze. "We never talked about the fact that you want children."

"We weren't exactly given the opportunity to discuss it, were we?" She clenched her fists, feeling as if she was dying inside. "Besides, I saw how you looked at that baby. You want children, too."

He looked grim. "It didn't cross my mind until I married you."

She stumbled back, grief slamming into her. How had things gotten so mixed up? How had she wound up here, married to Caleb and wishing for a real marriage with him?

"Why are you telling me this?" she scraped out.

He stood stiff and unmoving, fists clenched at his sides. "If we were able to have a child, you could raise him or her with the help of my family. My father and brothers would provide the proper male influences. You wouldn't lack for help. You could move into my cabin permanently."

Rebecca stared, heart thudding painfully against her rib cage. "You would do that?"

A breeze whipped his hair in his eyes, but he didn't bother to brush it aside. "For you. Because you would be an amazing mother. Because you didn't ask for this marriage, and I can't deny you a child of your own."

"And what about you? You would be content to only see him or her a couple times a year?"

Misery lined his features. "I'm not fit to be a father. You know that."

"I know nothing of the sort," she snapped, anger bubbling up inside. "I think it's unreasonable and even selfish of you to make such an offer. You haven't considered what your absence would do to a child, have you?" *Or to me,* she thought miserably.

"I'm merely trying to find a way to make you happy," he growled, ramming unsteady hands through his hair. "You deserved to marry the man of your dreams, to build a family with him."

"You keep saying I deserve to be happy and you don't. What makes me better than you? I make mistakes. I have faults. We all do. God alone is perfect. It's because of His compassion that He doesn't give us what we truly deserve. He chooses to bless us, to extend mercy and grace, because He loves us. So stop making yourself out to be the villain, because you're no worse than me or your brothers or anyone else in this town."

Rebecca marched off, unwilling to stick around for his response. And before she blurted a truth so shocking he'd never believe her—that *he* was shaping up to be the man of her dreams.

Chapter Twenty-Two

The first half of January slipped past in a succession of dreary days made more miserable by the wintry standoff between her and Caleb. Since the day she'd left him standing in the orchard, he'd done his best to avoid her. There were no more leisurely breakfasts. By the time she awoke each morning, he was already in the barn milking the cows. Rebecca wasn't sure what he did for lunch, but she suspected he either took a sandwich or stopped in at the main house. Supper was a strained affair. Their stilted conversations—if they spoke at all—revolved around the weather and farm workings.

There was absolutely no mention of the baby. Rebecca had gone to visit Kate and Victoria every other day, careful not to stay long and tire out the new mother. When she'd learned Caleb hadn't been back since the baby's birth, she'd known immediately what he was doing. Guarding his heart. Why get attached when he wasn't going to be around?

There'd been no more sightings of Samantha and her gang. Shane hadn't discovered any links between them and the locals, which meant Rebecca hadn't been off O'Malley land except for Sunday church services. Amy had to be escorted to and from school. She didn't complain, however, as she was perfectly content living with Sam and Mary. Rebecca suspected that for her sister, the older couple helped fill the gaping hole left by their parents.

Removing a heavy cast-iron skillet of corn bread from the stove, she plunked it on the cooktop and laid the towel aside. Boots thudded on the porch seconds before the door swung open and Caleb's imposing presence filled the space. What was he doing here in the middle of the day?

Her heart flailed at the sight of him. His black duster hugged his sturdy shoulders, the sides open to reveal a black vest, forest-green shirt underneath and black trousers encasing his long, muscular legs. A black-and-white handkerchief protected his neck from the cold.

Her husband had become a forbidding stranger, and it hurt. Especially when she recalled the tender moments that had passed between them—the way he'd held her hands as they'd exchanged vows, comforted her after Wendell and Samantha's visit, the expression on his face Christmas morning as he'd watched her open her gifts and the reverence with which he'd slid the gold band onto her finger.

She missed his crooked smile. She missed the heat and admiration in his eyes right before he kissed her—

"Are you busy?"

"I, uh, not really. Do you need something?"

"I need to go to the smithy." He paused, uncertainty marking his features. "I thought I could drop you off at Clawson's and afterward we could stop at Plum's for dessert."

He was offering to spend time with her? Hope flared. Despite the many problems in their relationship, she'd begun to treasure the reemerging friendship between them. Things would never be easy, but surely they could achieve some level of contentment.

When he's around, I mean. Don't forget he's leaving the moment Samantha's in custody. Don't expect more than he's willing to give.

Recalling the night he'd told her he didn't want her heart, that he didn't care if she loved Adam forever, pain lodged in her chest.

Caleb must've taken her hesitation for reluctance. "If you'd rather not go—"

"No." She quickly untied her apron strings. "I want to go. I'm just surprised by the invitation, that's all."

Shifting his weight, his gaze landed on the floor. "Figured you needed a change of scenery as much as I do. There haven't been any sightings of the gang in town since the last time. We should be safe."

Memories of that last trip to town and the resulting embrace slammed into her. She couldn't resist a peek at his firm, perfectly shaped mouth. Caleb looked up and caught her staring. Longing darkened his eyes. His hands curled into fists, and he half turned away. "I'll saddle up a horse for you. Unless you need the wagon?"

They'd stocked up on flour and sugar and other dry goods last week—she'd given Nathan a list of items, which he'd gladly procured for them. Besides, riding close beside him on the narrow seat would only make her want things she shouldn't. "No, thanks. I'd enjoy the ride."

Touching the brim of his hat, he closed the door without another word. Hurrying into the bedroom to change, she impulsively chose the dress from Nicole and her sisters.

His stunned expression when she emerged onto the porch made up for his cool distance of the past weeks. His gaze did a slow inspection from the tips of her leather boots—snagging on the snug bodice and waistline—to the matching ribbons in her upswept hair.

He came to assist her into the saddle. "New dress?"

Her mouth went dry when he took hold of her hand. His heated skin seared hers. "It was a wedding present from your cousins."

"Nicole does good work. Suits you perfectly. In case I haven't mentioned it, you've grown into a beautiful woman, Becca," he said as he handed her up onto Cocoa's back. "I'll be the envy of every man in Gatlinburg."

Tightening her hands around the reins to keep from burying them in his hair, she stared deep into his eyes. "And I'll be the envy of the women."

Shock parted his full lips. Then he surprised her by smiling. "They'll certainly wonder what you see in me."

Pushing off, he went to mount the horse he'd borrowed from Josh. By his easy movements, she couldn't tell he'd been injured at all. The tension had lifted, and the ride into town was pleasant. At Clawson's, he waited until she had her horse hitched to the post.

"I'll join you here shortly."

She stepped onto the crowded boardwalk. With warmer temperatures and the sun shining in a clear blue sky, shoppers were out in droves. "I'll wait for you."

Touching a finger to his hat's brim, Caleb nudged his

horse on down the street. Inside the mercantile, shoppers roamed the aisles and lined up to pay for their items. Rebecca spotted Nicole behind the counter helping customers and waved.

"Hi, Rebecca." Her eyes lit up when she noticed the dress. Pointing to a package she was wrapping, she shrugged and mouthed, *Talk to you later.*

Rebecca smiled and strolled to the paper goods section in the middle aisle. She didn't expect to see anything new—Emmett Moore stocked pretty much the same items from year to year. She wasn't here to shop, really. Just being in the presence of other people buoyed her spirits. And there was the dessert at Plum's to look forward to.

"Excuse me."

Rebecca turned to see an unfamiliar young lady approaching. Petite and smartly dressed with blond ringlets peeking out of her bonnet, her eyes were kind and set in a pleasant face.

"Good afternoon," Rebecca offered politely, all the while racking her brain for a clue as to her identity. She didn't resemble anyone of her acquaintance, but that didn't mean she couldn't be visiting family in the area.

"I apologize for my rudeness, but I overheard the shop assistant speaking to you a moment ago. Is your name by chance Rebecca Thurston?" Curiosity sparkled in her pale blue eyes.

"That's me. Although it's Rebecca O'Malley now."

The stranger's resulting smile was blinding. "Oh, you're married? How wonderful."

Thoroughly confused, Rebecca openly studied the girl. "Have we met before?"

Clapping a hand over her mouth, she giggled nervously. "Forgive me, you must think I'm a complete ninny." She thrust out her hand. "I'm Laura Tierney. You don't know me, but I've heard a lot about you."

Tierney. Rebecca limply shook Laura's hand, foreboding settling like cold mist in her bones.

"Laura, sweetheart, I found the—" A voice she hadn't heard in over a year drifted behind her, a voice that used to call *her* sweetheart. "Rebecca? Is that you?"

Feeling as if she was in a dream, Rebecca slowly swiveled to gaze dazedly at the good-looking man in the wheelchair. "Adam."

Her former love looked very much the same save for a light beard. His wheat-colored hair was cut short as usual, and he was dressed simply, having never made much of a fuss over clothes, as long as they were clean. Right this moment, his eyes were colored with consternation and regret.

"Rebecca, I had intended to pay you a visit." His voice carried a note of strain. He cast a glance in Laura's direction and grimaced. "I hadn't envisioned us meeting up like this."

"You mean here in front of everyone?" Already the banker's wife and another couple had abandoned their shopping to observe this most intriguing meeting between the jilted bride and her replacement. She should be used to this by now, what with Adam's abandonment and her forced marriage to Caleb.

"What's a little more gossip?" she quipped, hysteria bubbling to the surface. Turning to address the blonde woman, she said with false brightness, "You must be Adam's new wife. Welcome to our humble town. How long are you planning to visit?"

Laura's manner had turned uncertain. "I'm not sure. Adam indicated we may be here a week or two, at least. He hasn't been home to see his family in quite some time."

"Rebecca." Adam rolled the chair closer. "Can we go somewhere more private?"

Around them, chatter had ceased, and it seemed to Rebecca that all eyes were on her and Laura. *What does she give you that I couldn't?* she wanted to demand of Adam. Slightly nauseous, she clasped her hands tightly together and fought to appear calm.

"Please excuse me."

"Rebecca, wait—"

Ignoring Adam's quiet request, she plunged headlong down the aisle intent on escape.

The bell above the mercantile door dinged as Caleb entered. The unusual hush struck him first. Odd. Clawson's was full of people conducting business. There should be conversation and the sounds of scoops and weights and paper rustling as Nicole and Emmett assisted customers. Instead, everyone stood frozen, fascinated by something in the middle of the store. Nicole's mouth was pinched, violet eyes blazing with ill-humor. Something was wrong.

Clipped footsteps registered to his left. The skin on the back of his neck prickling, he turned and observed Becca heading straight for him along this outer aisle. Skin as pale as moonlight, cheeks hollow, she appeared to have suffered a severe shock.

She would've barreled right past him out the door if he hadn't laid a hand on her arm. "Rebecca, what's wrong?"

Her jade eyes were empty, blank. It was as if she didn't even recognize him. "I have to go."

"What's happened?" he demanded in a low voice, aware that everyone's attention had swiveled their way.

"Caleb?"

Becca went stiff. Caleb dropped his hand and, heartbeat thundering in his ears, searched out the owner of that voice. Couldn't be, could it? But there sat his childhood friend. The man he'd condemned to a wheelchair. The man who'd abandoned Becca.

Guilt and anger wrestled for victory, clouding his thinking to the extent he didn't try and stop her from leaving the store. She was gone in an instant, hurrying to her horse.

"What are you doing here, Adam?" The question came out more sharply than he'd intended, but all he could see was Becca's face. She was hurting, and Adam was responsible.

"My folks have been asking for us to visit for a while. I couldn't put them off any longer."

"Us?" He belatedly noticed the small blonde standing slightly behind Adam's wheelchair.

His old friend's smile spoke of true happiness. "This is my wife, Laura. Laura, meet Caleb O'Malley."

"Pleased to meet you," she said, keen interest on her face. "You're Rebecca's husband?"

Startled, his gaze swerved to Adam's. But he remained unruffled. "That's right."

Hands folded in his lap, Adam said simply, "My parents wrote me about your marriage."

The door opened behind Caleb as another customer entered. He edged sideways to give the man room to pass. Adam had a wife. No wonder Becca had run out of there as if her skirts were on fire. *She still loves him,* he thought, despair gripping him. *His wife was in love with another man and there was nothing he could do about it.*

"You should go and talk to Becca," Caleb said darkly, even as jealousy reared its ugly head. "She deserves an explanation, don't you think?"

He nodded in solemn agreement. "You're right, and I will. But first I'd like to talk to you."

"Not here."

Adam agreed. Laura offered to stay behind and finish her shopping. When she bent to kiss her husband's cheek, the affection she felt for him was plain as day. And while she seemed curious about Caleb, she gave him the impression that she fully trusted Adam and wasn't bothered by his ex-fiancée's earlier presence.

On the boardwalk, Adam paused. "I'll need help getting this contraption down the stairs," he said with wry humor. "Care to help a friend out?"

Caleb strove to hide his surprise. From his family's reports after the accident, Adam hadn't handled his paralysis well. Gritting his teeth, he grabbed the handles and maneuvered the wheels to the dirt street below. Talk about past mistakes slapping him in the face. How could Adam stand to look at him, let alone speak to him?

"Where to now?" Caleb grunted, noticing the stares of passersby.

"I seem to recall a spot behind the mercantile with a fine view of the river."

He tried not to jostle the man, but the dirt road wasn't

smooth and neither was the grassy expanse near the riverbank.

As if sensing his thoughts, Adam said over his shoulder, "Don't worry, I'm used to it."

When they'd reached the bench, Caleb dropped his hands to his sides. Moved around to face Adam.

"There's something I've needed to say to you since the night everything went wrong. I'm sorry. Sorry for daring you to break in. Sorry I couldn't help you when that stack fell." Confronted with the result of his reckless behavior, the remorse that had burdened him every day since weighed heavier than ever. He clenched his fists. "I know words won't change facts, but that's all I have to offer."

"My parents told me that you came to see me." Adam's gaze was steady, calm. Devoid of accusation. "They also told me how they turned you away. They feel bad about the way they acted, but haven't known quite how to approach you."

"I—" He clamped his lips together. He'd been about to say he'd deserved their ill-treatment. Becca's words from their conversation in the orchard slipped through his mind, something that had been happening with irritating frequency. He'd even opened his Bible searching for proof her words were true. And while he'd found quite a few verses to support her assertions, he'd had trouble applying the truth to his own situation.

"I understand they were hurting," he said at last.

"I was angry for a long time," Adam admitted. "At you. At God. Wasted a lot of time and energy on blaming my circumstances on everyone else but myself. Eventually I realized that I was responsible for my own choices. I went along with your plan because that's what

I always did. You were the leader, and mostly I followed you without question. Since then, I've learned to stand up for myself. Well—" he gave a halfhearted grin and spread his hands over his legs "—not exactly *stand up*. You get my meaning."

"How can you joke about it?" Caleb challenged.

"It's either laugh or wallow in self-pity," he said, and shrugged. "I wallowed until I could hardly stand myself."

Kneading his tense neck muscles, Caleb gazed unseeing at the wide river below them. Adam had clearly learned to live with his disability. Had found peace and, from the looks of things, happiness.

Adam spoke into the silence. "I know this is going to sound crazy, but I'm a happier man than I used to be. Do I wish I could do the things I used to? Sure. But if God hadn't allowed it to happen, I would've married Rebecca and made us both miserable. I would've missed out on God's calling for my life. Not only that, I wouldn't have met Laura. She's the love of my life."

Caleb stared hard at his friend. "Why would you say that? You and Rebecca were perfect together." As difficult as that was to admit aloud, it was the truth. They'd been happy. Most of the time. But what couple didn't have their issues?

Sadness stamped his features. "We were far from perfect, Caleb. In fact, now that I'm able to look at things objectively, I'd venture to say the two of you are more suited than she and I ever were."

Chapter Twenty-Three

Rebecca lingered in the O'Malley's barn, the shadows and the horses' nonjudgmental stares a balm to her ruffled spirits. The shock of seeing Adam had waned somewhat, allowing humiliation to pour in. What must Caleb think after she'd bolted like that?

The sound of creaking metal behind her had her lifting the brush from Cocoa's coat and twisting to see who had discovered her hiding place.

Adam's steady gaze searched her out in the semi-darkness. Although bright outside, the interior of the lofty barn was dim, and she hadn't bothered to light the lamps.

With a sigh, she laid the brush on the stall's edge and went out into the aisle. "Is Caleb with you?"

"He said he'd wait in the cabin."

Rebecca was afraid to imagine what he must be experiencing right now.

"And what about your wife? Where is she?"

Hands folded in his lap, he was at ease in the chair. "At my parents'."

Her brows lifted. "She doesn't have a problem with you visiting me?"

"Laura understands we have unfinished business. I've kept nothing from her."

"I see."

"Rebecca—"

She held up a hand. "All I want to know is why you didn't answer my letters. If you'd simply written to me and told me you'd found someone else, I would've ceased writing. And that embarrassing scene in the mercantile would've been avoided."

His grave countenance reflected his inner struggle. "I regret that I didn't have the courage to do what was right by you. At first it was just too painful. And then I met Laura, and I felt guilty. I left town an extremely bitter man, you know. I thought my life was ruined, that because of my disability I had nothing to offer. I never told you I felt God's calling to preach."

Surprise rippled through her body. Adam? A preacher? He'd been set to take over his father's farm. She'd thought he was content with that. Looking back, she realized they hadn't spoken of truly serious issues. Their relationship had been quite shallow, come to think of it. She hadn't shared her private thoughts with him. Nor he her.

"I had no clue."

"That was part of our problem. We held pieces of ourselves back."

"You're right. We did." *I don't have the same problem with Caleb, though, do I? I say exactly what's on my mind.*

"I couldn't accept that I was meant to be a preacher,

so I ignored what was in my heart. The accident stopped me from running."

"Are you saying you're a preacher now?"

"Not yet. I'm currently attending seminary. Laura and I are living with her aunt and uncle in Maryville."

She digested that information. "I lied," she blurted. His brows shot up. "I do want to know something else. What convinced you to give her a chance when you couldn't give me one?"

Regret flashed across his features. "The day Doc Owens told me I'd be bound to this wheelchair for the rest of my life, and that I would be dependent on others for the simplest things, I couldn't fathom being your husband. Or anyone's, for that matter. All I could see was the loss of my independence, my manhood. How could I support a wife and family when I couldn't even dress myself? I felt cheated. And I couldn't bring myself to face you. I knew that if I stayed here, I'd have to watch you fall for another man. I couldn't stand to watch someone else get the life I was supposed to have, so I left."

"I wish you would've talked to me," she said softly.

His fingers clenched on the wheels. "I wish I had, too. I don't think it would've changed our circumstances, but you deserved to hear my decision from me personally. I'm sorry."

Nodding, she scuffed her boot in the straw. "So you met her in Maryville…"

"I was still bitter over my lot in life when Laura came along. Unlike those around me, she called me on my self-pity, refused to allow me even an ounce of sympathy. She treated me as an equal. It was as if she didn't see my disability. She just saw *me*." His smile was quick and natural. He was content, something Rebecca never thought she'd witness in him again.

"Eventually, I realized I needed to let go of my former expectations about what my life was supposed to be like. I had to accept my new circumstances if I ever hoped to be content. Of course, this took me a while," he said, and blushed. "Laura got tired of waiting and made the first move."

Oddly, Rebecca couldn't summon jealousy for Laura or resentment for him. That part of her life was well and truly over. "I'm happy for you, Adam."

Cocking his head, he openly studied her. "I believe you mean that."

"I do."

"Caleb and I had an interesting conversation."

"You've forgiven him?" She held her breath. If Adam withheld it, Caleb might not ever be able to move forward with his life. He'd be stuck forever in the cycle of self-blame.

"Of course. After all, I agreed to go along with his scheme." Her shoulders sagged with relief, and his gaze turned knowing. "You care for him."

"That's none of your business." Sidestepping him, she paced to the door and pushed it open but didn't leave. The yard was empty save for a stray calico cat stalking unseen prey.

Adam turned the chair around. "Back when we were all friends, I suspected Caleb had feelings for you. I even found myself wondering if you harbored feelings for him, as well."

Pressing a hand to her rapidly beating heart, she

whirled to stare at him. "How can you say that? I was loyal to you, Adam."

"I wasn't questioning your loyalty." He arched a brow, then shook his head. "I don't know how to explain it. There was just something in the way you looked at each other sometimes. And after your crazy rescue of that kitten, you wouldn't go near the man. I confronted Caleb. I thought maybe you'd quarreled. But he was as confused about your behavior as I was." He kicked up a shoulder. "Anyway, my suspicions were confirmed the night after I proposed to you."

"What? How?"

"He paid me a late-night visit. Not to congratulate me, mind you, but to warn me. If I didn't treat you right, I'd have him to answer to. I asked if he cared for you as more than a friend, but he refused to answer. Just reiterated his threat and stomped off into the night. I'd never seen him that serious about anything before."

Rebecca sagged against the door. Could it be true? Had Caleb experienced the same mysterious pull she had? More important, had he cared for her? Truly cared?

Looking at her former sweetheart, she accepted that what they'd shared had been an immature love. Like a tree with shallow roots, it hadn't been able to withstand the fierce winds of life's trials. That was why he'd broken off the engagement, why her pledge of support hadn't been enough.

"I think he still cares, Rebecca," Adam said. "More than he'll ever admit."

Caleb thought he might climb out of his skin waiting for Becca and Adam to emerge from the barn. His instinct was to barge in there and see for himself what they were saying. She was *his* wife, after all.

Somehow he found the willpower to stay away. He tried reading his Bible but couldn't concentrate. Ended up pacing the floor, tiring his leg and driving himself crazy imagining their possible conversations—none of them satisfactory.

He jerked to a stop the instant she walked through the door. Closing it, she leaned against the smooth wood. "Adam's waiting outside. He said you offered to take him home."

Going to stand before her, he became frustrated when he couldn't read her expression. She didn't look particularly upset. Much more composed than when she'd fled the mercantile. "Are you all right?"

She nodded. "I apologize for running off like that. I didn't exactly expect to run into Adam today."

"I wasn't thinking straight, either. Should've seen you home." He shuddered when he thought about the danger she could have been in, alone and unprotected.

"We were both shocked."

Unable to resist touching her, Caleb lightly skimmed his knuckles along her cheek. Her lips parted, and the tiniest of sighs escaped. Only the knowledge that Adam—her first choice—was waiting kept Caleb from kissing her.

"Tell me the truth," he murmured, searching the jade depths. "How are you really? Seeing him with her couldn't have been easy."

"I told you the truth," she softly insisted, wrapping her fingers about his wrist. "I'm not suffering. In fact, knowing he's content and settled has actually given me closure."

Her equanimity coupled with her admission gave him hope. Did this mean her heart was free? Could she one day come to care for him?

Care for me? I am the reason she's trapped in this marriage. No doubt the chief emotion she feels is resentment.

Sure, Becca welcomed his touch, but that was likely loneliness talking. And plain old run-of-the-mill attraction. A spark had always existed between them, even when she'd been courting his best friend. Not that she'd ever admit it.

Edging back, he snagged his Stetson off the coatrack and shoved it on his head. "I've got to go."

"Wait." When he paused in buttoning up his coat, she clasped her hands behind her back. "What about you? Has seeing Adam again, speaking with him, given you closure, too?"

Unprepared for such a question, he dropped his hands to his sides and stared at her. "I know what you're really asking. Now that Adam has absolved me of blame, you want to know if I can forgive myself. Shed the guilt. Am I right?"

"Yes."

"And what if I can? Would you be happy having me around day and night?" He crowded her, need expanding in his chest until he thought his heart might burst. What was she doing to him? He used to be content on his own. She'd wrecked that. If he had to go back to living alone in the mountains, he'd surely go mad with wanting her, missing her. "Would you be willing to rescind our agreement?"

Panic stealing across her face, she held up her hands as if to ward him off. "You like solitude. You prefer it."

"Do I?"

"While I don't want you to shoulder the burden of guilt any longer, you and I should stick to the agreement we made. That's the only way we can survive this marriage."

Sorrow worked its way up from the soles of his feet. Hang the outlaws and the circumstances that had led him to her. He would've been better off if he'd stayed far away from Gatlinburg and the one woman who'd ever laid claim to his heart.

"If that's the theory you want to cling to, darlin', I won't challenge it."

Then he left before he proved himself a liar and set about changing her mind with actions instead of words.

Caleb steered clear of the cabin the rest of the day. He didn't dare go near his wife, not when his emotions were so near the surface, threatening to spill over at the slightest provocation. He could hardly believe he'd been foolish enough to fall for her. Rebecca, the girl who'd fascinated him with her zest for life, her ability to see beauty in the mundane, her compassionate nature. The girl he'd never been good enough for, not even before the accident.

He loved her. Even in the silence of the dairy barn, in the privacy of his own mind, the admission rocked him. Spooked him. Because this wasn't something that was going to go away. He'd have to live with this all-consuming emotion knowing she didn't love him back. That she wished him far away.

"What do you expect, O'Malley," he muttered, forking a wad of straw in the last stall. "You've caused her nothing but heartache."

"Talk to yourself much?"

Caleb turned to glare at his older brother. "What brings you here, Nathan? Surprised you could tear yourself away from that pretty little wife of yours."

Perching his arms on the stall, Nathan grinned over at him. "Ten-minute intervals is about all I can take. That's why I brought her with me. She's in the kitchen with Ma."

With a shake of his head, Caleb turned to his task. Maybe if he ignored Nathan, he'd go away.

"We've been to see the baby."

Then again, maybe not. He didn't respond, just kept mucking out the stall.

"When's the last time you saw her?"

"I'm guessing you already know the answer."

"She's your niece, Caleb," he said with a sigh. "While Josh didn't come right out and say it, I got the impression he's hurt by your neglect."

Stopping to lean his weight on the pitchfork handle, he snapped, "As soon as Tate's killers are caught, I'm leaving. You know that. So you can understand why I'm reluctant to play the part of the doting uncle."

"You don't have to leave. You can choose to stay here with the family, who needs you. That includes your wife and sister-in-law."

His fingers tightened around the handle. "Actually,

I do have to leave. I made a promise to my wife that I aim to honor."

"Why don't you talk to her?" Nathan entreated. "She may have had a change of heart."

"I have. And she made it perfectly clear that she wants me gone."

Looking decidedly unhappy, Nathan pushed away from the stall. "I'm sorry, Caleb. I had hoped…"

"Yeah. Me, too," he admitted. "But it's not to be."

After a constrained silence, Nathan jerked a thumb over his shoulder. "Why don't you have dessert with us? Ma made pie."

"I'm not in the mood for company."

Frowning, he turned and walked toward the double doors. "I'll be praying for you, brother."

Grateful, he nodded his thanks. He hoped God would have mercy on him and banish these feelings. That was the only way he'd survive leaving her. "Tell Sophie I said hi."

"Will do."

Losing himself in his work, he trudged home at half past eight, his empty stomach growling in protest. Should've stopped to eat hours ago. Hadn't been able to face the thought of another strained meal with Becca, however.

On the porch, he hesitated. "God, give me strength."

The fact that Becca was sitting on the sofa facing the door immediately struck him as wrong. Warning prickles pinched the skin between his shoulder blades.

"Caleb—"

The strangled note in her voice, the stark fear in

her eyes, registered the same time he became aware of their visitors.

"Well, if it ain't our witness," a burly man with shorn brown hair snarled from his position in the kitchen. The revolver in his hand was pointed straight at Caleb's chest. "Took your time comin' home, didn't ya? We've enjoyed gettin' to know your wife while we waited."

Nausea swirled. Fists clenching, his gaze slammed to Becca's paper-white face. Her wrists were bound with thick rope, and he could see the reddened, chafed skin beneath it. He did a rapid inventory—her hair wasn't mussed and her dress didn't appear wrinkled. There were no other marks on her exposed skin.

A second man, short and slender, moved from his spot in the corner to stand directly behind her, gun barrel glinting in the low firelight. "She's not much of a talker." His hand encircled her neck, and she flinched.

Lunging across the coffee table, Caleb landed on the cushion beside her and shoved the man in the chest, knocking him into the wall.

"Do that again, and I'll shoot you in the other leg." The man from the kitchen was suddenly looming over them, menace twisting his craggy features.

"What's stopping you?" Caleb growled, muscles trembling with fury.

"Please don't," Becca whispered in his ear. "I'm okay."

"Well, you see, we have a bit of traveling to do, and I'd rather not do it with an injured man." His teeth flashed. "I will if I have to, though." To his companion, he said, "The lady will ride with me. He'll ride alone. Don't drop your guard again, John."

"That's not fair, Wendell—" John rubbed his sore head.

"Shut up." He waved the gun at them. "Time to go, you two. The boss lady will be real happy to see you. Impressed, too, seeing as how she has no idea I left camp."

Wendell. As in, the man who'd accompanied Samantha to Becca's house. The one who'd frightened her with his attention.

Fear coiled like a viper in his belly. If they left the farm, there was a mighty good chance they wouldn't be returning.

"She will only slow us down, you know," he pushed out. "Leave her here, and I'll go willingly. I'll tell Samantha everything I know, and who I've told it to."

Reaching around Caleb, Wendell snagged Becca's arm and hauled her over to him. Her dismayed gasp speared through him, and it took every shred of self-control not to reach out to her.

"She's going. And the next time you take it into your mind to rebel, O'Malley, she'll get the punishment. Understand?"

Jerking a nod, he tried to tell her with his eyes that somehow, some way, he'd get them out of this mess.

Chapter Twenty-Four

Rebecca was going to be physically ill. With each passing mile they traveled farther from the O'Malley farm, the lower their chance of rescue became. Night cloaked the silent, massive forest. Behind her on the hulking horse, Wendell took advantage of the situation to pin her close, his arm a manacle about her waist.

She didn't dare risk a glance at Caleb. The last time she'd done so, she'd been tempted to do something rash like vaulting off the horse. Anything to reach him. To comfort him. Her husband had managed to look furious and ill with terror at the same time.

Bringing up the rear, John's whistling pierced the stillness, the jaunty tune at odds with the gravity of their predicament. Things certainly weren't in their favor. In fact, there was a good chance tonight might be their last.

Grief snatched her breath away. Caleb would never know how much he meant to her. He could very well die thinking she didn't want him around. She squeezed her eyes tight. Why had she led him to believe a lie? Why insist on sticking to that agreement when the thought of not being with him made her die inside?

I've made a huge mistake, God. I've lied to myself and to my husband because I was too frightened to take a chance. Too scared to give in to these feelings.

"If you're sleepy, little lady, feel free to rest your head on my shoulder."

Snapping her head up, she ignored the low growl from Caleb. "I'm not sleepy."

"I am." John stopped whistling. "When are we gonna bed down for the night?"

A sigh heaving his chest, her captor pulled up on the reins. "Next time, you're staying at the camp. Not sure why I let you talk me into letting you come. Should've brought Vance."

"I'm not useless," the younger man protested. "Besides, I'm the boss's nephew. That gives me the right to be here."

"It's after midnight, anyway." Wendell guided his horse to a level clearing on their right. Caleb followed and, sliding off his horse, strode to help her down before the other man could. At his reassuring touch, Rebecca blinked back tears. Then Wendell dismounted and shoved Caleb away.

"Tie him up," he ordered John.

"Where's Samantha?" Caleb demanded, brown eyes almost black with loathing. "How far away is your camp from here?"

Ignoring him, Wendell tethered the reins to a tree branch and reached for his canteen.

Rebecca edged closer to Caleb as John secured the

ropes, shivering when she noticed his wince. Her own wrists burned from the friction.

"We'll get there tomorrow around suppertime," Samantha's nephew told them amiably, as if he was some sort of mountain guide instead of their captor.

"Start the fire, John," Wendell snapped. "I'll be back in a jiffy."

When Wendell had stomped off into the forest, lamplight dwindling, Caleb brought his face close to hers. "I'll find a way to get you out of here. You have to promise to do what I say."

Tangling her fingers with his, she whispered fiercely, "You mean *us*. I'm not leaving you."

His forehead pressed against hers, warm breath caressing her face. "I'm so sorry I wasn't there for you. When he put his hand on your neck..." He shuddered. "Did they do anything—"

"I'm unhurt. John's not the one I'm worried about." Something in Wendell's eyes made her skin crawl.

His fingers tightened on hers. "We have to try and escape before we reach camp and the other men."

"I wouldn't let Wendell catch you two whispering together like that," John called, tossing another stick onto the growing pile. The single lamp did little to dispel the night's shadows.

"He's right." Caleb sighed before disengaging his hands and moving away. The cold crowded in again, and she was grateful that at least they'd been allowed to wear their coats.

"Do you have a wife, John?" Caleb approached the smoldering fire.

Wiping his hands on his pants, he shook his head.

"Nah. There's a girl I'm sweet on back home. My aunt needed my help, though, and I haven't been back in nearly six months."

"What's her name?"

"Hannah" His smile bordered on innocent. What was this boy—he looked all of eighteen—doing with roughened criminals?

"Think she's waiting for your return?"

"She said she would."

Caleb studied the other man with narrowed eyes. "What do you think she'd say if she knew you stood by while your aunt gunned down an innocent man?"

He put his palms up. "I wasn't there the night Sheriff Tate was killed. I stayed back at camp."

"But you knew what she was going to do, didn't you?"

"No," he protested. "All I knew was that she was planning to confront him."

"What did Tate ever do to deserve such a fate?"

A stick snapped, announcing Wendell's return. "What is this? A tea party?" Jabbing a finger in Caleb's direction, he snapped, "You. Over there on the grass. And you, little lady, over here on my side of the fire. Bedtime."

Caleb's cheeks flushed with anger. "She's sleeping beside me, you filthy—"

"Wendell, be reasonable," John interrupted. "They're married. What's it gonna hurt?"

"Stay out of this." His hand went to his gun.

"I'm getting kinda tired of you treating me like a child." John squared his jaw. "Keep in mind that my aunt will be expecting a report."

His lip curled in obvious disdain. "I'm Samantha's best man."

"But you're not family, are you?" To Rebecca, John turned surprisingly sympathetic eyes. "Stay with your husband."

Thank you for this small kindness, God. Limp with relief, she hurried to Caleb's side. His eyes burned with a fierceness she feared would get him into trouble. "Let's just try and get some rest, okay," she murmured, lowering to the stiff grass and lying on her side to face the fire.

After a brief hesitation, he followed suit, scooting behind her so that his big body sheltered her from the occasional frost-scented breeze. They didn't speak. Not until Wendell had bedded down and his snores rent the night. Having taken the first guard shift, John was sitting against a tree trunk doodling in a book and humming a tune she didn't recognize. How could he act so nonchalant?

An owl hooted in the distance. Far above, the forest canopy blocked the night sky. Would they live to see the stars? Or was this truly their final night on earth?

The ground's dampness seeped into her body, and she shivered.

Caleb scooted close. Until that moment, she'd wondered if he slept. He'd been so still and silent. His breath stirred the hair at her ear a second before he pressed a light kiss to her throat. "I'd give anything to be able to put my arms around you right now."

Try as she might, she couldn't stop the hushed sobs from escaping. In this moment, she desired more than anything a chance to be a true wife to him. She wanted a future with him, wanted to experience it all with him. The joy and laughter, the arguments, the highs and lows. *Too late. I was too stubborn to admit I loved him until it was too late.*

"Please don't cry, Becca," he begged, voice raw. "It's not over yet. We still have a chance."

Snuggling into his long length, she tried to take comfort in his strength, tried to block the looming terror. "I don't see how…"

"Hey." He lightly rested his chin against her hair. "Where's the brave woman I married?"

"Gone." Lifting her bound hands, she attempted to swipe the moisture from her cheeks.

"I don't believe that for a second, Rebecca O'Malley. You're the strongest, spunkiest woman I've ever met." He sucked in a deep breath. "I'm gonna need you to hold on to that strength in the coming hours."

"You have a plan?"

"Not yet. I'm thinking John might be of use to us. The most important thing we can do right now is pray and ask God to give us a plan."

Startled, Rebecca pushed onto her back and gazed up at him. While he'd accompanied her to church and she'd seen him reading his Bible in recent days, she hadn't expected him to suggest such a thing. "Do you mean that?"

The flames cast his eyes in shadow, highlighting his jutting cheekbones and firm mouth. "Your frequent speeches about forgiveness spurred me to search out the evidence for myself. One particular verse in 1 John stuck with me. 'If we confess our sins, He is faithful and just and will forgive us our sins.' What I take away from that is forgiveness doesn't hinge on me, because clearly I don't deserve it. He chooses to forgive because of His innate goodness."

For the first time since this ordeal began, Rebecca smiled. "I like this one from Psalms. 'He does not treat us as our sins deserve or repay us according to our iniquities. As a father has compassion on his children, so the Lord has compassion on those who fear Him.'"

"We need His compassion right now."

They grew quiet, each lost in their own thoughts. Or perhaps emotional exhaustion was kicking in. "Caleb?" she ventured, suddenly shy.

His face suspended above hers, his gaze returned to hers. "Hmm?"

"I wish I could hold you, too."

Caleb was rudely awakened by a boot in his shin.

"Get up," Wendell ordered, waving his hat toward the dawn-streaked sky. "Time to get a move on."

The burly man had bags beneath his eyes, and he was sweating. John, on the other hand, appeared almost cheerful as he readied his saddlebags. Plainly the lack of sleep hadn't bothered the younger man.

Amazed he'd slept at all, Caleb gently shook Becca's shoulder to rouse her. She bolted upright, blinking the sleep from her eyes, features wan with apprehension. Her mass of dark hair had long ago tumbled from the pins, bits of grass clinging to the ends. Dirt smudged her cheek where she'd rested her head on the ground. Yet she was more beautiful, more precious to him, than ever before.

He wished he could reveal what was in his heart,

but their predicament silenced him. He had to focus on keeping them alive. Besides, she'd made her feelings plain. She was determined to stick to their original agreement. A confession wouldn't change anything, particularly one made when the threat of death hung over their heads.

When Caleb had helped her to her feet, John walked over with a canteen and a small bundle. "Breakfast." His breezy smile irked Caleb.

"How are we supposed to eat?" he retorted, lifting his bound wrists.

"Right."

He set the bundle on the ground and, whipping out his pocketknife, sawed through Becca's ropes first. The inexperienced outlaw did it quickly, roughly, as if unaware of her pain. Caleb ground his teeth. John had finished cutting his ropes when Wendell burst out, "What are you doing, you fool? That was the last of our rope! What are we supposed to tie them up with now?"

"Oops. Sorry, I didn't think."

The guilty surprise on John's face didn't quite match up with the hard look in his eyes, which aroused Caleb's suspicions. He'd be watching this one more closely.

Handing them the water and bundle of food, he returned to his horse, seemingly unaffected by his cohort's continued rant. Caleb offered Becca a piece of bread and ham.

"I can't eat." Grimacing, she pressed a hand to her stomach.

"You have to try," he murmured. "You need to keep up your strength."

Nodding, she reluctantly nibbled on the ham while

casting anxious glances at their captors. Unlike Becca, he was ravenous. His last meal had been at lunchtime the day before. Not knowing when they might have need of rations, however, he forced himself to eat only half a piece of bread and return the rest to his coat pocket. A couple of sips of water helped ease the hunger.

"How's your leg?" Worry tugged her brows together as she studied him closely.

"A little sore," he admitted, "but holding up better than expected."

Taking a drink from the canteen, she handed it to him. Pink splashed across her cheeks. "I have to take care of a private matter."

For a moment, he considered telling her to make a run for it. But they were miles from town, and the possibility of her getting lost was too high. Not to mention she had no weapon to defend herself against wild animals. "I'll tell John."

When she'd slipped away, Caleb begged God for guidance. He needed assistance, needed to know when and how to act. Because if he screwed this up, it was their lives on the line.

Lord, please don't let me be the one to cause her pain again. Help me to be the man she can trust to take care of her, to keep her safe.

Becca returned after five minutes. His request that she ride with him was laughed off. Watching Wendell pull her onto the horse and imprison her in his arms while not being able to do a thing about it was the hardest thing Caleb had ever had to endure. Hot and cold shifted through his body, the fiery heat of rage shadowed by icy dread.

Vaulting into the saddle and nudging his mount into motion, he kept his gaze trained on the mountainous terrain instead of the horse in front. Familiarizing himself with the area helped keep the rage contained.

By midmorning, the sun had burned off the fog and raised the temperature to what felt like the high forties. Wendell abruptly halted his mount, causing Caleb to jerk on the reins to avoid a collision.

"What's the matter?" John called.

Sliding to the ground, the burly man dished something from his saddlebag and started for the forest, gait uneasy. "Wait here."

Becca twisted around to look at Caleb, her big eyes dark with anguish. Misery tugged at her generous mouth.

He said over his shoulder, "Mind if we stretch our legs a bit?"

"Why not?" John said, remaining in the saddle, one hand on his gun handle and manner watchful.

Becca sagged against Caleb the instant he reached her, her arms locked around his waist. He buried his face in her hair, the slight scent of lilac still clinging to the silky strands. The words *I love you* hovered on the tip of his tongue, but he clamped his mouth closed.

Wrong timing, O'Malley. Wrong place, wrong situation. Wrong man.

She admired men like Adam—sensible, dependable. Safe. Not men who made stupid mistakes that hurt the ones he loved.

"I can't stand this," she bit out, her breath heating his cold neck.

Taking hold of her shoulders, he eased away so that

he could look her in the eye. "I've never been more proud of you, Rebecca."

Tears shimmered in the luminous depths. "Don't call me that. When you do, it means you're worried. Or angry."

He was both of those things, of course. Letting her know that would only burden her further. Forcing a lopsided grin, he chucked her chin. "What would you rather I call you? Turtledove? Baby cakes?" His voice dipped. "My love?"

Her grip tightened on his waist. "Caleb—"

"He's coming," John warned in a quiet tone.

Daring to drop a swift kiss on her cheek, he returned to his horse and climbed into the saddle, thankful for the younger man's consideration but curious as to his motives. Was he merely trying to avoid conflict? He'd admitted to being unproven as a criminal. Maybe he was discovering he didn't have a taste for violence, after all.

Becca placed her boot in the stirrup, only to be halted by Wendell's barked order. "Ride with John."

The relief washing her countenance mirrored what was rushing through his veins. Between the two, John was the better option. Not ideal, just better.

"You don't look so good," John said to Wendell.

It was true. Wendell's complexion was washed-out, almost greenish, and he looked to be experiencing some discomfort.

"I'll manage."

When Becca walked past Caleb, the tiny smile she gifted him with was hopeful. And he got the distinct feeling that even in the midst of this ordeal, God was watching over them.

Chapter Twenty-Five

He'd called her *my love*. The way he'd said it—with such gravity—made Rebecca's heart flutter with impossible yearning. When he'd challenged her about the agreement, she hadn't been able to see past the daring in his eyes. Just now, however, she'd glimpsed deep emotion, an earnestness that had shifted the ground beneath her feet.

She studied the proud line of his shoulders and spine, the occasional view of his profile, as they ventured farther into a wide valley surrounded by blue-toned mountains. While she longed to be with her husband, riding with John wasn't terrible. His impartial touch didn't make her feel dirty as Wendell's did.

The despicable outlaw was physically sick. They'd stopped again an hour after the first time, and he'd returned from his jaunt in the woods sweaty and pale. Caleb watched him with narrowed eyes, and she could almost see him plotting a way of escape. *God, help us.* The sun was almost directly above them. By evening they will have reached the camp, and their chances of escaping would plummet.

Behind her, John shifted. "How about we stop here?" he called up to his cohort, indicating a sliver of a stream winding through the trees. "We can let the horses drink while we eat lunch."

Wendell wordlessly directed the group to the spot. When he'd dismounted, he took a long swig from his canteen and went to the stream to refill it. Caleb assisted her down, then quickly moved a few steps away, gaze watchful and lean, powerful body riddled with tension. Was he going to act soon? Fear for his safety knocked thoughts of his endearment—and the meaning behind it—from her head.

Rebecca stared at the trickling water, wishing she could soak her sore wrists but unwilling to go near Wendell. John presented her with an open tin of beans and a fork.

"Nothing fancy, but it's all we've got." He flashed an apologetic smile, then went and plopped down at the base of an old oak and dug into his own can with gusto.

Her stomach cramped with nerves. Sensing Caleb's attention, she forced a couple of bites before handing it to him. He pressed a slice of slightly stale bread into her hand. "Eat this."

It was from breakfast, which he'd clearly denied himself. "Only if you promise to eat that entire tin of beans."

He made a show of sniffing the contents. "Do I have to?"

The fact that he was attempting to lift her spirits made her love him that much more. Taking a bite of the bread, she firmly nodded.

"I don't really like beans, you know."

"I remember."

His startled glance gained him a small smile. Then

Wendell sprang from his seated position on the bank and shattered the moment. The bread lodged in her throat. He was glaring at them.

Hand rubbing his gut, he jabbed a finger toward the denser forest they'd recently vacated. "I'm going for a walk." To John, he growled, "Make sure you keep an eye on these two. If they get away, your aunt will hang for her crimes."

Swallowing hard, the brown-headed man lowered his fork to his lap and watched with a troubled expression as Wendell stomped off.

Caleb casually made his way to the oak tree, lowering his tall frame into a crouch, tin can in hand. Rebecca trailed behind him.

"What happened between Samantha and Tate?" he prompted. "What did Tate do to set her on a path of revenge?"

John's jaw hardened, and defeat settled in the lines bracketing his mouth. "She wasn't always like this. She used to be sweet-natured. Generous." His attention drifted to what Rebecca guessed were happier times.

"What changed?" Caleb said.

"She and Tate were sweethearts once upon a time. Planned to marry before..." He heaved a sigh. "My aunt was walking home one night when she was set upon by a pair of men. They abused her and left her for dead."

Caleb grimaced. Rebecca's blood ran cold.

"Tate couldn't handle it. If he'd only been there for her, she could've healed. But he broke things off and, after that, she went a little bit crazy."

"How can she surround herself with men?" Rebecca

blurted, thinking she would've wanted to keep her distance.

"She controls them," Caleb surmised. "My guess is it makes her feel powerful, something she wasn't before."

"I want to help her. That's why I came," John admitted.

Caleb set his tin on the ground. "Let us go, John. You know she's not going to let us live. Not when we can testify to her crimes. You don't want our deaths on your conscience, do you?"

Rebecca could see his obvious struggle.

"I can convince her to give herself up. You'll be fine," John said.

"I'm afraid your reassurances aren't good enough," Caleb said as he leaped on top of the smaller man. Unprepared, Rebecca clapped her hand over her mouth. She mustn't scream. While he scrambled to pry the gun from John's holster, she frantically scanned the forest behind them. Where was Wendell? He wouldn't hesitate to shoot.

The horses! Dashing over, she seized the reins of Caleb's mount. Slapped the others' rumps to scare them into bolting.

Angry grunts echoed behind her. Punches landed.

The click of a gun hammer froze her in place. *Oh, Lord, please let that be Caleb. Not John. Not Wendell.*

Afraid to look yet unable to refrain, she turned. Winded, one cheek bruised and his hair in his eyes, Caleb pointed the gun at John, who was sprawled in the grass. He looked stunned.

"Don't call for Wendell. If you do, I'll make sure you're punished to the full extent of the law. Keep quiet, and I'll ask for leniency." Spinning, he strode to her side. "Let's go."

* * *

His heart didn't return to its normal rhythm until hours later, when dusk had fallen and he was confident no one was on their trail. He didn't dare relax his guard until they reached Gatlinburg.

"Caleb, I need a break," Becca said softly.

She hadn't complained once about the punishing pace he'd set for them. Her shoulders were sagging, however, and her legs were surely as stiff as his were. Studying their surroundings, he chose a sheltered spot between a circle of pines.

Reaching the ground first, he turned and assisted her down, hands lingering on her slim hips. He told himself it was to steady her, not because he couldn't resist touching her in order to reassure himself she was all right. Safe.

She glanced around in trepidation. The thick pines mostly hid them. Still, there were gaps.

He released her and snagged the canteen. Half-empty. Giving it to her, he warned her to take it easy. They'd need to find a water supply soon.

"Amy must be worried sick," she fretted, arching her back and rubbing the knots from her muscles.

"They would've noticed our absence and come searching for us." But would they know which way to travel? Caleb couldn't help the feeling of foreboding lodged in his chest. "I meant to tell you earlier...great thinking running off the other horses. I'm impressed." He took a shallow sip of water and recapped the canteen.

"I didn't really think about it. Just acted."

Gently hooking her hair behind her ear, he said, "You were very brave, just like I knew you'd be."

"You're the brave one." She frowned. "I wish John wasn't mixed up with Samantha and her troubles."

"Me, too. He made his choice, however. He'll have to live with the consequences."

Hugging her middle, she rubbed her arms through her wool cape. Her fingers were pink from the cold. His ears burned from exposure.

Her jade gaze clung to his. "I won't feel better until we're inside our cabin with the door locked and a fire raging in the fireplace."

Caleb zeroed in on the word *our,* aware she didn't actually think of his cabin as her forever home. "Becca, I don't know how long it'll take to capture these people, but as soon as the danger has passed you can return to your cabin in the cove "

White teeth sinking into her plush lower lip, brow creasing, she merely nodded her understanding.

What had he expected? That she'd beg to stay with him forever? *I'm really a fool if I think she'd ever do that.*

He turned away to scan the mountainous, winter-cursed terrain beyond the opening. "We'll stay here ten minutes more, then head out."

"Okay." She sounded uncharacteristically unsure. Confused.

He brushed it off. No use punishing himself further. Nothing had changed.

Rose and russet hues streaked across the sky. Without a lamp, their progress was going to be slow. Walking the outer edge of the pines, he stretched his legs.

"Ready?"

Solemn, she accepted his boost up. When they set

out again, he reveled in the way she leaned into him, her slender fingers threaded through his. Once they reached the farm, they wouldn't be sharing this kind of closeness again.

An hour later, he made the mistake of lowering his guard. Whether due to fatigue or preoccupation with Becca, he didn't anticipate the riders emerging from the shadows.

"Stop right there."

The husky voice set off alarm bells.

Becca stiffened. "Oh, no."

Surprise flitted across Samantha's features. She hadn't been expecting them, then. Or searching for them. Her companion, a man who looked to be about the same age as her, wedged his mount beside hers.

"That scar," he said, eyes narrowing. "Is this our elusive witness?"

A hard smile lifted her lips. "Very perceptive, Isaiah." The gun she held on them was propped lazily against her thigh. "Rebecca, isn't it? I didn't realize our witness was in fact your husband. A shame. I warned you not to place your faith in a man."

"Not all men are untrustworthy," Becca said. Caleb squeezed her arm, a silent warning not to mention Tate at this point.

"Some people never learn." Samantha sighed. Her gaze sharpened on Caleb. "What are you doing so far from home?"

"Your man Wendell thought to deliver us to you as a belated Christmas gift." On edge, fingers itching to retrieve the weapon he'd lifted from John, he desperately tried to subdue his instincts.

"Is that so? He failed to mention it to me. Where is good ole Wendell, anyway?"

"Probably roaming the woods and cursing his existence. I think he got a hold of some rancid food."

She and Isaiah exchanged a look. Lifting her gun, she motioned with the long barrel. "Get down."

"You don't have to do this." On the ground, he blocked Becca with his body. "Your nephew told us what happened to you," he said gently. "Killing us won't make the pain disappear. I'm guessing killing Tate didn't help, either."

"Don't you dare breathe that man's name again." Expression thunderous, she jerked out of the saddle, boots striking the ground with force. Memories of the murder filled Caleb. Her hatred. Her utter lack of mercy. She must've endured terrible things to have come to this point.

"I don't blame you for despising him. Or men in general. He failed you, didn't he, Samantha? His rejection hurt worse than what those men did to you."

"Caleb." Becca breathed a low warning, gripping his arms from behind.

Isaiah joined Samantha, placing a hand on her shoulder. "What's he talking about, Sam?"

Eyes on fire, she flinched, dislodging him. "Touch me again, and you'll lose a hand."

He rolled his eyes. "Have I ever given you a reason not to trust me?"

"We'll discuss this later," she snapped, fury blazing in a face made more delicate by the severe haircut. "As for you, Caleb O'Malley, playing compassionate bystander won't alter your fate. In fact, throwing my past in my face has only served to shorten your time on earth. On your knees. Both of you."

He weighed his options. Time was running out. *Not again, Lord, I can't fail Becca again.* "Aren't you curious as to what happened to John?"

While she tried to mask her reaction, he saw her swallow convulsively. She cared about the young man at least a little. "Should I be worried?"

"How about we strike a deal? I'll spill about my time with your nephew after you release my wife."

Gasping, Becca dug her fingers into his skin. He winced.

"And have her hightail it to the authorities?" she scoffed. "No deal."

"All she cares about is getting home to her sister."

"I'm not a fool, O'Malley." Gesturing to the root-studded earth in front of his horse, she said, "I said get on your knees."

Defeat pounded at his temples. Even if he jumped the woman, that left her partner to deal with Becca. He couldn't risk it. There had to be another way.

Side by side, they lowered themselves to the uneven ground. He refused to believe this was the end.

Samantha moved to stand before them. "Tell me where my nephew is or I'll shoot her and make you watch as she takes her sweet time bleeding to death."

In that moment, he hated another human being. Rage licked his insides. "I left him hale and hearty after I relieved him of his weapon," he said.

"And where was this?"

"Half a day's ride north."

"Excellent. That wasn't so hard, was it?" When Isaiah leaned over to whisper something in her ear, Caleb took advantage of their momentary distraction.

Nauseated, he turned his head to stare deeply into his wife's eyes. "Rebecca, I—"

"Don't say it," she begged, a silver tear tracking down her cheek. "None of this is your fault."

Wait. She thought he was about to *apologize?* When they were staring death in the face? "You don't understand—"

"Stop your yammering." Both Isaiah and Samantha were watching them with impatience.

Beside him, Becca spoke with quiet dignity. "Have you ever thought about how your actions are affecting your nephew? He strikes me as an intelligent, fair-minded young man. Do you really want to take away his innocence? His future? Because if he stays with you, he'll spend the rest of his life in prison. Or worse."

For a split second, Samantha wavered. "I didn't ask him to tag along. He thinks he can help me." Her laugh was edged with scorn.

"I know I can." John materialized from the gloom-shrouded woods with his horse. He must've run after the animal the second they left.

The sun had dipped below the mountains. Lantern light only served to toss shadows over everyone. "If you'd only let me."

Momentarily disconcerted, Samantha stared as he approached with his gun outstretched. Pointed at *her*. Not them. Could this be the break they needed?

"What are you doing?" she sputtered.

"I can't let you kill another innocent person, Sam."

Isaiah kept his pistol trained on Caleb and Becca, but his manner hinted at uncertainty. Caleb could practically see him trying to decide what to do. Aim at the captives? Or the nephew?

"You're not gonna shoot me," she boasted, recovering her equanimity. "I know you, John."

"Let them go. Forget about what happened in Cades Cove. We can start over, you and me." His voice was steady, as was his aim.

Caleb leaned close to Becca. "Be ready to run."

Her big eyes took on a mournful cast. "I'm not leaving without you."

"Don't be stubborn," he urged. "Think of Amy."

"You'd never leave me—" her mouth twisted fiercely "—so don't ask it of me."

Battling frustration, he refocused on the scene playing out in front of him. If he jumped Isaiah, what would Samantha do? Was it worth the risk?

Samantha scowled. "What makes you think I want a fresh start? I like my life just fine."

"You're bluffing." Entreaty darkened his eyes. He lifted an outstretched hand. "Leave this violence behind. Come with me, Aunt Samantha."

"You sound like my brother," she said, disgusted. "A normal life is out of the question for me. Not after— Enough of this." She jerked her chin in their direction. "Isaiah, since my nephew is being particularly grievous, take Mr. and Mrs. O'Malley into the woods."

Isaiah grimly made to obey her. "Whatever you say, boss."

When he reached for Becca, Caleb didn't think. Just reacted. He launched himself at the man, knocking him off his feet. A growl of outrage pierced his ear.

A shot rang out, and Caleb braced himself for the inevitable pain.

Chapter Twenty-Six

Adrenaline surging, Rebecca grabbed a fistful of Isaiah's hair and yanked with all her might. "Get off him!"

Head snapping back, he howled an obscenity. Caleb scrambled for the gun. Rebecca watched the struggle, prepared to jump in a second time. She'd almost lost Caleb once to these maniacs. She wouldn't stand by and watch him get shot again.

Samantha cradled her left shoulder, face crumpled in more than physical pain. "Why?"

John scooped up her discarded weapon and holstered it, aiming his own at the man scuffling in the dirt with Caleb. "It's over, Isaiah." Then he handed his aunt a handkerchief to put on her wound.

To Rebecca, he said, "Are you all right?"

Jerking a nod, she slowly unfurled her clenched fists as Caleb rose to his feet, disheveled and dirty but otherwise unharmed.

"I don't understand why you'd do this." Samantha's composure slipped.

Regret carved deep grooves in his cheeks. "If I'd

known what you were planning the night you confronted Tate, I would've tried to stop you. I couldn't stand by and let you continue the cycle of violence." His gaze flicked to Caleb. "Besides, I may not know him personally, but I know someone very close to him."

"Who?" Caleb demanded.

"I work as a farmhand for Evan Harrison and his wife, Juliana O'Malley Harrison. Your cousin."

Startled, Samantha jerked back. Cades Cove used to be her home. Of course she'd be familiar with the residents. "The Harrisons are related to my witness? How did you know of the connection?"

"Juliana is always talking about her family. When I heard Wendell mention he was going after Caleb O'Malley in Gatlinburg, I figured I'd better volunteer to come along. Once I saw the scar, I knew I had the right man. I also knew I couldn't let anything happen to him. Not after the kindness the Harrisons have shown to me."

"Thank you," Caleb said gravely, his dark eyes full of gratitude sliding to Rebecca. If not for his interference, they'd likely be dead.

"Now what?" Samantha demanded as John rifled in her saddlebags for rope. "You're gonna hand me over to the authorities? You know they'll hang me."

He tossed the rope to Caleb, who then proceeded to tie up Isaiah.

His throat worked, and he had the demeanor of a graveside mourner. What a horrible position to be put in. "We don't know that. Maybe they'll show leniency."

"Tate was Cades Cove's sheriff." She snorted inelegantly.

John glared at her. "*Was* a sheriff. Now he's dead,

thanks to you. The fact that you don't appear to be experiencing any remorse bothers me."

"You don't understand." Stance rigid, her brokenness cloaking her in fury, she said, "You didn't see the way he looked at me...like I disgusted him. Like it was my fault—" She shuddered, and when John settled a hand on her uninjured shoulder, she flinched. "I thought he loved me."

"It wasn't your fault," he said firmly. "Tate was a blind idiot for acting the way he did. But he didn't deserve to die, Sam."

Rebecca startled when Caleb slipped his hand in hers. Absorbed in the scene playing out before her, she hadn't heard his approach. The troubled light in his eyes mirrored what she was feeling. This story could've had a vastly different ending. There could've been healing instead of destruction.

She squeezed his hand, knowing deep in her soul Caleb would never let her down like that. He'd support her no matter what. Studying his dear, familiar profile, she understood that he was the type of man she'd always dreamed of—noble, brave, honorable. Heroic.

The scar was no longer a reminder of lost dreams. Instead, it was a mark of lessons learned.

"Let's go." John dropped his hand. "You need medical attention."

His hands bound, Isaiah moved over to whisper softly to his leader. John loped over to Rebecca and Caleb. "I know you've been through a lot, and I apologize for the part I played. I hope you can forgive me."

"You saved our lives," Caleb said simply, as if that

wiped clean all that had gone before. "Sheriff Timmons will take that into consideration."

They mounted up, Caleb and Rebecca on the horse they'd taken, Isaiah on his mount and John and his aunt riding together. The return trek through the mountains seemed to last an eternity. She couldn't relax. Every noise potentially meant Wendell had caught up to them or Isaiah had gotten free. Caleb tried to reassure her, but she felt the tension humming through his body, as well.

As dawn split the darkness, they glimpsed Gatlinburg tucked in the valley below. The glorious view sparked relief and a deep sense of gratefulness. Their nightmare was over.

Sheriff Timmons wasn't there. The deputy informed them that he and a group of men, including Caleb's father and brother Nathan, were still searching for them. Frustrated at the news, Caleb had no choice but to leave the three in the deputy's care. They rode straight home. Mary and Amy cried when they saw them. After too many hugs to count, they proceeded to ply them with food and drink. When Mary insisted on drawing them baths in the main house, Rebecca didn't complain. She was cold and filthy, and her hair surely resembled a bird's nest. Best to rid herself of all the physical reminders of their ordeal.

The mental reminders weren't as easy to dispel.

Back in their cabin, Caleb turned to her with a determined air. His hair shone and the scent of soap clung to his skin, but he hadn't taken the time to shave. "I should go after Pa and Nathan. They need to know we're all right."

The horror of all they'd endured swamped her. Her

knees threatened to give out. Clad in fresh clothes, a thick quilt wrapped around her shoulders, she couldn't seem to get warm. She couldn't bear the thought of him venturing into those mountains again. Wendell and the other outlaws were still out there. "Don't go."

His brows shot up. "Believe me, I'd much rather stay here with you."

"Then stay. Caleb, you've had only snatches of sleep the past two days. Admit it, you're exhausted."

Indecision flared deep in his eyes. Weariness stamped his features.

Boldly taking his hand, she led him to the couch. "The truth is I don't want to be alone. That was as close to dying as I've ever been, and I can't get the images out of my head." Sinking down, she patted the cushion beside her. "Please stay with me."

His intense gaze bore down on hers. Easing down beside her, he rested his arm along the back edge. "I'll stay."

Her breath whooshed out.

"For today. If they haven't returned by morning, I'll have to go after them. Shane needs to know we have Samantha."

"Thank you."

A ghost of a smile flickered across his lips, there and gone again so quickly she might've imagined it. Getting comfortable against the cushions, he motioned with his fingers. "Scoot closer so I can warm you up."

Without a second thought, she nestled against him. He was like a furnace. The heat coming off his body leaked into hers, and she closed her eyes in delight. His arm came around her, and he tucked her head in the curve of his shoulder. His fingers trailed lazily, methodically, through her hair.

Rebecca felt as if this was where she belonged, where she'd always belonged but hadn't known it.

The caress ceased. He shifted slightly away from her. "Becca, now that we're no longer in danger, you and Amy can finally go home."

Rebecca eased her lids open, stared at his tanned fingers splayed across his thigh. Her stomach knotted up.

"And I can get back to what I do best," he continued.

Bracing a hand against his chest, she pushed away to look at him. "It's too cold. What if we get another blizzard?"

"Cold doesn't bother me."

She couldn't decipher his thoughts, not with that watchful guardedness, the way his features were schooled to blandness. The shadows beneath his eyes spoke of his exhaustion. She should be quiet and let him rest.

"Won't you be lonely?" she couldn't resist asking.

"I'll have Rebel to keep me company." His shrug struck her as completely natural, as if walking away from her would be the easiest thing in the world. "Besides, I'll be back in about a month. I'm going to hire a farmhand to take care of the repairs and ongoing upkeep since I won't be around."

Seared by the heat blazing through his cotton shirt, she dropped her hand to her lap and twisted her fingers together. "I know we had an agreement. However, I didn't consider the impact on your family. They will miss you horribly if you go." *I'll miss you.*

He smirked. Not the reaction she'd expected.

"They're used to me being gone. I'm sure they've already had their fill of me."

"But—"

He stopped her with a finger pressed to her lips. "Stop worrying, Becca. My family will be fine. I'll be fine. Most important, you'll have your old life back. You'll probably even reach the point where you'll forget you even have a husband."

Not possible.

His eyes darkened to burnt umber. He leaned forward, lowered his head. Her lids fluttered closed in anticipation of what was to come. Bliss. Connection. Unspoken witness to what was in her heart.

The kiss wasn't to be. The air stirred, and she blinked to see him disengaging from the quilt and surging to his feet. She stared up at him in what was surely open-mouthed dismay.

"Have you ever gotten so tired you couldn't sleep?" Striding to the kitchen, he yanked the tin of coffee onto the counter. "I'm afraid I can't relax. But you—" he waggled a finger her direction without sparing her a glance "—go ahead and stretch out. I'll be quiet."

Heart bruised and bewildered, Rebecca did as he suggested, curling up on her side so that her back was to the room. Sleep was impossible. So was baring her true feelings. Not when he was bound and determined to leave her and didn't appear the least bit bothered by the prospect.

What was it about her that made it so easy to walk away?

Chapter Twenty-Seven

Three days later, Rebecca ventured out alone, desperate to see her best friend. Meredith was as levelheaded as they came. She'd know how to put everything into perspective. That was what she was counting on, at least.

Meredith's excited cry and all-enveloping hug brought tears to her eyes. Tears that were too near the surface ever since Caleb had made his plans clear. He was sticking to their agreement. To her growing dissatisfaction, he hadn't bothered to ask if she'd changed her mind. She waffled between confessing all and shaking him senseless. Why did he have to go and become all responsible? Where was the hang-the-rules man she'd married?

"I've wanted to visit but my parents advised me to wait." Meredith released her, only to link her arm with hers. "I was frantic with worry when I first learned about the kidnapping. Tell me everything that happened." Concern clouded her eyes as they left the porch and walked along the path to the corral. The sun was warm on their backs, and there was no breeze to stir the cool mountain air.

Reluctant to rehash the sordid story but aware her friend was keen on details, Rebecca gave her the basic outline of what had happened. Meredith listened intently, gasping in places, frowning in others. "Caleb was so brave," Rebecca finished.

Dark brows met over her nose. "Sounds like you both were."

"No." Rebecca stopped before an oak tree, aware of the pair of cardinals perched in the bare branches, a brilliant shade of red against the nearly colorless sky. "I couldn't have survived without him, Mer. His strength kept me sane."

"If it had to happen, I'm glad he was with you. He's a very capable man, it seems."

Capable. Thoughtful. A little roguish. Without him around, who was going to make her laugh? Caleb had a way of lifting the tedium of ordinary days with his smile, a teasing word, an unexpected kiss. She'd miss his vitality, the way his presence expanded the room, made the air particles dance with anticipation of what he'd do next.

"You're looking sad," Meredith said. "What aren't you telling me?"

"He's packing our things as we speak. Amy and I are returning to my parents' cabin, and he's going on a hunting excursion in the mountains."

"How long will he be gone?"

"About a month. He'll be home just long enough to hire a helper." He hadn't left yet, but already there was an empty space where her heart should be.

Meredith nodded decidedly. "I think you should tell him the truth, Rebecca. Tell him you want a real marriage."

"It's that obvious?" She gasped, horrified. Did he suspect? Did his family?

"You're clearly miserable, my friend. And you haven't mentioned Adam or his pretty new wife, not even once. That's monumental."

"You met her?"

"At church. She struck me as a genuinely nice person."

Meredith wasn't the type to sugarcoat matters, not even to protect a friend's feelings. Rebecca wasn't upset. She was well and truly over Adam Tierney. "I got the same impression. I'm happy he's found someone he can share his life with."

"And you're clearly not sorry that person isn't you."

Disengaging, she turned and, sinking her hands in her pockets, surveyed the forested cove similar to her own. "When I think of how I went on and on about Caleb being my enemy, my immense disdain for him when he first arrived, I cringe with shame. It was more convenient and far easier to blame him for my misfortune than it was to deal with Adam's rejection. Blaming Caleb relieved me of any responsibility in the dissolution of my engagement."

"You weren't entirely without compassion," Meredith said loyally. "I was there. I saw how deep your concern went. Perhaps God used his brush with death to open your eyes to the truth."

"Perhaps." She'd entertained similar thoughts. "Still, I wasn't particularly nice to him, was I? I made sure he knew he wasn't welcome. And before we exchanged vows, I made him promise we'd have a long-distance marriage. If I go to him now and explain I've had a change of heart, who's to say he'll want to stick around? I have no idea how he feels about me. He could very well laugh in my face."

Meredith shot her a skeptical look.

"Well, maybe not laugh. He'd let me down gently." While he may project a tough attitude, her husband was sensitive in many ways.

"Go to him, Rebecca. Ask him what he wants. If you can't bring yourself to do that, you'll have to let him go."

The sight of the half-filled wagon outside Caleb's cabin jarred Rebecca. He wasn't wasting any time, was he? Was he that eager to be off?

Nerves frayed, mind pathetically blank, she found him in the kitchen placing half-eaten loaves of bread into a crate on the table. He looked up and, with a curt nod, continued his task as if on a deadline.

"How's Meredith?" he asked over his shoulder, reaching for the jars of muscadine jelly and sorghum molasses.

"She wanted to hear my account of what happened."

He hung his head. Then, squaring his shoulders, he pivoted to deposit the jars in the crate. With his head bent, his longish locks hid his eyes. "Are you sleeping better?"

Because they'd arrived home in the morning and slept on and off during the day, her schedule had been thrown off. The bad dreams didn't help. She thanked God that Sam and Nathan had returned the following day, preventing Caleb from having to search for them. They, along with Sheriff Timmons and some other local men, had caught up to Wendell. Timmons and the others had continued on to the camp and arrested Saman-tha's cohorts.

Crossing to the table, she gripped the chair for sup-port. "A little."

"I'm sure that will change once you're in familiar surroundings. In your own bed."

He wouldn't even look at her. How was she supposed to bare her heart when he was acting cold and indiffer-ent? It was as if his mind was already out there in the rugged country.

When she continued to stand there, desperately try-ing to come up with something to say, he motioned to the bedroom. "There's a trunk on the bed. Thought I'd leave the packing of your clothing and personal items to you."

"Oh." Her throat was dry. "Okay."

"I told Ma to have Amy ready to go in half an hour. Will that give you enough time?" His jaw was hard and unyielding. Looking at him, she could hardly rec-oncile him with the man who'd risked his life to save her, who'd kissed her as if her value was without equal, who'd held her in his arms, safe and warm and pro-tected.

Emotion clogged her throat. Would she ever see that man again? Or was this forbidding stranger here to stay? "That should be sufficient."

Steps wooden, Rebecca went into the space she'd made her own. A photo of her parents graced the night-stand, as well as her Bible and three of her favorite nov-els. Her clothes and shoes filled the armoire, her art supplies in the corner desk. She wasn't certain how it had happened or when, but this cabin—Caleb's cabin—had become her haven.

And it was all theirs. Alone.

At her family homestead, memories of Adam had lurked in the oddest places, keeping her mired in the past. In addition, memories of Caleb's terrible injury and the dreadful things she'd been forced to do to save his life had permeated the rooms. Fear and anger and bitterness had overshadowed any joy that tried to break through.

Moving here had given them a fresh start. A sanctuary untainted by the past.

Here Caleb had presented her with her wedding ring. Surprised her with a Christmas tree and decorations because she'd been sad without one. He'd cooked for her, cared for her. Comforted her.

This was their home. This was where she longed to stay.

She was going to miss it. Dreadfully.

Rousing herself, she threw open the armoire doors and began to take the dresses off the hangers. If he'd given her a sign, a small token of encouragement—a look, a smile, a touch—she could've drummed up the courage to broach the subject of the agreement. He'd done nothing.

He couldn't possibly walk away so easily if he loved her. If he felt anything close to what she felt for him.

Numb, overwhelmed with dread, she didn't say a word as he finished loading the wagon. Nor did she breach the heavy silence as they rode across town. Normally chipper, Amy sat slumped in the wagon bed between crates, Storm curled up on her lap. It seemed neither sister had wanted to say goodbye to the O'Malley farm.

Back at her old cabin, Rebecca stood in the middle of the living room as Caleb toted everything in. He'd gruffly waved aside her offer of help. Because of their prolonged absence, a layer of dust coated nearly every surface. The tree would have to be disposed of, the decorations packed away. Mindless tasks that would hopefully distract her from her melancholy.

When the wagon was completely unloaded, he filled the doorway and announced it was time to go. "I thought it'd be more convenient for me to sleep at home tonight. That way I can bring your milk cow and old Toby over in the morning before I head out."

He wasn't staying? Wiping damp hands on her skirts, Rebecca frantically searched for some means of delaying the inevitable. *Tell him the truth,* an inner voice prodded.

"I can have breakfast ready for you," she rushed to say. "Biscuits and gravy. Your favorite."

His eyes landed on her face. For a moment, she thought he might agree. Gloved fingers furling and unfurling at his sides, he gave a hard shake of his head. "I can't. I'll be leaving long before dawn."

"I see." Gritting her teeth, she fought to rein in the threatening emotions. "I guess this is goodbye, then. Be safe, Caleb." If he noticed how her voice cracked, he didn't show it.

"You, too, Becca."

Then he walked away without a single glance.

Caleb was a fool. More than that, he was a coward. That's what he'd been telling himself every day for the past two and a half weeks. Without Becca, the days bled into one another, empty and cold and pointless. He was sick of his own company. Desperate for Becca's.

Tucked into his pallet at night, a canopy of velvet sky far above, he'd dream of her. Sometimes they were innocent. Casual, ordinary moments. Other times they were downright frightening...like Becca dashing through the mountains trying to escape Wendell and Samantha. Either way, he woke with a throbbing ache in his chest and the distinct feeling he was missing out on something precious by staying away.

I'm honoring her wishes, he told himself every time he was tempted to return. *The bargain I struck at her request.*

He hadn't been able to venture far. In the midst of preparing to leave, he'd failed to ask his family to watch out for her. Maybe it was an excuse to be near her. Whatever the case, he'd resumed his role of anonymous donor. Once a week, he returned to her cove and left his offering strung on a nail inside the barn, safe from predators.

This evening he'd brought a single rabbit. Dusk was sinking into full-on darkness, the perfect cover. As he left the forest behind and strode quickly across the expanse, he kept his gaze trained on the cabin. Yellow light glowed in the windows. Wisps of thin smoke curled from the chimney.

He had to act fast. Before Becca or Amy discovered him. Before his willpower disintegrated, and he stormed inside and swept her into his arms.

Hesitating at the barn door, he pressed his ear against the wood and strained for sound. No voices reached him. No active movement that indicated someone was inside tending chores.

The rabbit dangling near his knees, he tried to ease the rickety door open but it snagged on a mound of raised earth. It took a little maneuvering, but he was finally able to get it closed. With a sigh, he turned around and found himself staring into a pair of striking jade eyes that haunted his waking hours. Eyes that were rapidly filling with suspicion.

"I can explain." Holding up a hand, he winced at his choice of words.

Becca studied the dead animal. "It's you, isn't it? It's been you all along."

Unable to help himself, he took a step closer. The sight of her, her sweet scent, wreaked havoc with his restraint. "I was simply trying to help."

"That's why Rebel made his way here in the snowstorm," she said with dawning understanding. "He knew the way because he'd been here dozens of times before."

"I should've told you, I know." He laid the rabbit on the ground. Removing his hat and flinging it onto a nearby hay square, he jammed his fingers through his hair to keep from reaching for her. Being within arm's length of his wife after a torturous absence was testing every shred of his self-control. "But I don't always do what I should. We both know that."

Her eyes suddenly shimmering, she whispered, "I do know that."

A resigned sigh shuddered through him. "How've you been, Becca?"

"Miserable."

A tear tracked down her pale cheek and dripped from

her jaw onto her shawl. Alarm speared through him. "What? Why?"

"Because you did the honorable thing. Because I knew if you didn't truly want to go, you wouldn't have."

Shock winged through him to the tips of his toes. "Hold on a second. Are you telling me you're upset because I did what you asked me to?"

She bit her lip. "Yes."

"I think you'd better explain, Rebecca." If there was a harsh edge to his demand it was because he was desperately trying not to let hope take root.

"I'm miserable because I'm a coward. Because on your last day here, I tried a million different times to tell you…to ask you…" Her eyes squeezed shut. She looked unnerved. Becca didn't do unnerved.

Absurdly, that bolstered his courage. "Ask me what?"

Squaring her shoulders, she stared deep into his eyes. Lifted both hands, which he noticed weren't quite steady. When she cradled his face, he forced himself to stand very still, to let her come to him. His chest heaved as if he'd just finished a race. Slowly, she went up on her tiptoes and, before he could react, placed a featherlight kiss on the scarred flesh fanning out from his right eye. Astonishment rendered him speechless even as a violent shudder racked his body.

Easing back, Rebecca's hands slid down to rest on his shoulders. "Will you stay with me, Caleb?"

"What about the agreement? I thought—"

"What if there was no agreement? Would you *want* to stay?"

Caleb was having trouble processing her meaning.

The words coming out of her mouth were not ones he'd ever dreamed he'd hear. Not from Rebecca.

When he didn't speak, the anguish that twisted her features told him she was serious. Pulling away, she edged backward.

"Don't." Snagging her waist, he anchored her to the spot. "You have to give me a minute to compose my thoughts," he said on a shaky breath. "You have to realize how unexpected... I mean, after the past two years—"

"I thought you'd forgiven me." The abject misery in her eyes wounded him.

"I have."

Her chin went up. "But a real marriage with me is out of the question. I understand why you can't. Won't."

Covering his hands with her own, she attempted to dislodge his firm hold. Not happening. He pulled her closer, reeling her in slowly but surely.

"Do you? Because I don't recall saying such a thing. In fact, I don't recall giving you an answer yet." He watched as tears pooled in her eyes. Unable to restrain himself another second, he cupped her cheek. "My dear, sweet, brave wife. I thought there wasn't room in your heart for any other man but Adam."

"That's what I thought, too. But then you came crashing back into my life, and I realized that what I felt for Adam was immature, the shallow love of a naive girl. You asked me once why my behavior changed after those days in my barn trying to save the kitten. The truth is...you frightened me."

"What?"

"Let me clarify. What I *felt* for you frightened me. There was a connection between us, something bigger than me, more powerful than I had ever experienced before."

He relaxed. "I know. I felt it, too."

"I couldn't be around you, Caleb. I didn't trust myself not to fall for you." Her eyes pleaded for forgiveness. "I'll always regret hurting you."

He lovingly caressed her face. "We were both young and immature."

"In case you haven't noticed, I'm all grown up now." She gifted him with a tremulous, hopeful smile. "The love I have for you, darling husband, is rich and strong and pure. You're the only man I want standing beside me when life's storms come. I know without a shadow of a doubt that I can depend on you."

Her conviction, her confidence in him, melted any lingering uncertainty.

"From the moment I said 'I do,' I've longed for this marriage to be real," he said. "You thought the reason I avoided the new baby was because I was leaving. While that had something to do with it, mostly I couldn't be around her without wishing for a child of our own. And when Samantha and Isaiah had their guns trained on us, you assumed I was going to apologize. I wasn't." He stroked her silken skin with his thumb. "I was going to tell you that I loved you."

With a small cry, her arms, which had been idle at her sides, went around his neck, and she buried her face in the curve of his shoulder. Tears wet his shirt. "I love you, Caleb. Stay with me for endless days and nights. Have children with me—"

She didn't get any further, because his lips sought hers in a kiss that claimed her as his own. When the

heat building between them seemed about ready to ig-
nite, Becca pulled back.

"You still haven't given me your answer."

"What was the question again?" he teased.

"Stay with me for always?"

"Try and stop me, wife."

Epilogue

June, 1882

"I have something for you."

Seated on her in-laws' sofa, Rebecca ceased her fawning over Kate's baby to smile up at Nicole. "What's this?" She accepted the parcel tied up with a bright pink ribbon. "My birthday isn't until August."

"Just open it." Hands clasped at her waist, Nicole stood serene yet aloof. In the months since her and Caleb's marriage, Rebecca had attempted to draw the other girl out. And while her responses were amiable, she never completely relaxed her guard. A pity, for Rebecca genuinely liked her. She just couldn't figure out how to get close to her.

Beside her, Kate transferred a fussy Victoria to her shoulder, patting the tiny back while pressing butterfly kisses to her cherubic cheek. Light hair, the same wheat color as Josh's, covered her head. "I have an idea what it might be."

Curious, Rebecca released the ribbon and peeled the paper away, gasping when she saw the contents. Made of pristine white cotton and trimmed with white satin ribbon, the nightgown was the perfect size for a newborn. "This is our very first baby gift," she said, throat suddenly thick with emotion.

The tears weren't unexpected. The past couple of months had wrought major changes in her body, and the ease with which she cried was downright scary. It hadn't occurred to her to complain, however. Not with this miracle growing inside her. Caleb's baby. Wonder spread through her chest every time she thought about it.

Fingering the delicate material, she told her, "I'll be sure to tell people this is your work."

"That's not why I made it. Not this time."

At Rebecca and Kate's exchanged glances, Nicole looked over her shoulder at the three brothers huddled around the chessboard. Caleb's carefree laughter burst forth in reaction to something Nathan said. Shaking his head, Josh chuckled and stroked his goatee. Seeing her husband relaxed and happy with his family flooded her with gratefulness. *I'll never tire of thanking You, God.*

Lowering her voice, Nicole said, "Because of you, Caleb is finally at peace with himself. Happy, too. I never thought I'd see that."

How sweet. "That's kind of you, Nicole. When you settle down and have children of your own, they'll be the best dressed in all the county."

She looked dumbfounded. "Me? A mother?" Her petite nose screwed up. "That's not the path I have in mind for myself."

"You may find God has a different plan for your life than the one you're envisioning," Kate gently reminded, her expression knowing. "I certainly didn't journey here with the intention of marrying my sister's ex-fiancé."

The men, having gone silent, had turned their attention to the ladies' conversation. At Kate's remark, Josh's blue eyes warmed with affection, and he winked at her.

Lucian, who'd entered the living room a step ahead of Megan, spoke up. "Nor did I plan on marrying the local storyteller."

Curving into his side, Megan gazed adoringly up at him. "That's certainly true. You were dead set on returning to New Orleans and marrying the first dutiful debutante."

"That was an idiotic plan," he murmured. "I would've been miserable without you."

When Lucian kissed his wife's cheek, Nicole rolled her eyes and announced somewhat smugly, "Mark my words, I will not waver from my plan. I won't marry before the age of thirty, and *if* I decide to have a child, it won't be until I'm successful enough to hire a full-time manager for my boutique."

Sophie breezed into the room. "'In their hearts humans plan their course, but the Lord establishes their steps,'" she quoted, a verse from Proverbs.

Sensing Caleb's intense scrutiny, Rebecca looked at him, her insides going all fluttery. Or was that the baby?

Unfolding his long length, he strolled over and slung an arm about his cousin's stiff shoulders. "Please don't take this the wrong way, Nicki, but watching your plan disintegrate is going to be extremely entertaining."

Around the room, feminine gasps were punctuated by deep chuckles.

Her eyes narrowed to slits. "That's not very nice," she said through clenched teeth.

"I'm simply speaking from experience." His affectionate gaze fastened onto Rebecca. "Trust me when I say you might not like it at first, but God's plan really is better than what we plan for ourselves."

Then he dropped his arm and extended his hand to Rebecca. "And now, if you all don't mind, I'd like to have a word with my wife."

"You can talk to her right here," Nathan drawled as he took hold of Sophie's hand and tugged her down to fill the empty space beside him. "We don't mind."

"What I have to say is for her ears alone," Caleb retorted drily, assisting her to her feet and settling his hand low on her back. He was very careful of her these days. She was curious how he'd cope as her time neared, which wouldn't be until autumn.

Out on the porch, she said, "What's the big secret?"

He urged her in the direction of their cabin, framed by the thick forest. Flower beds along the porch added splashes of vivid color. They'd decided to put her family's homestead up for sale and move here permanently. Caleb had offered to build an addition for Amy, but her sister had decided to remain with Sam and Mary—an arrangement that greatly pleased the older couple.

"No secret." He flashed her an endearing smile. "I'm craving your undivided attention, that's all."

At the heat in his dark gaze, a thrill zipped up her spine. "Is that so, Mr. O'Malley?"

"Allow me to demonstrate." Shutting the door and cocooning them inside their cozy home, he pulled her against him, only to laugh when her small, rounded tummy proved a barrier.

"This is only going to get worse." She laughed along with him, fingers playing in the silky hair at his collar.

"I don't mind," he murmured, dropping his head to

plant a kiss against her lips. "You're only going to grow more beautiful."

"You mean rotund, don't you?" She grinned. "Barrel-like. And you can forget graceful."

Admiration blazed in the brown depths as he led her to the sofa, their favorite place to curl up together, and urged her to get comfortable. He went on his knees before her and placed his hands on her belly. Warmth spread outward from the contact.

"You are giving me the most precious gift on earth. Believe me when I say that I find you irresistible." Leaning into her, he kissed her with immense tenderness and reverence. Her insides grew lighter than air, buoyant, effervescent. A solid kick low in her womb caused her to stiffen with surprise.

"What is it?" Caleb pulled away in alarm.

A slow smile spread across her face as she moved his hand over the spot and, fingers covering his, applied slight pressure. The nudge came again, harder this time. His sharp intake, the way his eyes went wide with wonder, would be forever impressed upon her memory.

"That's our baby moving?" he whispered.

"Our little blessing."

"God has blessed us, hasn't He?" At her nod, he said, "I'm going to spend every day of the rest of our lives appreciating you and our children."

"We have to make the most of every moment." Settling a hand on the back of his neck, she tugged his head down for a kiss.

He smiled against her lips moments before he took her in his arms. "I intend to do just that."

* * * * *

WE HOPE YOU ENJOYED THIS BOOK!

Love Inspired®

SUSPENSE

Uncover the truth in these thrilling stories of faith in the face of crime from Love Inspired Suspense. Discover six new books available every month, wherever books are sold!

Carolyn Wiebe will do anything to protect her late sister's children from their abusive father—even give up her Amish roots and pretend to be Mennonite. But when she starts falling for Amish bachelor Michael Miller, can they conquer their pasts—and her secrets—by Christmas to build a forever family?

Read on for a sneak preview of
An Amish Christmas Promise *by Jo Ann Brown, available December 2019 from Love Inspired!*

"Are the *kinder* okay?"

"Yes, they'll be fine." Uncomfortable with his small intrusion into her family, she said, "Kevin had a bad dream and woke us up."

"Because of the rain?"

She wanted to say that was silly but, glad she could be honest with Michael, she said, "It's possible."

"Rebuilding a structure is easy. Rebuilding one's sense of security isn't."

"That sounds like the voice of experience."

"My parents died when I was young, and both my twin brother and I had to learn not to expect something horrible was going to happen without warning."

"I'm sorry. I should have asked more about you and the other volunteers. I've been wrapped up in my own tragedy."

"At times like this, nobody expects you to be thinking of anything but getting a roof over your *kinder*'s heads."

He didn't reach out to touch her, but she was aware of every inch of him so close to her. His quiet strength had awed her from the beginning. As she'd come to know him better, his fundamental decency had impressed her more. He was a man she believed she could trust.

She shoved that thought aside. Trusting any man would be the worst thing she could do after seeing what Mamm had endured during her marriage and then struggling to help her sister escape her abusive husband.

"I'm glad you understand why I must focus on rebuilding a life for the children." The simple statement left no room for misinterpretation. "The flood will always be a part of us, but I want to help them learn how to live with their memories."

"I can't imagine what it was like."

"I can't forget what it was like."

Normally she would have been bothered by someone having sympathy for her, but if pitying her kept Michael from looking at her with his brown puppy-dog eyes that urged her to trust him, she'd accept it. She couldn't trust any man, because she wouldn't let the children spend their lives witnessing what she had.

Don't miss
An Amish Christmas Promise *by Jo Ann Brown,*
available December 2019 wherever
Love Inspired® books and ebooks are sold.

LoveInspired.com

LIEXP1119

Looking for inspiration in tales
of hope, faith and heartfelt romance?

Check out **Love Inspired**® and
Love Inspired® **Suspense** books!

New books available every month!

CONNECT WITH US AT:

Facebook.com/groups/HarlequinConnection

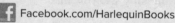 Facebook.com/HarlequinBooks

Twitter.com/HarlequinBooks

Instagram.com/HarlequinBooks

Pinterest.com/HarlequinBooks

ReaderService.com

"You won't have to stay on our account, and we can look after Ernest's place, too. I can hire a man to help me. Someone I know I can..." Ruth's words trailed away.

Trust? Depend on? Was that what Ruth was going to say? She didn't want him around. She couldn't have made it any clearer. Maybe it had been a mistake to think he could patch things up between them, but he wasn't willing to give up after only one day. Ruth was nothing if not stubborn, but he could be stubborn, too.

Owen leaned back and chuckled.

"What's so funny?"

"I'm here until Ernest returns, Ruth. You can't get rid of me with a few well-placed insults."

She huffed and turned her back to him. "I didn't insult you."

"Ah, but you wanted to. I'd like to talk about my plans in the morning."

Ruth nodded. "You know my feelings, but I agree we both need to sleep on it."

Owen picked up his coat and hat, and left for his uncle's farm. The wind was blowing harder and the snow was piling up in growing drifts. It wasn't a fit night out for man nor beast. As if to prove his point, he found Meeka, Ernest's big guard dog, lying across the corner of the porch out of the wind. Instead of coming out to greet him, she whined repeatedly.

He opened the door of the house. "Come in for a bit." She didn't get up. Something was wrong. Was she hurt? He walked toward her. She sat up and growled low in her throat. She had never done that to him before. "Are you sick, girl?"

She looked back at something in the corner and whined softly. Over the wind he heard what sounded like a sobbing child. "What have you got there, Meeka? Let me see."

He came closer. There was a child in an Amish bonnet and bulky winter coat trying to bury herself beneath Meeka's thick fur. Where had she come from? Why was she here? He looked around. Where were her parents?

Don't miss
The Hope *by Patricia Davids,*
available now wherever
HQN™ books and ebooks are sold.

HQNBooks.com

Looking for more satisfying love stories
with community and family at their core?

Check out **Harlequin® Special Edition**
and **Love Inspired®** books!

New books available every month!

CONNECT WITH US AT:

Facebook.com/groups/HarlequinConnection

 Facebook.com/HarlequinBooks

 Twitter.com/HarlequinBooks

 Instagram.com/HarlequinBooks

 Pinterest.com/HarlequinBooks

ReaderService.com

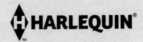

**ROMANCE WHEN
YOU NEED IT**

HFGENRE2018

Inspirational Romance to Warm Your Heart and Soul

Join our social communities to connect with other readers who share your love!

Sign up for the Love Inspired newsletter at **www.LoveInspired.com** to be the first to find out about upcoming titles, special promotions and exclusive content.

CONNECT WITH US AT:

Facebook.com/groups/HarlequinConnection

 Facebook.com/LoveInspiredBooks

 Twitter.com/LoveInspiredBks

LISOCIAL2018